Darkness Our Shadows Cast

Book XIV of The Quietus of Fate

By Brian C. Kershner

All of the characters in this book are fictitious, and any resemblance to actual persons, living or dead, is purely coincidental.

ISBN: 978-1-942082-27-9

Acknowledgements

Each book takes on its own character, and I find sometimes that I'm not sure what character it will be until it is finished. More often than not, I am writing these acknowledgements when I have already finished a book and perhaps even a book or two ahead. It is during the editing process that I figure out the final order of the chapters and how they will flow into one another. Sometimes the prologue of one book was intended to be the epilogue of another, or other times the order in which events happen have to be altered as I learn the fate of characters during the writing process.

Now, as I sit writing this acknowledgement, I look back on the outline of the book, at the events of several chapters, and knowing what comes next, I find myself at a loss to sum up exactly how I feel about this book. As the title suggests, there is a lot of darkness and foreboding contained in this book, but there is just as much hope and uncertainty. Just as each of the characters are moving through their own journeys that will ultimately culminate, so too am I moving through the journey of writing. The end of this journey is in sight now, and the closer I come to it, the more I find myself relying on the characters themselves to determine their own endings.

Some of these endings will be justified, some bittersweet, and others maddening. But each character's journey is their own, and I have grown to respect them all (even the ones I don't like) enough to tell those endings in full, no matter how deserved or undeserved they may feel. I find that I have far more to say about this, but some will have to wait until the next book, which itself is a departure from the structure that I've set to this point.

In every way, this book is the beginning of the end of this story, and I thank everyone who has come this far with me. I look forward to seeing how it all turns out.

B.K.

Table of Contents

Chapter 117

Chapter 118

Epilogue

Appendicies

The Creator teaches,
That the darkness fears the light,
The voice of the Word preaches,
Nothing can stand against the Creator's might.

But in the darkness there is a lesson,
One that seeks every heart and mind,
It's haggard voice causing distress in,
Those who wander and leave faith behind.

Faith is fragile, and must be cared for,
It must be guarded against all attacks,
Whether with the shield or with the sword,
Even should it lead to life's climax.

The Creator has granted life to all through grace,
Requiring devotion beyond transgression,
To die for such a gift is a duty to embrace,
With the ultimate rewards to be reaped in Heaven.

- *The New Verses of The Word*
  From Baeta Catrinel
  High Priestess of the
  Church of the Creator

Prologue

Eulogy of a Hero

Year Two of the Divine Empress and Child of the Creator Marlae Tamerlane, Creator's Calendar Year 1872

When I was younger, I had an idea of where I wanted my life to go. Of course, what I thought were the facts of my life were only half-truths, but I suppose that could be said by any child anywhere. We all have this view of our parents when we are children, a view that is cobbled together mostly by inference. My formative years were an even more incomplete view of reality than most as I only had my father's less than forthcoming nature to contend with. Yes, I knew from an early age that my father was a warrior, but I didn't understand until much later exactly how special he was. Of course as a child I looked at my father like he was a god, and knowing that he was a soldier made him even more of a hero in my eyes. But he would have been a hero if he had been a ditch digger in the army. My father had been one of the elite, and I never knew until after he was gone. And then there was my brother. I only remember him fondly from my childhood. Later I would find that he hated me, not for something that I had done to him as a child, not for some imagined slight, but for my very existence. That was the kind of hatred that never truly goes away. It festers in the soul and in the mind and clouds everything it touches. To me he hid the hatred well, at least for as long as he stayed home. He was tolerant. Where the strain was felt was with my father. If my brother hated me, he hated my father a hundred times more intensely. He blamed me for my mother's death, but he blamed my father more. She had died giving birth to me, and so, I suppose my brother was right in saying that I took her from him. But where he blamed me, he also pitied me. I would never know her love. My brother blamed my father for being selfish, for wanting another son. Of course, neither of us knew why she really died, that it wasn't my fault, or my father's. Our mother was just another pawn in a game we wouldn't understand until so much later.

And I suppose that was the story of my life for so long. Always out of control without really seeing it. My mother dies because of the actions of others. My father dies, my brother abandons me, and I'm left with just my friends, my house, and my worries about a future that I can't even begin to fathom. Then the worst thing that could possibly happen to a young man with no guidance happens to me. I fell in love. I fell hard. She was everything, simply everything. When I looked at her, I could see nothing else. When I thought of her, she crowded out all thoughts in my head. When I was with her my heart pounded so hard that I thought it would burst out of my chest, and when I wasn't with her I thought my heart would never beat again. She made me feel stupid and brilliant at the same time. I could never find the words to make sense of how I felt, and I could never say the right thing in her presence. The words just evaporated, erased by the awe of her. Her smile filled me with a warmth greater than any sunbeam, and her withering stare shook me to the core so that I never wanted to upset her ever again. Yet at the same time, I reveled in making her cross with me just so that I could make her laugh again. And that laugh. It broke on me like a wave, glorious and full. She was my greatest strength and my greatest weakness. The worst part of it all was that she knew the effect she had on me. While she loved me too, she knew that I was not what she needed, even if I was what she wanted. I wasn't ready for her, and she knew it. But of course I couldn't see that. I was too young, too stupid, and too sure of myself. So she taught me a lesson. She showed me that while she loved me, and while she needed me, she was willing to live without me.

It made me crazy, and I was angry. The craziest thing about it though was the fact that as hard as I tried to be angry at her, I could only be angry at myself. I wanted to convince myself that I was right, that I was the wronged party, but I couldn't fool myself, not for long anyway. So I ran, I ran far away and thought that I was justified in doing it. I had no real ties, no real responsibilities. The world seemed so wide and so full of opportunities and I could wrap myself up in the dream that everything I was doing was for her, to impress her, to show her that I was more than what she thought I was, and in a matter of time I would be able to make her proud of me. But again, I was the fool and she knew all along. And so in those still nights when I was alone, I had only my pride to keep me company and it left me cold. Unwilling to admit my mistakes. Unable to live up to the expectations that I set for myself. As much as I wanted to go home, go home to her, I couldn't. I just couldn't. I was afraid, I was a fool, and I thought that my pride had cost me her love forever.

But like all things that are meant to be, fate, or at least what looked like fate at the time, intervened. Suddenly I was thrust into a role that I had dreamed of from the time that I was a boy. But just like the woman I loved, I was not prepared for what was coming. Unlike love, the role of a hero has a cost greater than any that can be imagined. We hear tales of glorious battles when we are children, the triumph of heroes over villains and monsters, but we never truly hear about the cost. In children's tales the smell of burning flesh, or the broken bodies of loved ones are not detailed the same way as glorious feasts and conquests of light over darkness. And so, when the forces of the Shadow fell upon my little home town, I felt the true cost of war before I even had a chance to fight in my first battle. People I had grown up with, people who had taken care of me, been kind to me, and taught me what it was to be a responsible adult were gone. Just gone. No goodbyes. No closure. Just gone. And there wasn't even time for tears, it was just the bloody and stinking beginning to a torrent of bloodshed that would follow. Everywhere that I went, every part of the quest, there was blood. People died by the hundreds just because of who I was. And then the greatest cosmic joke was played upon us all. I was not even the hero of the story. People died for nothing. Despite what happened for the rest of the quest, that fact left me cold. Even when we were victorious, I still felt that loss, and victory was a hollow word.

It was here that the story diverges. Not because of anything I wanted to happen, or needed to happen, but because we were all just pawns in a game we were just beginning to understand. But that understanding would not come for a great deal longer, and not before thousands more felt the sting of their mortality. From a moment somewhere before we battled what we believed to be the ultimate evil, the Creator allowed for the paths of every person on our world to split. Two worlds came into being at that moment, one where the forces of the Light would prevail and hold an advantage into the next generation, and one where a pyrrhic victory would give the Shadow a path to total domination. And while these two worlds initially didn't know the other existed, that secret could not be kept for long. In the end, none of what happened to us in either of those realities mattered. We lost. I'm not sure there is any other way to look at it. We didn't understand the stakes of the war we were fighting and we lost our world in the process.

And so I found myself here, on this world, another imperiled by the pointless game being waged by infantile dictators and their enigmatic father who cared nothing for the lives they were destroying every day. But I was not ready to act, not ready to be anything other than the broken man that landed upon this world confused and conflicted. It took a long time for me to reconcile my two selves. The first was the family man who had gotten his happily-ever-after. He defeated the evil, married the woman he loved, had a child, and died in his bed. Excepting of course that he was murdered by the man who was supposed to be his patron after a year of terrifying nightmares about the apocalyptic future to come. Then there was the other man, the man that I still feel closest to. The man who lost everything. His love, his future, his world, even himself fighting an impossible war. He became what he reviled in an effort to find victory, and yet the cruelest truth was that there was no possibility of victory.

For a long time I watched and waited, wounded to my core in a way that could never heal. And so when I began to see the seeds of the conflict that had taken everything from me sprouting on this world, I began my millennia long work. I formed an order dedicated to saving those people who would inevitably be caught up in the war to come. I preached the dangers of the worship of the Creator, and made a great many enemies along the way. I conspired with former friends and enemies alike, gathering forces for the day when the conflict would begin again. And yet, after almost two thousand years of preparing, we were still not ready. We still did not understand the enemy that we were fighting or the depths that He would go to remain in power. And so the losses mounted. Friend and foe alike fell. Innocents were slaughtered by the hundreds, and I was forced to do the unthinkable. I killed my best friend. And as I lay in a pool of my own blood, my friend's lifeless body beside mine, his head in my lap, I could think only one thought as the blackness came.

It's not over……not like this…….

****

I often wonder how it's possible that we constantly find ourselves losing to the humans. We were bred to be their destroyers. To be eternal. To be their conquerors and their betters. We were made to be the exemplar of everything that made them monsters at their cores. Their pettiness, their rages, their lusts, the cold that wrapped around their soul and prevented them from becoming more than they were. For a time, we were the plague we were designed to be. We hunted and murdered them by the dozens. We leveled whole cities. Wiped out generations with a snap of our fingers. We were the gods of monsters. What we did not understand was that cruelty of that kind, warfare of that kind, is not sustainable. Creatures of hate and violence will eventually succumb to their own natures and target their own kind. And so we fractured. We sought our own power away from the collective. We plotted against one another, fought private wars, and secretly desired to unseat our master and rule over everything we could see. Like the humans we were made to despise, we were blinded by the extent of our grasp, and did not see what lay beyond. We were creatures that were made to last forever that could not see past the moment. Perhaps that was why we as a collective failed.

But I know where I failed. I know where my story deviated from what it was meant to be. I was the first-born daughter of a god. With a thought, I could make fire rain from the sky. I enslaved kingdoms who dedicated themselves to my beauty. Then he came into my life. The scourge and blessing that would be by my side for untold years to come. He was recruited into my army without my knowledge, and impressed everyone, and then quickly rose through the ranks. It was then when I first saw him, in formation, in his uniform, and he was stunning. In that moment, I could think of nothing more than having him as my momentary diversion. My arrangement with my husband of convenience made my dalliances a two-fold blessing. It gave me the opportunity to spite my husband and show him that I would never be truly his, and it also gave me a place to focus his murderous rages and keep them firmly away from me. He could work himself up and drive himself crazy choking the life out of my conquests which made him believe he wasn't a powerless cuckold. Meanwhile I would do whatever I wished and gained more and more control over our military assets. The arrangement worked well until that man inflamed me.

He was as attractive as he was infuriating. He beguiled and frustrated with every word, and it seemed that there was nothing that could take the lightness from his heart or his mood. He disarmed with a glance and had a smile that could melt the coldest heart. While I thought I was entrapping him with my wiles, he was entrapping me with his. When I was in his arms, I felt something for the first time, and I was never the same again. I was in love and in lust with this impossible man, and I would never feel whole without him again.

But like all star-crossed lovers, we were not meant to be in that or any other life. We had our time together, and then he was gone, taken from me by my own family. An old story, a common one. Political bickering, battles for power and attention, petty back-stabbing disguised as expediency for a greater agenda. In the greater scheme of things, our time together was so brief, I did not even grieve. But together we had our son, and though it pained me to do so, after he had been properly prepared, I sent him off to war with an old ally, one I knew I could trust. On the outside, it seemed like a tactical move of someone who was trying to gain every advantage that she could. On the inside, it was because I could not stand to see his face. His eyes, his chin, his nose, they all reminded me. They all tugged at my heart, and they all created weakness in me that I could no longer indulge.

Then he came back to me. First in part, in the body of someone I thought to be my enemy, and then later in the body of a woman who came to me as a friend. But those were just shadows, preparation for the moment he returned to me in full. And even as the world tore itself down around us, we could not tear ourselves from each other's embrace, not knowing if those stolen moments would be the last we would ever have together.

The Creator however was not done with us, and so we were allowed to live life together for almost two millennia in a way that we did not ever believe was possible. But we both knew, perhaps from the very start, that those days were numbered. And even for creatures like us who would endure for as long as time was time, the years passed as though they were moments. We both knew that soon they would come for us. For us, and for our family. Our family, our extended family that is both blessed and cursed. Those that share my husband's blood, and those that share his legacy, all marked for something greater and more terrible than any of us could possibly truly understand. There is one facet however, one truism that regardless of how many years have passed since my birth remains imprinted on every fiber of my being. I was born for death. I was born to make mortals suffer. And then I was to be returned to the fire that forged me.

But I never imagined that I would be plunged back into that fire by my own son….

* * * * * * * * * * * * *

The last vestiges of the setting of the twin suns was still in the sky, the deep blues and purples shading the bottoms of the thick clouds in the sky over the broken Kingdom of Hedorah. Some of the light streamed in through the open balcony doors of the Royal Palace of Hedorah, shining into the quarters that used to house the Celestial Empress Marlae Tamerlane during her brief time in Hedorah. Now however, the chamber was home to a much grizzlier pair of occupants. From the open door to the balcony to the wall of mirrors stretched a long smear of blood across the perfect white tile floor. There on the floor, his back against the wall, Logan Ranthall sat, his eyes closed, his breathing barely strong enough to move his chest. In his arms, pulled close to him was the limp and nearly lifeless body of Bryn Aplee-Seth. Whatever energy he had left in him after dragging himself on his hands and knees across the length of Hedorah to the palace, he had poured into Bryn in an effort to mend the nearly mortal wounds inflicted upon her. The exertion had nearly cost him his own life, and there was still a very real possibility that they would both die. But at least they would not die alone. Even if Bryn never woke again, she would die in the arms of someone who loved her. Logan owed Aerith that much.

Logan drifted between consciousness and unconsciousness for an unknown amount of time. It could have been minutes, or hours, or days. Every so often, Logan thought that he could feel another presence in the room, but with all the blood and power that he had lost, it was probably nothing more than a delusion. Finally, Logan felt his eyes flutter open. The light in the room was low, but there across from him, sitting on the edge of the foot of the wide bed across from them was a woman in white. She was both frail and powerful at the same time, a wave of cold emanating from her lithe form. The aged white gown that wrapped around her seemed as much as part of her as her skin, and was the same color as her hair, streaked with shadow. It seemed as though all of the color had been drained from her form, with the exception of her brilliant green eyes that hummed with power, and her red-stained fingertips were folded neatly in her lap. Logan's eyes found the woman in white's and he held her gaze for merely a moment before he smiled meekly and shut his eyes again. A warmth filled him, and he knew that his story had not yet ended.

* * * * * * * * * * * * * *

Humans, for all their complaining about the lack of control in their lives, have the innate ability to determine their path through their limited understanding of their reality. Unlike my siblings who trampled across the landscape grinding the bones of their enemies into dust, I studied those that I was loosed against, trying to determine how best to help them destroy themselves. What my brothers and sisters didn't realize in their march toward subjugation was that Emries did not design the humans to be anything more than pawns in his battle against his siblings, and therefore they were disposable. But even the lowliest of creatures had its uses, and most of those uses were hidden to the eyes of the untrained and unimaginative. For the large part, my siblings are brutes who tromp, snort, and bellow. They are ruddy beasts no different than the sheep they were birthed to slaughter. And so, as I studied those pathetic humans, I saw in them a glimmer of something greater. They had aspirations, they had dreams, and they always saw in themselves the ability to transcend their station and become greater than they were. In most, this drive was limited and covetous. The desire for wealth. The desire for comfort. The desire for gratification. These base goals were always easy to manipulate and turn to more sinister pursuits. However there were a few, a precious few, that distilled within them a fire that could never be quenched. A need for advancement above their place and station that could not be denied. For many this fire consumed those around them, and they became villains in their own right, because the core nature of the human was to sacrifice everything for their own needs. They were built to be engines of chaos and fodder in a war. But in every generation it seemed that there were a handful, those elevated even above the special, that seemed to weave fate around them, and turn the world to their desires. They were the best of the humans, and were they to be allowed to do what their hearts and souls guided them toward, they could have elevated the whole of their race. However, Emries knew that these people existed and so he turned them to his will, first as his Erieal *and then finally as his* Coromors.

My siblings never saw these people coming until it was too late. It cost us one of our own in Aryx Terian, as he could stand the killing no longer, and it cost us perhaps the greatest of us in Kamen, who was sacrificed so that more of us could be brought into existence. Then more of us were sacrificed for their arrogance. Grawn, Bryn, and Ellis were purged from the Brotherhood because of Aerith Seth, not the last of us to be lost to his interference. But it was when the hero Cedric Binosear emerged, I knew that an opportunity had presented itself. It was clear that Cedric was to be Emries' chosen champion against Shau-ling, but what was not clear was whether or not Cedric had to be that champion. Was his will strong enough to resist the pull of Emries' crusade? Could he be turned to another path? So my course became clear. It was a simple enough task to dispatch the woman that Cedric loved from afar and then replace her. It was even simpler to capture his affections and set them ablaze. But before I had my chance to turn him to another path, I was betrayed.

Once the next generation dawned and I was reborn, I set upon my task again, and yet again I was thwarted in my attempt to seduce and repurpose Emries' chosen hero. But something was different in my connection to Logan Ranthall. He had touched a part of me that I did not know existed. I would not call what I felt for Logan love, but it was a kinship that I had never felt with those of my own kind. There was a doubt within him that I touched within his mind that I had never felt from Cedric. Cedric Binosear for all of his faults was a force of nature, driven by demons and angels that he did not fully understand. But always there was the push forward. The need to be and do better. The need to conquer an adversary or a challenge. A destiny that he was always chasing. His companions were the same. They were heroes, they were legends in the making, they were elite amongst the elite. But Logan and his fellows, they were different. They were flawed, doubting, determined, and uncertain. They fumbled against the pull of destiny, stumbling down a path that threatened to strike them down at every turn. And it wasn't because Logan was playing the part meant for his brother. There was something else. They asked questions, they doubted, they felt too much and thought more. They would not be blindly lead, not by Emries, not by Cedric, not by me. They clung to each other, and used each other as beacons in the darkness.

When the next generation came, and the lies were exposed, Logan and his fellows showed the true heroes that they could be. Logan sacrificed himself to ensure that the war would end, even at the cost of their own world, and I stood beside him as long as I could. But my path would take me elsewhere, and I thought perhaps my story would end there at the hands of Emries' pawn. But in the void, the green glow found me and pulled me away from the abyss. Dorovar offered me a new purpose as the highest of his heralds. Unlike those that would follow, he did not lie to me about my purpose. He did not hide from me the reason that he chose me. He saw my conflict. He saw my love for Cedric Binosear, he saw my admiration for Logan Ranthall, he saw my hate for Emries, and he saw my dispassion for Shau-ling and the phasia. He would use me to sample the power of the Blaze and find a way to thwart its effects upon him. He would use my abilities to walk into the minds of others and turn them to his will. My powers and abilities became his, magnified by his anguish and his pain, amplified by every soul that he added to his Chorus. I became the tip of the sword that would be used to pierce the heart of the Creator.

But what Emries did not understand, what Halicon did not understand, and what Dorovar does not understand is that fate's cruel and unpredictable fancy cannot be shaken from those she sets her sights upon. Try as they might to thwart destiny's call, those that had risen to shake the foundation of the Creator's order could not be shaken fully from their path. Cedric Binosear, dead by the hands of a friend, dead again by the hands of his greatest rival, had risen yet again to shake his fist at fate. Aerith Seth, sacrificed at the altar of Emries' greater ambition, content to give away his powers and live life with the woman he loved, was drawn back into the war he never wanted but was made to fight. The fiery Bryn Seth, born to kill and die for her master, she instead found the one thing she never wanted and never thought she needed, the love of a man who stoked her fires to greater heights. Together they slaughter angels, make deals with devils and sire children upon whose souls the whole of Creation seemed to be turning. Even the redoubtable Pike Rhuiden, a man who saw himself as the hero but could not help but become a villain, had done his part to try to shape fate in his image and in some ways had succeeded. And of course there were the Sandars, the maddeningly stoic and efficient Gwydeon and the irascible Midarin, the unlikely lovers whose mortality always seemed a greater strength than an impediment.

And then there was Logan. Logan the farmer. Logan the thwarted savior. Logan the reluctant hero. Logan the tortured soul. Logan the quixotic villain. Logan the heretic, Logan the guru, Logan the mender of lost souls. And most recently the thorn in Dorovar's side. At every turn Logan had proven to be too much for Dorovar's Heralds, and fortunate that the dragons and Raenera had thus far drawn Dorovar's considerable ire. But that fortune would soon end, and Dorovar would soon begin to deal with those that vexed him more directly. Logan would not be ready for that, no matter what new abilities had allowed him to defeat not only Death but Conquest. There is still so much for him to do, and the hardest part of his road is still ahead.

There is not a rule that I have not broken. And this moment will be no different, even if it costs me everything…

* * * * * * * * * * * * *

Jerah rose from her position at the foot of the bed and moved to where Logan sat with Bryn pulled tight to him. They were both drenched in blood, their own and each other's, and neither looked as though they would last more than another few hours. Logan had done his best to heal Bryn's wounds, but the effort was sloppy and incomplete. Regardless of his injuries, he had never been that adept at using his powers for healing. Jerah knelt down and reached out a single blood drenched finger. Inches from Logan's forehead she hesitated. The two halves of her were not so much divided as they were unsure. Dorovar would instantly know what she had done, as would Rhain. But the time had come for a change. A change that no one could have seen coming. Steeling herself for the few seconds she would have before Dorovar's retaliation, Jerah let her finger touch Logan's forehead.

A faint green glow passed down Jerah's arm and through her finger into Logan's failing form. The ghostly glow suffused first his body and then Bryn's knitting all of their wounds and restoring all of the vitality that had been stolen from them after a series of battles. But Jerah was not content with merely restoring her former compatriots to health. Like all of Dorovar's Heralds, Jerah had the ability to tap into Dorovar's so-called

Chorus of Souls. But unlike the other Heralds, Jerah had been granted the ability to bestow power to those who could be made to serve Jerah's will and Dorovar's agenda. But Jerah had different intentions this time. Dorovar thrived on using the abilities of others against them, and now it was time to take some of that advantage away. Jerah needed only a second to plant a seed inside of Logan, something that would allow him to learn everything he needed to know about the Chorus of Souls, and perhaps everything he would need to destroy Dorovar.

And perhaps it would let him put Caris' soul to rest once and for all.

Chapter CX

A Matter of Faith

Year Two of the Divine Empress and Child of the Creator Marlae Tamerlane, Creator's Calendar Year 1872

The hour was late when Anabel Binosear made her way to the room that had been prepared for her near the private garden where the meeting with the High Priestess Baeata Catrinel had just ended. The room itself was well appointed, with a comfortable looking bed and finery that you might have expected to find in a smaller regional palace of some second-tier lord or lady. The Heart of Stone was an impressive fortification, but it was clearly not interested in the finery of station. Those that called the Heart home were devout people and believed in the humility of their work, and thus the humility of their surroundings. While of course there would be dignitaries that would come to visit the Heart, they would be forced to make due with less than their station demanded, and would do so without the ability to complain. In some ways, Anabel's political mind viewed it as a reinforcement of the standing of the Church of the Creator in Cadaria. If someone wanted the favor of the Church of the Creator, they would have to play the game on the Church's level. Whether or not that was the actual thought process when the Heart was designed and its chambers configured mattered little. The implication was clear.

No longer required to be the proper lady she had been for the majority of her life, Anabel slumped into the chair by the door, suddenly feeling the weight of all of her years on her shoulders. So much had happened in just a few days, and Anabel had not given herself the time to even think about it all. But that was how she had always been. If she slowed down to truly consider all of the tragedy around her, she would never have the strength to fight it. Others could spend their time consumed by worry for their loved ones, or the ultimate consequence of their actions, but not Anabel. She had been making life and death decisions from the moment she was thirteen years old, and had not looked back since.

On Onea, Marcwell was an important kingdom even before it became the home of the Lord Lion and his entourage of celebrated warriors. Anabel's father, or at least the man she had believed for her early life to be her father, was an important man. He had built Marcwell into a power without the force of arms. He had been a brilliant strategist and master of trade and economics. Through negotiation, bargaining, and diplomacy, he had been able to craft agreements with all of his surrounding kingdoms and manufactured the most complex trade networks that their world had ever seen. Of course, the one hold-out to those arrangements and agreements had been the Kingdom of Trelon. Trelon in those days was stubborn and steadfast in their adherence to might. While Illimar had an impressive navy, Brea had the world's best archers, and Alimidar had the mercenary forces that could be bought by anyone with coin, Trelon was renowned for the whole of its military. The lord of the kingdom, a man by the name of Balthazar Trelis, was a fourth-generation solider, and the rumors were that his father had fought with the Hand of the Light before they were destroyed at the hands of the forces of Shau-ling. Of course, very few people actually believed in Shau-ling at that point. That was nothing more than a ghost story that was told to the children or the ramblings of the old hermits the Moridon. Everyone was ignorant of what was coming, except perhaps for the military of Trelon. Lord Trelis did not respect the intentions of the Binosear family and did not respect the manner in which they insured peace. Lord Trelis was not the most eloquent man, nor did he have patience for the niceties of court. But, when it became more and more difficult to acquire the supplies needed to keep his soldiers in fighting shape, Lord Trelis was faced with a choice. He could either mobilize his military and attempt to take what he needed from the rest of the kingdoms, or he could make a deal. It was not as clear-cut a decision as one might think.

CHAPTER 110

Lord Trelis had absolute and complete faith in both the abilities of the military and in his own combat prowess. Already Trelon had some of the richest farmland at their disposal, and enough food and water to sustain extended campaigns against even the most fortified kingdoms. However, in assaulting Illimar, would Brea come to its defense, pinning Trelon's army between the archers and the sea? If Trelon assaulted Kandor, would the mercenary army of Alimidar assault from one side while the military of the twin towns assaulted them from the other? Assaulting Marcwell was out of the question, because allies would come from all sides, leaving Trelon to be crushed. But still, for weeks and months Lord Trelis met with his advisers and most brilliant tacticians in an attempt to determine whether or not such an undertaking could be successful. What Anabel would discover later, to the horror of her heart, was that an outside voice intervened and changed the course of history for the entirety of the world.

During her time as the Queen of Trelon, Anabel had access to the official records that were kept from those days, including the secret writings of Lord Trelis himself. In one passage Lord Trelis wrote of the day that a new adviser appeared in Trelon offering his advice on the quandary facing Trelon and the lack of options that were vexing Lord Trelis. Though he may not have been much in the way of a diplomat, Lord Trelis had been an excellent chronicler and meticulous note-taker. He recorded every detail of the meeting with the strange non-descript man with penetrating blue eyes. He said that the man gave his name only as Emries, and that he had a clear solution to the problem at hand, but it would require a great sacrifice. The man calling himself Emries offered that if Lord Trelis were to march on any of the allied kingdoms, he would quickly be defeated by the combined strength of the alliance. While Trelon would have been able to inflict some losses, it would not be enough to stave off the ultimate defeat. Emries instead suggested that Trelon march its army against the town of Lakestone. Lakestone, like Trelon, was not part of the alliance of kingdoms, and it did have a significant military presence. The lord of that kingdom, a man by the name of Alek was disliked by most of the other kingdoms, and had made clear his dislike of most of the other lords. Rumors were rampant however that Lakestone's prospects were beginning to fade, much as Trelon's were, but to a much faster degree. In Lord Trelis's notes, he surmised that Lord Alek was in the process of negotiating a marriage alliance between Lakestone and Marcwell, and that in a matter of weeks,

Lord Binosear's only son Wolfric would be wed to Lord Alek's oldest daughter. If this took place, it would severely damage Trelon's ability to negotiate a beneficial alliance with Marcwell. So, Emries suggested, while Lakestone's disposition was in question, Trelon could launch an attack on Lakestone, remove the universally disliked Lord Alek, demonstrate their strength and worthiness, improving their bargaining position.

Lord Trelis jumped at the chance to flex his military might and planned the invasion of Lakestone over the next few days with Emries' help. Emries was emphatic that the defenses of the city needed to be completely destroyed if Trelis was going to prove the power of his military resources. The siege went precisely to plan, all fortifications around Lakestone were destroyed, and Lord Alek was killed in the final assault on the palace, as he led his troops personally rather than surrender. What Lord Trelis didn't know until much later was that Emries had paid one of Lord Trelis' lieutenants to ensure that Lord Alek's entire family was executed. There would be no marriage alliance between Lakestone and Marcwell, and Lord Trelis returned the rule of the city to its people. The second part of the plan of course came to fruition mere weeks later when Marcwell sent an envoy to open diplomatic relations with Trelon. It took little time for the bargain to be struck, a bargain that would send Lord Trelis' only daughter to Marcwell to wed Wolfric Binosear. Of course before her ultimate arrival in Marcwell, Christina Trelis found herself in the arms of a rogue by the name of Aerith Seth. Emries with one subtle manipulation had crafted one of the most important alliances that would stand against Shau-ling, while at the same time creating the very battleground where Shau-ling and his minions would time and time against launch their assaults against the rest of the world. In doing so, he also created the first prophesied vessel that would carry his mantle.

Anabel had been raised, as her brother Cedric had, to be the leader of a great kingdom. Cedric was to be the lord of Marcwell, and Anabel was to be the lady of Trelon. When their mother passed away when the twins turned thirteen, Anabel was declared to be the ruler of Trelon, a position that would be held in trust by Lord Wolfric Binosear until Anabel reached the age of sixteen. While that proclamation held true, it did not stop Anabel from being involved in the day-to-day business of the Kingdom of Trelon. Her grandfather Balthazar had also passed on by this point, and so

Anabel was the only true member of the nobility of that family left other than her brother. Balthazar had been an oddity in Trelon, the only male ruler of the kingdom for nearly a thousand years. However, Balthazar's wife had died giving birth to their daughter, and he held the throne in trust for her until she reached the proper age. But when the time came, Balthazar would not relinquish control of the kingdom. While it ruffled the feathers of many within the kingdom, Christina Trelis took great pains in ensuring that the people knew that she was not concerned with her father's temporary leadership, and that he only had the best interests of Trelon at heart. The return of a woman to the throne, once Anabel was officially installed, was heralded with great celebrations throughout the whole of the kingdom. It was supposed to be a return to prosperity and peace. Of course, soon the whole of the world would be embroiled in war, and Trelon would be right in the middle of everything that would occur.

Anabel rubbed her temples, the memories of the past more of a burden to her than they were fond remembrances. If she tried hard enough she could find memories of playing hide and seek in the halls of the palace, or laughing with her brother over little things. But most of the memories that came unbidden were filled with pain, sorrow, regret, and frustration. She had been surrounded by death for so long, and she could not see a change on the horizon.

A knock at the door shook Anabel from her momentary distraction. Baeata said that she would arrange for a bath for Anabel despite the late hour as well as some food. Anabel opened the door and let the robed initiate push the half full tub of steaming water into the room. Another robed individual brought in two pitchers that were filled to nearly overflowing with steaming water as well as a plate which contained a small cask of oil and a wedge of soap that smelled of flowers. The two robed figures made for the door, and Anabel ran her fingers through the water. She heard the door close behind her and then sat on the edge of the bed to unlace her boots. It was then that she noticed one of the robed figures still standing by the door.

"I require no additional assistance," Anabel managed in her best regal tone, "you may go."

The robed figure made no move to leave, instead letting the hood fall away from his face. The short wild black hair and irritated eyes were recognized immediately, but Anabel made no motion to either attack or flee. She simply returned to unlacing her boots. When she spoke again, she made no attempt to hide the annoyance in her voice.

"What do you want Jeroch?"

Jeroch let the robe drop to the ground and moved to the chair where Anabel had been seated only a few moments earlier.

"I take it you aren't surprised to see me."

Anabel looked up from unlacing her boots and gave Jeroch a withering glare.

"I may not be as practiced with my abilities as the others, Jeroch, but I can still feel when a portal opens close to me. I didn't know that it was you, but I was certainly expecting someone to come sooner rather than later."

Anabel looked back down at her boots.

"So who sent you?"

Jeroch felt indignation rise within him.

"Sent me?"

Anabel exhaled slight frustration and shook her head before looking back up at Jeroch.

"I have no intention of wasting nicety or diplomacy upon you, Jeroch. You have never been one to stand on your own to do anything. So I ask again, who sent you?"

Jeroch had several thoughts run through his mind at the same time, but whatever anger he thought to muster instantly faded. Whatever pride had once been the trademark of the Lord Shadow had been lost as he watched three of his powerful siblings sacrifice themselves in an attempt to save one of their one-time deadliest enemies and strike a blow against an immortal madman from another world. Kamen's loss had been particularly difficult on Jeroch, and he had still not come to terms with it. But Rhain had been right, there would be time for sorrow and recrimination later. Now, the goal was to ensure that they all survived what was coming. That meant that old grudges would need to be let go.

"I suppose that depends on your point of view," Jeroch said finally. "I am here on the orders of Rhain Seth, the new Mistress of the Blaze, but I also suspect that I am here on behalf of the so-called Divine Empress, Marlae Tamerlane."

Anabel looked up, relief on her face.

"Isabella was able to get her out. I've been worried, but haven't had time to consider the possibilities. Logan, in true Logan fashion, sent me here with Baeata in an effort to keep our standing with the Church of the Creator and negotiate in good faith with the High Priestess. I trust that Jillian, Isabella, and Leonora made it there safely as well?"

Jeroch nodded.

"They did."

The silence held for a long moment. Anabel didn't want to ask the next question, but she had no choice.

"And Logan?"

Jeroch shook his head.

"All I know is that his fight with Rhuiden went poorly. Kamen, Rael, and Trece sacrificed themselves in an attempt to give him a fighting chance. All we know is that Rhuiden was defeated, but Rhain has not been able to determine whether Ranthall survived the conflict. I would say that the man is too stubborn to die, but even Logan Ranthall has his limits."

Anabel pulled one of her boots off and then began to unlace the other.

"So why are you here, Jeroch?"

Jeroch leaned back in the chair, crossing his arms.

"I'm not a diplomat, Lady Lion, nor will I ever be."

Anabel looked up at the title.

"Don't call me that."

Jeroch frowned.

"Would you prefer Anabel Seth?"

In one smooth motion, Anabel picked up the boot from the floor and sent it flying toward Jeroch's head. The phase snatched it out of the air with little effort.

"Never again, Jeroch. I don't ever want to hear that cross your lips again, or I swear I will rip out your tongue with my bare hands."

Jeroch let the boot drop to the ground and stood. He moved half way across the room toward Anabel before speaking again, his voice filled with frustration and barely-restrained anger.

"You may not be proud of your lineage, Anabel, but you can no longer deny it. Aerith and those loyal to him may be the only ones able to save us from the fire that the Creator intends to rain down upon this world, and we need every one of you fighting with us. You can't bury your head in the sand anymore."

Anabel dropped her other boot to the floor and stood. She was easily head and shoulders shorter than Jeroch and had to look up to him, but her presence more than made up for her lack of physical size.

"I am contributing in the way I think is best, Jeroch, and I will certainly not be dictated to by the likes of you no matter who you represent. I am a diplomat and a negotiator, and if I can help to hold these fragile alliances together, I will do the best that I can. Now, deliver whatever message you intend to deliver and then go back where you came from. I'm tired, I need a bath, and I have no intention of wasting more time than necessary on this conversation."

Jeroch sighed, shook his head, and walked toward the door.

"Rhain wanted me to tell you that a war is coming here. It may be the last big war. I know that Marlae was trying to make sure that the Church of the Creator stood with her, but now you need to make sure that the Church stands with us. The angels, the Servants, who knows what's coming, but it's going to be hard for the faithful to take. No matter what it takes you have to hold everything together, even if you have to take over this kingdom yourself."

Anabel shook her head.

"You understand nothing about diplomacy. But I take your meaning. When the time comes, I will make sure that the Church of the Creator will stand with us."

Anabel waited, but Jeroch did not leave.

"Is that all?"

Jeroch considered his next words very carefully.

"You need to make peace with your father."

Anabel started to retort, but Jeroch held up a hand.

"With what is coming, with how important all of you are, we can't afford you to hesitate because of ancient bad blood. If you have the chance, you need to try to make it right."

Jeroch started to say something else, thought the better of it, and then opened the door. The robe that he had discarded floated off the floor and wrapped itself around his shoulders before he stepped out into the darkened hall. When the door closed, Anabel slumped back onto the edge of the bed, her heart sinking and her mind filled with more and more questions and doubts. She would need to rededicate herself to her responsibilities because there was no time for worry. Logan, Aerith and all the rest would have to take care of themselves.

* * * * * * * * * * * * * *

Aelind shivered as the wind whipped around her. She had crawled out onto the thin ledge that stretched around the whole of the third story of the

Heart of Stone, where the guest quarters were situated. The cruel dagger clutched in her hand, she inched down the ledge, her destination never leaving her vision.

Aelind had left her boots in her room and walked barefoot on the cold stone floor from her quarters, up the stairs to the unused room at the end of the hall from where Anabel Binosear would be staying. For a long time Aelind crouched in the shadows behind the door, her eyes cast down the length of the hall, waiting for Anabel to emerge. She wasn't sure how long she knelt there, her feet and legs beginning to cramp before her quarry appeared. Finally, Anabel emerged from the private garden where she had been meeting with the High Priestess. Anabel had been assigned to the quarters nearest to the garden in order to ensure that she would not be disturbed and also to make sure that the High Priestess did not have to explain her presence until it was necessary. Once Anabel entered her room, Aelind waited. If the High Priestess left the garden and returned to her rooms, Aelind would have to abort her mission tonight and find another opportunity. But, Aelind had guessed that because of the late hour, Baeata would take advantage of the small bedroom that was attached to the garden. The door to the garden opened once more, and Baeata emerged. Aelind cursed under her breath and began to plan her retreat when Baeata stopped at an acolyte's door half-way down the hall and knocked lightly. The acolyte answered, words were exchanged, and Baeata returned to the garden. Aelind remained hidden, watching as the acolyte left his room, moved quickly and with purpose down the stairs. Aelind heard some hushed voices below, and after several minutes, two hooded initiates returned with several large pitchers of steaming water. One of the initiates stopped by a door near the end of the hallway and pulled a rolling tub from the supply room. The two initiates quickly emptied the pitchers into the tub, and by the time they were at Anabel's door, a third initiate appear carrying two more pitchers, oil and soap. One of the initiates stayed outside while the other two took the bath into Anabel's room.

Aelind waited and watched as one of the initiates emerged from the room. The two hooded men returned downstairs, but the third did not come out of Anabel's room. Several minutes passed, and Aelind began to wonder what was taking the initiate so long to emerge. Finally, the door opened again, and the hooded initiate exited the room and walked slowly down the hallway toward the stairs. There was something strange about his gate, and he carried himself far too proudly for his station. As the initiate reached the top of the stairs, he looked in the direction of where Aelind knelt. He continued to gaze in her general direction for several moments before slowly walking down the stairs. Once Aelind could no longer hear the man's footsteps, she closed the door and walked as gingerly and silently as she could to the window.

Every part of Aelind was cold as she inched her way towards the window to Anabel's room. Her feet were numb but somehow she still felt the cold. The wind whipping around her caused her to shiver, and her heart was beating so fast and so hard that she was sure Anabel would be able to hear it before Aelind got near to the window. Finally, she had reached the window, and chanced a quick look inside. The tub was set in the center of the room, and Anabel had already submerged herself in the water, her back to the window. As silently as she could manage, timing her movements to the howling wind, Aelind crept into the room. Inch by inch, she edged across the floor, the cruel dagger practically dragging her forward towards her target. Aelind's mouth was dry, her heart pounded in her ears, and her feet felt as though she was walking across sandpaper with every step. She was less than a half a dozen steps from her target when Anabel started and whirled around. Aelind started to charge forward, but then she felt a strong hand grasp her shoulder. Shocked, Aelind whirled around, slashing wildly with the dagger. It was only out of the corner of her eye that she got a glimpse of the man that had taken a hold of her. The next thing she knew, however, the man with the short wild black hair had taken hold of her wrist squeezing so tight that she dropped the dagger. She pulled hard against his grip, trying her best to free herself. She kicked hard, landing a strike on the man's knee, freeing herself from his hold upon her. What she didn't realize was how close she was to the window. Aelind reset her feet and made a lunge for the dagger, but the man was ready. He intercepted her charge, and pushed her backwards. Her lower back collided with the windowsill and she lost her balance, falling backwards. The man tried to grab her to arrest her fall, but he was too late. Aelind closed her eyes and said a silent prayer before the pain shot through her body and her life was forced from her.

****

Anabel pulled a robe around herself and joined Jeroch at the window. They both looked down on the broken body of the personal assistant of the High Priestess, and then looked at one another.

"I'm glad you're the diplomat," Jeroch said finally. "Otherwise this might be trouble."

White, Grey, and Blood

Year Two of the Divine Empress and Child of the Creator Marlae Tamerlane, Creator's Calendar Year 1872

Coriden's eyes shifted to the woman who emerged from the swirling blue portal. She clearly had ability and from the green flicker in her eyes, she had a much greater level of control over her powers than even the Dark God Alderin had. The woman Chelsea and the so-called empress were no challenge to Coriden, and Alderin had been neutralized. Once he took care of this new interloper, he would be able to take the Sacred Weapon from Chelsea. He would take no pleasure in ending the woman's life, but at this point it was a matter of principle. The woman stopped several feet from where Coriden stood. She looked like a commoner in her simple pants and shirt, her lithe form obscured by the unflattering fabric. They were a man's clothes by the cut of them, but she seemed to pay no mind to the unflattering garments. She carried no weapons, but Coriden knew that mattered little. Those who had command over the Blaze had access to any weapon that their minds could conjure. Coriden's dark skin glowed in the dying light of the day, his white hair whipping about in the gentle breeze that began to blow. He pointed one finger at the new arrival and let his cold emotionless voice fill the void between them.

"I have no quarrel with you. My only goal is to acquire the Sacred Weapon from Chelsea Zarova. If she surrenders the weapon, I will leave in peace. You care little for its disposition, so surrender it."

Leonora let a sword of pure Blaze fire appear in her hand. The sword resembled the one that Cedric had trained her with all those years ago, a simple but effective weapon with no ornamentation, designed for killing.

"You may not wish to have a quarrel with me," Leonora responded, "but that won't prevent me from having a quarrel with you. You raised a weapon against my allies, and so you will not leave this place."

The phantasmal green glow intensified around Coriden consolidating around his left hand until it formed into a cruel-looking crescent shaped blade.

"Very well," Coriden said finally. "I shall not weep over your body."

With that, the white-clad member of the Adhradair stepped forward and lowered his sword and his body into a combat stance. His sword was held low, a stance that would take full advantage of his blade's unique shape. Leonora took the moment to size up her opponent. The blade in his left hand would create unique angles of attack that Leonora was not used to defending against. The curve of the blade meant that it would not be used as a thrusting weapon, but as a slashing one. The slashes would be wide and come from odd angles, as the blade was made for chopping and dismembering opponents. Leonora fell into the stance that Cedric had taught her. He had showed her how to keep her weight balanced between her feet so that she could defend from multiple angles simultaneously. Her weapon she pulled up so that it was perpendicular with her chest, both hands on the hilt of her blade. Her right elbow was held high, ready to bring her sword down in a low block, or up in a guard. Because she did not know the full capabilities of her opponent, she would not strike first. Cedric had tried to instill in her patience, but it was never her strongest suit. Once Cedric had told her that the fighting style that he was teaching her was not his own, but rather one taught by one of the greatest swordsmen he had ever seen in combat, a man by the name of Gwydeon Sandar.

Though she did not intend to strike first, Leonora edged closer and closer to Coriden, daring him to strike. Coriden was the picture of relaxed concentration. No expression clouded his face or his eyes, and he took in everything about Leonora's movements. Coriden raised his blade slowly as Leonora approached. Once he had raised his blade so that the center of the blade matched the level of Leonora's he extended it away from his body until their swords touched. They stood like that for several long moments, each quietly daring the other to strike. In the next second both combatants moved in unison, drawing back their blades and swinging fully at their opponent. The two swords met with a shower of green sparks and otherworldly moans. Leonora and Coriden leaned into one another, testing each other's power and intention. Coriden gained a momentary leverage advantage, pushing Leonora back, but with a simple application of the Blaze to the muscles in her legs she was able to nullify any of Coriden's strength advantage. She had to be cautious. Leonora was unfamiliar with the capabilities of the green glow that powered Coriden's abilities, but she could feel the strength of it flowing through his strike. Their blades still joined, the two combatants circled one another, waiting for the opportunity to strike. Leonora delayed, not willing to tip her hand, preferring to let her opponent make the first move. The more information she was able to gather about Coriden's abilities, the greater chance she had to defeat him. As Leonora intended, Coriden was the first to strike in earnest. In one single deft motion he disengaged his blade from Leonora's and leapt at her with his sword raised high. The blade came down in a hard downward slash aimed at her right shoulder. The strike would not have been fatal had it connected, but it would have disabled the woman. Leonora raised her blade and parried the blow. But there was such power behind the attack that it forced Leonora to one knee. The strike parried, Leonora angled her blade away from her body, letting the momentum of Coriden's strike carry him away from her. She spun away in the opposite direction, creating distance between them once again. With her weapon, Leonora had the advantage at distance, while Coriden seemed to have the advantage in close. Coming back to a knee, Leonora slashed at Coriden's knees, but the man was far too fast for such a pedestrian strike to connect. Coriden hopped back, away from the stroke, his blade low, his eyes never leaving his opponent. Leonora rose slowly to her feet, her eyes locked on Coriden, and the two warriors began to circle one another again. Each wary of the other's hidden abilities.

This time it was Leonora that struck first, a direct thrust marking Coriden's left shoulder as the target. The lunge was foiled as Coriden moved faster than Leonora expected, sidestepping the blow. However, Leonora's charge had brought her in range of Coriden's blade, and he brought it down hard intending to end the battle then and there. The strike easily would have cleaved the head of a lesser opponent, but Leonora was the prize student of the Lord Lion and was not going to die so easily. Whether or not her skill was equal to Coriden's was still to be determined, but she was up to this task. As soon as she sensed that her lunging stab would miss its mark, Leonora pulled her sword in and allowed her momentum to carry her into a roll that brought her under the path of Coriden's sword. At the end of the roll, Leonora popped up to a knee and brought her sword up in time to stop Coriden from hurrying into another strike. Instead, Coriden thought better of pressing a perceived advantage and stayed a safe distance from Leonora as she rose back to her feet. The deadly game continued moments later, the two circling again, the pace still slow and deliberate. The respect was there, and the combatants were ready to fully test the skills of the other. Coriden lunged forward, but instead of targeting a body part again, Coriden targeted Leonora's blade. His intent was to test her hold on her powers, and as to whether the constructs of the Chorus of Souls were stronger than the constructs of the Blaze. Their swords met time and time again as the two tried to find some inch of opening that they could exploit to draw first blood. Blaze fire flashed against otherworld spirits and sparks flew as the two swords challenged one another for superiority. The light from the crossing blades blurred the motion of the combatants, making it difficult for each to keep up with the movements of the other. They danced around one another with deadly precision, not willing to give the other an opening. Slashes flowed into blocks which flowed into parries, the margin for error so small that it was impossible for the two to maintain the impregnable defense for long. It was as if any moment one of the two would slip, and a strike would land that would prove to be fatal. In a battle like this, first blood was liable to be last blood, as the one who slipped would end up with a sword in the heart, or the loss of a head. It would only be a matter of time.

The combatants broke apart again. However, Leonora planted her foot and charged seconds later. Coriden was ready. As the two combatants passed one another, both charging at full speed, time slowed to a crawl. Plumes of blood burst forth from each of the combatants, and as they ended their lunges and turned back to face one another, pain was etched on each of their faces. Blood flowed down Leonora's side coating her shirt and pants in hot blood. Only a trickle of Blaze energy was required to knit the wound, but the pain continued to rocket through her body. Clearly the energy from the Chorus of Souls had some lingering effect. Coriden too seemed worse for the exchange, his white clothing also stained red with blood. The wound had sealed, but Blaze fire danced around the edges of the wound still threatening to burn the ancient man from the inside out. Coriden let a smile curl one corner of his lips, impressed with the proficiency of his opponent. Coriden brought his sword up to rest on his shoulder and let a taunt cross the air between them.

"It seems that you are well trained for a mortal. But no amount of training will prevent your death. I have seen your skill and tasted your power now. This battle is over."

Leonora sneered.

"You talk too much."

Leonora's charge came the next moment, the blade constructed of the pulsating force known as the Blaze coming down in a long hard slash. Coriden's blade dropped from his shoulder and he brought up his curved nearly ethereal blade. The two weapons struck again with a flash of light and thunder. Leonora was taken off her feet by the force of the strike as Coriden poured more of the power of the Chorus of Souls into his blade. It took several moments for Leonora to be able to pull herself back to her feet. Rather than brushing the dirt off her hands and arms, Leonora forced herself back into a fighting stance, channeling more of the Blaze energy into her aching muscles. Coriden stood very still watching Leonora's recovery, his glowing phantom blade showing its inner power with that haunting emerald glow, ready to block whatever attack Leonora saw fit to launch against him next. Leonora felt the rage surge within her, the kind of rage that Cedric had always cautioned her against in their training. Despite herself, Leonora held the rage at bay and slowly approached the man who clearly had the potential to match if not exceed her own abilities. With several long, yet carefully considered strides, she stood before Coriden again, her blade in a ready position, but the leverage in her body not ready for a quick decisive strike. She kept her weight as balanced as she could even though every fiber of her being was telling her to be as aggressive as possible. Coriden regarded the woman's body language and saw the casual ease with which she was walking and tried not to be unnerved by it. He had dealt the woman a substantial blow, one that had reminded her that her life was on the line. But it seemed that Leonora was trying to entice Coriden to lower his guard by the matter-of-fact nature of her approach. Coriden was unsure whether Leonora was going to strike or wait for Coriden's attack due to the casual ease of her stance. That next moment, the blade constructed of pure Blaze energy lashed out in a quick arch and Coriden sidestepped and brought his own sword to bear. Leonora had been testing his resolve, and it was a test that Coriden was too practiced and disciplined to fail.

Leonora frowned. She had hoped to catch Coriden overconfident and not paying attention. However, the opening had not been there as Leonora would have expected. She would not make the same mistake again. She had been thinking too much, and if Coriden had been more aggressive, he possibly could have overpowered her yet again. Leonora did not believe that Coriden was invincible, but he certainly was practiced and careful. Coriden began to feel that he had gained an advantage in this battle and was ready to take the fight to Leonora. He would eliminate this troublesome impediment and then visit his justice upon Chelsea, Dominique, and Alderin. Once they had been eliminated, Coriden would claim the Sacred Weapon and return the imprisoned soul of Judoc to the living world. The first blow of a new assault came quickly raining down on Leonora as the hard downward slash struck the flat of her blade. Leonora's parry was quick and concise, exactly as one would expect from someone trained by a master of the sword. Undeterred by Leonora's defense, Coriden recovered and continued with two quick slashes. Each slash was intended not only to overcome Leonora's close defense and expose an opportunity to land a fatal blow. Despite her growing irritation and rage, the practiced reflexes ingrained in her by Cedric's training took over and Leonora parried each of the blows harmlessly away. Coriden sensed that there was no reason to maintain a deliberate pace any longer and began to increase the frequency and intensity of his blows. Leonora became lost in the flow of the battle, no longer thinking about defending Chelsea, or anything other than defeating her opponent. Her focus was solely on the blade in her hand and the opponent across from her. He was her whole world, and nothing else existed. One by one, each of Coriden's attacks were blocked or harmlessly parried aside while Leonora remained on the defensive. With each attack, Leonora got a better sense of his timing and his pace, until she began to see the flaws in his form. Finally, Leonora had seen enough, and she was ready to take the fight fully to her opponent.

Leonora countered what appeared to be a lazy slash and stepped into Coriden, locking the guard of her blade against the guard of Coriden’s. Coriden pushed hard against Chelsea’s advance, but this time he could not push the woman away. Redoubling his efforts, Coriden dug in and summoned more power from the Chorus of Souls and let it reinforce the musculature of his legs. He tried to gain the upper hand in this test of strength, but regardless of the power that he brought to bear, he could not gain the upper hand on Leonora. For her part, Leonora too began to exert force on the crux of the two weapons, channeling more and more of the powers of the Blaze into her body. There was no subtlety in her application of the Blaze, there was only raw power; raw, unrestrained power. They had reached a stalemate. The heightened senses granted by her application of the Blaze allowed Leonora to hear the tensed muscles and the gritting of Coriden's teeth. It seemed as though he was putting in everything that he had to their contest of power. With a single additional push, Coriden was sent sprawling across the ground. The crescent-shaped blade disappeared from Coriden’s hand as he struck the ground, but as he pulled himself quickly back to his feet, the sword reappeared. The aura of phantasmal energy flared brighter around Coriden, the sound of the wailing souls growing louder and louder. It was clear that Coriden was far from finished with this duel, and he was ready to pour every last ounce of his power into the final act of the duel. Leonora could see the change in the intensity of the haze of the Chorus of Souls, the power sustaining and reinforcing Coriden’s defenses. Without warning Coriden charged forward, the cruel blade chopping toward Leonora’s head. Leonora countered the charge with one of her own, ducking under the high slash and bringing her blade to the recently healed flank of the member of the Adhradair. Once again, the Blaze-charged sword ripped through Coriden’s flesh, drawing a fresh plume of blood. Leonora turned after the strike, determining whether she would be able to follow-up with a final blow, but Coriden, despite being wounded, was fast enough to bring his defenses back to bear.

This time Coriden did not waste the power to knit the wound in his side. Leonora could see the fires of Blaze energy tearing through her opponent, slowly sapping his strength as it fought with the Chorus of Souls in an effort to burn Coriden from the inside out. For her part, Leonora could still feel the impact of the Chorus of Souls on her insides. She was shaken, her balance not quite right. It felt like there was a steady vibration running through each of her limbs, and occasionally her eyes would lose focus for no reason. At the very edges of her hearing, she could vaguely make out what sounded like whispers, and those whispers would rise and fall, giving way to screams and moans. She wasn't sure that she was going to be able to keep up the pace for much longer. Cedric had always warned her against prolonged use of the Blaze, and she knew that the more she drew on the nearly limitless powers of the Blaze, the greater chance it had to burn her alive.

"Your powers are fading," Coriden chided. "How long can you keep this up? I think perhaps one more pass, and you will no longer be able to stand."

Leonora smiled.

"Then I better kill you now."

With that, Leonora launched herself at Coriden again, this time with more fury. Blow after blow rained down on Coriden, each one parried in turn. Coriden was not content to simply parry, turning the parries into counters, forcing Leonora to block more blows than she was attempting. In only a matter of seconds, Leonora was totally on the defensive, and was stumbling backward against the flashing assaults of the cruel crescent blade. Leonora began to feel a rage building inside of her like she had never felt before. In the back of her mind, she saw all of the horrors that Dorovar had inflicted on the people of Cadaria in just a few short years. She could see the bodies lying in the streets of Rashaleb once the Herald of Dorovar had turned the once-proud kingdom into a ghost town. She could see every victim of the Crawling Plague and the Wasting Disease. She heard the cries of anguish from people that she knew from when she was a child. She saw the broken bodies of soldiers from her kingdom laying on the field outside the Academy of Arcane Arts in Jelan. She saw the creature named Death nearly wiping out the whole of the Heart of Stone, and the attempted execution of her friend Hannah Ironheart. But it was Cedric's face that she saw in her mind. The man that she loved. The man that she thought was dead. The woman that she met named Jillian who was Cedric's daughter. In her mind were visions of a life that was stolen from her. A world where she and Cedric were happy. A world where they had a family together. A world without Dorovar. A world without Kaitain. A world without the misery and suffering that had been visited upon the people day after day and year after year.

Leonora in that moment countered a crushing blow from Coriden and brought one of her own raining down upon him. The wailing of the Chorus of Souls increased tenfold when her blade of Blaze energy struck Coriden's crescent sword. Coriden reeled from the impact, but was able to bring up the blade in time as the next hard downward slash hit. The force of the blow was nearly enough to force Coriden to one knee. It was the third slash however that forced Coriden down, one hand on the hilt of his spectral sword while the other braced the blade in an effort to block the continued onslaught. Over and over, the fiery blade slammed into coalesced emerald force, the intensity of the wail from the Chorus of Souls echoing like a hurricane forming around them. The sound was deafening, and as it increased in intensity, the ache in Leonora grew and grew. Despite the pain, Leonora continued the assault, unrelenting as she pounded down upon her opponent over and over again. A cry of rage and pain tore from Leonora's throat as she brought the blade crashing down. The sound that came from the Chorus of Souls was unlike anything that Leonora had ever heard before and then there was an explosion of energy that radiated in all directions. Leonora was blown off her feet, sent flying backwards dozens of feet. When her head hit the ground, she was robbed of consciousness for several moments, and when her eyes opened again, she didn't know where she was for a moment. Then when her memory filled in the pieces, part of her expected to see Coriden standing over her, ready to take her head. But all she saw above her was sky.

It took Leonora several moments to regain her equilibrium, but once she did, she pushed herself back to a sitting position. While her first inclination was to form another weapon out of Blaze energy, she found that when she reached for the fickle green power, it would not respond to her call. Feeling utterly defenseless, Leonora scrambled to her feet looking for Coriden. Regardless of where she turned, the white-clad man was nowhere to be found. She wasn't sure whether or not the explosive wave of energy from the Chorus of Souls had meant his death or if it had merely been a way for him to enact his escape. Either way, Coriden was gone. The battle was over for now, but something inside Leonora told her that she would be seeing the man again.

Leonora got back to her feet, moving to where Chelsea and Dominique knelt beside Alderin. The young man had already started to regain consciousness, and whatever damage Coriden's attack had done was already beginning to mend. Satisfied that the young man would recover, Leonora turned her attention to Chelsea.

"What are you doing out here, Chelsea?"

Chelsea looked up at Leonora for a moment and then stood. The two women had always had a good relationship, and so it was quickly apparent to Chelsea that something had changed in the older woman.

"Protecting my charge. Doing my duty."

Ordinarily that answer would have been enough for Leonora, but the woman gave Chelsea a withering stare before speaking again.

"That's not an answer."

Chelsea crossed her arms.

"I'm escorting Dominique to Iltorp, the Keep of the Serpentine Knight. We're hoping that from there we can unite Saldarine and Thorigald under the banner of Quyhn Ravenheart. As the last recognized heir to Kaitain's throne, she has the most legitimate claim to be Empress of Cadaria. Dominique has put her support behind Quyhn, so have the Peregrims of Lordhill, and several members of the Dark Gods."

That brought an immediate reaction from Leonora.

"What Dark Gods?"

It was Alderin's voice that answered.

"Gwydeon and Midarin Sandar and their daughter Camille, my nieces Mirana and Liara Ranthall."

Alderin had pulled himself to a sitting position and Chelsea could see the relief growing on Dominique's face.

"I suppose we are all finding ourselves working with interesting allies these days. But as to who is in the best position to rule this empire, we may find ourselves at cross-purposes. I've recently become loosely allied with Marlae Lorien, though she's calling herself Marlae Tamerlane these days. I say loosely because my affiliation is through Logan Ranthall and Rhain Seth."

Alderin made his way to his feet with Dominique's help.

"Rhain sent you to find me?"

Leonora nodded.

"And to bring you back."

Alderin quickly shook his head.

"I'm sorry, I can't. I gave my word that I would escort Chelsea and Dominique safely to Albitonin, and I intend to do that. Then I'm going after Darrien. Rhain is just going to have to wait."

Leonora considered for a moment.

"Then I'm going to travel with you. You can fill me in on what you and your allies have been up to, and I can tell you what I know. I'm sure you'll find it quite illuminating."

Eclipsed by Destiny

Year Five of the Just Emperor Kaitain "Dragonsbane" Lorien, Creator's Calendar Year 1872

Kaitain stalked around the small abbey a day's ride from the capital of Zevarit, his heels clicking on the ancient cobblestone floor. Only two hours before, this place had been home to a small order of monks whose mission was to preserve the teachings of the Creator in exacting detail. Eighteen hours a day they slaved away over meticulous illuminations of what was considered the oldest remaining copy of the Words of the Creator, the teachings that formed the foundation of the Church of the Creator. Though all fifty of the brothers that called the abbey home knew the words of the text by heart, still they slavishly worked to reproduce every blemish, every imperfection, and every stroke of the pen. They even went so far as to smear their own blood on the cover of the book once it was completed. Legend had it that a member of their order had saved the book at the end of the Founding Wars by tucking it into his robe while fleeing a battle that had raged around his abbey. The abbey was said to be burned to the ground on the very ground where this abbey stood. The monk was struck in the shoulder by an arrow as he fled, and the arrow pierced him through from back to front. His blood smeared across the front of the book as he fled. When the monk reached the safety of another abbey, it was said that he died the moment he put the book into the hands of another monk.

CHAPTER 110

Kaitain stopped at the reliquary doorway again and stared at the book. He had already stopped here a dozen times since Alise departed, and each time he found himself walking away and touring the rooms of the now empty so-called holy place. After their fateful meeting with the being that called itself Dorovar, Alise and Kaitain happened across the abbey. Despite her recent failures, Alise proved herself to be a capable enough killer. In a matter of minutes, she had bloodily dispatched every member of the small monastic order. Their corpses were left in pools of their own blood, vicious claw marks across chests and throats. Her grizzly work done, Kaitain allowed Alise to go after the Dragon's Tear alone. She wanted to prove herself, and Kaitain considered that if she succeeded, he would be in possession of the Tear, and if she failed, she likely would not return at all.

The first thing that struck Kaitain was how small and ugly the abbey was. There were no tapestries, no finery, and no sense of anything beyond the stone and dankness. How anyone would willingly live like this baffled Kaitain. The rooms that the monks inhabited were tiny, barely large enough for the small thing that passed for a bed. There was no frame, no thick mattress, or thick comforters. The bedroll that lay on the ground might as well as been parchment considering how thin it was, and there was only a simple sheet pulled over it. Zevarit could be very cold in the winter, and these men were content with something that could never keep them warm. Kaitain always had a dozen pillows on his bed, full and fluffy, like clouds. These men had but a single pillow stuffed with what must have been plant stalks and grain husks. It was disgusting.

What irritated Kaitain the most was what he found in the lead monk's office. Someone with that amount of responsibility should have demonstrated it through the trappings of his office. This man, this pathetic excuse for a leader had only a large wooden chair that could in any way, shape, or form be considered out of the ordinary in this place. Though he rarely chose to get his own hands dirty, Kaitain had to make his temporary home as presentable as possible. Dragging the chair from the small office into the chapel was difficult but not impossible. The tight doorways and hallways made the enterprise more annoying than an exertion. Of course, once he got the chair to the chapel Kaitain had to upend the altar to make proper space for it. Once in position, Kaitain set about the more gruesome work.

The pews were easily pushed aside, opening space for the makeshift throne room. One by one, Kaitain dragged the bodies of the monks into the chapel, bent their bodies until they were on their knees, face down, with arms extended. While the undertaking could have been considered frivolous by some, to Kaitain it was a perfect use of his time. Once finished, Kaitain sat down on his makeshift throne in front of his deceased supplicants his feet resting on the ancient Words of the Creator. It did not take long for the annoyance with his surroundings to begin to grate upon his nervous. Fortunately, however, his torment did not last long.

At the far end of the impromptu receiving hall, a swirling blue portal winked into existence. First out of the portal was a young-looking girl who could only have been Tess Annis, the Dragon's Tear. She was beautiful without a doubt though plain to Kaitain's eye, but it was an eerie, nearly unsettling beauty. Tess was pale, almost white, and her body was very lithe. Her long brown hair hung loose falling to one side and resting on her right shoulder. However, it was her eyes, those golden eyes that immediately drew Kaitain's attention. Her features were flawless, and her skin looked smooth and supple. Pale rose colored lips, and high cheekbones. She easily would have fit the description of a goddess for most, but for Kaitain, she was nothing more than a tool. She was his path to transcendence. She was his path to total domination of Espre. Quickly following Tess was Alise, looking less pleased with herself than Kaitain would have imagined. The look on her face was more one of puzzlement and uncertainty. They were unusual emotions for a killer such as Alise to exhibit. Kaitain did not move from his position and watched impassively behind his cruel mask as the two women walked down the path between the supplicants. Tess stopped two feet away from the ancient book, her hands clasped together at her waist, her face expressionless.

"So, this girl will reshape reality at my whim."

Alise moved past where Tess had stopped and moved to Kaitain's side. Kaitain did not let his gaze leave Tess's face.

"Did she give you any trouble?"

Alise looked first to Kaitain and then to Tess. She could have lied of course. Even with Kaitain's ability to detect falsehood, Alise had always been able to hide her dissembling from him. Perhaps it was because of the nature of her birth, or perhaps it was because of the magicks that even enabled her to live, but whatever the reason, she did not fear his lie detection. But in this instance, she was curious to see Kaitain's reactions to the truth.

"No, she did not. She came willingly."

Alise felt nothing from Kaitain. He did not shift in the simple wooden chair, nor were any emotions rolling from him. He was an island of calm in a world gone mad, and perhaps that was far more disturbing than puzzlement or irritation.

"Interesting," his voice intoned coldly. "Very interesting."

Tess and Kaitain kept their eyes trained on one another for several long moments before Tess lowered her head and spoke softly.

"You've seen it too."

Kaitain nodded slowly.

"Yes, I have. I have seen the great battle ahead. I have seen the destruction and the blood. I have seen you at the heart of it all."

Tess closed her eyes and kept Cedric in her mind.

"I don't have to be the cause of that."

Kaitain did not respond for a moment, and then kicked the book out from under his feet so that it skidded to a stop in front of Tess.

"Oh, my dear deluded girl. You won't be the cause of it. It's already happening."

It was clear by Tess's reaction that she was not expecting Kaitain's actions or his words. There was a softening around her eyes and just a speck of confusion that touched her gaze. It lasted a fraction of a second before the calm descended on her features once more, but it was clear to Kaitain in that moment that whatever the girl was, whatever power she had sequestered inside of her, there was a fragility there. She was a tool, not a person. She needed to be treated as one.

"You need to look no further than that book at your feet and your own history. You are not the cause of destruction and blood. Destruction and blood are the natural order of the Creator's universe. Everything that he has created is coated in pain and suffering. Even the so-called divine are not immune to this. Dorovar, the dragons, the Dark Gods, all victims."

There was a barely perceptive nod that came from the girl, and Kaitain pressed, sensing the weakness within her. Kaitain was an expert on human weakness and how to turn it to his advantage. Could the weakness in a Dark God be that different?

"If the Creator willed it, could He not end war? Could He not end hunger? Could He not end suffering? Of course, He could. Now that book at your feet will tell you that all of the suffering we experience is so that we can overcome it. So we can better know the Creator's love. So, the love of the Creator is conditional upon suffering? It is conditional on death and depredation and despair?"

Tess shifted uncomfortably and made no attempt to hide it. Kaitain was supposed to be evil. He was supposed to be one of the forces that destabilized this world, and if that was so, he should not have been able to make sense. Cedric said that people could have good motives for evil acts; that even villains could seem to have goodness in them. But when was it actual goodness and when was it an act? It was clear that the reverse was also true. Look at her own father. Pike was supposed to be a hero and yet he was capable of such terrible things, and of so much death. Her own sister spent years covering up their father's misdeeds. Even Cedric had killed in the name of what he thought was right only to find out that it was all a lie. He spent centuries trying to make up for acts that it could be argued were not his fault. And now sitting before her was Kaitain Lorien. A man who fomented war everywhere his feet touched ground. A man who killed and destroyed people simply because of their beliefs. So why was it that his words sounded less like those of a madman and more like someone fighting against a true evil? Why did he speak like a hero?

"You see the conflict, don't you?" Kaitain continued. "I remember the moment that I saw it."

Kaitain stood slowly, careful to not make any sudden moves that would threaten the girl.

"Many in my position, knowing what you are, would give you some grand show of their good intentions. I have no desire to lie to you, and thus I will tell you perhaps the worst story I can of myself. You see, my brother, Feyd, was the darling of the court. He was a good man, a better man than I, and I think that my father would have preferred that he inherited the throne and not I. But the lot of the younger brother can be a blessing. He did not have the responsibility awaiting him. He did not have the weight of his name perched as firmly on his shoulders. What he did have however was love. Everywhere he went Feyd engendered love. But there was one love, one woman, who inflamed Feyd more than any other. Her name was Teairra."

Kaitain balled his fist.

"Love stories only exist in books, Tess. The world is much too ugly for them to really exist."

Tess nodded.

"Yes, the world is too ugly for those stories."

Immediately images flashed into Tess's mind. Her father and the broken bodies of those who had shared his bed over his lifetime. The look of horror on Devlin Rannoch's face when Tess reached into his chest to stop his heart, all for the crime of loving the woman that Tess herself loved. Lissa watching over the sleeping form of the man that she loved for thousands of years unable to rouse him from his slumber. Darrien and Alderin, locked together as much in love as they were in shame for their actions. Midarin, spending her days with part of her heart missing for over a millennium. All the great loves that Tess had known were filled with misery.

"And so, my brother, my younger favored brother, found this love and knew without question that this woman was the one he would spend the rest of his life with. However, I was the older brother. I was the one who was to rule the empire. I was the one who should have had everything he wanted. Nevertheless, I found that the more I had, the more I wanted. That was what my father made me to be. He made me to be the man that would rule not just an empire, but a world. Everyone wants to remember my father as the Just Hand. The even-tempered man who strove to treat everyone equally. That was not the man I knew growing up. My father encouraged competition between my brother and I in everything we did. Moreover, if I were not the best, my father would lord it over me for weeks. Of course, my brother did not receive the same treatment because he was not the heir apparent to the throne. He was just another tool that my father used to teach me lessons."

Kaitain paused and held out both of his hands palms up.

"And so here I was left with two choices. I could respect my brother and allow him to have what he wanted even though I knew and was taught to take that which I desired. Doing so would have probably drawn the ire of my father and would have left within me a hole that I would have never been able to fill and would have engendered even greater resentment for my brother than it does now. Or I could take what I wanted regardless of the cost. Because that is what I am. That is what I was made to be."

Tess looked between the man's hands. In her mind she heard the lessons of her own father and the lessons of Cedric Binosear. The lessons of the man calling himself Emries. She even heard the lessons taught by her beloved Camille. They were the lessons of power. The application of power. The restraint of power. The responsibility of power. The allure of power. The corruption of power.

Pike taught that all those who had power would seek to use it, and never for the pure intentions that may have started their quest. However, Pike was a corrupt man who did not seek to rule over people, but instead sought to rule himself and his thwarted ambition. Emries taught that power could remake the world, power could remake the Cosmos, and that the power itself created the right to do what you wanted with that power. This was how the Children viewed their worlds. They would not seek to see another way because power was the genesis of what they were and the thing that would always define them. It was not corruption; it was the natural order.

Cedric did not discourage the use of power, but he did seek to show how that power could be used to better or worse effect based on the intention of the user. Even when Cedric sought to do good with the power that he had, death, destruction, and pain followed in his wake, none more profound than the pain he carried inside of himself. Camille's lessons were less specific, as she always preached seeing as many angles as possible before making a decision, and that no matter what there was never a perfect option. It was always a matter of balancing the good with the bad.

"But you could not be who you were not," Tess said finally. "And so, you took what you wanted."

Kaitain tried to keep the joy from coming to his eyes.

"I did." He kept his voice flat, matter of fact. "I arranged to have my brother transferred to a forward position where there was fighting between two of the great kingdoms and where there was a better than average chance that he would not return. However, I knew my brother and I knew the men that would follow him into battle. Of course, he would come back. But that didn't matter. What mattered was that Teairra believed he might not come back, and that she was distraught because of the possibility. I went to comfort her, and though she objected to my advances, I would not take no for an answer. There was much effort put behind my machinations and I would not be denied my prize."

Kaitain returned to his chair and sat.

"So, I took what I wanted. And once I had had my prize, the rest did not matter. Such is the application of power that I chose."

Tess saw immediately her father sitting before her. That attitude, that flippant nature, and that complete disregard for anything other than the wants of the moment. It was disgusting. And yet at the same time it was completely and totally understandable.

"Which brings me to the moment I saw the conflict that I spoke of. My brother returned from the front and Teairra returned to his arms. She confessed to him her dalliance, and he forgave her, though of course he would never forgive me even if he did not understand the depths of my betrayal. They married, they made a life, they had a child. And though I found my own bride, and had my own child, my eye never fell far from the happiness that my brother had found despite what I had done to them both. It was as though he had taken back from me the victory I created. That somehow the very nature of their love and devotion was greater than a stolen moment. It inflamed me."

Tess nodded.

"Because you did not see that what they had was a power you could not command. It was outside of you, regardless of the extent of your reach."

Kaitain's eyes widened.

"You see it."

Tess nodded again.

"Yes. I have taken what I thought was mine. And when it was claimed by someone else, I felt I had no choice but to crush the man who stood between me and my prize. I put my hand into his chest, and I stopped his heart. His love could never be greater than mine, and so it had to end. The delusion had to end."

As if mesmerized by the words, Kaitain rose again slowly, his feet dragging him forward.

"And just the same, I could not abide Feyd overshadowing my power with his lesser status. He could not be allowed to surpass me with his happiness."

Tess finished Kaitain's words.

"So, you took from him what he did not deserve. You arranged for his wife to be murdered. His suffering had to mirror his hubris."

Kaitain's mind whirled. He knew that the girl had the power to shape reality, but he did not know what other abilities she could manifest. Was she reading his thoughts? Was she looking into the past and watching him issue the order that ended Teairra's life? Or did she simply see the impacts of his deeds on his soul? What she said next shocked him even further.

"But that wasn't enough. Simply taking from him what he had could only be the beginning. You had to surpass that which he had created. He had a child with the woman that he loved, a child that could surpass your own child. So, you had to create something that would surpass that child. You had her created."

A chill went through Alise. She was not ignorant to her origins, but to hear it so plainly and matter-of-factly explained was jarring even for the unflappable killer. Kaitain for his part felt his lips twist into a cruel smile behind his mask.

"Not unlike my own nature," Tess continued. "I was made to be a weapon. I was made by one of the Children of the Creator to destroy all that which the other Children held dear. I was made to rip the Creator from his Throne. I was made, like your Alise, to be a killer and a destroyer. That is why my dreams are filled with blood. That is why death has always swirled around me. And that is why I am here."

Tess reached down and picked up the ancient Words of the Creator from the floor and held it out to Kaitain.

"You spoke of the conflict, the love supposedly embodied by the Creator, and yet He allows the wicked and the powerful to take and destroy and corrupt all that they touch. My father, the leader of the Dark Gods killed indiscriminately to satiate his carnal needs and to quiet the self-loathing in his soul. That was how he expressed the great power given to him by the Creator. You, the leader of the people of Cadaria, you send people to die in frivolous wars to glorify yourself. You kill those who get in your way, and you rape and steal to ensure that no one rises above you."

Kaitain's blood burned at the characterization, but if Tess felt his rage building, it did not seem to faze her.

"And I, perhaps the most powerful being on this world, what do I do to make it better? I kill the lover of a woman I adore simply because her eye found him and not me. I ripped apart a man who wanted to bring peace to this world. I nearly killed my sister and her lover. And now I stand here willingly before the man who is supposed to be my enemy, ready to help him to make the visions in my nightmares come true."

A small peak of fire appeared on top of the ancient book.

"The Creator will banish this world to fire if he succeeds in his aims. Those who fight against him are trying to prevent this. But they are deluded. That is what I have learned from my tutors in power. Cedric tried to show me a better way to fight, but he knew in his heart that there was no avoiding the death and destruction that was coming, and he more than anyone knew that many would have to be sacrificed for the greater goal. There is no avoiding what will come. This world will burn."

The fire sparked brighter and the whole of the book began to crumple and turn black in Tess's hands. But the fire did not touch her skin, and her golden eyes flashed with power.

"And so, Emperor Kaitain Lorien, I shall walk beside you, and I shall advance your goals in bringing this madness to the whole of the world. The worship of the Creator must be snuffed out. All who follow must be shown the error of their ways. They will follow you, or their delusion will be burned out of their soul. From one end of this world to the other, we will tear down all vestiges of the Creator. Every church, every abbey, every temple. There will be nothing left until at last the Heart of Stone is torn down and the flames of righteous rage touch the souls of the Divine Empress and High Priestess and rend every last element of faith from their soul. There must be nothing left for the Creator. We must take everything from him upon this world before we take everything from Him in the Heavens."

Her eyes flashed again, and Kaitain could feel the power roll from her like waves. Part of him knew that he should be afraid of the girl, but all he could do was laugh. The laugh came from the part of his soul that reveled in every kill. The part of his soul that found solace in the torment of others. The monster beneath the skin of the man.

"I shall rip the wings from every angel. I shall burn them with their own fiery swords. And when I stand before the Golden Throne, I shall turn it black with the blood of the Creator's servants. If the Creator's worlds were made in pain and conflict, the next reality shall be made from blood. Blood and vengeance. Those are the only constants. Those are the only truths."

Tess reached out and laid her hand on the side of Kaitain's mask. Kaitain felt a cool energy run through his body. The next instant the mask was gone, and the girl's hand was touching his cheek. The damage from the poison had been healed.

"We shall take back everything that was taken from us. We shall take everything that we are owed. We will take everything our power allows." Tess's voice was icy and powerful. "We will take until this world has nothing more to give, and it burns beneath our feet. And then the Heavens will feel our rage, a rage that will blot out every star, and consume every speck of light."

Fear gripped Alise's heart as she heard her father and the girl begin laughing. It was a laugh that froze the blood and fractured the soul. It was a laugh of a madness that would consume everything it touched and eclipse all sanity left in Creation.

Shadows of Hope

Year Two of the Divine Empress and Child of the Creator Marlae Tamerlane, Creator's Calendar Year 1872

Marlae awoke with a start, for a moment not realizing where she was. However, the moment she felt Rhain's smooth skin against her own, whatever anxiety had roused her from her contented slumber was immediately banished. Marlae nuzzled up against Rhain, pulling them tighter together. Rhain had already been awake for quite some time, watching her lover in her gentle slumber. Now that Marlae had roused, even slightly, Rhain let her hand move to the back of Marlae's head, stroking her hair softly. They lay there like that for a long time until Marlae looked up into Rhain's eyes, smiled slightly and then pulled herself up to kiss the taller woman. Rhain let Marlae's lips linger against hers for a long moment before she pulled Marlae tight to her and kissed her back passionately. Marlae went nearly limp in Rhain's arms and then pulled away, her eyes fluttering closed and her head resting on the much older woman's chest. Marlae draped herself across Rhain, feeling safe and loved for the first time in a long time. But whatever contentment was holding Marlae in that moment, she knew that it could not last forever. There was much to be done, and no time to do it all.

"This cannot last, can it?"

Marlae's voice sounded small, smaller than Rhain had ever heard it. Whatever Marlae had been the last time that she and Rhain had been together, clearly that version of the woman no longer existed. There was no trace of the haughty princess that desired to rule the world and felt that she deserved to simply because she existed. There was no trace of the vindictiveness and pettiness. Marlae had grown up and embraced the woman that she always had the power within her to be. But there was more, and it was the more that troubled Rhain. Whatever else had led Marlae to her new existence, she was the chosen vessel of the Creator's authority on Espre. For all intents and purposes, she was the right hand of the enemy. But what was still unclear was whether or not the Creator could control Marlae. The trepidation of what would come next consumed Rhain, and part of her was not sure she would be able to face the consequences. She could have left it to Jeroch, could have shied away from the pain that it might cause. But the part of her that was her father's daughter would not allow her to shirk her responsibilities, and the part of her that was her mother could not stand to let someone do a job that she was singularly capable of completing. With her next words, Marlae surprised Rhain again.

"So how do you figure out whether you can trust me or not?"

Rhain stayed silent and stroked the smaller woman's hair. The answer was complex at best, and overly simplistic at worst. After a few moments of the silence that held them both, Marlae pulled herself free of Rhain's embrace. She sat near the edge of the bed, one leg tucked up under her while the other hung off the edge, her toes barely scraping the rug on the floor below. Marlae turned fully to face Rhain, and then as if suddenly realizing that she was nude and that her new life required more modesty than she had shown in the past, a slight color came to her cheeks, and she reached for the simple dressing gown that she had worn the night before. After draping the gown over her shoulders, she returned her gaze to Rhain. Rhain made no effort to cover herself, feeling that moment more connected to her mother, a pillar of confidence in a repressed world. The silence held again, and Marlae felt the utter weight of it.

"And if you can't trust me, that means you have to kill me, right?"

Rhain ground her teeth but could not keep the corners of her mouth from twisting into a frown. She pulled herself straighter and let the cool wood of the headboard attempt to quench some of the fire that was crawling across her skin. Pulling one knee up but resisting the urge to hug it to her, Rhain instead rested her elbow on top of the knee and then let her chin fall to the back of her hand.

"I'm faced with several bad options, Marlae," Rhain said finally. "You have been touched by the Creator. What that means is anyone's best guess. Is he seeing through your eyes? Does he know everything you know? Can he control your actions? If he thinks we're holding you prisoner or going to harm you in some way, does that mean he will send the whole host of the Heavens after us?"

Rhain closed her eyes for a moment, her next words she knew she could not say looking in Marlae's eyes.

"And if I were to kill you, the Creator could just bring you back. And if he did that, what would happen to your soul? Would you still be you? Or would you just be a puppet on his strings just like the Servants?"

When Rhain opened her eyes, she saw that a single tear had rolled down Marlae's cheek, but there was no sorrow in her eyes, and her posture had not changed. Silently Marlae nodded, and then spoke in a very calm yet confident voice.

"You've been careful to keep me away from your plans, and I have to applaud you for that. I learned a lot in my time as the selfish and plotting Marlae Lorien, and my father would always say that anyone you could not completely trust was a spy and you could never completely trust anyone. Strangely enough, the Creator and my father seem to have a lot in common."

Rhain could not help the small chuckle that forced its way from her lips. The thought was absurd, and yet could not reasonably be denied. Both of the violent dictators trafficked in subjugation and fear, just on much different scales.

"But I am more than what the Creator shaped me into. Another lesson that my father taught me was that if you are not a user, then you are allowing yourself to be used. It's clear that for whatever reason, I am a piece that others have been trying to use for some time. Whether it was my father, or the Creator, or Dorovar, or even you my dear sweet Rhain, there is something about my former life that appealed to the users of this world. But that was before. I've learned a lot since then, and I've had some help to find my new path. I don't want to be used any more Rhain, and I don't want to be a user. There has to be another way through this."

Rhain could not suppress the smile that curled her lips.

"You sound like someone I know."

There was a quizzical sparkle that came to Marlae's eyes, but before she could ask the question that was beginning to form in her mind, Rhain leaned forward and took Marlae by the hand.

"What you're asking, Marlae, will not be easy. I'm not even sure what you're asking can be done. In my heart, I can trust you, I know I can. But my heart is not enough. We are faced with such dire consequences for every action, I cannot allow any situation to be guided by blind faith. So yes, I must know if you have been compromised to the point that you cannot be trusted, and if that is so, I must know what to do with you to minimize the damage you can do to our plans."

Marlae nodded slightly.

"Whatever you need to do."

The smile faded from Rhain's lips and she took hold of Marlae's hand.

"I can't promise this won't hurt."

Marlae lifted her hand with Rhain's, turned her lover's hand over and gave her a long kiss on her palm.

"I trust you."

* * * * * * * * * * * * *

Marlae was very aware of the beat of her heart and each breath that moved through her body. She felt as though she were floating in a vast dark ocean under a black sky, no concept of up or down. At the same time, she could not shake the feeling that she was locked in place. Her head felt as though she had far too much wine, and no matter how hard she tried she could not hold onto a thought. Her mind was equal parts panic and peace. It was too soon after the disturbing dream that had threatened to take everything she had fought so hard for away from her. She tried to think of Logan's cottage, tried to form a picture of it in her mind to ground her, but she couldn't make the walls or the floor materialize. All there was was blackness. A moment later a voice found her ears. It was muffled, as though it were being whispered through a thick cotton wall.

"I'm here with you, Marlae," the voice said, "do not fear."

The voice was familiar, but no matter how hard Marlae tried to find the identity of the voice, she could not. Thoughts slid away from her mind before they could form, swallowed by the blackness that held her. There was a gentle touch, like fingertips on her cheek and the voice came again.

"Relax, Marlae," the gentle voice cooed, seemingly closer this time, "do not try to think. Just let everything slide away from you."

* * * * * * * * * * * * *

Sweat began to bead on Rhain's forehead as she pushed through the formidable layers of protection that the Creator and others had erected around Marlae's soul. She would only get one chance at this, because as soon as the Creator realized what Rhain was attempting, the walls around Marlae would be sewn so tight that no matter the exertion they could not be pierced. As it was, Rhain was taking an unbelievable chance. She may have had the powers of a Child of the Creator, but she was not one. Already Halicon's powers had burned through Sabrina Binosear, and if Rhain was not careful she would be another victim of the strain of the powers upon her very mortal body. Already she was weakened from the exertion that reunited Logan Ranthall's powers as the Lord Phoenix with the other parts of him, Kamen, Rael, and Trece. But what she was doing had to be done. There was no other way. Rhain knew that she could have reached out through the powers of the Blaze and drawn upon the remaining members of the phasia to bolster her strength, but to do so would alert them to the danger that she was in. Their missions were far too important for that. No, no matter the outcome, the burden was on Rhain and Rhain alone. All of her life had prepared her for this moment, to face down the challenge that her mother and father had been grooming her to face. And the only thing that could stop her was her own fear. Marlae was worth the risk. If her father had taught her nothing else, love was worth the risk.

* * * * * * * * * * * * *

Light exploded in Marlae's mind. It was a hot searing light that threatened to burn everything out of her memory. She had felt this light before, it was the same light that had woven through her body when she had been chosen as the Divine Empress, the embodiment of the Creator's will upon Espre. But something was different. When that light had been introduced into her, she had felt calm, ease, and grace. It had taken some of the wickedness from her and suffused her with the capacity to do more and to be more. What she had not known at that time was that it also infused her with a portion of the soul of the woman who had once been Elwyne Tamerlane. This woman would become Marlae's teacher, her inspiration, and the reason that she left the petulant life that she had lived since her birth behind. But this was different. Where the blackness had made it impossible to hold on to a thought, the searing white created so much pain that thoughts could not form. It was as though it was trying to hollow her out, leaving only the light. The voice came again, strained, distant, and almost a whisper.

"Hold on Marlae. Hold on to me. Hold on to my voice. I'll catch you if you fall. Remember that. Remember that no matter what I will catch you."

The words sparked something inside of Marlae, and she tried her best to hold on to one thought, to any thought. Rhain's red hair, Rhain's soft skin, the taste of her lips. She had to hold on. She had to find her way back into Rhain's arms again.

* * * * * * * * * * * * *

Blood began to stream from Rhain's nose with the exertion. She knew she was taking on too much, but she had the ability to heal her own wounds, where Marlae did not. The defenses wrapped around and through the woman's being were impressive, but not unassailable. But there was something else, something more. Something that she was missing.

"This isn't wise, Rhain."

There was movement out of the corner of Rhain's eye, but she didn't have to turn her head to find it. A moment later, Sabrina Binosear's lithe and diminutive form came into view. She sat at the very end of the large bed, smoothed her blue dress, and shook her head before bringing her gaze up to meet Rhain's. Rhain's jaw clenched.

"You're not here," her voice growled. "This is a trick. The Creator is just using you to stop me from what I'm doing."

Sabrina frowned.

"Why would the Creator use me? Why wouldn't he use someone else, like your father or your mother? The reason you're seeing me is because I'm one with the Blaze now, and I'm the only way that the truth you are denying can get out. You know you shouldn't be doing this. It's an unnecessary risk. Marlae may be important to you Rhain, but look at the bigger picture. If you kill yourself now trying to save her, then how can you stop the Creator or protect the phasia like you promised you would? This doesn't make any sense."

A predatory smile came to Rhain's lips.

"Sabrina would never argue against saving one life, no matter whose life it was. Sabrina knew that what she was doing would kill her when she protected us in Celidar's throne room. But she did it anyway. At every turn she would never value her own life above anyone else's. Now, please leave. I have work to do."

The apparition was gone before Rhain could blink. It was clear that she was on the right path. She just needed to press harder.

* * * * * * * * * * * * *

CHAPTER 110

Pain rocketed through Marlae and she thought she was dying. Every part of her body felt as though it were on fire. Each of her finger and toenails felt like they were being pulled from their nail beds, and her hair was being ripped free at the root. Marlae's eyes burned so hot that she couldn't open them, and each breath was liquid fire that filled her lungs. Needles punctured every inch of her skin, and each joint felt distended and stressed to the point of breaking. But regardless of the pain that wracked her body, Marlae still held on to the voice that was now so distant that only the memory and not the sound of it remained. She held fast to the fleeting and failing memories of the woman that she loved, even though she could no longer remember the woman's name. There were echoes of red in her memory. Perhaps it was the color of a dress that she wore, or maybe the color of her lips. It didn't matter. Marlae knew that she existed, knew that she was loved and safe. Knew that there was someone waiting for her once this torment passed. And the torment would pass. It had to. The only alternative was death.

"That's right, Marlae. Just let go."

The voice was back. But was it the same voice? It felt like the same voice. It was muffled, and distant, and oddly comforting.

"This pain can all stop. All you have to do is let go. Let the light and the fire take it all. Just let everything go and sleep in the light. All of the pain will stop. All of the torment will stop. There will be no more conflict. There will be nothing but peace. Sleep in the light, Marlae. Just sleep."

Marlae wanted the pain to end. Wanted it to all stop. Maybe that was best. Maybe letting the light take her was the right thing to do. Why was she fighting in the first place? Was there someone? Was there a reason? Why did she keep thinking about red?

****

Blood was now streaming from Rhain's nose as well as the corners of her eyes. She could feel Marlae slipping away, the light that was binding her soul was threatening to burn it away. The gamble was not paying off, and in a matter of seconds, Marlae could be lost forever. However, Rhain could not give up, she could not allow herself to give up.

"There's no shame in losing, Rhain dear. No matter what your mother and your father may have taught you."

Rhain recognized the voice immediately. Early in her life, the woman that came to visit that her mother had called Aunt Isa was very special to Rhain. She was kind, but not overly so. She was intelligent, and even at a young age, Rhain knew that the woman was tolerating the child's ignorance. Later in life, Rhain learned that Isa was actually Bryn's sister Ellis, a member of the Brotherhood of Phasia, and the second born female member of that deadly society. Ellis was a killer, like Bryn. She was cold, she was calculating, and she reveled in killing.

"You've never been one to accept losing, Ellis. Even if it took you several lifetimes, you would find a way to get your revenge."

Ellis appeared from a shadow in the corner of the room, moving slowly and deliberately toward the foot of the bed, her long white hair shimmering in the flickering candle light.

"There is no shame in losing, Rhain. The shame, unlike what your father may have taught you, is fighting a losing battle and knowing that you are going to lose no matter what you do. You know that what you are doing is folly, Rhain, and you knew it before you even began. So here we are. You're on the edge of sacrificing yourself for an outcome you cannot secure. In a matter of minutes, both you and Marlae will be gone. The only difference is that Marlae will awaken moments later somewhere else. She won't be the Marlae you remember of course. She will be far more pliable, obedient. She will no longer have that petty need to better herself, or that cloying superior voice in her head. She will be the tool that she was meant to be, and it will all be because of you and your fatalistic love for the pampered princess."

Rhain felt a bolt of pain rush through her as though she had been stabbed in the back and in the chest simultaneously. Jolts of pain and numbness ran down both of her arms, and for a moment she could not see. Still she held her connection to Marlae. Part of her work was to separate the searing hot white tendrils of divine power from Marlae's glimmering soul, while at the same time rooting her essence to the Blaze as a form of armor.

"You knew before you started that the Creator would not allow his chosen vessel to be taken away from him. You knew that the moment you began to interact with the power of the divine that you would be stopped. Did you think the Creator so arrogant or so blind that He would sit by and let you do what you wanted without repercussion? Of course, you knew this would be the result. You knew that the Creator would kill Marlae before He let her go. You knew that the Creator would kill you before allowing your interference to bear fruit. So what was the point of this elaborate suicide? Some futile gesture of antiquated love? What a waste."

Rhain could feel the strength fleeing from her.

Don't listen.

A burst of strength ran through Rhain. It was as though something had slapped her across the face and pulled her attention back to the here and now. There was a voice, she was sure of it. But Rhain didn't know if she heard the voice or if she felt it. The Ellis shadow continued to drone on, but Rhain could no longer pay attention to that distraction. She redoubled her efforts on Marlae, and continued to extract the needles of white light from Marlae's soul.

Careful. You're missing it.

The voice again came like a slap. There was something familiar about it. Something close. But it was enough to draw Rhain's attention to what the voice was talking about. It was there, hidden deep in Marlae's core. Under everything, under the Creator's influence, under the brilliant blue haze of Elwyne Tamerlane that crawled across the shimmering core, there was a what seemed like an infinitesimally thin spectral green vine that clung like a web to Marlae's soul. It seemed that the more of the white needles had been removed, the stronger the hold of the ghostly web had become. Whatever Rhain was going to do next, she would have to address the web and the needles at the same time. She summoned all of the strength that she could muster and began to focus attention on the diametrically opposed forces. At first, the web would not budge. No matter where Rhain tugged on the construct, it simply constricted somewhere else. But then something tugged at Rhain's mind. It was as though she suddenly was injected with a wealth of new knowledge, and it was critical to what she was about to attempt. Looking up and wiping away some of the blood that had streamed from her nose, Rhain locked eyes with the shadow of Ellis.

"Just answer me one question," Rhain said, a sly smile coming to her face. "I know from Halicon that the Creator didn't use to be this petty tyrant fixated on setting his children against one another. He allowed the Children to fight their ideological war, but without the malevolence that seems to permeate his current actions. When did the Creator learn to hate?"

The shadow's eyes flashed with brilliant white light, and the next time that it spoke, it spoke not with Ellis' voice but with a mortal approximation of the Voice of the Creator.

"HATE.....YOU DARE ACCUSE ME OF HATE? EVEN AERITH SETH DID NOT PRESUME TO ACCUSE ME OF SUCH A BASE AND PETTY EMOTION. HATE IS NOT WHAT DRIVES ME. I DO NOT HATE. HALICON KNOWS THAT I DO NOT HATE. ALL OF MY CHILDREN KNOW THAT I DO NOT HATE."

Rhain's smile twisted into a sneer.

"If you do not hate, then I pity the alternative. You kill without thought. You destroy worlds on a whim. If you do not hate, then you are simply indifferent. But if you were indifferent, why would it matter which of the Children won? It has to come back to hate. It has to come back to you responding to an insult to your pride. Because you are clearly vain and proud. You clearly are worse than those you created. Base and petty emotions could have come from nowhere else."

A primal scream of rage came from the shadow, and Rhain capitalized on the few seconds that the shadow was distracted. In one focused burst of power, she pulled away both the spectral web and array of divine needles, wrapping them into a single collection and manifesting them outside of Marlae's body. The morass looked as though it was trying to pull itself apart, the two forces at war with each other. The shadow realized what was happening the moment Rhain propelled the ball of power in its direction. A single outstretched hand stopped the attack and held the ball of power at bay.

"In your weakened condition, child, you could not hope to use this power against me."

Rhain smiled.

"It was never intended to hit you."

The confusion came to the shadow's eyes a moment before the tip of the sword erupted from the shadow's chest. The cacophonous scream filled the room and then the shadow simply exploded in a flash of brilliant white light. When Rhain's vision cleared, she was relieved to see the two figures standing behind where the shadow had once been. Logan's cheeks immediately filled with red and he averted his eyes.

"The least you could do is put some clothes on."

Bryn clicked her tongue.

"For a disciple of my husband, you are incredible prudish."

Rhain could not contain the laugh that escaped her lips, and for the first time since inheriting her terrible burden, she felt like herself and could perceive the echo of hope all around her.

Chapter CXI

To Purge Lingering Doubt

Year Five of the Just Emperor Kaitain "Dragonsbane" Lorien, Creator's Calendar Year 1872

The Pritan Island chain, while considered beautiful by all was largely inhospitable to all but a few pirate bands that chanced the wild animals, unfriendly tides, sharp rocks, and poisonous plants. The Cadarian Empire at various points had sent expeditions to the islands to determine the feasibility of establishing a new kingdom that could be used as a staging point for military action against the Dark Continent of Mythryn or could reinforce Cadaria's southern shipping routes. However, all of these expeditions were met with some kind of misfortune, and few if any of the explorers returned. Those that did return told stories so wild and unbelievable that few if any gave them any credence. However, at some point the stories and the losses broke the will of those in the Imperial leadership that were pushing for expansion and the expeditions stopped coming. The Pritan Islands returned to the quiet monotony, only disturbed by the few brave or immortal souls that called it home. However, as the Days of Star Fire ended and a new year began, the newest inhabitants of the island chain were beginning to make their presence felt.

Storm clouds began to gather over the islands, blocking out all light from the moon and the stars above, blanketing the land in darkness. All that remained was the eerie green glow that pulsed from the Chorus of

Souls that surrounded Dorovar. Standing opposite the immortal creature was ostensibly one of his servants, the cold and unflappable Seisyll. She was clad in her flat black armor that seemed to absorb all light and stretched from her feet to her neck. The only light was reflected from her gauntlets and the edge of her sword. Her short black hair also reflected some of the haunting green light, but her eyes shown with their own angry brilliance. Dorovar for his part was feeling the same rage begin to grip his heart, and regardless of how he tried to push it away, he could not.

Dorovar had predicated his new existence on the absence of the emotion that led them all to this point. The Adhradair had been corrupted by their desires for revenge, just as Dorovar had been corrupted by his desire to fulfill the goals and desires of his goddess. Raenera had been the focal point of all of Dorovar's love and devotion, to the point where it bordered upon obsession. Dorovar wanted so much to serve and to be of service, so much to advance the goals of Raenera. But his hubris had led him to believe that his dreams and visions were in fact providence and not a clever deception perpetrated by those who wished nothing more than to see Raenera's dreams burn. And so, as he floated impotent above the shattered fragments of his dying world, rage built within him. Dorovar wasn't sure how long he floated in the nothingness, just staring at the remnants of the life he had taken for granted. Perhaps that was the greatest sin perpetrated by the Adhradair in their attempted defense of their world. Raenera's design had been so simplistic and yet so complex. Assign each person from the moment of their birth to an immutable role. Perfect perpetual harmony as there could be no opportunity for strife and discord. There could only ever be harmony because that was all that could ever be allowed. Imposition of perfection by rules so strict and stringent that they were invisible. Everyone simply accepted that the way that it was is the only way that it could be. And so, to the Adhradair when the threat came from the dragons there was no thought that they could be defeated, no thought that their perfect order could be disrupted, even by the ancient, winged lizards.

When the war began, it was not arrogance that forced the Adhradair to fight in the manner in which they did. The people of Loinn were not soldiers, and they knew no other way of life than the one that was assigned to them. So, it was only the guardsmen of the great temple that could have been depended upon to commence an attack on a seemingly unbeatable foe. But again, the strictures of the perfect order would not allow the guardsmen to abandon their posts and take the fight to the dragons. It was left to those who did not know how to fight using tools that were never intended to be weapons. There was no way that the defenders of Loinn could succeed while at the same time not understanding how they could possibly fail. That contradiction held in Dorovar's soul for hundreds of years. He floated in nothing, only his rage to keep him company, as he learned the limits of his new abilities. After an untold amount of time, Dorovar allowed his body to be cast onto the stellar winds, carried from one star to the next. He watched as worlds that teemed with life floated by his vision. Each world that passed made the rage inside of Dorovar burn that much brighter. Finally, he floated close to a star around which circled three separate worlds that had been seeded with life by the Children of the Creator. Which of the Children were responsible for the life mattered little to Dorovar. All of the Children were guilty of crimes that could never be atoned for. Therefore, Dorovar resolved at that moment to be the deliverer of punishment to the Children and freedom to their creations.

Floating next to the blazing blue star, Dorovar let the rage within him coalesce into something tangible. It radiated from him as the light did from the star he beheld. The hate flowed like a black tendril from the depths of his soul into the heart of the radiant star. For long moments, there was nothing, just Dorovar and the star. Then finally, deep within the heart of the star, the black rage began to boil. Slowly, the blue tint began to fade from the star's light, a shadow darkness replacing it. Finally, the light from the star was completely extinguished, leaving only a massive ball of smoldering hate in its place. Just as in Dorovar, the hate began to grow and expand, feeding on everything around it. It fed on the life that crawled across the worlds; it fed on the worlds themselves, it fed on the dust and the light of the neighboring stars. It grew and it fed, and it grew and it fed. Finally, the hate could not be contained by the boundaries of the star. The hate exploded in all directions, engulfing the trio of worlds, extinguishing the life there before they knew there was a threat to their existence. The worlds shattered, Dorovar looked on, expecting that the rage inside of him would diminish; that he could see an end to the hate the filled him. However, he was not diminished. The rage still burned, and it burned hotter than it had before. Dorovar cast himself onto the stellar winds again; floating to another star whose surrounding worlds had been blessed with life by the Children of the Creator. Again, the star was no match for the rage that burned within Dorovar, and it was snuffed out including all life on the surrounding worlds.

The Creator would finally be motivated to focus some attention on Dorovar's assaults on the worlds under His purview, sending flights of angels in an attempt to arrest the rage-filled beast's advance. No amount of the winged annoyances proved to be a deterrent for Dorovar. If anything, they only proved to strengthen his resolve. And then it happened. Then the futility of his cause became apparent. No matter how many worlds he destroyed, no matter how many angels he killed, no matter how many populations he wiped out, it would never be enough. The rage would never be sated. Revenge would never be found. The Creator could simple make more worlds, more angels, more disposable mortals. It would never end. Dorovar would just be a forest fire, burning out the old and useless to make room for the new and different. In that moment, more than when his world was taken from him, Dorovar felt that his existence mattered little. Desolation set in and he floated among the stars full or rage, disappointment, and impotence. It was there in the void that he first felt it. He felt the call of the souls of all of those who were sacrificed to the vanity of the Creator and his Children. They reached out across the emptiness and found comfort in the torment of Dorovar's soul. They felt the kinship in the loss that consumed him. The rage that had fueled his rampage had prevented him from hearing their call for too long. But when he finally made his mind quiet, the call was unmistakable. It took years to be able to understand their words, even longer to decipher all of the different languages and modes of communication. Before long however, all of the disparate voices sang the same heartbreaking story. They told of the disrespect shown to them by their supposed betters. How they had been cast aside by the Children, betrayed by their Creator. Despite their pain and their anger, they did not seek vengeance. They did not seek to punish those who had misused them. The souls wanted only to see the cycle of pain end. So there in the darkness, a pact was made. Dorovar would use the power to ensure that the Children would never again create a world just to watch it be torn apart by their ideological war. That was when the Chorus of Souls became Dorovar's to command, and that was when all rage was banished from Dorovar's mind and heart. For centuries and millennia to come,

Dorovar would be the eye in the storm of pain, motivated only by the goal of returning Creation to a more civilized order.

Those thoughts led Dorovar back to the present, his eyes locked onto his former ally. Rage burned in Dorovar to the point that the very ground he stood upon had begun to shake. The clouds above gathered in thicker masses, green lightning dancing between them.

"There is no advantage in this course of action," Dorovar said as calmly as he could manage. "The enemy is the Creator and the Children and those who have taken their power. We are destined to forge a new order upon Creation. If I am destroyed, there is no path to that victory."

Seisyll did not lower her blade or change her posture.

"That victory was never yours to have, Dorovar. You have been a traitor from the first moment you uttered your pronouncement, and you damned our world as well as your brothers and sisters of the Adhradair to the hellish prison that Talisia had created for us. Your life should never have been allowed to continue. There would have been no deal with the dragons, there would have been no incursion by Emries and Talisia. Loinn may well still exist, or at the very least we would not have been the cause of its unmaking. These humans and Dark Gods seem to do well fighting the Creator and his ilk. Perhaps you should leave it to them and accept the judgment of the High Priestess upon your soul."

Dorovar's eyes flashed red.

"You dare to speak to me of the High Priestess' judgment? You dare to presume to speak for her? You spin a tale of suicide at Raenera's order, and somehow that places you in position to judge me? No, Raenera betrayed us. She betrayed us by allowing us to fall. She betrayed us by not helping us to combat the dragons. She betrayed us by letting the corruption of her siblings to enter into our ranks."

Dorovar steeled himself. He could feel the fires building to a point that he would lose control. The song of the Chorus of Souls was becoming weaker in his ears, and the mass of green ghostly energy was pulsing with the erratic beat of his heart. He attempted to calm himself once more before letting the next words come out as more of a hiss than eloquent language.

"She betrayed us by not letting us die."

Seisyll flinched for a moment at those words, the tip of her sword dipping ever so slightly. Dorovar saw the opportunity and pressed forward, taking slow steps toward Seisyll.

"We were all victims of Raenera's neglect, Seisyll. Your tormented souls were allowed to be trapped by Talisia, the High Priestess's soul stolen from us when she took her own life, and I was left to watch as our world tore itself apart. We are all outcasts from paradise, all remnants of a life that could have been so much more to the whole of Creation. But we can have it all back now. We can make Loinn live again through the rest of Creation. There need be no more death that is senseless, no more suffering, no more want, and no more pain. We can forge harmony."

With his last words, Dorovar stopped walking forward, the tip of Seisyll's sword barely touching the black fabric of Dorovar's robe.

"We need only find the High Priestess's soul, Seisyll. Bring her back to us and let her lead the way."

Again, the tip of Seisyll's sword dipped slightly.

"You would relinquish control of the Adhradair to the High Priestess once she is freed? You would follow her commands as it has been decreed by Raenera?"

Dorovar frowned.

"No, Seisyll. I cannot relinquish control. You misunderstand my words. The High Priestess will lead the way. Once her soul is merged with the Chorus of Souls, her connection to the divine will make the power of the Chorus unmatched in the whole of Creation. Not even one of the Children will be able to stand against me. I will be able to absorb each of their powers into myself. And with the strength of the Chorus led by the High Priestess, the powers will harmonize within me, and I shall ascend to the Golden Throne and destroy the Creator. And then you, my loyal

Adhradair, will take your places at my side as the new Servants of the Creator, and we shall craft something new out of the shell of the old. The Perfect Order will be born anew, and we shall take comfort in the perfection we shall bring to life."

Seisyll's sword steadied.

"Perfection cannot be created from corruption, Dorovar. You cannot be allowed to take the Golden Throne, for the thing that you will create will be as much of an abomination as you are."

Seisyll thrusted the tip of her blade forward to punctuate the last word, and Dorovar leapt back to avoid the strike. The fog of the Chorus flared around Dorovar and as Seisyll charged forward, Dorovar parried her strike away with his hand coated with the ghostly green glow. Again and again Seisyll stabbed and slashed, each strike knocked harmlessly away by Dorovar's enchanted hands. Finally, Dorovar dodged one of the strikes and charged forward landing a palm strike to the very center of Seisyll's chest. The phantom woman was thrown back a dozen feet where she landed on her back, her sword clattering from her grip.

"Do you begin to see, Seisyll," Dorovar said as calmly as he could manage, the ire within him rising, "the futility of standing against me? Despite your training, despite your power in your former life, you are but a shadow of what you once were. I however have ascended. I have transcended the limitations of Raenera's teachings. I have moved beyond what it was to be Adhradair. I am something new. Something different. I have taken life from worlds that you could never imagine. Watched whole stars blink out of existence at my whim. Millions, perhaps billions, have known their end at my hand. Now though I can give that death meaning. I can create life. Life that will never know that horrors that we have known. Peace."

Seisyll rose from where she fell, not bothering to collect her sword. Instead, she pointed a finger into the sky.

"Do you see this, Dorovar?"

Dorovar looked to the sky and he saw the clouds tinged with the phantasmal emerald glow. He saw the lightning that arched from cloud to cloud.

"Do you know what that is, Dorovar? Do you know why you cannot control that? Why it continues to rage after all the millennia of you trying to purge yourself of your rage?"

Dorovar's expression remained controlled.

"Of course you do not know. You have been blinded to what is around you, just as you were blinded on Loinn. You were blinded to the deception of the dragons and Emries and Talisia, and it cost us our world. Now you are blind again. This time you are blind to your own fallibility. You are blind to your rage. You are blind to your need. You hide behind words like rebirth and order. You hide behind the promise of salvation for all, because you desperately want salvation for yourself. But salvation cannot be born from a lie. Perfection cannot be born from chaos and death. Your soul is damned no differently than that of the Creator. Whatever you would make from the Golden Throne would end just as perverted as this farce of a reality. Do you see, finally, that there is nothing but folly in your crusade? Do you see finally that you are nothing more than the monster that you seek to destroy?"

Seisyll reached out and a tendril of phantasmal green extended from her hand and took hold of her sword, drawing it back to her grasp. The next moment, streaks of lightning from the clouds above struck down at Seisyll's feet. The ghostly energy crept from the ground like an ill mist until it suffused her armor with its power. Every edge and crevice glowed with the power, but as the seconds passed, the green began to change to red, beating angrily like a tormented heart.

"You are afraid of your rage, Dorovar," Seisyll said finally. "You know that it means you will fail. It means that the Chorus of Souls is not what you imagine it to be. You see purity in the death of these miserable souls, but you do not want to face the truth. While some of these souls were wrenched from their mortal forms by the indifference of the Children of the Creator, there are a great many, millions and perhaps billions by your own reckoning, that found their way into your Chorus by your own indifference. You did not care how many you killed as you floated in your rage. You wanted to destroy every world. You wanted to snuff out every vestige of life that the Children had touched. How were you different from those that you hated?"

Dorovar stumbled back several steps.

"There is a poison running through your Chorus of Souls just as there is a poison running through your own soul. This is why you will fail, and this is why you must fail."

Seisyll charged forward again, feinting high and then striking low. Dorovar was prepared for the tactic having seen Seisyll train for many years on Loinn. However, this time when he brought his hand down to parry the blow, the blade of her sword bit his flesh. Dorovar felt the pain rush through him, blood flowing from the open wound for just a moment before the powers of the Chorus sealed it. Dorovar again shrank back from his advancing opponent. The blow had shaken Dorovar's resolve for a moment, but also brought more of his rage bubbling to the surface. He could feel the heat of it laying across his forehead and gathering in his cheeks. It took only a thought to fashion a blade from the incandescent souls that circled him, but the action felt forced and less instinctive than it should have. Dorovar was not practiced in martial combat as Seisyll was, and he had depended upon his mastery of the Chorus of Souls as well as the interventions of his Heralds for any physical trials. Seisyll, despite the fact that she was merely a shadow of what she had once been, seemed to lose no edge to her ability, and now that she had suffused herself with the angry ghosts of Dorovar's victims, she had gained the power to breach Dorovar's near invulnerability.

Seisyll, sensing the advantage she had gained for herself, charged in again, abandoning any pretense of tactics. Again and again, she brought the cruel black blade down upon Dorovar's spectral weapon, the force of each blow stronger than the last. Finally, one of the blows pushed Dorovar down to one knee. The next shattered the spectral weapon sending an ear-shattering wail in all directions. In that moment, the Chorus of Souls dissipated from around both Dorovar and Seisyll, leaving the two allies staring at one another, diminished, but no less intent on ending their conflict. Seisyll placed the tip of her blade under Dorovar's chin and locked her gaze upon his.

"I take no pleasure in this action, Dorovar. In my heart I still see you as a brother, a compatriot, and the man who was to marry my greatest friend. But this thing that you have become, Dorovar, is not that man. And so, I must end you."

Seisyll raised her blade and struck true. Her blade entered Dorovar's body at the junction of his neck and his right shoulder, passing diagonally through his body until it erupted just above his left hip. Seisyll took a step back, pain rocketing through her arms. The sword in her hands felt suddenly impossibly heavy, and her fingers spasmed, letting the blade clatter to the ground. Her purpose had driven her to this moment, her duty her only companion through her long millennia of imprisonment. She sank to her knees and felt the tears welling in her eyes. This was not the end that she wanted, nor was it the end that any of the Adhradair deserved, but at least they were free. They could pass to the nothing beyond and finally be at rest.

"The greatest lessons are often learned through the greatest pain."

Dorovar's voice shocked Seisyll. Her eyes widened as she watched Dorovar's head lift. There was no expression on his face, and the crimson light in his eyes had not dimmed from his apparent death at Seisyll's hand. The wound was still visible across his chest and stomach, but blood no longer flowed from it.

"You have given me a great gift, and done me a great service, Seisyll. In fulfilling your promise to the High Priestess, you have also fulfilled the wish of those rebellious souls within the Chorus that you were so easily able to wrest to your call."

Dorovar stood, the green light beginning to coalesce around him again. Try as she might, Seisyll could not summon the strength to stand, and could barely raise her head to keep her gaze on Dorovar's face. She began to feel stretched, insubstantial, lost.

"You were correct that there were souls inside my Chorus that raged against their deaths at my hand. They wanted to see me punished as much as they wanted to see the punishment of the Creator and the Children. What better way to appease their lust for blood than to see me humbled and cut down at the hands of one of my own. The fact that I was willing to stand against you, knowing that I was no match for you in combat showed the value of my cause. It removed the last vestiges of doubt and fear from the members of my Chorus. Their strength has been redoubled, and we are wholly committed to the cause of justice."

Seisyll hung her head.

"I have failed the High Priestess."

Dorovar knelt before Seisyll and lifted her chin, gazing deep into her eyes.

"No my dear Seisyll, you have not failed. You delivered unto me her message and have insured that I will follow it. As you said of the High Priestess, she was victorious in defeat because her pride and duty could not be taken from her. You too, Seisyll will be victorious in defeat. You will take your pride and your duty with you into my Chorus, and you will teach them to sing of the strength of our cause. Duty transcends life and death. It cannot be snuffed out by millennia imprisoned, and it cannot even be taken from us when those we love betray us. It is the constant, the edge that cannot be dulled by time, and the path that cannot be obscured by distraction or diversion. I am purpose. I am the arrow launched from the bow, knowing only the purity of my role in the cosmos. More than ever there can be only one end to this game."

Dorovar stood again, reaching down to take Seisyll by the hand.

"Our High Priestess, our Adhradair, served the teachings of the Goddess, not the Goddess herself. Those teachings endure, even as our belief in the one who gave us those teachings has fled. The Perfect Order will endure, Seisyll, and nothing that I have been through shall change that. You say that I am a monster like the Creator, but unlike the Creator, I do not believe myself to be infallible. I am not the idea, I am the teacher. I am not the ideal, I am the one who will carry its light into the shadow. I am not the destination, I am the way. All of Creation will be able to see the glory of the Perfect Order once the Golden Throne has been shaken loose from its fraud of an occupant. There will only be peace, my dear friend. And you shall help me craft it."

Dorovar pulled Seisyll up by her hand, and suddenly all of the burden was gone from her. The weight and the pain had been taken from her and she felt only the joy of being of service to the Perfect Order. She felt as though she was on Loinn again, among her friends, confident in her path, knowing that there was no other way but to follow the path laid for her from the moment of her birth. She vaguely noticed the woman in black armor slump to the ground as she rose to her feet. She smiled at Dorovar as she rose into the sky. There around her were faces that she recognized. They were from the Great Temple on Loinn, and the farmers from the surrounding countryside. She was home. She was at peace.

Dorovar watched solemnly as Seisyll's spirit joined the Chorus of Souls. With a gentle nudge of his foot, the discarded shell of Seisyll's body fell off the edge of the cliff into the sea.

"The only shame in sacrifice is the sacrifice you are unwilling to make."

Dorovar's words echoed into the night as he looked out over the turbulent sea, beyond the horizon, beyond the stars, to the Heavens and the Golden Throne that lay waiting for him.

To Light a Candle is to Cast a Shadow

Year Five of the Just Emperor Kaitain "Dragonsbane" Lorien, Creator's Calendar Year 1872

The battle near the site of the former Imperial Palace of Aldere had ground to a halt, all eyes turned upward to behold the impossible sight that floated above them. The brilliant green and gold bird's shrill call had forced the attention of all of the combatants, and several of the men of the Lordhill rebellion had dropped their weapons and staggered backwards from their angelic opponents. Fortunately, the warrior angels did not press the advantage that the stunned fear created, instead choosing to split their attention between the massive creature and their commander. The Spirit and Midarin Sandar also had ceased their deadly dance, albeit at considerable distance from one another, and it seemed as though the Spirit was unsure how to proceed. The only person on the battlefield that did not hesitate was Gwydeon Sandar.

Gwydeon had seen this trick before, long ago, as had Midarin, but Gwydeon was unsure whether his wife's hatred for her opponent would allow her to look through the moment and see the opportunity that it had presented. Duncan's trick would only afford them a few moments. As impressive as it may have been visually, Gwydeon knew in the instant that it happened that it would have two unavoidable consequences. The first was that the Spirit would focus all forces against Duncan. The second was that when that tactic was ineffective, the Spirit would attack Duncan directly. Duncan would not survive that conflict, but perhaps Duncan would be able to force the Spirit to retreat. Either way, Gwydeon's course was clear. Leaving Rhionna standing sentry in front of Mirana and Liara, Gwydeon quickly slashed and tore his way through the stunned warrior angels, severing heads from bodies before they knew they had been engaged in combat. As he charged forward, he ordered the troops back to where Mirana and Liara were still maintaining the shield above their heads. If the remaining soldiers could form a screen around the twins, they would not need to exert as much energy and therefore would be able to protect everyone more completely once Duncan had fallen. It took only a matter of seconds for Gwydeon to make his way across the field to where Arent Fox was attempting to keep the soldiers fighting and in some aspect of a formation.

"Arent," Gwydeon commanded skidding to a halt beside the man, cutting down another warrior angel, "get the men back to the command point. Defend Quyhn while the distraction holds."

Arent didn't answer. His eyes floating between the dual impossibilities of his men fighting against angels and the massive fiery bird that floated over the battlefield.

"Arent!"

Gwydeon's stern voice shook Arent away from his distraction and he nodded wordlessly before starting to bark orders in every direction. The men of the Lordhill Rebellion were well trained, and though it took Arent several more attempts to secure their obedience to the new orders, it was understandable given the circumstances. Arent's rallying cry was soon doubled and tripled through the ranks, and the men disengaged from the angelic host and reformed around the carriage that had become the command point for the army. The warrior angels did not make any attempt to advance on the retreating ranks. Gwydeon stayed deep in the battlefield, his eyes moving between his wife, the Spirit, and the great bird. There were no angels within reach of his blade, but if something changed, he would have been overrun in a matter of seconds. He used the precious seconds to channel all of the power that he could into his muscles. He would be faster, stronger, and more agile than any of the angels, and he hoped that the power would hold out through whatever aftermath would follow Duncan's defeat.

****

The Spirit dodged one more volley of arrows from Midarin and then watched the great green and gold bird appear in the sky. She could feel the power rolling from the creature, the impossibly bright primal power of the Blaze raging uncontrolled. At the center of the bird, the Spirit could feel the mortal desperately trying to hold the form of power together while at the same time trying to keep himself from being torn apart.

"Impressive," the Spirit said finally, "but ultimately futile."

With a wave of her hand, a dozen warrior angels leapt into the sky from where they stood on the battlefield, the flaming swords set to pierce through the undulating wall of Blaze fire that served as the flank of the enormous bird. The first two warrior angels struck at nearly the same moment, one to the bird's right and one to its left. There was no shock or pain that came from the form of the creature, instead there was a brilliant pulse of green light, and the two angels were simply gone, their flaming swords falling impotent to the ground below. The next three warrior angels met the same fate the moment their blades attempted to pierce the flame barrier. Though she cared little for the fate of the warrior angels, the Spirit also had no desire to waste resources. She motioned again with her hand and the remaining angels attempted to abort their charge. Duncan however had other plans. A wave of pure Blaze fire expanded in all directions from the bird, engulfing the remaining angels, utterly obliterating them.

The remaining massive guardian angel strode forward, brandishing its spear, ready to lance its point deep into the heart of the fiery bird. This time however, Duncan was not intent on being defensive. The bird's beak opened wide and a stream of brilliant white fire erupted, speeding toward the center of the guardian angel's chest. The angel raised the giant gleaming white shield in an attempt to deflect the assault, but the moment the column of Blaze fire struck the shield, the metal popped and hissed, beginning to glow bright red before shattering like glass. Deterred for only a moment, the roiling flames collided with the angel's chest, burned through in less than the blink of an eye and erupted from its back. The guardian angel's head rolled back, its massive helm dislodged from its head. Glowing white hair flailed around its head as the massive creature fell backwards. When it struck, the ground shook for miles, and the angelic glow faded from the corpse.

The Spirit hung in mid-air, watching as the guardian fell. Finally, she let her voice catch the air so that everyone on the battlefield could hear.

"I must commend you on the inventive use of power. But all it has accomplished was to delay the inevitable. A dozen warrior angels and one guardian are hardly noticeable losses to the angelic host. But what have you lost? How many soldiers are dead or lay dying on the field below you? How many have fled never to return. Your great rebellion is broken, and once I have dispatched you and the other so-called Dark Gods, there will be no one left to remember your failure at this place. But if you give me the girls Liara and Mirana, I will withdraw my forces and let you continue your pointless mortal conflicts. It is a small price to pay after all. The choice is clear. Give me the girls, and you live. Make me take the girls, and you will all die."

Silence held the field, but the Spirit could sense the doubt that her words had created.

"You mortals," the Spirit pressed. "You do not need to die here for these fallen and treacherous Dark Gods. Give me Mirana and Liara and you will be able to go home to your families. You owe no allegiance to these creatures. Cast away your blasphemous actions and obey the will of the Creator."

Before anyone could respond to the Spirit's combination of offer and threat, Duncan gave an answer of his own.

* * * * * * * * * * * * *

A portal opened on the edge of Aldere, and two women emerged. Because of the amount of power being expended by the great green bird in the sky as well as the massive shield that protected the men and women of the Lordhill Rebellion, no one paid the emergence of the portal much notice, if they felt it at all. Taya Viruci and Jillian Corven stepped onto the field, immediately awestruck by the sight before them. Jillian recovered her wits quickly, having come to terms with the impossible by the side of the enigmatic Logan Ranthall. Taya however did not react. She stood straight and tall, her hand on the sword at her hip. Jillian drew her sword and started to move toward the conflict, but Taya's hand took hold of her arm. Jillian's face was incredulous when she turned to face Taya, but the look on the woman's face robbed the angry words from her tongue. Jillian had expected to see determination or perhaps concern on Taya's face, or at the very least the seemingly constant anger and determination. Instead, there was sorrow in her eyes, tinged with the barest hint of shame.

"We have to help, Taya," Jillian said finally.

Taya sighed and hung her head.

"I'm sorry, Jillian. I really am."

With a wave of her hand and a small expenditure of power, Jillian's eyes rolled back into her head and she slumped to the ground. It wasn't difficult to put the woman to sleep but keeping her that way would require a significant amount of Taya's attention. Already Taya could feel Jillian's conscious mind attempting to break through the fog that had descended upon it. But this was what needed to be done. Her father's message had been clear. Jillian needed to be taken to Gideon as quickly as possible if there was any chance of winning this war before the Creator unmade everything. Taya had tried to rationalize the decision. She was not betraying Jillian, Rhain, or even Sabrina's memory. They all wanted this war to end, and they all wanted to minimize the casualties in the process. She was doing what needed to be done. Picking up Jillian's limp form, Taya reached into her pocket and recovered a black and green flecked stone. A small exertion of power pulled the edges of the stone open, and the portal sparked into existence. It had been many years ago when Taya had stolen Aerith's stone that was keyed to her father. During her long voyages she would often visit him in Raenera's home, and they would sit for hours planning this very moment. It had not however made the execution of that action any less stressful. But regardless, the path was clear. Taya carried Jillian through the portal. As the portal closed behind them, Scaleripper gleamed in the flashes of lightning in the sky, forgotten in the abduction of its wielder.

* * * * * * * * * * * * *

Lightning continued to flash above the battlefield, but the strikes that rained down on the shield maintained by Mirana and Liara had slowed to almost nothing. However, the twin girls would not allow the slowing in the assault to make them complacent. They were responsible for all of the lives of the soldiers who could not hope to survive a direct assault by the Spirit. However, Liara was torn. She had known the moment before Duncan's gambit what he had planned to do. She had seen it in his mind. What none of the other members of her family knew, what no one knew, was that Liara's intuition expanded far beyond the bounds of what anyone would have dreamed possible. She was connected to all who shared power, all who had been touched by the Children of the Creator. She knew all who walked the world who had been touched, and could feel through their blood. Through her blood. Duncan Rhuiden was special, the son of Pike Rhuiden and Cairyn Binosear. A distant cousin by blood, Liara knew his power the moment she laid eyes on him. What's more, Duncan knew also. His time with Logan Ranthall and Kamen in the Order of the Flickering Flame had opened his mind to the possibilities that he would never be able to reach with his limited time and expertise. But the true power inside of him, unlocked by the understanding of need and sacrifice instilled in him by all the events of his life, was that Duncan could see beyond his limitations to the needs to the moment. He had taken the stories told to him by Logan, combined them with Kamen's lessons, and codified them into being by sheer will.

Liara and Mirana had been sharing the burden of the shield equally, and though the size of the shield no longer required as much exertion, it was far easier with two of them totally dedicated to the task. Liara however had to do something. She could feel Duncan's control beginning to slip. The Blaze threatened to grow out of his control. At best, it would simple burn him into nothingness and then dissipate like a cloud on a sunny day. At worst, the uncontrolled Blaze energy would burst forth in all directions, destroying everything that it touched. It was possible that Liara and Mirana were strong enough to protect the soldiers from the assault, but Liara was not sure. Besides that, there were still many outside the reach of the shield, including Midarin and Gwydeon. If nothing else, Liara rationalized that what she was about to do served to increase all of their odds of surviving the next few minutes.

Slowly she began to transfer more of the responsibility of the shield onto her sister. Liara didn't need to see Mirana's exasperated look to know it was there.

"Lee!"

Liara didn't answer. She simply extended a hand in the direction of the great fiery bird, channeling power that she hoped would help to reinforce Duncan's control. The next moment, Liara felt a hand on her shoulder.

"What are you doing?"

Rhionna's voice was cross, concerned, and confused all in the same moment. But Liara didn't hear it. The sudden surge of energy that tore through her muted all sound.

"I'm sorry."

Liara's mouth moved to make the words, and to give them sound, but she wasn't sure that any sound came out. It wouldn't have mattered much anyway. Reaching back through the physical connection, Liara seized on the untapped power within Rhionna's blood, the dormant energy inherited from her father, the former Coromor of the prophecies, Korrd Ranthall. The surge almost caused Liara to lose her hold on the shield, but a moment later, she redoubled her efforts and sent the new mass of power flowing into Duncan. Liara felt Rhionna's hand slip from her shoulder as the strong woman collapsed to the muddy ground unconscious. There would be time enough for proper apologies later if they survived. If they didn't, it wouldn't matter much. Invigorated by Liara's bolstering, the emerald flames that made up the body of Duncan's phoenix, flared brighter. Liara watched in wonder and terror as once against the impossible manifested itself before her eyes.

* * * * * * * * * * * * *

Duncan floated in the air in the form of the phoenix, but in the roiling heart of the Blaze fire that surrounded him, Duncan felt only a mixture of pain and disconnection. He was vaguely aware of his physical body at the heart of the bird, but the longer he held the form, the less he became connected to it. All that drew his focus now was the Spirit and the host of angels that held positions below. Lightning flashed above, some bolts attempting to lance through the body of the bird, but the Blaze snuffed them out of existence without effort. Already Duncan could feel the new power filling him. Liara had done what she could to prolong his control, and he would not waste the opportunity. Duncan reached out with his awareness and found each and every angel that was on the field of battle. With a massive cry, the Blaze flared once more. Hundreds of beams of Blaze energy shot out in all directions, including from the phoenix's beak and eyes. Those three larger beams sped toward the Spirit, while the others each targeted individual warrior angel. Their self-preservation motivating them to act, the angels scattered like a startled flock of birds attempting to outrun the assault. It was too late. Though they tried to dive and climb and swerve their way out of the path of the impossibly hot flames, one by one they all succumbed to the attacks, the oppressive angelic host reduced to ashes and burned feathers in a matter of seconds.

The Spirit fared much better against the assault, at least initially. She conjured a shield of pure divine energy, deflecting the trio of beams in all directions. Where the attacks struck the ground created massive fissures and craters. But as the seconds passed, the shield was being pushed back. Midarin, sensing the opportunity, let loose with a volley of arrows hoping to catch the Spirit unaware. The tactic was successful, and one of the arrows cut across the Spirit's left cheek, drawing blood, and robbing her concentration for a split-second. The trio of Blaze columns struck true and the Spirit cried out in pain before plummeting to the ground below.

Midarin watched the woman fall, and for a moment entertained the hope that the battle had been won. However, a moment before the woman struck the ground, her form righted itself and hovered inches above the ground, her eyes cast up at the fiery bird. Brilliant white light surrounded her form, and for several seconds nothing happened. But when the light flashed around the former Rachel Core, Midarin looked on in horror, transfixed by the transformation that occurred before her eyes.

CHAPTER 111

The incredible divine energy that surrounded the woman's form began to pulse with power, and each pulse created visible change in the Spirit's form. Formerly pinkish skin and armor fused together into a singular covering, making the woman look naked and fully clothed at the same time. This new physical covering lasted only a moment before converting to gleaming white and golden scales, and the brilliant white that infused her eyes took on a golden glow. Slowly, each of the Spirit's appendages began to thicken and lengthen, the trunk of her body growing in commiserate and colossal scale. The middle two fingers on each hand grew together, becoming one as the hand flexed back, shifting on the wrist with the thumb being pulled back until the hand had more of the character of an eagle's claw. Each of the massive arms bent backwards at the elbow, spikes growing from the new joint that hummed with divine power. The claws sprouted long and wicked-looking golden talons, wreathed in haunting white and red divine fire. Each talon was roughly eight feet in length once the transformation had been completed. The gleaming gold and while scales cascaded down each of the altered appendages, the transformation of the knees and feet mirrored by those of the hands and elbows. The Spirit's torso expanded and the gold and white scales seemed to erupt from the former humanoid's pores. As everything else on the body expanded and enlarged, the Spirit's neck lengthened. With each addition to the length of the neck, the gold and white scales appeared to cover the human skin of the previous section. As the neck continued to lengthen, the Spirit's head also grew and deformed. The jaw jutted forward and lengthened as the nose sank back into nonexistence, the creature's head flattening and drawing wider and longer. The upper jaw grew in length with the lower, and the whole head shifted so that it was in line with the neck rather than at a right angle. The whole transition to this new form was accompanied by the stomach-churning sound of snapping bones and ripping flesh. Lengthening from the human tailbone, the newly formed tail rivaled the neck in terms of length, and was easily as long as the rest of the creature's body combined. Three massive talons erupted from the end of the tail; their lethal gleam clear for miles in all directions. On the newly formed dragon's back, the wings of the Spirit grew, black and white feathers losing their color, until they simply glowed a nearly translucent ghostly gold. The wings looked insubstantial, as though they were nothing more than decoration, however once the transformation was complete, the wings beat just once and twin tornados formed, casting soil and stone in all directions. When the wings beat again, the dragon pushed off the ground into the air and hovered so that it was eye to eye with the phoenix. The dragon's size dwarfed that of the fiery bird.

The phoenix cried out in a shrill that threaten to deafen everyone on the battlefield before charging forward. The dragon attempted to bite at the neck of the bird, a move that would have ended the battle quickly and decisively. However, the smaller bird feinted low and dragged its talons across the flank of the dragon. Gold and white light cascaded from the wound, but before the phoenix could attempt another attack, the long tail whipped around, the tip of one talon scraping the bird's side. The phoenix shrieked and toppled for a moment before righting itself. Again the bird charged, this time intending the bury its beak in the dragon's heart. At the last possible second, the wings of the dragon beat hard, and the massive beast was carried above the strike. Again, the phoenix tried to avoid the counterattack as the dragon's fore-claws snatched and grabbed at the bird's wings. This time, the phoenix was able to avoid being struck, but as it came up again, the dragon was ready. A beam of brilliant white light shot from the dragon's open mouth, striking the bird square in the face. The phoenix tumbled out of control, plummeting to the ground at deadly speed. Everyone looked on in horror assuming the battle was over, and that the Spirit would move on to destroying the rest of the Dark Gods in its new incarnation. Duncan however had other ideas.

Just as the Spirit had done only moments before, the phoenix arrested its fall mere inches from the ground. However, instead of coming to a stop to re-evaluate its tactics, the phoenix used the speed of its decent to slingshot it back towards the dragon at impossible speed. There would be no more feinting, no more tactics. Duncan's control of the Blaze had reached its end, and there was only one card left to play. The phoenix sped toward the dragon, and despite the impressive dexterity that the gargantuan creature had displayed in close quarters, there was no time to dodge what was coming. Had Duncan intended to hit a specific part of the dragon, perhaps the Spirit could have evaded, but in this case, Duncan only needed to make contact.

The explosion that followed the contact of the phoenix with the dragon could be seen across the whole of Cadaria. For several moments it appeared that a new sun had simply flashed into existence, its green-gold corona beautiful and haunting. But just as quickly as the new star had come into being, it faded, leaving only sparkles of green and gold at the edges of the clouds where the star had once been. On the battlefield, everyone was forced to look away, but when the light faded and all returned their gaze to the skies where the two massive creatures had once been, neither could be seen. However, floating in the middle of the space, back in her former guise was the Spirit looking none the worse for the conflict.

"Fools! I am the embodiment of the Creator's power! The powers of the Children pale in comparison to the reserves of strength I have at my disposal. To stand against the Creator is folly. To take arms against the angelic host will bring only death. I am the Spirit. I am eternal. I am…"

The Spirits next words died in her throat and were followed by a blood-curdling scream. As if her wings had been clipped, she plummeted to the ground, but this time did not arrest her fall before she struck the ground. Gwydeon and Midarin were upon the fallen angel at nearly the same time. The sight was gruesome; limbs turned at unnatural angles, blood pooling from dozens of open wounds and open fractures. Half of the woman's face was so caved-in that it was unrecognizable. However, as soon as Midarin looked at the woman's face, her good eye opened and locked onto Midarin. Erratic breathing gave way to blood-filled coughing and then finally words that were filled with spite and rage.

"The tenets have been broken…." the Spirit's voice ragged, its power fading. "A Child has assaulted the Father. The end is coming."

Midarin and Gwydeon shared a quick look.

"Weep and cower," the fading voice said finally. "This world too shall burn."

Before Gwydeon knew what was happening, the blade had formed in Midarin's hand and struck true, cleaving the head from the Spirit's broken body. For several long moments Midarin did not break the gaze of the Spirit, watching the light fade from her eyes. Finally, Midarin let the blade disappear from her grasp, and then turned away walking back toward where the army was gathered, not knowing whether to cheer or flee. Gwydeon barely heard the words that came from his wife's mouth, as he was so fixated on the Spirit's final proclamation.

"Not this time," Midarin said coldly. "Never again."

The Calling of the Blood

Year Two of the Divine Empress and Child of the Creator Marlae Tamerlane, Creator's Calendar Year 1872

Rhain pulled the covers up over Marlae and kissed her lightly on the forehead. The ordeal had taken much out of the young empress, and it remained to be seen what the true ramifications of Rhain's actions would be. Marlae's tie to the Creator had been severed, and whatever connection she had to Dorovar had also been removed, but what that would mean to the woman that remained was anyone's best guess. All she could do now was wait. But there were other matters to attend to now, matters that could no longer wait. Rhain left the large bedroom, pulling the door closed behind her, and moved to the antechamber where her two guests waited. The appearance of Logan Ranthall and her mother had been unexpected by not unwelcome. And as much as she wanted to take time to take solace in their presence, she knew that she did not have that luxury.

In the antechamber, Logan stood in the far corner of the room away from the door, his back to the wall and his arms crossed over his chest. He did not look the worse for the wear from his recent conflicts, but Rhain could no longer feel him the way that she should have. Logan was a member of the Brotherhood of Phasia, and more than that he was possessed now of the powers of three other members of the Brotherhood.

His tie to the Blaze should have been stronger than any of the others, but in her mind Rhain only saw him as a shadow. He smiled when he saw Rhain, but instead of making any moves, he nodded in the direction of the other occupant of the room. Bryn stood in front of a high-backed chair, her recognizable red hair pulled over a bare shoulder. What was unusual however was the tight-fitting black dress that covered her from neck to knee. While her shoulders and arms were completely bare, the rest of her was covered, including the lace black stockings that continued beyond the hem of the dress to her feet. Something was also different in Bryn's eyes. The woman had always been intense, but there was something new, a resolve that could not be denied. Before Rhain made a move toward her mother, Bryn took two steps toward Rhain and the two women met in the center of the room and embraced. Bryn held the hug much longer than Rhain expected. Her father had always been the more affectionate of her parents, and Rhain was genuinely surprised at the intensity of the emotion she felt from the much older woman. Whatever she had been through, it had clearly left a mark on her soul. Finally freed from the embrace, Rhain took a step back only to find Logan beside her, instantly encircled by his arms. His embrace did not last as long, but it was filled with no less emotion. Their relationship was admittedly complex, but was not nearly as loaded as the relationship she had with her mother. When Logan pulled away, he kept his hands on her shoulders and looked deeply in her eyes. The frown that twisted his lips sent a shudder through Rhain's body. It was clear that he knew.

"That was very foolish," Bryn said as Logan stepped back. "If we hadn't intervened, that shadow probably would have killed you. You know it was a piece of the Spirit don't you?"

Rhain turned slightly to regard Bryn, without shifting too much of her attention from the growing concern in Logan's gaze.

"I wasn't aware that the Spirit could split itself like that."

Logan's voice was distant.

"There's a lot of things we didn't know the Creator and his Servants could do. I don't think they're going to be holding back any longer."

He reached up and took hold of Rhain's chin to bring her eyes back to his. She held the gaze for only a moment before pulling away and sinking down into the chair that slid into place behind her. Logan's frown deepened and he took position behind the chair across from her, leaning lightly on the high-back, his eyes fixated on her. Bryn also sat, looking not at Rhain, but at Logan.

"What is it?"

Logan lifted his head, pointing his chin in Rhain's direction, his voice low and gruff.

"Ask her."

Rhain's nails dug into the arm of the chair, but she tried to keep the irritation from finding its way to her face.

"Logan, we don't have time for this."

Logan closed his eyes and shook his head.

"That's exactly the point. How long?"

Rhain frowned.

"After all that you've been through…."

Logan tossed the chair so hard against the wall that it broke.

"Dammit Rhain, how long?"

"Weeks," she blurted out, shocked at the violence of his actions. After she realized what she had said, her voice calmed, but was grave. "A month at the outside."

Rhain's eyes shifted from Logan to Bryn, but her mother had no concern on her face. Whatever was going through the ancient predator's mind, she did not allow it to come to her face or to her eyes. Logan folded his arms across his chest again, his countenance not angry but rather contemplative.

"I suspected as much. I knew that Kamen could not have done what he intended without your help, and now after that stunt with Marlae, Halicon's power has to be burning through you pretty quickly now."

Rhain sighed.

"I did what needed to be done, Logan, no different than you."

Logan nodded.

"None of us have made very intelligent decisions recently. But at least we continue to fight for what we believe in, that's something at least."

Bryn clicked her tongue.

"Despite your saving of my life, Logan, you are still far too idealistic for my liking. Or would you have us all sit and hold hands and sing songs while the world burns around us?"

"I'd pay to hear you sing," Logan retorted, "just once."

Rhain could not stifle her laugh, and the withering gaze from her mother quickly dissolved into a smile.

"So, daughter," Bryn said finally. "It seems that you have been busy since last we met."

Rhain nodded.

"Only because Logan causes trouble everywhere he goes."

Logan put both hands up.

"I come by it honestly. I trust everyone from Hedorah got here safely."

Rhain nodded.

"They all arrived safely. But I've had to send them along on other errands."

Logan's smile faded.

"Yes, Logan, even Jillian. But Taya is with her with strict instructions to keep her out of danger and to send her back here if things become difficult. I couldn't have her just stalking around the halls while everyone else was doing something. With not knowing what happened to you coupled with the loss of Kamen, it would have been too much. She is a woman of action, and keeping her active was the best choice."

Logan nodded. What Rhain said made perfect sense.

"If you knew what I knew," Rhain said softly, "you would probably not be happy with my choice, but we have time enough for that later. As it stands, we have much to discuss, and much to plan."

Logan held up a hand.

"I think we should wait a moment. We're going to have another troublemaker join us shortly."

As if on cue, a swirling black and red portal appeared in the center of the room. First through the portal was the Black Snag, it did not open to reveal its eyes and teeth, instead it bounded across the room to where Bryn sat. It made as though it were going to bounce up onto her shoulder as it would other members of the Seth family, but Bryn's outstretched hand caused it to simply sit in place at her heel. Next through as expected was Aerith Seth, looking as though he hadn't bathed in a week. His hair was streaked with dirt and sweat, his clothes ripped and torn. He turned first to see Rhain, but her eyes went past her father. Aerith turned on his heel and saw Bryn. She had barely pushed herself up from the chair when he crossed the distance, pulled her into his arms and pressed his lips to hers. For many long moments they were locked in a passionate kiss, causing both Rhain and Logan to avert their eyes. When Aerith finally pulled away from his wife, he rested his hands on her bare shoulders and looked her up and down.

"This is new. Nice. A bit, well, understated for you."

Bryn patted Aerith on the side of his face twice, and then gave him a half-hearted slap.

"As though you would know anything about understated."

This time it was Bryn that pulled Aerith in and kissed him before pushing him away. Aerith laughed and then turned to his daughter who was already approaching him. She snaked her arms around his waist and rested her head on his chest for a long moment. Just before she pulled away, he kissed her on the top of her head and smoothed her long curly red hair. As Rhain pulled away and moved back to her chair, Aerith made his way to Logan. A step away Logan put his hand out.

"No kissing."

Aerith's laugh was quickly followed by laughter from Bryn and Rhain. Aerith clapped Logan hard on the shoulder twice and then moved behind the chair where his wife sat. He leaned forward, resting his arms on the back of the chair, one hand idly winding its way through her hair. For a moment annoyance read on Bryn's face, but it faded quickly.

"So," Aerith said finally, "what did I miss?"

Rhain relaxed back in her chair and Logan took a position against the wall where he could see the other three members of his dysfunctional extended family.

"Nothing much really," Logan responded. "You know, dying, coming back from the dead, dying again. Pretty typical."

Bryn scoffed.

"Getting bored, Logan? To be fair you were only mostly dead."

Logan nodded.

"Still closer than I would have liked Bryn. But at least I didn't get stabbed in the back, twice."

Bryn's scowl was half-playful.

"Once in the back, just once. The second one I saw coming. I couldn't believe it, but I still saw it."

Rhain cleared her throat.

"Perhaps, this once, we should all say what we mean instead of relying on old games. There is too much at stake to risk any misunderstanding."

Bryn sat back and crossed her arms.

"You sound like Halicon."

Rhain smiled.

"Thank you."

Aerith let a small chuckle escape his lips.

"Alright Rhain. Where would you like to start? I have questions myself that I need answered."

"Then by all means," Rhain said indicating her father with an extended hand. "Ask away."

Aerith squeezed Bryn's shoulder and then moved around from behind the chair to take a position in the center of the room.

"The Creator said something to me when he was mocking me. When he was using Bryn as bait. 'Your family will not end without first fulfilling my design'. He talked about you being the inheritor of Halcion's power, Gideon tasting power, Cedric about to, Anabel in position. He was mocking me knowing that I didn't have all the pieces, and I think he was counting on me not being able to get them."

Bryn was the first to answer.

"You're making a dangerous assumption, Aerith. We have to assume that the Creator knows everything we are doing and is simply choosing not to intervene."

Logan interjected next.

"Even with his angels stretched thin, down one Servant, and without the power of the gods or the Children, He's still keeping up with the multiple fronts this war is being fought on. Straight up, we'd lose. But with so many wild cards we're at least still fighting."

Aerith turned to Logan.

"How can you say that? After all we've been through? The Creator is clearly scared of something that we are doing, otherwise He wouldn't have bothered to warn me off. I know there's something I'm missing; I know it deep down in my bones."

Rhain raised a hand.

"In this, father, I'm afraid you are quite correct. But as usual, you only have a piece of the puzzle. Logan has a piece of the puzzle, and I believe, unless I miss my guess, that mother has a piece of the puzzle as well. Perhaps she would be willing to justify the risk that she took in invading Halicon's memories."

Rhain could feel Bryn's frown without seeing it.

"Really mother, you don't think that you could scan through Halicon's memories without my knowing about it, do you? You and father taught me enough to know when you were rifling through my thoughts."

Bryn scowled.

"I never know what you listened to and what you didn't. You have far too much of your father in you. He never learned lessons very well either."

Rhain demurred.

"I wasn't as terrible a student as Ayden. And look where that got us."

Bryn's scowl deepened.

"There will be time enough to deal with Ayden later. For now let us deal with my little indiscretion where it came to Halicon's knowledge." Bryn paused for a minute, and Logan was a bit surprised at her admission to making any kind of mistake. "What I found in the Heavens was unexpected to be sure, but the information may be the difference between winning this war and losing everything. And despite how much it pains me to say this, as my husband tends to believe that everything revolves around him, this time he happens to be partially right."

Aerith took a facetious bow, which prompted an immediate eye roll from Bryn and a chuckle from Logan. Rhain on the other hand was completely silent and without reaction to the revelation.

"The Creator is concerned about you Aerith, but not because of the annoyance you always make of yourself, but rather because of where your power comes from, and by extension where the power of our children comes from. 'The Creator did not grant Aerith his power, nor was it some fluke of faith. The Cosmos itself has bestowed power upon Aerith, a foil, an end to conflict in all its forms. One who thrives on conflict cannot itself learn without a threat. The Cosmos has ensured that there has been a path to challenge and defeat the Creator. That path lies through Aerith, and though he sees, he does not believe. Once he does, he will come into the truth of his role.'"

Aerith stood stunned, his jaw slack. Logan let a low whistle hit the air, and Bryn's hard gaze turned to him.

"Don't think that you are outside of this, Logan Ranthall. 'Logan has also begun to see, though he does not know what he thinks he knows. It is merely a piece. The one called Wolf, the inheritor of Pyrrus' power also has begun to understand. But he too only sees shadows cast by the greater light. Already they know too much, they are too dangerous, and steps are in place to remove them from the game permanently.'"

Logan's eyes went first to Rhain and then to Aerith who had turned to face him.

"You did something," Aerith said, his voice weak because his thoughts were elsewhere. "I felt it, for a moment. A surge of power, like you were dying. Like you died that day when you took the Flame's power."

Logan looked down to the ground.

"It was when I fought Dorovar's Herald, the one called Death. Seems like a lifetime ago now. He was strong, stronger than anything I had ever fought before. But then again, I wasn't exactly at my best. That's when I learned that Dorovar could negate the use of the Blaze against himself and his Heralds, because of Caris. Then Death made a mistake. He told me that Pike had become one of Dorovar's Heralds, and everything kind of clicked into place. Dorovar was collecting abilities. He needed to taste each and every type of power so that he could defend himself against it. He took Caris to learn how to negate the Blaze. Makes sense that would be one of his first gets. The phasia are powerful, and almost all of us from Onea can touch it these days. It robs us of a pretty big weapon. By taking Pike, he touched divine power, at least after a fashion. The Dark Gods aren't on the same level of the Servants, but there is something about them that is different. But Pike also had the remnants of his connection to Emries. Halicon may have severed that connection in the Dark Mirror, but something tells me that there is more than enough of it left for Dorovar to craft something. So, if Dorovar could combine powers, that means someone else could too. And since I had already figured out a way to use myself as a conduit for power when I became a member of the Brotherhood by tapping into Kamen's power, maybe there was a way I could do it again."

Bryn shook her head.

"Another completely Ranthall maneuver."

Logan smirked in her direction.

"It shouldn't have worked, and by all rights it should have killed me. I knew that Korrd was out there, and whatever Dorovar had gleaned from Pike as far as the power that Emries had once gifted him with as a member of the Erieal, I gambled that it couldn't have been equal to the power that a Coromor would be able to touch. Dorovar pulled on powers linked to him by those slaved to his Chorus of Souls, so I thought I would have a chance to pull on power through the blood that I shared with Korrd. So, using Aerith's mantle to hold me together, just like I did when I tried to absorb the powers of the Flame, I reached back through my blood and tried to touch Emries' power that inhabited Korrd. And thanks to Aerith I knew that my son had become the vessel for Pyrrus' power. So, I reached for those too. It shouldn't have worked, and it should have killed me. It almost did. The three powers fought in me no differently than they fought their ideological battles over the millennia. But finally, they fell into a kind of harmony. And with that power I was able to destroy the Herald, at least temporarily. It wasn't until after my fight with Pike though that I started to put together what Dorovar was doing. The way that the powers harmonized when I fought Death, the way that I was able to push away the Chorus of Souls with the combined powers that I inherited from Kamen and the twins. Dorovar isn't just going to nullify the powers of the Children, he's going to combine them within himself. He's going to force the five powers to converge within him because he thinks that will be enough to defeat the Creator."

Aerith nodded and started to speak, but Logan put his hand up.

"Let me finish. That may be what Dorovar thinks is going to happen, but he's wrong. And with the information Bryn just shared, I know why. The key is you. Your powers. The ones that come from the Cosmos. In me, they acted as the glue that forced the powers to harmonize, but I have the sinking suspicion that that was what the Creator wanted me to tell you. What he wanted us to think."

Bryn nodded. She too had worked out this part.

"That's why what Liette told me didn't make sense. It was too easy. Whatever the source of Aerith's powers, that wasn't what she wanted me to get out of that conversation. She wanted me to be shocked by the fact that Gideon was alive and had inherited Raenera's powers. The Creator didn't send Ayden to kill me because I had learned about the source of Aerith's power, it was because I had started to guess that He was the one putting our children into position to inherit the powers of the Children."

Aerith blinked hard twice, and then put a hand to his forehead.

"I must be extra thick today because it sounded like you said that the Creator wants our kids to inherit the powers of the Children so that I'll have the ability to destroy him."

Bryn eased herself from her chair and moved to Aerith. She smoothed his hair for a moment and then took his face into her hands.

"As brilliant as you may be my love, you have always been thick. Which is why you are where you are, and why we are where we are. But, if you would have been more thoughtful and less impulsive, the Creator probably would have eliminated us all a long time ago."

Logan chanced a look over to Rhain.

"I hate to say this, but should we even be having this conversation?"

When both Aerith and Bryn looked at him, he hooked a thumb in Rhain's direction. All eyes shifted to Rhain, who had steepled her fingers under her chin, and was looking down at the ground contemplatively.

"A valid concern, Logan, and despite my recent direct affront to the Creator's power, the power from Halicon cannot be separated completely from its adherence to divine mandate. If anything, I have brought more scrutiny upon my actions by attempting to save Marlae. But I believe, both from the interaction I just had with the shadow of the Spirit, as well as based on this conversation, that regardless of what I do, the Creator will not take direct action against me."

Bryn crossed her arms and glared at her daughter.

"Faith or fact?"

Rhain smiled.

"Fact. Again mother, as adept as you are at intrigue, do you really believe for one moment that the Creator would have allowed you to extract the location of the Tomb from Halicon's memories had He not wanted you to go in the first place? And again, as you have theorized, the reason the information was given to you was because the Creator wanted you to have it. He is putting us where He wants us. I have Halicon's power, Gideon has Raenera's."

Rhain hesitated for a moment and turned to look direct into Logan's eyes.

"And now, Cedric has taken Emries' power."

Logan's eyes went wide for a moment, but then he felt a pain rushing through him. It was not a physical pain, but rather one of inevitability.

"That means Korrd and the others may be free from that influence, or it may mean they have become even more dangerous."

Rhain nodded.

"Wolf may have Pyrrus' power now, but he is nothing more than a waystation. The Creator's ultimate design will be for Ayden to steal that power from him. Meanwhile, Talisia's power is currently in the body of Darrien Annis, and she is on her way to deliver it to Anabel. Once those two pieces have been put into place, the Creator will force the endgame."

Aerith frowned.

"And do you know what form that endgame will take?"

Rhain shook her head.

"Whatever it is will be quick and bloody."

Silence held the four of them for a long time before Bryn finally spoke up.

"So, do we just stand here and let the world fall down around our ears again, or do we do something?"

Aerith smiled and kissed her gently on the cheek.

"Oh, we're going to do something alright. I think we need to look in on our wayward children dear."

Rhain sighed.

"Anabel is in Albitonin."

Aerith nodded.

"Good. Hannah is on her way there now, and there is about to be a lot of trouble. I'll make sure that Hannah knows what to do once she gets there. Anne may not like being a part of this, but she will do what needs to be done."

"I hope so," Rhain replied. "Darrien is on her way there, and unlike the rest of us who have become the inheritors of the Children's power, Darrien is unstable and not coping well to the change. It is unclear as of yet who is actually in control, Darrien or Talisia."

Rhain turned her attention back to Logan.

"Gideon is in Thorigald. From what I know, Korrd and the others are close to there, as is the Herald War. That is the most dangerous potential location as Gideon is acting on Raenera's instructions, enacting a plan that has been millennia in the making. Gideon believes in the rightness of his action, and thus it may not be possible to dissuade him from loosing the calamity he is preparing. But if anyone can stop him, Logan, it would be you."

Logan scratched his chin.

"And if I can't?"

Rhain's face was grim.

"Then we may have even less time than we thought to figure out how to keep the Creator from destroying everything. Dorovar has almost freed all of his compatriots, and it's only a matter of time before he makes his play for Aerith. We can't let that happen. Not until we know the true endgame of this war."

Aerith looked over the faces of his compatriots and frowned.

"All this time, all this information, and all this loss, and we're still mostly in the dark. We think we know what Dorovar's plan was, but even that now seems to be cast in doubt. With Talisia off the board, we don't know how she was planning to use Dorovar against the Creator. Now with Raenera's mystery plan, and whatever Emries was doing…"

Rhain's head bowed.

"I was hoping that I wouldn't have to divulge this, but there is really no choice now. Even with my connection to Halicon, there are things I don't know. The Children of the Creator were connected, and they shared some thoughts with one another in the same way that they shared their thoughts with the Creator. Over the millennia they've learned to shield their true intentions, but when power transferred from a Child of the Creator to the new vessel, for just a second there is an opening to ferret out some information. Raenera was too careful though, there was not even a crack in the protection around her thoughts when she transferred her powers to Gideon. I think she had been planning it for some time. She never intended to see the end of this war. But that didn't mean that she wasn't going to try to force its conclusion. She sacrificed herself to Dorovar in an attempt to atone for her sins on that world, that much I do know, but what Gideon intends to do, or how he intends to do it, I have no idea."

Rhain paused. Logan could see the beads of sweat forming on her forehead and could hear the momentary waver in her voice. He knew what he was seeing, and he didn't like it.

"Emries' pride wouldn't let his voice be silent. He used Tess Annis to bring Cedric back and was training her to become the weapon that she is supposed to be. She is the Dragon's Tear, and she was at least part of Talisia's plan. Between the Tear and Dorovar, they were going to be able to unmake reality, stop the Creator, and then, I'm not sure. That was where Talisia's secret takes over. Emries knew something, and he was hoping to exert his own control over the Tear so that when the time came it would be Emries and not Talisia who would take control."

Aerith frowned.

"That sounds like Emries. Plot and scheme and use others to the last. Which means one of us has to go to Cedric and find out what he knows. I think, my lady love, that should be you. I'm not sure that he and I will have much to say to one another."

Bryn nodded.

"What about Ayden?"

Logan shrugged.

"I guess the real question is, do we let Ayden get Pyrrus' powers, or do we try to stop him? The Creator is angling this so that all of your kids get the powers of the Children. Do we let that happen? Can we even stop it? And if we do stop it, will that just trigger the Creator to end this whole thing? I don't want to sacrifice my son unless I know that his death will either buy us time, or give us a chance to win."

Everyone turned to Rhain.

"I wish I knew, Logan. What I do know is that regardless of what we will try to do, Ayden will inevitably kill Wolf and take Pyrrus' power. I think Pyrrus knows that too. In the end, I think that we have to let things play out as the Creator intends until we understand why."

Logan nodded. He didn't like it, but the plan did have the best tactical merit. Aerith cleared his throat.

"So Bryn is going to talk to Cedric, Logan is going to go talk to Gideon, Hannah will deal with Anne and Darrien, we have to leave Ayden alone, and Rhain is safe and sound here. So what am I supposed to do?"

Bryn patted Aerith on the head.

"Poor thing. Are you feeling left out?"

Aerith playfully frowned and then turned back to Rhain. He held his hands out, palms up, waiting for a response.

"Something terrible is about to happen in Celidar. Jerrard and Erika are gone."

Logan started to say something, but Rhain's outstretched hand restrained him.

"I know, Logan, the losses are mounting. But we do not have the luxury of grieving. Father, you should collect Arin Ranthall in the south of Zevarit and go to Celidar. I fear that your abilities may be needed there."

Aerith turned to Bryn.

"I thought she took more after me, but she gets bossier and bossier the older she gets."

Bryn playfully patted his cheek again.

"She finally exercised the intelligence that we both know she always had and has become her mother's daughter."

Rhain rolled her eyes.

"Father, a stone if you would?"

Aerith turned, reached into his pocket, and recovered a speckled white stone. With an easy gesture he flipped it in Rhain's direction, and she caught it without effort. Holding it in her hand, she concentrated for a few moments before tossing it back in Aerith's direction.

"That stone should get you to Cedric quickly, mother. Father's stone that is keyed to him will no longer work because the Cedric now walking is not one from our reality. Tess did not so much bring him back to life as she pulled him from a possible reality to this one. She has become quite advanced in the application of her powers, which does not bode well."

Aerith handed the stone to Bryn.

"Shall we?"

Bryn shook her head.

"You and your toys. I'll never know why you keep using these things."

Aerith shrugged.

"Well, it's not like I need to sneak into bedrooms anymore."

Bryn's eyes went wide and she scowled. As if escaping a chiding that was on the way, Aerith pulled another stone from his pocket and quickly pulled it open to a swirling gray portal. He blew Rhain a kiss and saluted in Logan's direction before retreating through the portal, the Black Snag bounding after him. Bryn watched him go, the look on her face melting from incredulous to playful. The instant Aerith's portal closed, Bryn held out the stone. Logan watched as the stone floated from her hand and opened itself into a portal.

"You have to admit, my way is far more elegant."

Bryn nodded to both Logan and Rhain before stepping through. The portal winked out of existence leaving Logan and Rhain alone. Logan hesitated only a moment before moving to the side of Rhain's chair and dropping down to a knee. He took her hand in his and looked up into her eyes.

"How bad is it?"

Rhain slumped in the chair. There was no reason to hide how she felt from Logan, not after what he had experienced with Sabrina's death.

"I can feel the power burning inside of me, Logan. It's terrible. It's like a fire that is growing out of control, and no matter what I do its going to burn me from the inside out."

Rhain patted the back of Logan's hand.

"I know I shouldn't have done what I did for Marlae, but if we can't use the power that we have to save the ones we love, what is the point?"

Logan smiled meekly and started to stand up, but Rhain held on to his hand and kept him in place. For several long moments she remained silent until finally she sighed and spoke.

"I need to tell you about Jillian, Logan. And then I'm afraid I have a terrible task to request of the Lord Phoenix."

What We Are and What We Can Be

Year Five of the Just Emperor Kaitain "Dragonsbane" Lorien, Creator's Calendar Year 1872

Korrd Ranthall woke with a start. He didn't know how long he had been unconscious, nor did he know even what day it was. All he knew was that it was in fact day, and that he was still alive. But everything he knew and everything his body told him was that he probably shouldn't have been. He wasn't sure what had happened, but he knew that he felt different. He was changed, diminished. Before the confrontation with the Herald calling itself War, Korrd could feel the brilliant white light that was Emries' power suffusing his being. While he had carried Emries' mantle when he was anointed as the Coromor on Onea, it felt alien to him. The powers were no different than tools, like a hammer, that when properly applied would accomplish an intended task. But when Korrd was reborn on this world, the powers were different. They were brighter, stronger, more all-encompassing. He could feel the light with every breath, with every beat of his heart. It was boundless and powerful, and it was also incredibly painful. There was a near-constant hum in the back of his mind, and if he did something that Emries did not approve of, the hum became an ache. If he persisted on the unapproved course of action, the ache became blinding pain. Korrd in the beginning thought that he would be able to resist the pain, simply endure through it. But what he learned very quickly was that the pain became so intense and so engulfing that Korrd would eventually lose consciousness. Once divorced from his conscious mind, Korrd would simply cease to exist for a time, leaving Emries to do whatever he wanted with Korrd's form. Korrd soon learned that the new dynamic could not be defeated, and Emries had engineered the situation to get what he wanted whenever he wanted. Eventually, Korrd stopped fighting against the hum in his head and just did what was expected of him.

Korrd soon found that he was not alone in his predicament. Others who had been touched by Emries' power also soon found themselves co-opted by his will. Naturally there were some that ended up immune, a fact that vexed Emries a great deal. When Emries would have to override Korrd's consciousness and take control of his body, there would be remnants of Emries' thoughts left within Korrd's memories. There were many things that vexed Emries about the new world that he had been forced to inhabit, but the majority of those memories were too complex or distant for Korrd to attempt to recall. It was only memories about those he had a strong connection with that he was able to bring forth. The most prominent of those were about the members of the Erieal from Onea that had been reborn onto Espre.

There were twelve Erieal that were reborn onto Onea, fourteen if you count people rather than positions. That still would not have been enough to directly challenge the phasia that would be reborn, but it was a start. Korrd knew that Emries was still obsessed by the confrontation with his brother Halicon, and he wanted nothing more than to avenge the defeat suffered at his hands on Onea. Emries recruited Draven before his rebirth, keeping him from being drawn back onto Halicon's side of the war, and Basille was not given formal rebirth because he was still tied directly to Wolf Ranthall. Because Wolf had not died, but rather had ascended to the Heavens, that tie was never broken. That brought the number of phasia down to nineteen. Caris was co-opted by Dorovar at some point after her rebirth, and that was another member of the phasia out of the equation. Lastly, the Creator himself made the odds even closer by using Taron as the host of the Will. Both sides realized that the other could not be allowed to gain any level of control over the very human ruling class that would emerge from the Founding War. Of course, Grawn was not satisfied with letting the humans control Espre. He gathered those of like mind to himself in a bid to take over the whole world in the name of the phasia. Of course, what everyone knew was that Grawn had no intention of sharing the spoils of his war. It was not, in truth, in the name of the phasia, but in the name of Grawn.

Grawn was the object lesson, but not the only one. Emries was not shy in attempting to make his impression upon the fledgling warlords of the Foundation Wars. At the outset of the war, there were at least a dozen warlords that were vying for control of what would become Cadaria. These factions would become the seeds that would grow into the Great Kingdoms. Terrik Lorien was not the favorite to win the war in the beginning. In fact, when the Foundation War started, Terrik was not the leader of his faction. Terrik was the younger brother of a much more experienced and much more feared leader. Terrik's brother Eerick was the oldest of four brothers and as ruthless as any member of the phasia. He also was a man who could draw those soldiers to him who dreamed of glory in battle. But like other early warlords, he was not established enough to defend against the type of power that Grawn and others like him represented. So, when the ranks began to swell around the Lorien brothers, Grawn employed the skills of his sometime brother and sometime ally Erdric Yarrow. It took little effort for Erdric to infiltrate the Lorien camp and assassinate Eerick. Terrik was able to escape the assassin's blade, but the act was nearly enough to destroy any chance of Terrik ascending to the throne of what would become Cadaria. Many of the mercenaries that flocked to the Lorien banner moved on, thinking that they would not have the opportunities for battle that they once thought they would. Terrik was considered more of a negotiator than a warrior. But what the loss of Eerick allowed was for Terrik to remain out of the fierier incidents of the war and was there when it mattered the most.

Other members of the phasia and the Erieal were not content to wait out the results of the conflict, but were not as bold as Grawn to become warlords themselves. Many worked quietly, acting as generals or advisors. Some openly recruited soldiers to the various causes. The most prominent of these recruiters was Arathorn Geoffry. He openly used the banner of the Lion to rally troops to the cause of one of the minor warlords who operated out of what would become the Kingdom of Steel. Cedric took Arathorn's actions as a personal betrayal and made sure that the man was put down. Of course, Arathorn was acting on behalf of Emries, supporting a warlord that he felt had the most opportunity to be controlled by Emries' subtle and not-so-subtle direction.

The first generation of Erieal, Arathorn, Mailock, Aryx, and Diana all had very different dispositions when it came to how Emries chose to handle them. Aryx and Diana were completely out of his reach because they had become ascended beings. Their inclusion in the Dark Gods returned some level of vulnerability to Emries' influence, but not enough in the early years to make them targets for Emries' manipulation. However, Korrd began to suspect that Emries believed that in time he would find a way to crack through the armor that their ascended status had given them and be able to directly influence their actions. Of course, Aryx and Diana would have the last laugh, sacrificing themselves and their powers before Emries had a chance to pervert their powers and beliefs. Arathorn's fate was set the moment Emries pressed him into using the banner of the Lion to recruit for a warlord. In hindsight, perhaps Emries was trying to draw Cedric out, or perhaps he was using Cedric's reaction as bait in an attempt to figure out which others of those who had been touched by his power had been influenced by the conspiracy headed by Sabrina Binosear, Gwydeon Sandar, and Aerith Seth. Either way, Arathorn was lost to Emries very quickly in the game. The play that Emries made with Mailock in the early days of the Foundation Wars was ingenious. As he did on Onea, Emries tried to influence religion on the world of Espre. Mailock introduced himself as the prophet of the Creator, bringing the Creator's Book of Laws to the people. However, it was the book that had been introduced on Onea, the one that named Emries as the true Creator. However, because of the positions of two of Aerith Seth's loyalists among the members of the Servants, that gambit was doomed to failure. Mailock was cut down, and the true Book of the Creator was introduced, ensuring that the people of Cadaria would know the true Creator and not the false one.

The second generation of Erieal also proved to create unique challenges for Emries, not the least of which were the unclear dispositions of two of its members. Arin Domae and Talon Aielin were quickly accounted for. Arin was a professional soldier and Emries was able to keep him hidden, as he did with Korrd, though the whole of the Foundation Wars and for many years after. Talon Aielin was slightly harder to keep quiet, as his boisterous personality did not lend itself well to blending in. Emries had to take direct control of Talon's will often, stopping the man from acting out. But where Talon was most effective in the expression of Emries' will was as a bard and a chronicler. Emries would order Talon to travel the countryside, spreading stories and information that Emries wanted spread. He would ensure that some of the warlords became popular while others became feared. He would use the spread of false information in an effort to draw out enemies or potential enemies, or he would use such stories to mislead his opponents. Talon's inherent skill and charisma made him a natural choice for the task, and it was easy to disguise his identity as the years stretched into centuries and millennia. Talon became perhaps one of Emries' most important tools in the early days of the war. His impact was no more clearly felt than after the Day the Heavens Fell and the emergence of the Dark Gods. It was Talon who spread the fear and trepidation about the Dark Gods and the danger that they posed to the fledgling Cadarian Empire. The other two members of the second generation's Erieal offered Emries no opportunity to reacquire their services. Pike Rhuiden had his connection to Emries removed by Halicon near the end of the war on Onea. Gideon Viruci disappeared from Emries' view and could not be accounted for.

It was the third generation of Erieal that offered Emries the most fertile ground to draw allies from, both by his own manipulation of bloodlines, and by quirks of the timeline created by the Dark Mirror. First of the group and most vulnerable was Gwillim Crill. Gwillim was only alive because of Emries' manipulations, and he was always intended to be leverage against Gwydeon Sandar and Korrd Ranthall. Gwillim would never have agency in his life or a choice in his actions. He would always serve Emries. Rand Merin was another professional soldier who had little choice in his path. In life he had been corrupted by the phasia, manipulated, and enslaved by those of stronger will. Emries tapped into that same weakness in Rand's character and used it for his own nefarious purposes. Like Arin Domae, Rand was easy to hide generation after generation in the ranks of the many armies across the face of Cadaria. Soldiers were often faceless and nameless, only the very best rising to the attention of their betters. Practiced soldiers who had been through the kind of conflicts that Rand and Arin had been through could serve well but without distinction. Like her mother Diana, Lissa Terian was protected by her status as a member of the Dark Gods, but that protection was not what kept her from the side of Emries and his schemes. Lissa was a pawn in one of Talisia's extended games and so Emries had chosen not to pay her any mind. Where Emries gained an advantage was the inclusion of the Mystic children in the ranks of the Erieal. In the light reality, Storm Mystic was a member of the Erieal and his sister was not. However, the Dark Mirror version of Taya, the daughter of Gideon Viruci and Erika Belnosian, was. Emries, in a subtle manipulation of the exercise of his mantle, chose to remove Taya Viruci's status as an Erieal and confer it upon Taya Mystic. Because of the prominent positions of the Mystics in the Kingdom of Celidar, Emries chose to keep the Mystic siblings in quiet and unassuming positions. He moved them often, keeping them largely in the ranks of the Church of the Creator, where they could subtly influence doctrine and dogma over the many centuries. Both were learned people, and were natural choices to find their way into positions as functionaries and scholars for the Church.

Korrd found his way back to his feet slowly, the pounding in his head forcing him to abort his attempt several times. He staggered away from where he fell in the general direction of where he saw his son Gwillim fall. The veteran warrior was injured, but not seriously so. It appeared that his right arm was broken and there were a great many cuts on his face and arms. All in all the damage could have been much worse. Korrd reached for the powers granted to him as the Coromor in an effort to heal Gwillim's wounds, but the power would not obey his command. The power was still there, but it was faint, almost non-existent. More than that though, the power seemed to be sealed away, restricted from his touch. In addition, Korrd could no longer feel the primal strings coming from Talon and Gwillim. If he wasn't seeing Gwillim breathing with his own eyes, he would have thought the man was dead. Gwillim was still unconscious, likely due to the pain, so Korrd found himself stumbling in the direction of where Talon had landed. Talon wasn't in nearly as bad of shape as Gwillim, no broken bones, but many cuts and bruises. Talon was just regaining consciousness when Korrd arrived at his side.

"Well that could have gone better," Talon said, his eyes finding Korrd.

Korrd nodded and helped Talon back to his feet. Together the two men made their way over to where Gwillim lay and sat back on the muddy ground. They sat in silence for a long time, the suns cresting over the mountains to the east. They were still the better part of a day's walk from Thorigald, where War was no doubt laying waste to the citizenry there. But in their current condition, there was nothing that Korrd or the others could do about that. Even at their best, they had only been able to delay the beast. In their current condition, what hope would they have had against it? Talon finally looked at Korrd and asked the only question that mattered.

"Do you feel different?"

Korrd nodded silently.

"We're cut off from our connection to Emries."

Talon cocked his head.

"Could it have been what War did to us?"

Korrd thought for a moment. It was an option that he had considered, but he didn't think that a Herald of Dorovar was powerful enough to sever their connection to a Child of the Creator. Besides, if the Heralds did have that kind of ability, would they not have used it when they were fighting Logan? Of course, Logan had to use some unconventional tactics in those battles, but he had still prevailed.

"War is powerful, of course, but I don't think he's that powerful," Korrd responded. "At least, I hope not."

Talon nodded.

"Alright then, was it Emries' idea or someone else's?"

The implication of Talon's words was clear. There were only two possible reasons that their connection to Emries would be severed. The first and most likely was that Emries was irritated by their failure to stop War and had chosen to punish them. That meant that the access to their abilities would be returned at some point. That also meant that the control would be reasserted as well. For the moment, their minds were their own. The fact was a double-edged sword. They could think for themselves without consequence, but they were also forced to face the thousands of years of terrible deeds in the name of their benefactor. While not the most pleasant of circumstances, it was better than the alternative. The alternative of course was that Emries had finally been defeated. Korrd wondered if that might not have been the better alternative. It meant of course that Korrd and the others would not be getting their abilities back. That alternative meant that Korrd and the others were free, but that freedom had a very high price.

"If Emries is dead," Korrd began, "then we need to figure out what we're going to do next. If he isn't I'm sure that we'll know it soon."

Talon frowned.

"We've done a lot of terrible things, Korrd, a lot of terrible things. And there are a lot of people out there, people we used to call friends, that would just as soon see us dead. It's not like we can go back to Logan and the others."

Korrd nodded. Talon was right. He had only been cut off from Emries' power for a few minutes and already his head felt clearer. Throughout his life, Korrd had done terrible things both for himself and in the name of others. But what he had done for Emries defied description. He had murdered, destabilized kingdoms, and betrayed a woman that he loved all in the name of Emries' long con. Would they be able to find forgiveness anywhere for the actions they had taken? Would Logan forgive him? Would Chelsea? And now that they were without the ability to fight the war on the scale in which it was being elevated to, they would only end up in the way.

"The way I see it, Talon, we have two choices. I don't really like either of them. We can make for Saldarine, catch up with what is left of the Army of Fire, and try to figure out what side of this war we want to be on. Or we can head toward Albitonin. We can find refuge in the Heart of Stone, and maybe we could find use there."

CHAPTER 111

There was a cough that came from Gwillim, and his eyes opened. With the help of Talon and Korrd, the larger man got back to a seated position. Gwillim tried to speak, but his voice came out raspy and was interrupted by another cough. After settling himself, Gwillim swallowed gently and then spoke.

"I have another thought."

Talon put his hand on Gwillim's shoulder.

"And I have a feeling I'm not going to like it."

Gwillim locked his eyes on Korrd.

"You know what we've done, Korrd. You know all the ways that we've failed ourselves and our principles. I don't think we can just run. And I don't think we can just hide out in Albitonin. We have to finish what we started with War."

Talon couldn't stifle his laugh.

"Are you crazy? No, don't answer that, I know you're crazy. Four of us, with all of our powers couldn't touch that thing. Not only that, it swatted us around like flies and even killed Arin. And you want to take another shot at it with no powers whatsoever? I mean I know we did a lot of bad things, Gwillim, but I'm not interested in committing suicide on principle."

Gwillim looked over to Talon, the gravity of his suggestion showing fully in his eyes.

"It's not about what we've done, Talon. It's about who we are."

Gwillim turned his attention back to Korrd.

"Once long ago you came to my defense not knowing who I was. You had no reason to save me from the Light Keepers, you had no reason to take me along with you on your journey, and you had no reason to put the trust in me that you did. But something told you it was the right thing to do. It wasn't Emries, it wasn't Shau-ling, and it wasn't any other outside force. It was you."

Korrd felt a pang of shame strike his heart.

"Emries lied to us all. But we still tried to do what was right. We did it for our family, we did it for the innocent, and we tried to do it for the sake of our world. We may have failed on Onea, but that doesn't mean we have to fail here. We can fight. We can reclaim our honor, and we can do what needs to be done because it's the right thing to do."

Korrd sighed and nodded.

"Foolish and futile it is."

Talon shook his head.

"You don't have to come with us if you don't want to, Talon," Korrd said finally. "I'm sure you can find a place to ride out the rest of the war."

Talon smiled.

"Foolish and futile. How could I pass that up?"

Korrd nodded.

"Alright then, I guess we should get moving then."

****

It was nearly nightfall when the trio made it to the capital city of Thorigald. In their approach, they had heard the sounds of battle coming from the city itself, but there were no signs of people fleeing the battle from the surrounding villages. This made Korrd fear the worst. It was possible that War had methodically eliminated all of the innocent villagers around Thorigald before taking his assault to the heart of the city. As they moved through the streets of the city toward the city center, the sounds became louder and louder, but still there were no people to be found. As Korrd passed one of the houses, he saw that the front door was open. He brought his allies to a stop and moved into the house. The sight he saw there turned his stomach. Blood was smeared across the walls and floors, knives and forks from the kitchen strewn across the room, many resting in pools of gore. There were severed fingers as well as some bits of skin and bone laying in the room; the clear signs of death. Clearly, War had inflicted a great deal of damage on the city and its citizenry.

Leaving the house, Korrd, Talon, and Gwillim continued to pick their way through the abandoned and empty streets. More and more pools of gore dotted the pathways as they moved toward the city center. Finally, the city center was in clear view, and all three men were astonished by what they found there.

Standing in the center of the wide-open area was the hulking presence of the Herald War. Surrounding the massive creature clad in mottled armor was an army of the dead. Some were ancient fallen soldiers that had been forced from their tombs, while others seemed to be the slaughtered innocents who had once called the city of Thorigald home. Talon tugged at Korrd's sleeve and pointed past War. There, standing in front of War, looking up at the colossus was Gideon Viruci. From behind him, there was a clattering of weapons and armor, the sound of an army on the march. In a matter of moments, a new army took the field in the center of the city. This army wore gleaming white armor and brandished weapons that glowed with a cool white light. From the distance that they stood from the ranks of the army, Korrd could not make out any features of the inhabitants of the army. Perhaps they were just animated pieces of armor. But regardless of whether or not there was anything in the armor, the array of troops was massive. The green glow of the Chorus of Souls intensified around War, and the ranks of his army of the dead prepared for battle. The next moment, the army in gleaming armor charged, and battle was joined.

Chapter CXII

Fangs and Claws

Year Two of the Divine Empress and Child of the Creator Marlae Tamerlane, Creator's Calendar Year 1872

Carnage awaited Saurn as he stepped through the portal from the quiet confines of the headquarters of the Shadow Guild. His Shadow Guild he continued to remind himself. Yes, Rhain Seth had appeared as the new leader of the Brotherhood of Phasia, the Mistress of the Blaze, and taken command of the agents of the guild, but Saurn was still its leader and its architect. There was a part of him of course that resented Rhain. Resented her very existence. But this was not Onea. This was not millennia ago during the war between Shau-ling and Emries. In that time and in that place he might have used the resources that he had pioneered to make an attempt on Rhain's life. He may have taken what he knew about the power-stealing daggers and used it to become the master of the Blaze himself. He could have accomplished the goal that he once set for himself, and become the leader of the Brotherhood, the master of the phasia, and the most powerful of his race. However, the petty jealousies of that world died with that world. There was no more War for Ascension. There was no more time for hatred between the phasia. They would have to defeat their own worst natures and find ways to work together. If Jeroch and Saurn could find ways to work together, then it was possible for all the phasia.

There were only three of them left now. Jeroch, Bryn, and Saurn. They were the only members of the phasia that still walked. That was why the loss of Kamen, Rael, and Trece was so devastating. How could the three of them, even as powerful as they were, hope to change the tide of the war with the Creator? Saurn tempered himself. Caris was still out there, though she called herself Jerah now and ostensibly worked for Dorovar. However Jerah seemed to have her own agenda, and just as in her life as Caris, that agenda was difficult to determine. As a member of the phasia, Caris was cagey, keeping her own council and refusing to share or work with the others. Then of course there was Logan Ranthall, the so-called Lord Phoenix and youngest of the new phasia. The one-time enemy turned friend, Ranthall could be counted on to do what he thought was right and had no agenda that would be recognizable to the goals of the Brotherhood. Of course, that was on Onea. Now, the agenda was clear. Survive.

In addition to the three remaining phasia and their wayward brothers were the phasia-adjacent. Those were the ones that Rhain had dispatched Saurn and the others to find and rally. And so, here Saurn was, hunting down another old enemy in Arin Ranthall, and potential allies in Orren Eldrath and Felicia Lorien. But what Saurn didn't expect was to discover them in the condition that they were in. Arin Ranthall lay on the ground a nasty gash on the side of his head that dripped blood onto the dirt. His arms and legs were covered with superficial cuts. Arin however was lying in a pool of blood, which had to be coming from a much larger wound that was not apparent from Saurn's vantage point. Reaching out through the powers of the Blaze, Saurn could tell that Arin was still alive, and that he was using his powers to slowly knit his wounds. It was still unclear how long it would be before Arin would regain consciousness, but at least he would. Orren Eldrath was also worse for wear with a broken arm, a broken leg and several pieces of shrapnel lodged deep into his flesh. Orren apparently had not yet learned passive application of his powers. He was not healing, and if there was no intervention soon, the man would bleed to death. Felicia was in the worst condition of the trio. She lay limp and nearly lifeless, her chest barely rising and falling with breath. All around her were the metallic remnants of Nightwing, that creature seemingly destroyed. Several broken ribs had burst through her chest and stuck up in various directions like broken teeth. Blood leaked from the wounds in her chest, as well as the open fractures in both of her legs. There was also a very good chance that her skull was fractured. Like with Orren Eldrath, Felicia did not appear to be healing herself. If Nightwing had still been part of Felicia, then it would have taken over the innate healing. Now, it was only a matter of time before she too would bleed to death.

Standing in the middle of the carnage looking as though she had not been affected in any way was a woman who at the very least could be referred to as striking. Her glowing white eyes had turned to regard Saurn, her white-blond hair ruffled slightly by the breeze. The form-fitting dress that she wore looked to be a type of leather with simple metallic plates sewn through it that could be considered armor. The woman however appeared to be completely unarmed with the exception of a faint phantasmal green glow that surrounded her. She did not speak for several long moments after Saurn's arrival, content to let him survey the scene and determine the extent of damage inflicted to the others. Once she was satisfied that he had gathered all of the necessary information, the woman folded her hands behind her back.

"Your allies made this harder on themselves. It was unnecessary. If they would have surrendered the Sacred Weapon, if they would have allowed me to free my imprisoned sister, then they would most likely still be standing. But they resisted. Your kind always resists needlessly."

Saurn's violet eyes flashed in the advancing moonlight.

"You know little of my kind. We do not resist, we conquer."

Drust blinked her eyes slowly and then let her head loll to one side, not letting her gaze leave Saurn's.

"I know more about your kind than you might want to believe, Saurn Macco, the Lord Viper of the Brotherhood of Phasia. You were the dominant species on your world, and yet you were defeated by lesser creatures because you chose to fight amongst yourselves rather than unite to defeat your enemies. In the end you proved to be as foolish as we were."

Saurn kept his hands at his sides, trying to present the most non-threatening posture possible. However, deep inside of himself he was gathering the powers of the Blaze slowly and deliberately. He hoped that the gentle build of power would escape the woman's notice.

"I assume that this information comes to you from my sister Caris."

The woman nodded.

"That would make you one of Dorovar's servants."

There was the subtle hint of a scowl that flashed across the woman's features, but it lasted barely a heartbeat. Saurn wondered if it hadn't been for his enhanced senses if he would have been able to perceive it at all.

"In life, I was a member of the Adhradair, the leadership caste on my world. I was Drust, and my role was to facilitate, mediate, and negotiate on behalf of those who lived under my purview."

Saurn's eyebrows arched.

"I know a little about the world that you come from through my allies. It was a world of perfect order, was it not? A world where there was no strife, no disagreement, and everyone had their place. Why then would your world need a mediator? It seems as though you would be an unnecessary and redundant member of your order."

Drust's unblinking response unnerved Saurn.

"I hardly think a schemer such as yourself would understand the subtle nature of my world or the systems that kept the Perfect Order just that. I find it strange that you were a servant of Halicon. Your pursuits seem much more suited towards Emries' predilections."

The woman's knowledge was starting to unnerve Saurn. It was clear that Dorovar had done more than sample Caris' power. She had given him complete access to her memories and knowledge about the other members of the phasia. That could prove to be a serious impediment in the future.

"If you do know what you claim to know, then you will realize that the phasia were made to exploit the weaknesses of our enemies."

Drust again showed no expression.

"How did Halicon consider that a benefit? If you were made to exploit, your use was limited. If you were made to uplift and empower as the Adhradair were, there was no limit to what you could accomplish. Our way was superior."

A vicious smile curled Saurn's lips.

"And yet you still fell."

Drust's tone was no longer confident.

"Yes."

Saurn sensed an opportunity, so he pressed.

"But it wasn't some betrayal by dragons or Emries or Talisia that dragged down your Perfect Order, was it? That is the lie that Dorovar has told himself all these years, but you know the truth, don't you, Drust?"

This time the corner of Drust's mouth curled into a slight smirk.

"Is your intention to keep me talking until your friends have had enough time to recover so you can then launch a coordinated assault? Or is your plan to continue gathering power until such time as you feel you have enough to overwhelm me in one frontal assault?"

Saurn had to admit that Drust was far more intelligent and observant than he had anticipated.

"It's always good to have options," Saurn responded.

Drust's smile faded.

"Very well, Saurn. I will humor you. But let us make clear the situation first."

The eerie emerald glow emerged from Drust and hung around her like a fog. From the fog, tendrils grew and stretched toward the three fallen adversaries. The tendrils sprouted claws that embedded themselves into the chests of each of the three, drawing unconscious gasps from each. The claws in place, Drust spoke again.

"The situation is this. While I had no intention of harming your associates when I came here, they refused to follow simple commands and return to us the Sacred Weapon. Because of that they forced us to take what we needed. While we did succeed in freeing our sister, the cost was my ally Zaraven. That cost was too high to pay. Now, while I held no animosity coming here, I am well within my rights and my power to exact retribution. If any of your fallen allies attempts to rise, I will kill them. If you so much as take a step forward, I will kill them. If I feel threatened in any way, I will kill them. In fact, the likelihood that you will provoke me into killing them is quite high. But, if we can come to an amicable solution and you answer my questions honestly and fully, I will give you my word that I will let them live."

Saurn nodded.

"Very well, Drust."

Drust nodded.

"I shall give you the answer to your question first, Saurn, as it matters little if you have this information. Yes, I was a mediator, and a lessor mind would not be able to comprehend why such a role was vital to the continued operation of the Perfect Order. There were those whose roles on our world were more important than others. But there were not always ready replacements when the inhabitants of those roles died. It was my responsibility to determine which of the members of that role's caste were the best fit for the abandoned role. And then once the ordained replacement came of age, I would oversee the peaceful transition of power from one to another. There was no conflict, but my role was also not simply functionary. There was tradition, there was ritual, and there was import to the practiced adherence to Raenera's will. But in theory, my mandate was to oversee all potential communication with other worlds, other races, and the Servants of the Creator should they ever visit our world. There were those among the Adhradair who believed that Dorovar exceeded his role by speaking supposed prophecies from Raenera. In a purely technical sense, he exceeded his role by entering into negotiations with the dragons."

Saurn was fascinated by Drust's description.

"So Dorovar was responsible for the fall of your world. Why is it then that you serve him as he usurped your responsibility and doomed your world?"

Drust shook her head ever so slightly.

"Again your intelligence is overestimated, Saurn. How is it that you think you see something so clearly and yet understand so little? You clearly know what occurred in the final days on my world, and I have told you my role in the Perfect Order. And yet instead of using what you have heard for constructive purposes, you waste breath attempting to foment discord. It is quite pathetic really."

Saurn felt as though he was struck and could not keep the irritation from coming to his face.

"Poor Saurn, your ego has been bruised by my words. But I care little. As you are not competent to discern the truth of why I continue to tie my fate to Dorovar, I shall tell you. Though you are correct that Dorovar usurped my role by making the arrangement with the dragons that brought them to my world, it was not that negotiation that proved to be the doom of Loinn. When the dragons started killing my people, the Adhradair were committed to finding a way to defend our world. We were overmatched from the start, hopelessly and completely unprepared for the savagery of our opponents. And so, we failed. Time and time again we failed. When it seemed hopeless, and our goddess ignored our prayers, Emries and Talisia appeared. It was I that negotiated the deal with Talisia that gave us the power we needed to fight against the dragons. It was I who made it possible for us to destroy our own world through our need for vengeance. I serve. I follow. I fight because I was the one who slaughtered our world."

Drust sighed slightly, blinked once, and then reset her gaze upon Saurn.

"And now that you have heard my tale of woe, you understand how little it truly matters. But you have made your agreement with me for the lives of your allies. Now you will fulfill the terms of our bargain, and answer my questions. Tell me everything that you know about High

Priestess of Loinn and where Talisia hid her soul. If Raenera knew, then Halicon knew. If Halicon knew, I am sure that the new Mistress of the Blaze imparted the information to you. It would be a suitable weapon to use against Dorovar."

Saurn kept his expression as passive as possible.

"If Rhain knows anything about the disposition of your High Priestess's soul, then she has not shared that information with me."

Drust blinked but her expression did not change. For several long moments, the silence held between the two. Drust again slightly shook her head before speaking again.

"Conniving and stubborn to the last I see," she said finally. "Being the chosen mediator of the goddess required skills that your overrated intelligence obviously did not account for. I could not be expected to effectively negotiate or mediate if I could not feel the motivations of others and know instantly if they were being honest or not. Even someone such as you, Saurn, who dissemble as easily as you breath are nothing short of transparent to me. There is no lie that you can spin that I cannot decipher. There is no web of deceit that you can construct that I cannot burn down. But you really have no choice in the matter, do you? You are what your master made you."

A green tendril of the spectral force burst forth from the fog around Drust and wrapped itself around Saurn's neck. In response, Saurn tried to release all of the Blaze energy that he had been quietly gathering in himself, hoping that it would have been enough to disrupt Drust's hold on the others and give Saurn an opportunity to attack the woman. But when he reached for the power of the Blaze, he found that he was cut off from it the instant that the tendril touched him. The tendril lifted Saurn into the air by his throat.

"Again I find myself utterly disappointed in you, Saurn. The great Lord Viper, the one of your breed whose schemes almost succeeded in overthrowing Halicon. You are the pinnacle of what the phasia have to offer as resistance? Did you not anticipate that Dorovar's subjugation of your sister Caris would give me the ability to disrupt your hold on the

Blaze? Now, understand that I must alter the terms of our agreement as you are not honorable enough to be trusted in fulfilling your part of it. Now here are my new terms. One by one I will rip apart your allies. After each is destroyed, I will ask you again about the soul of the High Priestess. If you do not answer, I will rip apart the next. Their deaths will be slow, painful, and unnecessarily bloody. I will keep each of them alive to feel as much pain as possible before the very end. They will each watch as their organs and limbs are removed one by one, until finally there are not enough pieces of them left to sustain life. I will let you choose the one that will assuredly die. Then, after that one no longer draws breath, you will give me the answer I seek. If you do, I will kill the rest of your allies quickly. But make no mistake, Saurn, if you make me rip apart your three friends without giving me the information that I seek, I will not hesitate to rip you apart as well. Your life has no meaning beyond the information you possess, and yet as you are not the only one that possesses the information, I have no great investment in keeping you alive. Now, who shall I kill?"

Drust looked deep into Saurn's eyes, even as he struggled against the tendril that held him aloft. When Saurn made no move to indicate her target, Drust looked between the three fallen opponents, and pointed in the direction of Felicia.

"The little princess does not appear that she will live very long. Should I be merciful and let her be the one to die first? I think perhaps…"

Drust's voice trailed off as a strange sound filled her ears. The sound was something like purring, but was low and had a disconcerting tone. Before she could search for the sound, a black ball of fur rolled between her legs from behind and came to a stop approximately five feet in front of her. The ball of fur sat motionless for several moments before it started to bounce up and down in place, the deep purring becoming louder as the moments passed.

"And just what are you?" Drust said calmly.

"A distraction," the voice came from behind Drust a moment before a sword strike passed through the air where her head should have been. Drust, though not a warrior by nature, was a woman who learned quickly and had an understanding of her surroundings at all times. Though she had not felt the moment when the man and beast had set foot onto the ground, she felt his emotions rise as he came in for the kill. Drust was able to dodge away from the attack, using the speed granted to her by the Chorus of Souls to evade and pull away from the attacker. The maneuver however caused her to lose concentration on her other targets, the green tendrils disengaging from their fallen forms. Saurn however remained restrained. He was still a threat, and if Drust allowed the phase to regain his control over the Blaze, she would perhaps be able to be outmaneuvered.

"Don't worry, Saurn," Aerith Seth said calmly as he squared up to the woman, "no puns about your neck being on the line or being hung out to dry. Though you might want to hang around for a while. This should be a good show."

Drust did not react to Aerith's words.

"Nothing? Really? Not even an eyeroll? I would have at least gotten an eyeroll out of most of the people I've fought. I even get dismissive snorts from dragons. But from you, nothing."

Drust's unblinking gaze was unnerving.

"You are the one they call the Heretic. You are Aerith Seth."

Aerith gave a slight nod.

"Normally I would bow, but I don't think you would appreciate it, since you don't appreciate my puns."

Drust's expression remained cold.

"Those who talk for the purpose of talking have very little of worth to say."

Aerith smiled.

"You may not have much in the way of a sense of humor, but I do like your style when it comes to insults. I think you and my wife would have a lot to talk about."

Drust blinked.

"Dorovar says that you are not to be touched. That he will deal with you when the time comes. However, as you stand before me, you carry the prisons of two of my fellow Adhradair. There need not be continued conflict between us. Relinquish to me the weapons that you call Valor and Discipline, and I will let you attend to your allies. The ones you call Felicia and Orren have very little time left. I project that within the next three minutes they will have expired due to loss of blood if no effort is made to stabilize them. The forcible withdrawal of the tendrils of the Chorus I fear has hastened their decline. Now, despite your reputation and your considerable prowess, I suspect that I can keep you at bay for three minutes. Are you willing to risk the lives of your compatriots on that wager? Give me the Sacred Weapons, and I will leave. Then you may play the hero once more and rescue your friends from their dire predicament. What is your answer, Heretic?"

Aerith knew that time was growing short to act. He didn't know if he could chance taking out the woman with so many fading away so quickly. He wasn't worried about Saurn of course, he could well take care of himself. Perhaps he and his companion could overwhelm her quickly enough to force her to withdraw, or maybe it would just force her to lash out and finish off the wounded. Felicia was clearly in the worst shape, and even with intervention she might not make it. What was clear though was that Aerith could not give up both of the Sacred Weapons. That was a bridge too far. He had time for a quick round of diplomacy, and then he would have to act. Maybe the woman didn't know what the Snag could do, and maybe that would be the one advantage that Aerith had to draw from.

"You know I can't give you both of the weapons. I value these people, but the price is too high. One of the weapons. And I pick which one."

Drust blinked again.

"You have no intention of giving up either of the weapons, Heretic. And your attempted deception has cost you the lives of your allies."

The ghostly aura around Drust flared, and the tendrils shot out again. This time their aim was to kill Orren, Felicia, and Arin. Aerith seized his powers and shook the ground beneath Drust's feet. He hoped that she would be taken off-balance long enough for the next part of the plan to materialize. Drust proved to be a hearty opponent, but the attack had the benefit of making her change her tactics. Instead of the three tendrils striking the fallen heroes, the three converged on Aerith. Immediately Aerith felt the life being crushed out of him.

"I suppose Dorovar will forgive me for your death. Once you have been removed from this game, I will kill your allies and take the two Sacred Weapons. It seems to be a beneficial…"

In her haste to attack Aerith, Drust had lost sight of the black ball of fur. The Snag had opened a portal beneath itself and dropped through, reemerging on the other side, fifty feet above Drust's head. As it fell, the Snag's razor-sharp tail emerged from where it was concealed, and the Snag began to spin rapidly. When it reached the level of Drust's shoulder, the tail whipped out to its fullest extension, ripping through skin, muscle, and bone, decapitating her. Body and head slumped to the ground at nearly the same time, and the green phantasmal glow of the Chorus of Souls exploded in all directions. A scream filled the air unlike anything Aerith had ever heard before. It overwhelmed his senses, and before he knew what was happening, his vision blurred, and his consciousness was stolen from him. Saurn too could not keep his hold on the waking world, and before his head hit the ground, he wondered if he would see the twin suns again.

Monuments

Year Five of the Just Emperor Kaitain "Dragonsbane" Lorien, Creator's Calendar Year 1872

Quyhn Ravenheart emerged from her supposedly safe hiding place onto the finally quiet battlefield. It had been several minutes since the ominous thunder, yelling, and hellish roars had ceased. When the door to the coach first opened, Rhionna whirled around and gave Quyhn a look of concern. The implication was clear. Rhionna did not want Quyhn to be disturbed by what she was about to see. However, Quyhn knew that what she did in the next moments could very well determine the future of the Lordhill Rebellion, but also the Cadarian Empire as a whole. She was the current recognized successor to the throne of Cadaria, and she had been entrusted by Dominique with the responsibility of leading those who were still loyal to the empire and not to the madman Kaitain Lorien. If her first act as that sovereign had been accepting the assistance of the Dark Gods, her second act would be what she did on this battlefield. However, once she set foot onto the field and took in the sight, she almost regretted not heeding Rhionna's warnings.

Bodies of men and warrior angels littered the field, half-buried in the quagmire of blood and mud. Discarded and broken weapons were strewn everywhere. The size of the detachment from Lordhill had been reduced to merely a third of its former number, and the only member of the command staff that was still breathing was Arent Fox, and he did not look as though he would survive the night. Mirana and Liara were moving through the troops, healing what wounds they could, but because the majority of the wounds were inflicted by divine weapons, there was only so much that even the twin Dark Gods could do. Arent had been pierced through the gut by a blade, and while he was still on his feet with the help of one of the soldiers. Liara did her best to take away as much of the pain as she could, but eventually the poison would seep into his blood, he would take a fever and then die. There was nothing that could be done other than to make him as comfortable as possible. There were several soldiers with similar vicious wounds, and before the night was done, at least two dozen more graves would need to be dug. Arent saluted the best he could manage as Quyhn inspected the troops. It was clear in his eyes that the man knew his condition, even before Liara made her attempt to heal him.

"Your men fought well, Arent," Quyhn said after a moment. "You should be proud."

This time Arent pulled himself up and gave a proper salute. His chest swelled with pride despite the pain that raced through him. Quyhn looked over the faces of the men and then took several steps back. She hesitated for a moment, and then let her voice hit the air. She knew that the longer the horrors of what had occurred had to ruminate in the minds of the soldiers, the harder it would be to get them to refocus on their cause.

"Men of Lordhill," Quyhn began, her voice faltering for a moment before finding its strength once more, "you have suffered great losses today, losses that none of us expected. I did not say that we suffered losses, because as much as I would like to think that those men fought and died to defend me and the new empire that we could build, I know that they died for an ideal. They died because they believed in Connor Peregrim, they believed in his wife Gabrielle, they believed in their commanders and their duty, and they believed down to their very core that what they did was necessary. Their duty is done. Mine is just beginning. I have to prove that I am worthy of the sacrifices that these men made. I have to make good on the promise of that new empire that will value those men and what they represent, not simply for how they can enforce the will of the person sitting on the throne. But standing here in front of you, I am heartened by what has been accomplished here, despite the cost."

Quyhn turned back toward the battlefield for a moment, and then turned back slowly to face the soldiers, letting her hand sweep back in the direction of the collection of bodies.

"When we set out from Lordhill, we expected resistance from those soldiers who were loyal to Emperor Kaitain. That battle by battle we would drag our empire back from the brink of madness and restore some kind of order. But when this battle was joined, it was not against men whose agenda could be boiled down to money or fear. This battle, which we could not have predicted when we rose this morning, was against angels and servants of the Creator. How many of you believed that you would ever draw your blade to fight against an angel? How many of you stand here today having struck down one of those creatures in defense of your homes and what you believe in? Today, on this field, you fought side by side with Dark Gods, and were victorious in the face of odds the likes of which you have never seen before and likely will never see again."

A cheer went up from the men, a cheer that was not forced or demanded, but a cheer that was utterly heart-felt and pure. Quyhn let the cheer continue until it started to organically fade away. Just as it began to flag, Quyhn held up and hand and spoke again.

"But what we must not forget is that this victory was not without incredible cost. Our march was to take us to the site of the former Imperial Palace of Aldere, a place that we could rededicate and start anew. But all that lay in that place are ghosts of betrayal, pain, and depredation. That is not the fitting place for a new beginning. But here, on this blood-stained soil, the blood of patriots still fresh upon the mire, is a fitting place to build. Let this new capital of Cadaria, the new heart of the empire be built upon the sacrifices made here. Let us honor our dead. Let us erect a new foundation for everything that will come after. And at the center of this new empire shall be Fortress Peregrim, the seat of power for Cadaria."

The cheer went up again, this time louder and sustained for longer. Letting the troops enjoy the moment, Quyhn did not silence them with raised hand, but instead let the cheer die out before speaking again.

"We make camp here. Post guards and patrols, form burial details to give proper rest to our honored dead. We will burn four pyres tonight. We honor the Peregrims, Strum Anvilguard, and Duncan Rhuiden for their sacrifices."

Their orders given, all of the men snapped to their duties. Quyhn took a deep breath but did not allow any relief to show on her face. There was still much to be done, and she would not relax until camp had been made and she was alone and secure in her tent. Ignoring the mud, Quyhn walked back toward where Arent Fox sat.

"Commander Fox," Quyhn began.

Arent held up a hand and forced his best smile.

"We needn't worry about ceremony," he said in as sly a voice as he could, "from what Liara tells me, I will likely die in my sleep either tonight or on the morrow. Perhaps it is just as well."

"Arent," Quyhn said softly, "I am sorry that I must put matters of the army first…"

Her voice trailed off, but Arent gave no outward sign of dissatisfaction with her words.

"Connor used to say that a true leader looked to the good of his men and the good of his mission before counting the dead. You need to make sure that you don't forget that."

Arent looked past Quyhn to Rhionna.

"Rhionna Winter," Arent said in a voice that any of the surrounding soldiers could hear. It was a tone of command, the tone of a leader.

Rhionna stepped forward, saluted, and stood firm, waiting for Arent's next words.

"As the highest ranking military officer remaining from the command staff, I am passing command of the army to you, and awarding you a field commission of general."

Rhionna began to speak, but Arent waved her off.

"I understand your concerns, Rhionna, and I sympathize. The army needs you as much as the Empress needs you. Depend upon your men, depend upon your allies, and view this less as a burden than as an opportunity. I would recommend you convene your command staff and discuss how you intend to continue. The situation has evolved considerably since the last time the command of this army was discussed."

Rhionna saluted and turned away. She immediately fell into the new role she had just been assigned, ensuring that the encampment was properly formed and that all of the soldiers were doing what they needed to do. The men of Lordhill were well trained and needed little oversight, but all the same they needed to become accustomed to hearing their new commander's voice. It took only a matter of hours for the encampment to be squared away and properly erected, and most of the bodies of the soldiers to be extracted from the mud. Rhionna's last orders before summoning the regimental commanders to the command tent were to disperse foraging crews to gather wood, supplies, and food. The burials would take time, as would the assembly of the pyres, and likely would not be completed by morning. However, the troops were exhausted, and she didn't want to put more strain on them than necessary.

When Rhionna entered the command tent, she found the Dark Gods waiting for her. Midarin stood by herself in the corner of the tent looking angrier than Rhionna had ever seen her. Mirana and Liara were sitting together holding each other's hands. Liara looked distraught, obviously the death and the suffering that had been inflicted because the Creator wanted to gain control of the twins was weighing upon her soul. Gwydeon looked distracted, but not as emotionally impacted as the others. Rhionna acknowledged Quyhn, who stood in the far corner of the command tent where she could observe everyone. By the time that Rhionna had crossed to the center of the tent, the three regimental commanders entered. Rhionna regarded them for just a moment before issuing orders.

"I understand that these are difficult times, and that none of you expected to have new commanding officers or having to keep your troops together in these circumstances. But you have all performed well. Fortunately for us, we have a great deal of experience that we can now rely upon, and we would be foolish not to do so given how well we all just worked together. As the general of the army, my responsibilities will need to be split between the direction of the army and logistics as well as ensuring the protection of the Empress. To that end, Quyhn Ravenheart's protection detail will consist of Mirana and Liara Ranthall, with myself in support."

Quyhn immediately broke into a wide smile.

"I could ask for no better protectors. Mirana and Liara saved countless lives today with their strength and quick thinking. If they can defend me against the fury of Heaven, they can easily stand against Kaitain Lorien and the rest of those who would stand against us. That is, if Mirana and Liara consent to this assignment."

The two sisters shared a silent conversation for a moment, and for the first time since the battle color returned to Liara's cheeks. She had gone ghostly white from the moment of Duncan's death, and Mirana had spent much of her time consoling her sister when she wasn't attempting to heal the wounded or save the sick and dying. Mirana was the one to answer Quyhn's question.

"We would gladly continue to ensure that Quyhn will lead all of us into a world where the people of Cadaria and the people of Mythryn can live in peace."

Rhionna nodded and turned back to the regimental commanders.

"Bowmen and artillery troops will now take their commands directly from Midarin Sandar. Her experience in ranged combat is unparalleled, and we would all benefit from her tactical expertise. The infantry will take their orders from Gwydeon Sandar. The orders will come from me in service of our greater agenda. I expect guard rotations and duty rosters by the morning."

The three men saluted quickly.

"Very well, dismissed."

As one, the three men turned and left the tent. Rhionna took the opportunity to slump down into a chair and pull the piece of fabric that held her hair in a tail away. Her blond hair, full of sweat and grime, fell in clumps around her face. After several long moments, she looked up and locked eyes with Midarin.

"I'm sorry if I overstepped. I know that the two of you are used to being in charge."

Midarin shook her head.

"I have no desire to be in charge of your troops, Rhionna, either with your blessing or without. But I understand the need to play well together at this point in time."

Rhionna frowned.

"That was not the response I expected."

Gwydeon interjected.

"You'll have to forgive my wife," he said calmly, "she tends to be like this when the Creator or the Children try to kill us. It makes her cranky."

Rhionna didn't even see the bow or arrow form in Midarin's hand, and she barely was able to track it from her fingertips to the tent post beside Gwydeon's head. She did know that it passed barely an eyelash's width from his face.

"I am not cranky. I have never been cranky, nor will I ever be cranky. What I am, however, Gwydeon my love, is not in the mood to be trifled with."

Gwydeon didn't bat an eye at the violent rebuke.

"This is what happens when you're married for millennia. Subtlety in communication is much more difficult."

Neither Mirana nor Liara could stop themselves from laughing, and Quyhn too had to take a moment to stifle the chuckle that threatened to escape her lips. Finally, Midarin too could not help but laugh at herself.

"I apologize Rhionna. I know you're only doing what you must."

Rhionna didn't give any outward sign that she was insulted by Midarin's words, but there was relief that flooded through her. There were a thousand things running through her mind, but before she could give any of them voice, Quyhn interjected with perhaps the most germane question to the situation at hand.

"So what do we do now?"

Gwydeon looked first at Midarin and then at the twins before answering.

"Well, we certainly have some complications that we didn't have before, but in the greater scheme of things I'm not sure that it greatly changes our original plan."

Gwydeon could feel Midarin's stare.

"How could it not change our plans? The Creator just sent a massive amount of angels as well as the Spirit against us. Who's to say that the Voice and the Will aren't on their way next with an even greater force of angels?"

Gwydeon rubbed his chin.

"I don't think so."

He took a long moment to look down at the ground and then over to the twins.

"It was something that the Spirit said. Nothing that we did brought her down, it was something else. She said that one of the Children had acted against the Creator. The break of the covenants would be of primary importance. We know from our time in the Heavens that there are very few absolute laws. One of them of course was the fact that none of the Children were able to act directly against the Throne no matter what. They were also not to act against the Servants, but it seemed like that was far more of a guideline than a rule. If one of the Children, or rather one of the people that had inherited the powers of one of the Children, had directly attacked the Creator…"

Mirana was the one who responded, her hand to her chin, slowly winding the ring around her thumb.

"I don't think it was anything so direct. It must have been the Spirit that someone acted against."

Quyhn frowned.

"But wasn't the Spirit what you were fighting?"

Liara was the one who responded, picking up her sister's train of thought.

"The Spirit isn't one creature like the rest of the Servants. It is literally the physical embodiment of the Creator's power on the mortal plane. As far as we know from our time in the Heavens, the Spirit can be many places at the same time, with the only limitation being the Creator's desire to let his power be extended in such a way."

Midarin picked up the thought.

"Which means it's possible that someone with power, real power, inflicted so much damage on one of the personifications of the Spirit that it cause this version to feel its shadow's pain. I'm not sure that anyone other than someone with the power of a Child of the Creator would be able to inflict such damage."

Rhionna rubbed her temples.

"I'm sorry, but I don't understand why that means we should not expect another assault by angels and servants. Surely the Creator won't give up coming after Mirana and Liara just because one of the shadows of the Spirit was defeated."

Gwydeon frowned.

"I'm not sure that we can be certain that the Creator won't send more forces, but I think that perhaps we are not the priority we once were. If the

Creator now has to worry about taking the fight to the Children, we may be nothing more than a luxury."

"Or," Midarin countered, "acquisition of the girls may become a higher priority. There is really no way to know."

Gwydeon nodded.

"Which means that we need to continue with our goal. We create a defensible position here, and install Quyhn as the rightful ruler of Cadaria. We draw in all of the innocents that are being displaced by this war, and we do everything that we can to protect the people."

Rhionna's troubled voice answered.

"And how do we make this into a defensible position?"

Gwydeon smiled.

"That will have to wait to the morning. It's been a long day, and everyone should get sleep while they can."

Rhionna and Quyhn left the tent after a few moments, leaving the four Dark Gods. Liara and Mirana left next, the two wrapped in their near-constant silent conversation. Midarin made motion to leave the tent but hesitated when she saw that Gwydeon was not moving. She knew the look on his face, and it was concerning. Gwydeon was confused and conflicted, two things that were never good when it came to Gwydeon Sandar.

"You're thinking."

Midarin's words broke him away from his thoughts and he turned to his wife and smiled.

"I have a plan, Midarin, but I need your help. The problem is, I'm not sure you're going to want to help me when I tell you what it is I have planned."

Midarin leaned against the tent post.

"Does it need to be done?"

Gwydeon frowned.

"That's what I'm trying to figure out."

Midarin crossed her arms.

"And you're afraid to tell me what it is, because you think I'll say no."

Gwydeon nodded. Midarin crossed the distance between them and stood before her husband, placing both hands on his shoulders.

"You and I have been through too much for you to be afraid to tell me things, Gwydeon. But the fact that you're hesitant reminds me of that night before you went to face Terrik Lorien. You knew that night you would not be coming back, and that my world would be irrevocably changed. So is that why? Is what you have planned going to irrevocably change my world yet again?"

Gwydeon tried his best to smile, but the instant he attempted, he knew it looked forced. Finally, he sighed and held his wife's gaze.

"Alright. But remember you asked."

* * * * * * * * * * * * *

It was just past dawn when Mirana and Liara returned to the command tent. Neither of the girls had been able to sleep and they had hoped to find that both Midarin and Gwydeon's moods had lightened from the night before. What they found however was Midarin slumped in one corner, her face still streaked with tears, and Gwydeon sitting in a chair on the other side of the tent, his eyes so filled with sorrow that it caused the girls' hearts to hurt. Midarin looked up when the girls entered, but instead of more tears and the sorrow that was in Gwydeon's eyes, Midarin greeted the girls with a hopeful smile. Liara was the first to Midarin's side while Mirana went to Gwydeon's.

"What happened, Midarin?" Liara said with concern thick in her voice.

Midarin lightly touched the girl's face.

"I didn't know," Midarin started. "I didn't remember all of the things that we did."

The tears started again, and she pulled Liara into a long and emotion-filled embrace. Mirana looked deep into Gwydeon eyes, trying to find some answers.

"It was something that Aerith said," Gwydeon said finally. "Something about truth. All of us that survived the Dark Mirror were only half of what we should have been. Deep in us were the memories of both of our lives, but some of us just chose to deny it. It was easier for me, because in the light reality, the one that Midarin clung to, I was dead. There was nothing for me to reintegrate. For Midarin though, there was pain of loss that she couldn't accept, and the pain of something that was stolen from her that she didn't want to remember. But for what comes next, this new fortification and beacon of light that we intend to build, I needed Midarin to remember herself the way that I remember her. I needed her to remember the life that we had in that place. Even though we were surrounded by death every moment, even though we fought and struggled every day to be able to survive, and even though we were constantly under assault from our enemies, we crafted a life together. We were strong, and determined, and we would not yield no matter who came trying to knock down our walls. I needed that Midarin, and more than that, I needed her memory of that place."

Mirana's face was filled with confusion.

"Then why?"

Gwydeon sighed.

"Because in unlocking her memory of the life she wanted to deny, I saw the memories of the life and pain that she held on to so tightly. All the things that she did to survive, and all the sacrifices that she made in the name of winning a war that could not be won. We never talked about some things that happened, and now I know why."

Mirana started to say something, but Gwydeon waved her off.

CHAPTER 112

"There's time enough for all of this later, Mirana. Right now, it's time to present our surprise to Quyhn. A monument to all who have fallen here and on all the other worlds in defense of freedom in the face of tyranny."

The Reaper and the Dead

Year Two of the Divine Empress and Child of the Creator Marlae Tamerlane, Creator's Calendar Year 1872

Gideon Viruci could not help but smile as the troops that Raenera had spent so long assembling marched into the central square of the capitol city of Thorigald. While Dorovar may have had dominion over the souls and bodies of the dead mortal beings created by the Children of the Creator, Raenera had crafted a much more ingenious reservoir of potential disposable soldiers. When the Creator started to encourage the open warfare between the Children of the Creator through different ideological means on the worlds that He had created, the possibility arose that the Creator would need more than just the Servants to enforce His will upon the worlds of the Children. Another potential threat to the Creator of course were the dragons, but that potential in those days was quite small. Raenera, as the most trusted of the Children of the Creator in those days, was tasked with creating a force that would be loyal primarily to the Creator, then to the Servants, and then finally to the Children. And so, it was Raenera that created the warrior angels, the guardians, and all of the other divine enforcers that called the Heavens their home. The angels were the first expression of Raenera's Perfect Order and were tied to her in that regard. Though they were crafted with divine power, and infused with the power of the Creator, they also had a small measure of Raenera's power woven into them. Naturally, because of the limitless divine power available to the Creator, there was little need to worry about what would happen to the angels when they were destroyed. Raenera on the other hand, the consummate thinker and calculator, determined that the destruction of any angel left a void in the fabric of the Cosmos.

The beings that the Children of the Creator brought into being on the different worlds within Creation were made with the elements found on those worlds. Angels on the other hand had no tie at all to the material world, they were divine energy. But Raenera soon learned that the angels could not simply be motivated by the will of the divine, they required a level of autonomy that allowed them to act in the interest of their mission. Mindless automatons would not benefit the Creator, and would be no match for those that they would be dispatched to fight. So that was why Raenera included in the warrior angels a piece of her own spark. The angels would be able to learn, make decisions, and determine the best way to accomplish their missions. Experience would temper that learning, and the more the creatures experienced, the more powerful they would become. What Raenera would discover thousands of years after the first of the angels was created, was that her creations were more than simple tools.

It was on one of the worlds that Talisia experimented upon. She had chosen to create forms who thought of nothing but violence, without any sense of remorse, morality, or fear of consequence. The creatures were more than just mindless savages, they had enough intellect to not only torture and torment one another but also to perceive that there were other worlds and other types of life. One member of this race, a brilliant yet utterly corrupt scientist, was perhaps that world's most efficient killer. In addition to weapons, the scientist created means of manipulating nearly invisible elements in the air to attack his enemies. He created all manner of poisons, toxins, and plagues that he would introduce into the food and water of rival kingdoms. But the prospect of other worlds that could be conquered and laid waste to was too much of an opportunity to let go by. He secluded himself away for a dozen years constructing a machine that would allow him to travel instantaneously from one place to another. There were rumors of beings that came from the Heavens and written accounts of gateways that would appear out of nowhere leading to all manner of realms beyond. So, if these legends were true, and these portals existed, it was only a matter of time before the brilliant scientist would be able to make them a reality for himself.

The first few attempts at creating the portal once the machine was built were met with abject failure. However, each such failure was met with opportunity for increased knowledge, and eventual success. Soon, the machine was able to create portals that were stable, but determining their destination became the new challenge. Time and time again, the portal would open, objects would pass through, and they would not emerge where they were supposed to. But finally, even that challenge was overcome, and despite the fact that the first two human subjects died once they reached the other side of the portal, the machine worked. That of course was when matters became untenable. The Creator would not allow a mortal creature to move between his worlds upsetting the great ideological war between the Children. Therefore, this became the first true test of the warrior angels. One hundred were dispatched to eliminate the scientist and destroy all of his work. Though the angels were successful in their assault on the scientist's stronghold, a third of their strength was destroyed by the soldiers loyal to the scientist. This was when Raenera discovered what happened to her creations when they were destroyed.

The operating theory was that the once an angel was destroyed, the divine energy that held the creature together would be returned to the endless pool that was wholly at the Creator's discretion. What Raenera had not anticipated was the pieces of the angels that allowed them to think and learn did not return to the repository of divine energy. This remainder, this echo of what the humans would eventually call a soul, remained in the ether, in the gap between worlds. As the years passed, more and more of the angels were destroyed enforcing the Creator's will, and more of these echoes were left to float in the formlessness. Because these remnants were tied to Raenera's power, it took little effort when the time came to harvest those echoes. However, without the construct of the angel to house the echo, they could not be properly leveraged. Fortunately, Talisia made a fatal mistake, and she did not eliminate Arturious Demascious once he had crafted the Sacred Weapons.

Emries was the first to theorize what he called exemplars. In every race of being that was created there were those that were special. They exceeded the average in a way that put them above all others of their race. Emries theorized that these exemplars were an expression not of the powers of the Child of the Creator who made them, or even an expression of the divine energy that helped to form them. These exemplars were something different, they were a potential; a path by which an entire race could eventually become more. When the first exemplar appeared, Emries did not understand what it was, or what its purpose was. So, Emries watched. He watched the creature for its entire life, seeing how it seemed to pull all advantage to it. It seemed to be able to make its own fate, defy any challenges and prevail beyond any of its fellow beings. Emries watched with interest, and when this exemplar died, Emries waited. The next generation of beings did not contain an exemplar, and Emries began to wonder whether or not this creature was a lone occurrence. Emries was elated to see that in the third generation of beings, there was not one but two of these exemplars. He watched with interest as these exemplars divided the whole of the world between them. They marshalled forces, acquired power, and then, they set upon exterminating one another. It seemed that there was not room on the little world for two of these special beings. The resolution of the conflict was no different than Emries expected. The forces of the two exemplars killed each other for years, burning crops, tearing down cities, murdering innocents. In the end, there was nothing left. The whole of the world had been reduced to a tomb, and all because of these two extraordinary beings.

Emries made it his mission to study these beings on every world they occurred upon. And it was clear that all worlds had them. They would occur randomly, infrequently, with no discernable pattern, but they always occurred. Emries began to suspect that they were not an expression of the Creator's curiosity, but rather an expression of the Cosmos's. Naturally Emries could not monitor all of the worlds on his own, so he involved his ancient sometime ally, Talisia. And just as Emries did not share all his information about exemplars with Talisia, she did not share her information with him. Both began to identify and manipulate the exemplars, not letting whatever natural evolution existed take its course. Some Emries turned into his servants. Some he eliminated in order to discover the impact that it might have. In the end, when he came to Onea, Emries began to utilize the exemplars as his way of combatting Halicon. From them he created the Erieal and eventually the Coromor.

Raenera watched all of this with detached curiosity. Each time either Emries or Talisia manipulated or murdered an exemplar, the next group seemed to be stronger. When the stronger group failed to resist the meddling, there were more exemplars, but weaker. Onea seemed to be the last straw. It seemed that the Cosmos had tired of Emries and Talisia meddling with its own exploration of its boundless domain, and so it created one last exemplar. One that would defy any attempt to usurp its function. And yet even as Raenera took note of this occurrence, Emries and Talisia did not. They continued their petty games, continued their assaults on their siblings, and dreamed of the day they would unseat the Creator. When Onea fell and the Creator gave rise to the last world, Raenera watched as Talisia identified the one exemplar that would make her schemes a reality.

Arturious Demascious was brilliant and excelled at everything he touched. But where his proficiency truly manifested was in the working of metal. He became so adept at it however that he became bored. He moved on to other forms of material: wood, rock, precious minerals. It was this attempt to find a more challenging and rewarding canvas to work his skill upon that led him to his fateful collision with the door to the Vault of Terrors and the touch of Dorovar. While the conventional wisdom of the time believed that Arturious had gone mad in his quest for his obsessions, the truth was far more sinister. Talisia had determined that Arturious was an exemplar, but despite her best efforts, she could not influence the man as she had influenced so many others in the past. But she knew that Dorovar, who was at least marginally mortal, had the ability to wrangle the wills of others. So, it was Talisia that nudged Arturious in the right direction, letting him find information about a potential pure vein of obsidian in the crater. While Dorovar had not been able to subsume his will, Arturious was nonetheless diminished by the encounter. When he returned to his forge, Talisia was there waiting. She delivered the captured souls from the Adhradair of Loinn and set the man to work creating the prisons that would eventually be known as the Sacred Weapons. That work done, Talisia just abandoned Arturious to his madness, to his eventual self-destruction.

Raenera waited until Talisia had abandoned Arturious, and then she watched and waited longer. She wanted to be sure that none of her siblings would return for the man. When no one came, and the man looked as though he was spiraling into the final stages of his madness, Raenera appeared to Arturious in her true form. The artisan blacksmith was stunned to silence, his constant mad gibbering dying in his throat. Raenera offered the man an option. He could be taken to a safe place where he could work for the remainder of his days, or Raenera would free the man from his madness then and there. Arturious agreed to follow Raenera, and the two withdrew to her fortress in the farthest reaches of the Northern Wastes.

It was in the expansive forge that Raenera's plan was revealed. For millennia the echoes of the destroyed angels had been collecting in the ether. Now, Raenera had at her disposal a mortal who could create arms and armor that could hold those echoes. As each set of armor was completed, Arturious would embed the echo of a fallen angel within the armor, where it would wait to be activated by Raenera's power. The army could be as large as any that had ever been assembled upon any world multiplied by a factor of ten or more. The only limitation to the size of the army was the time Arturious had to make the armor. The man worked for nearly twenty hours a day, every day, for over fifteen hundred years. He was prolific, and dedicated, and he had made Raenera's dream of an army that would sweep across the face of the world, sweeping everything away to make room for the new Perfect Order, a reality. Once Arturious' work was complete, nothing would stand in the way of Raenera's vision, not even her own death.

So as Gideon saw rank after rank of new white-clad soldiers file into the square, he was filled with an alien sense of pride. That pride of course came from Raenera. However, there were other feelings that were surfacing in Gideon. He was afraid of what was about to happen. He was afraid for his old friends and allies that were still fighting upon this world. This action of unleashing Raenera's army would make every living being that walked upon Espre his enemy. The position was not enviable to say the least, but it was the undeniable reality.

Each of the soldiers was identical for most purposes. Naturally there were individual imperfections into each suit of armor that could be used to differentiate the soldiers. Beyond the imperfections in the armor, there was nothing unique or individual about any of the creatures. The armor itself was completely white. It was not painted, rather the metal itself was tempered and layered in such a way as the very character of the amalgamated metal turned white. The metal itself was steel, but the steel had been folded many times over, enchanted with power and coated with powdered diamond. Each of the individual plates of armor were styled like the limb of the human being it would ideally cover. Faux musculature was carved into every plate, with the exception of the gauntlets and the sabatons. Each gauntlet was oversized, close to one and a half times the size that it should have been and extended well beyond the joint at the elbow. The additional protrusion ended in a dagger point, sharpened on each edge as well as the tip. The fingers of each gauntlet also ended in sharpened points that glowed with lethality when touched by light. A cloak covered the broad empty helm of the armor, obscuring the open space that would have revealed eyes or other facial features. Instead, there was just a shadowed void that was only broken by the occasional glint of the armor beneath. Flaming angelic swords were clutched in the gauntlets of each of the soldiers, and from the creatures' backs sprouted wings made not of white feathers, but instead the same endless divine flames that made up the blades of the swords. Once several ranks of the soldiers had entered the square, they came to a stop and waited for orders. Gideon took a step toward War.

"No way ta end 'dis now," Gideon said with finality in his voice. "Gonna have ta take yer head."

The next moment, the front two ranks of the armored echo soldiers charged, their blades held high in the air. The sound of jostling armor filled the air with each step. War stretched one of its massive hands forward, and the ranks of dead men and women lumbered forward to meet the advancing enemy. Dozens and dozens more of the dead warriors emerged from the streets that converged in the city square, and the walking corpses appeared to be trying to outflank the echoes. One by one the echoes brandished their weapons and struck at the advancing corpses. The strikes were precise and deadly, separating heads and limbs from the on-rushing horde. Those corpse warriors that did not fall when their heads were removed found the rest of their desiccated bodies set ablaze by the power of the angelic weapons. More and more of the army of the dead fell, and as they fell, the divine fire spread from soldier to soldier, passing through the ranks like a deadly plague. The corpses continued to fall, but War was not to be defeated so easily. With a wave of his hand, the green fog of the Chorus of Souls spread through the ranks of the army of the dead, stifling the divine flame and reanimating those bodies that fell. More of the corpses swarmed forward. Robbed of their ability to simply reduce their enemies to ashes, the echoes changed tactics, quickly dismembering enemy soldiers, either with their blades, or with their clawed gauntlets. Piles of body parts began to collect at the feet of the front rank of the army of echoes, but the oncoming enemy seemed to pay no mind to the prospect of crawling over the bodies of their former fellows to strike at their enemy.

War was not content to stay silent once battle was joined. He took hold of his massive broadsword and waded forward. His stride toward the ranks of echo warriors crushed several of his own troops, but the moment that his foot lifted, those troops attempted to continue their advance toward the enemy. War lifted his massive sword to shoulder level and then brought it sweeping across the front rank of echo soldiers. The first echo that was struck by the massive blade came apart. The pieces of armor lost cohesion and dropped to the ground in a pile. The blade continued to the next soldier, but while this one did not fall apart, it was knocked from its feet. Three more of the soldiers also ended up on the ground from that singular blow. The army of the dead surged forward behind the aggressive attack of their commander, swarming over the fallen echoes, attempting to rip pieces of the armor away from the whole. The ranks of echo soldiers were unaffected by the minimal losses, and continued to flood into the city center, slashing and clawing in all directions.

Gideon too was not shy about joining in the battle. As he danced through the ranks of the army of the dead, daggers flew in all directions. As one left his hand, another materialized to replace it. Part of him wanted to take full hold on the powers given to him by Raenera and level his opponents. However, the more he drew on Raenera's power, the more it would destroy him. If he was going to use any of the borrowed power, he would have to save it for War. Out of the corner of his eye, Gideon saw three familiar forms down one of the side streets fighting against a group of gibbering and clawing corpses. One face Gideon recognized immediately. It was the face of a man he had travelled with for a long time, a man that he considered a friend, Talon Aielin. Gideon's first inclination was to send several of the echoes further into the city to both draw the enemies away from the trio of men, but also to diffuse the fighting throughout the city. However, despite their friendship, it served no benefit to save Talon, or the other two men, whom Gideon quickly identified as Gwillim and Korrd. Soon all of his old friends would be dead. It would either be at the hands of the army of echoes, or it would be at the hand of one of the other doomed factions who thought they had a claim upon Cadaria or Espre. However, tactically it was sound to have more of the echoes push forward through the streets. For now, they would be ordered to ignore the living, but that would not last.

War saw Gideon's advance through the ranks of the army of the dead and decided to address the largest threat on the field. There were enough of the corpses to deal with these troublesome angelic armored beings. A hard downward slash of his sword shattered the stone street that Gideon had stood upon only moments before. Pieces of stone flew in all directions, one of the sharp pieces ripping across Gideon's cheek. Gideon had easily dodged the attack, and quickly sent four sharp daggers flying in War's direction. The massive Herald made no attempt to dodge the attacks, and the daggers were deflected harmlessly away by the thick plates of War's armor. War lashed out again, this time with a quick tight stab, the speed of which Gideon underestimated. Gideon barely spun out of the way of the strike, but the razor-sharp edge of War's blade ripped through the flesh of Gideon's back. The wound was not deep, but it was long and jagged and rendered forth a great deal of blood. War sensed that his opponent was at the edge of death and repeated his tactic with three quick controlled thrusts at Gideon's head. Gideon ducked the first thrust, side-stepped the second, and then leaped over the third. From the leap, he landed on the flat of the Herald's blade and started to run up the wide blade toward War. War slammed his gauntlet down on the flat of the blade, launching a wave of emerald energy at the advancing thief. Gideon tried to leap over the strike, but the wave of energy stretched vertically, catching Gideon at the knees and sending him flying backwards. Gideon landed on the ground with a sickening thud, the back of his head colliding with the ground. Corpses began to swarm the fallen man, but a motion from War dispersed the opportunistic horrors. War approached slowly, his booming voice preceding his thunderous steps.

CHAPTER 112

"I am War," the booming voice called, shaking the very buildings of Thorigald, echoing through every street and alley. "I am the wave of destruction and devastation that will cleanse the path for Dorovar's ascension to the Golden Throne. The people of this world will shed their own blood gladly at my call to free their souls from their mortal prisons. They will join with the Chorus of Souls and Dorovar shall become the most powerful being in all of Creation."

As War continued, Gideon could feel his hold on consciousness starting to slip. His ears were ringing and his head hurt in a way he had never felt. His best guess was that his skull was broken, and from the heat he felt on the back of his head and neck, he was probably bleeding profusely. He could afford a small measure of power to mend the wound so that he would not bleed to death before he had a chance to act against the Herald. But he had to be careful. If Gideon used too much power, he might inflict so much damage upon himself that he would not be able to complete his mission. If he used too little, the attack would be ineffectual and War would probably kill him anyway.

"There will be nowhere to hide from the march of War. There will be no force that can hope to resist the tide of violence. Those who feel the touch of War can rise again to serve the Chorus of Souls. Those souls freed by the march of War will be spared the agony and torment that will be theirs at the hands of the Creator and the Children. The fate of all souls left to those demons is unfortunate and unfulfilled. The freed bodies, under the control of War will have the opportunity to free others from their fate, free others from their delusions, and free others from the hell of captivity that they currently live in. The march of War is a path of hope, the embodiment of freedom from ruined destiny. Those touched by War are spared the lie of potential, a lie that Dorovar will extinguish forever, and a lie that forces all men to watch the deeds of their lives reduced to bitter failure. As more of this lie is uncovered, and more spared from it, the Chorus of Souls shall swell, and Dorovar will cleanse not only this world, but the whole of Creation from its villainous touch."

War stood over Gideon, raising his sword high, ready to drive the tip through the chest of the fallen man. Gideon's eyes were closed, but he was aware of everything around him. He slowly drew power into himself, ready for the moment that could mean the end of his life.

"Those in the path of War will not be allowed to repeat their failures, and those who have failed can embrace their fates and find redemption," War continued. "One by one, you shall all be redeemed. One by one, you will all know the love of the Chorus of Souls, and the forgiveness of Dorovar."

Gideon felt the strike coming. War lifted the hilt of the blade high above his head and then drove the tip downward. A moment before the strike ripped Gideon in half, the former thief opened his eyes, reached out with both hands, and caught the massive blade mere inches from his chest. Gideon's eyes filled with white fire, and his voice boomed louder than War's had. But it was not Gideon's voice. Instead, the voice had a clearly feminine tone, but echoed across multiple octaves at the same time.

"You do not need Dorovar's forgiveness," the voice said full of malice and disgust. "You need mine!"

CHAPTER 112

Chapter CXIII

Don't Hunt What You Can't Kill

Year Two of the Divine Empress and Child of the Creator Marlae Tamerlane, Creator's Calendar Year 1872

Hannah stepped back out onto the rain soaked ground, the door closing behind her. She knew that Kiara would be following quickly behind, but Hannah took the few moments of silence to process and breathe. There had been precious little time to do either over the past few days, and Hannah expected there would be even less in the days to come. As Hannah looked over the past few years of her life, she did not recognize the person that she had become. In the protected world of the Heart of Stone and the Church of the Creator, Hannah had been one thing. She had been a member of the faithful, and then she had become the leader of the faithful. They were two sides of the same coin, and Hannah had begun to see the fact that she was once just a currency to be spent. She was used by the Church to do the work of the Creator, work now that she understood was in the service of a lie. And yet, she did not look at those years spent in the heart of the Church as a failure. Those years, despite the force behind the intent, were filled with good intention. Hannah's core tenant was to help people. That is what she wanted more than anything. And for those years in the Church, Hannah knew that she helped people. She saved lives. She made a difference. Or at least at the time it felt like she had. Now, in light of the greater narrative, she was unsure.

Hannah's thoughts immediately drifted to Aerith Seth, to the man he once had been. Hannah did not have access to all of the man's memories, and parts of his past were shrouded from her. What she did know however, was that Aerith never intended to be what he became. But did Aerith even have a chance? Everyone was vying for his powers, for his attention, for his very soul. As Aerith was placed in the path of occurrences that would forge his destiny, he could only do what he was being enticed to do. The walls had been erected all around him, forcing him in one clear direction. Perhaps if he had been a different kind of man, a more thoughtful man, he would have found ways to break through those walls. However, Aerith was conditioned to think that he was a blunt instrument; a hammer that was made only to demolish the adversaries that stood in his way. He was not meant to make decisions of his own. Taken from his family; he was put in a crucible meant to distill his ability and prove that he was special. Moved from the hellish pit reductively referred to as a mine, Aerith fell under the tutelage of a villain whose only goal was to exterminate his enemies and the enemies of his lord and master. His theoretical training complete, he was thrust into his new practical role as a general. From general he moved to sacrificial lamb, the role that had been his to fill from the moment of his birth. Had it been unavoidable? Could the road leading to that end have been different? Or was the fire he was forged in what made the sacrifice possible?

That thought brought Hannah back to herself. Her dedication to the Church had cast her in the role of a Knight of the Flashing Blade. The role had put her first in the path of the so-called Hand of Chaos and then ultimately in opposition of the Emperor of Cadaria. But it was not until her faith and her humanity collided that she was forced to make the choice that had brought her to this point. She had accepted the danger that Aerith Seth represented as the better alternative to the Creator's love. Now Hannah had fought gods, dragons, monsters, and demons. How much more good had she done in the service of Aerith Seth than she had done in the service of the Church? Was there any way to measure that? Even as Hannah could feel the days of her world grinding to a rapid demise, she still had hope that they could find a way to save the innocent, save their world, and save the souls of those who fought for the good of those who could not fight for themselves. The responsibility was one that Hannah took seriously, one that she had dedicated herself to from the beginning, and one that she was more able than ever to actually accomplish.

The door opened behind Hannah, and she turned back for a moment to see Kiara walk out. Hannah felt for the young woman and the path that she had taken to be at this point in her life. Hannah had tried to remember Kiara from her time at the Heart of Stone as an initiate, but she could not. There were many initiates, many acolytes, and though Hannah should have known all their names, she did not. If there was one thing from her time in the Heart that she regretted, it was that. As the High Priestess, she was not only responsible for the souls of all those who followed the teachings of the Church, but she was also responsible for all of those who showed the bravery and conviction to dedicate their lives to the Church's service. One evening, she and Gregor were having a conversation about the burdens of command on and off the battlefield. This was a time when Hannah had just been inducted into the Knights of the Flashing Blade, and the new responsibilities of that role had been cast upon her. Gregor had told her during that conversation that he knew the names and faces of every single man who served under his command, and should he have to send word back to the family of a fallen soldier, that the message would not be filled with empty platitudes, but true sentiment. Gregor believe that those who were willing to sacrifice their lives for a cause deserved that respect. Hannah then told Gregor of her guilt over not knowing the names and faces of all of those at the Heart of Stone. Gregor's response had been something that had stuck with her every day since. He said that an army was different from an organization. An organization functioned with necessary detachment so that disparate jobs and responsibilities could get accomplished without infringing upon one another. Armies had to function as a single entity, with one clearly defined goal. If the army did not function as one, men would die. Hannah took that characterization to heart, and she endeavored from that moment forward to learn all the names of all those who fought in the army of the Creator's love. Yet here she was, so far from that world, and so far from the Creator's love.

Hannah turned back and looked in the direction of home, or at least the one home she had always known. Albitonin was not far from where she stood by foot, but with a portal she could be there in a matter of seconds. At that moment Hannah began to consider how she intended to return to Albitonin. It wasn't as though she could simply walk up the steps to the Great Temple and announce herself. Perhaps the best option was for Hannah to create a portal and enter through the private garden that was reserved for the meditation of the High Priestess. The likelihood of anyone being there was relatively small, and if there was someone in that garden, it would be the new High Priestess. Between the two women they would be able to find the best way to explain Hannah's reemergence. From Aerith, Hannah knew that some of that groundwork had already been done, but it was highly likely that he had done far more damage than intended. It was then out of the corner of her eye she saw a figure approaching.

The woman drew immediate attention from both her posture and the ease with which she moved. There was a confidence to every step, and the baring of the woman instantly began to set off every danger sense within Hannah. The wind caught the edges of the white cloak that was draped around the woman's form, letting the loose-fitting garment flow around her. Beneath was the glitter of shimmering metal, which could have been nothing other than armor. As the woman began to draw closer, Hannah's now enhanced eyesight allowed her to take in more details about the armor that was supposed to be concealed beneath the cloak. There was heft to the armor, but the weight of it didn't seem to impede the woman's movements. Many of the heavily armored troops that she had commanded and battled in the past moved so deliberately because of the weight of their armor, they looked almost mechanical. This woman had none of that restriction and glided with ease through every step. The armor itself appeared to be an emerald green in color with heavy gold accents at the shoulder, the collar, and at every joint. The woman did not wear traditional gauntlets, preferring to leave her hands exposed. But there were thick golden bracers on her forearms that looked thick enough to block any incoming attack. A wide golden belt covered her stomach and hips, and appeared to give extra support to the armor in that region. She wore no helmet, instead choosing only to cover her head with the hood of the cloak. The woman stopped several yards from Hannah and slowly pulled the hood away from her head. Sandy blood hair in a tight braid appeared and she pulled it around to her left shoulder. The woman's eyes were turbulent, a stormy green that shifted to accents of gold like a heartbeat. Her expression was stern, matronly, and unflinching. Standing there she looked Hannah up and down once, and then her lips turned into a wide frown.

CHAPTER 113

"You are the one called Hannah Ironheart?"

The woman's voice was cold, devoid of emotion, except for the slightly palpable haze of disgust. A chill ran through Hannah, and for the first time in a long time she felt a twinge from her Sacred Weapon, Spirit. The weapon did not like the woman, or perhaps was afraid of the woman. But at the same time, there was almost an elation underpinning those emptions. Hannah was confused, but she steeled herself against the alien emotions. She focused her gaze on the woman and let a warrior's ease fall over her.

"I am Hannah."

The woman nodded almost absently.

"I think that I might not be so cavalier about claiming the identity of a traitor."

The word hit Hannah's ears like a sledgehammer. Her cheeks burned and rage threatened to break through the calm that she tried to impose on her now rapidly beating heart.

"And I would not be so cavalier about lodging such accusations."

The woman's hands disappeared behind her back, and Hannah felt herself tense, but no attack came. The woman's judgmental eyes again roamed Hannah's features.

"But is that not what you are, Hannah Ironheart? Were you not the most loved by the Creator upon this world? His High Priestess? The spreader of the word and love of the Creator to all of his flock and faithful? A trust that you broke when you joined the one that even the Creator refers to as the Heretic. And so now you have abandoned your flock, and what has become of them in your absence? They are hunted. They are persecuted. They are enslaved. You were supposed to protect them, Hannah Ironheart. You were supposed to defend them from all threats to their beliefs. Now every death of a member of the faithful is on your head. What other word is that for that kind of betrayal other than traitor?"

Hannah's heart lurched. All she wanted to do was take hold of the ancient mace at her side and bash the woman's head in. She wanted to keep smashing the woman's head until there was nothing left but a smear of red on the ground.

"And what about your vow to your Emperor? Why do you not stand at his side? You quickly threw away your vows to the Emperor in favor of his daughter. Another betrayal because the daughter represented better prospects? Or perhaps you had designs on the position yourself. After all, you are now consorting with a man who overthrows kingdoms, kills gods, and is a self-professed monster. Are you so eager to follow in your new patron's footsteps that you will forsake every vow you have ever made?"

There was no nuance to the woman's attacks. She was pulling at every shame in Hannah's heart, trying to incite her emotions to keep her off balance. It was an effective tactic, and Hannah could feel her control starting to slip. Even for a woman who had spent her entire life controlling her emotions, controlling her pain, controlling her every reaction, there were cracks in that emotional armor. Those cracks had been further exacerbated by her conversion away from her life in the Church. All of those days and years serving what was ostensibly a lie had changed her definition of faith, challenged her definition of self, and placed her in an unfamiliar position. She had to find out who she was without the Church of the Creator and without the comfortable blanket of religion that she had always depended upon to defend her against the cold and uncertainty of the world that she had sealed herself away from.

"And what of your vow to your husband? How much value did that vow have, Hannah? Where is Gregor Quicksilver now? Do you know?"

Hannah steeled herself the best she could.

"Gregor made his choices. He was a man of faith, and the Creator rewarded him for that faith. While now his path and mine may have diverged, the respect that I have for him has not diminished. Though one day we may find ourselves on opposite sides of a battlefield, it will not change my respect and admiration for him."

The woman scoffed.

"Spoken like the acolyte of a man who sees every alliance as a convenience to be depended upon until it is no longer convenient. How many of Aerith's allies has he abandoned? How many has he left behind when it suited him? And you are proving to be just like him."

The woman's hands reemerged from behind her back, and she held them to her sides, palms out, like she was trying to show to Hannah that she was no threat. Hannah of course new better. This woman was a threat at every level of the word.

"I bring you this truth Hannah, because I want you to see what you are allowing yourself to become, and what it is costing those who you once cared about with every fiber of your being. Your husband despite his ascension was still a man, was still your husband, and was still afraid when he was facing his death."

Hannah's heart froze.

"He died as he lived," the woman said coldly, the violent green and gold eyes filled with malice and scorn. "He was on his knees, begging for the aid of the Creator who would never come. And no, his death was not painless. He was ripped apart. His wings were torn from his back, his limbs broken and crushed, his heart ripped from his chest and stepped upon to ensure that there would be nothing left of the former Servant. He was sacrificed. Needlessly some might say. The Creator dispatched him to bring justice to a Herald of Dorovar. The Voice against Conquest. Gregor with all of his power and all of his faith was no match for Conquest, no match for the Chorus of Souls, and no match for Dorovar. And so he died, broken, bleeding, and cursing the Creator that had led him to ruin."

The woman paused, sighed, and shook her head.

"Such needless death."

Hannah gritted her teeth.

"All of the death that Dorovar inflicts upon this world is needless."

The woman's frown deepened.

"Spoken like a fanatic."

Hannah's face contorted into a quizzical glare.

"And what does that make you? You serve a monster who wanted to kill every last person on this world so that he can use their souls to create a path for him to ascend the Golden Throne. How is Dorovar worthy of reshaping the destiny of Creation? How is Dorovar any better than the Creator with his pettiness, greed, and endless need for supplication and devotion? The Creator with his Servants, Dorovar with his Heralds. The Creator with his Children, Dorovar with his, whatever you are."

For the first time a pang of irritation twisted the corner of the woman's mouth.

"I am not a fanatic. I am Redissa. I am a member of the goddess's chosen, the Adhradair. We were entrusted with the protection of our world, and though our world was lost, we are the protectors of the Perfect Order. We will make the Perfect Order a reality once again when Dorovar ascends to the Golden Throne. There will be peace on every world forever after. You and your patron stand in the way of the Perfect Order, and that cannot be allowed."

The woman's right hand pointed downward the next second and clutched something invisible. The next moment a sword materialized in her hand, stretching down to the ground. The hilt and pommel of the blade were clearly designed to be wielded with two hands, the blade wide and thick, gleaming from both edges with clear sharpness. A green glow clutched to the edges of the blade and circled around the whole length like a fog. Redissa did not raise the blade or make any threatening movements, but Hannah knew it was only a matter of time before the jibes and insults would become physical attacks. Redissa extended her other hand toward Hannah with her palm up.

"Your end does not have to come here, Hannah Ironheart. You may continue fighting your futile war at the side of your patron, and hope to make the difference that will make sense of your myriad betrayals. The disposition of your soul is not my concern. However, in your possession is the prison within which the soul of one of my fellow Adhradair is confined.

Surrender the Sacred Weapon that you insultingly refer to as Spirit, and free the soul of my sister Ninian. Surrender the weapon willingly, and there need not be conflict between us. Refuse, and I shall have no choice but to destroy you."

A sudden calm came over Hannah. Unbidden she felt Aerith's presence in her mind. The haze of power that had been referred to as his mantle filled her body. She felt stronger, she felt at peace, and she felt the singularity of purpose. In her mind the training of a thousand lifetimes entered her mind, and she wasn't aware until after it happened that two crystalline blades appeared in her hands. A sly smile came to her face, and the words that came out of her lips were in her voice, but were the words of the man who would not compromise in the face of the challenge that the Adhradair represented. Beyond that, Aerith was angry. He was angry about Sabrina, he was angry about Rhain, he was angry about Bryn, he was angry about Ayden, and most of all he was angry about Logan. It was that rage that fueled the next words.

"Conquest may have killed Gregor Quicksilver, it may have robbed the Creator of the Voice temporarily, but one thing that Conquest could not do was defeat Logan Ranthall. That makes two Heralds that Logan defeated all by himself. Add to that the one that Arin Ranthall killed and that makes three that the allies of Aerith Seth have taken from Dorovar. So why is it that Dorovar thinks that he's so superior? Now, as to the Sacred Weapon. If you want it, you're just going to have to take it. Because you may not want to fight me, but I certainly want to fight you."

Redissa charged in the next moment moving impossibly fast. A downward slash was supposed to catch Hannah by surprise and split her in half from her right shoulder all the way to her waist. But Hannah was ready. The sword in her left hand came up and blocked the blow and the block flowed into a spin that brought her right sword around in a wide arcing slash that Redissa was only just able to back away from. As it was the tip of the sword scratched against the metal belt at the woman's waist, sending a shower of sparks in all directions. Redissa's retreat lasted for only a moment and she charged forward again, the tip of her blade heading directly for Hannah's heart. For all of the woman's apparent agility, it was clear that she was not skilled in swordplay. Her attacks were intended to be lethal in one blow, and there was no art to the assaults. Hannah sidestepped the thrust, and then in one motion brought the flat of her left blade down on the back of Redissa's hands while the pommel of Hannah's right blade struck Redissa on the side of the face. Blood exploded from the woman's mouth and she lunged back yet again. The attack on her hands had been intended to make Redissa drop her blade, but the woman proved more tenacious than Hannah had anticipated. Whatever the woman lacked in skill, she made up for in fortitude and guile.

Before Redissa could reset her feet, Hannah charged forward, feinting high and slashing low. Redissa was able to block the low blow with her sword, but left herself open for the crushing elbow strike that landed on the other side of her face. Such an intimate maneuver however left Hannah open for a quick counterattack. Redissa extended her right hand in a palm strike that landed in the middle of Hannah's chest. The strike sent Hannah flying backwards, but she was able to regain control quickly, letting her feet drag across the ground until she came to a stop. Hannah smiled even as she could taste the faintest metallic taste of blood in her mouth. Redissa was quick to press her advantage, but chose not to rely on her unpracticed sword technique. Instead, three tendrils of the phantasmal green energy of the Chorus of Souls lanced out from the extended fingers of her right hand. One made for Hannah's throat while the other two intended to capture her wrists. The tendrils were fast, but with Aerith's powers, Hannah was faster. With one blade she chopped one of the tendrils away, with the other caught the other two attacks. The tendrils wrapped around her sword pulled the weapon from her grip. But this was exactly what Hannah intended. The very same moment that the blade left her hand, Hannah threw the other sword in Redissa's direction, using the tendrils as a momentary obstruction to Redissa's vision. The white-cloaked woman saw the strike a moment before it connected, and was able to move to the side enough that instead of the tip of the sword embedding itself in her heart, it instead took her full in the shoulder. Redissa's arm hung limply at her side. Even robbed of one arm, Redissa held her sword firmly and seemed ready to defend herself from Hannah's next attack. However, that attack would never come.

Behind her, Hannah heard the stifled cry come from Kiara. Hannah half-spun, not willing to turn her back on Redissa. Behind Kiara stood a man clad in matte black armor who was head and shoulders taller than the former initiate. The man's gauntlet was wrapped around Kiara's neck from behind, the cruel black metal studded with thorn-like protrusions. Some of the thorns must have been on the inside of the gauntlet's surface as well as Hannah could see trickles of blood flowing down Kiara's neck and squeezing between the fingers of the large man. Like Redissa, the man had sandy blond hair, but his eyes were a stark sky blue that pulsed with white. His expression was pure malice, his lips turned into a snarl with teeth bared. With his other hand, he pointed at Hannah.

"Enough of this. You will surrender the Sacred Weapon or I will make you watch as I crush the life out of this little girl. And make no mistake, Hannah Ironheart, as fast as you may think you are with the powers of Aerith Seth at your disposal, I am faster. Lay the weapon on the ground, step away until Redissa can recover it, and then we shall let you and this girl leave in peace. Defy me, and I will crush her, and then Redissa and I will crush you. Do not doubt the words of Haricos. For my word carries with it the weight of Dorovar, the Chorus of Souls, the whole of the Adhradair, and the vengeance we shall have in the name of the innocents lost on our world of Loinn. Surrender, Hannah Ironheart, you have no other option."

Tears of Blood

Year Five of the Just Emperor Kaitain "Dragonsbane" Lorien, Creator's Calendar Year 1872

Alise Modrall trailed behind her sometime father Kaitain Lorien and his new dangerous companion Tess Annis as they slowly walked in the direction of the capital city of Zevarit. There were a great many things on Alise's mind, and each step seemed to deepen her concerns. The first thought that struck Alise of course was the fact that she had never known Kaitain Lorien to walk anywhere, especially not over terrain and not without a significant protective presence. Yes, the remaining members of the Imperial Army were reforming just outside of Zevarit, but they were still several hours walk away. But moreover, why walk at all? Alise could have easily created a portal, or certainly Tess Annis could have managed the same. There was no need to walk. But something had changed in Kaitain since the moment of his conversation with the creature calling itself Dorovar. Though Alise had not been alive long, she had enough experience and empathic knowledge to recognize the changes in Kaitain. He had always been dark and border-line obsessive, but those traits had taken on a new edge. And now that he had been coupled with Tess Annis, the obsession had begun to transition to madness.

Alise Modrall was part of Kaitain Lorien's rather eclectic collection of servants, sycophants, and usurers. She was, in truth, a living and breathing representation of Kaitain's lack of trust in anyone and anything other than himself. Growing up in the Imperial Palace of Aldere, Kaitain had been exposed to the inner workings of the empire and the subtle and not-so-subtle organizations and alliances that made smooth operation of the empire possible. Whether it was the Academy of Arcane Arts that assured no people with the ability to touch the arcane forces of reality could become a threat to the empire, or the Shadow Guild whose responsibility it was to find and neutralize threats; each and every piece of bureaucracy had their own realm of attention. This fact was what Kaitain found the most troubling. While these actors all had responsibility to the empire, very few had concrete ties to the Emperor, and could in fact operate against the emperor for the good of the empire. This was an intolerable environment in Kaitain's mind, and so he would need to ensure the loyalty of everyone around him, even if it meant destroying the structures that had been in place in Cadaria for thousands of years.

The first of these monoliths of antiquity of course was the Academy of Arcane Arts. Kaitain had always detested them and their morally superior ways. Why would any organization exist that would consciously make people less than they could be. The Masters of the Academy could use their abilities to shake the world if they willed it. They could have overrun the government and seized control. But instead, they chose to hide in their school and teach their students to be servants and scholars instead of conquerors. Fortunately, over the years the Academy had collected many enemies for their short-sighted ways and resistance to change. The most famous of course was Orren Eldrath, who was expelled when he refused to stop his research into forbidden topics, but he was far from the first to question the teachings of the Masters.

When Alistair Ravenheart was just a novice at the Academy, the Master of the Academy was a man by the name of Dorin Cahlain. Cahlain was a traditionalist of the highest order and had no patience for anyone who would question either his authority or the strictures of the Academy. At the time, Cahlain was consistently challenged by one of the newer Masters of the Council, a man by the name of Yaron Telsin. Yaron had been a controversial addition to the Council, and the vote had been split two to two. However, because Dorin voted for his inclusion, his vote was the deciding one. But from the moment Yaron joined the Council, he debated every decision the Council made. He argued for the expansion of the teachings, argued for a more active role in the defense of the empire, and argued for the creation of a specialized program that would train acolytes in the offensive use of their powers against the dragons and the Dark Gods. Naturally all of these suggestions were rebuffed by the other members of the Council. However, it was the studies that Yaron committed himself to beyond his duties as a Master that would eventually put him at odds with the rest of the Academy.

Yaron Telsin had no desire to be in a leadership position at the Academy of Arcane Arts. He knew that he would not be able to influence policy. Becoming a Master was necessary so that he would be given access to the Academy's archives. In the archives Yaron would be able to spend hour after hour and day after day studying not just the foundation of the teachings of the Academy, but also the knowledge that was forbidden to teach. Yaron was fascinated by the natural and unnatural forces that could influence life and death. Yaron had a brilliant mind and believed that he discovered paths to create life as well as accelerate its development. These studies and eventual experiments were discovered by the other Masters and Yaron was expelled from the Academy. Of course, his knowledge and curiosity were quickly welcomed by Talisia and her Hand of Chaos. Talisia gave Yaron everything he needed to continue his studies and his experiments. Those experiments would eventually result in the creation of two other members of the Hand of Chaos; Xavier Cormea, the man who could wrangle the will of even the strongest mind, and Dimitri Sulano, the man who could speak with the spirits of the dead and lost. Even before Kaitain Lorien had ascended to the throne, Yaron Telsin approached Kaitain and proposed the creation of a group of arcane warriors who would be loyal to Kaitain and Kaitain alone. This was the birth of the Black Academy. While Kaitain did not fully trust Yaron or his motivations, what he did trust was the man's lust for power and destruction. Men like that could be used for a time, no matter what his ultimate goals were.

It was Yaron's inclusion into Kaitain's inner circle that made it possible for the subversion of the Shadow Guild. While Kaitain understood the need for the Shadow Guild in principle, he objected to any body that had the ability to act against the emperor unilaterally if the Grand Master determined that the emperor posed a threat to the stability of the

Empire. In Kaitain's mind, the Shadow Guild would be the first body that he would need to eliminate. But there would be troubles that Kaitain would face that required quiet remedy. So Kaitain approached Yaron Telsin with a plan to create a perfect assassin, an assassin that combined the training of the Academy of Arcane Arts with the proficiency and ruthlessness of the Shadow Guild. Alise Modrall was the result of that experiment, and she had been Yaron's crowning achievement. She was perfect, exactly what Kaitain had wanted, and from the moment of her birth and accelerated growth to adulthood, she had eliminated threat after threat. Of course, more of the threats that Alise eliminated were potential or imaged threats rather than actual threats. But what irritated Alise the most was the fact that she was not loosed against the true threats. She was only allowed to support the assassins of the Shadow Guild that were dispatched to murder Feyd and Felicia Lorien. She was never allowed to take direct action against the Masters of the Academy of Arcane Arts. And there was of course the mysterious man named Wynne, the thought of which made Alise's blood burn.

Alise wanted so much to track down that man and destroy him. She had already made the request to Kaitain once, and if she pressed the matter any further, he would perhaps respond badly. Now that Tess was at his side, that poor response could translate into reprisal in the form of swift and painful death. Many feared to incite Kaitain's ire before his new alliance, now none would dare tempt fate in such a way. And so, Alise followed silently as the two monsters born of power and privilege trudged slowly across the landscape.

But it was Tess Annis who concerned Alise the most. As a trained assassin, Alise viewed the world in absolute terms. There were targets, obstacles, threats and collateral damage. Targets were simple. Kaitain told her who to kill, and she would die before she let that target get away. Obstacles were those people and things that got in the way of a kill. Obstacles could be walls, armies, family members, other assassins, what have you. Some of those obstacles could be overcome, some could be avoided, and some just needed to be eliminated. This of course would lead to the fourth category, collateral damage. There were times when a target was not alone, but time was of the essence. Everyone around the target needed to be eliminated to ensure the death of the target, or to send a message. There were many times when death was the greatest communicator of intent. Threats however were another matter entirely. Alise prided herself on knowing the capabilities not only of her target but of those who surrounded that target. Was there a guard who was particularly accomplished in hand-to-hand combat? Did the target have a tolerance or immunity to a toxin? Did the target have access to arcane ability that had gone undiscovered by the Academy. If the target lived in Galateria, did they have access to the strange and unique forces that sometimes called that place home? And now, after the confrontation with the Serpentine Knight Vallic Ultiv and his companion, were they perhaps members of the Dark Gods in disguise? Alise never viewed other assassins as threats. Even with the impressive training that that Shadow Guild instilled in their top operatives, they were no match for Alise, with the possible exception of the Grand Master himself, but even there Alise had her doubts.

Tess Annis was a different beast altogether. The depth and breadth of her abilities were completely unknown. Kaitain had alluded to the fact that her role as the Dragon's Tear gave her the ability to reshape reality. But what did that really mean? To most sane and rational people, what the Dark Gods did reshaped reality. What was reshaping reality if it was not making possible what one thought was impossible? But clearly there was more to this little girl than met the eye. What unnerved Alise the most about the girl was her seeming calmness. Despite all of her power, she made no effort to resist Alise's advances. Despite her self-professed training, she seemed to quickly fall under the sway of Kaitain's growing madness. But was it truly Tess who was under Kaitain's sway, or was it Kaitain who had fallen under the power of the Dragon's Tear and what it could potentially do to advance his goal of becoming a god? Regardless, Alise would study the girl to determine whether or not there were weaknesses that she could exploit should the Dragon's Tear become a threat to Kaitain's life. Something within Alise however told her that Tess was already an existential threat to Kaitain's life, as well as to all life in Cadaria.

Just as the twin suns began to dawn over the horizon on the morning of the first day of the new year; Tess, Kaitain, and Alise arrived at the crest of a hill which overlooked the city of Zevarit which lay in the valley below. Zevarit was an unusual city by the standards of other capitols of Cadarian

Kingdoms. Zevarit was never intended to be the capital of the Kingdom of Blood. In truth, it was nothing more than an oversized mining town, the center of one of the largest coal and precious mineral mines in the whole of Cadaria. The fuel harvested in Zevarit were critical to the smelting operations in the Kingdom of Iron, Pellatori and in the Kingdom of Steel, Celidar. Moreover, the foundries in the Flying Kingdom, Hedorah would have fallen silent without continued shipments from Zevarit. But the work in Zevarit was not without cost. That cost took the form of bodies that were extracted week after week from the depths of the mines. Those of nobility avoided Zevarit, choosing instead to direct from a distance rather than have to deal with the loss first-hand. However, Zevarit thrived despite the tragedy. They advanced safety processes and technology that would ensure futures for their miners, while at the same time pioneering community relationships and programs that provided for the families that had lost loved ones in the depths of the mines. Zevarit was the lifeblood of the empire, but at times, it was also the truest representation of the compassion that the empire could have for its people in times of darkness. But because significant investments of wealth and time were made below the ground, it left little opportunity to invest in advancement above. To the eyes of royalty and nobility, Zevarit was a backwards place, still little more than a mining town with delusions of grandeur. Most of the dwellings in and around the city were small and focused on the needs of the families of the minors. Even the palace and estate of the Ruby Knight of the Flashing Blade were small compared to their counterparts in other kingdoms. Zevarit was a hard-working and humble place whose inhabitants took great pride in what they had built. That pride extended to the Army of Blood, who were considered some of the most highly trained and motivated soldiers in Cadaria. Under the tutelage of first Ivan Quicksilver, then Gregor Quicksilver, the men of the Army of Blood were disciplined, professional, hardened, and confident. Under normal circumstances, the Imperial Army would find combatting the Army of Blood challenging on a neutral field, even with their superior arms. Defending their homes, the Army of Blood would be a tenacious and potentially undefeatable adversary. But these were not normal circumstances.

Standing looking down at the city below, off in the distance Kaitain could see the banners of the Imperial Army forming up. It would not take long before the Army of Blood would become aware of their presence and begin to mobilize. Before Kaitain could make known his orders or his intentions, Tess spoke calmly, yet ominously.

"You should order your troops to move back beyond the ring of cliffs," her emotionless voice intoned.

Kaitain did not respond, instead turning to Alise and relaying the order with a wave of his hand. Alise bowed shallowly and then opened a portal to inform the soldiers of their new orders. Whatever Tess had planned for the city of Zevarit, it would spill out over a great distance and she was trying to avoid damaging Kaitain's ability to continue his crusade. Once Alise had gone and she saw the troops begin to move away from the city, Tess began to speak again.

"Do you know what blood really is, Kaitain?" Tess began.

As she spoke, she extended her hands to her sides, a golden glow beginning to coalesce around them.

"Blood is poison. Blood is a toxin that runs through your veins, killing you every moment from your birth. Some it kills quicker, and some it kills slower, but it kills all the same."

As the golden light continued to gather in Tess's hands, black clouds gathered above Zevarit, an eerie red glow around the edges of the clouds.

"We are born with the poison inside of us, you see. We are corrupted by the hate and enmity that holds between the Children of the Creator. We were made to be pawns in their eternal war, and we are nothing more than expressions of their hate for one another. But more than that, we are expressions of the disdain that the Children have for the Creator. They hate each other for the game they play and they hate their father for having to play the game. We are born of hate. We are born of intolerance. We are born to suffer and die in the furtherance of that hate and intolerance. We are damned all of us, and so what does it matter that we are poisoned and suffer in that damnation? The Children care little. The Creator cares less. And so we suffer, ignored and in darkness with no hope of ever seeing the light."

CHAPTER 113

In the clouds above the city, red flashes of light began to pulse inside the clouds. As Kaitain looked on, he noted that the light pulsed in time with the words that Tess spoke. In his heart he knew he should have felt some trepidation or fear as to the potential power of the girl in front of him. But all he felt was elation as she continued to speak.

"But the poison is more than just the evil of the Children of the Creator. The poison in our blood comes from the crimes of our parents and grandparents. Their prejudices, their fears and projections. All of the slights and disappointments. They cannot help but pass those on to their children and their children's children. The poison of crime. The poison of racism. The poison of hate. The poison of fear. All of those flow through us, diminishing us. And beyond all of that is the poison injected into us by our teachers, our tutors, our friends, and our enemies. We continue to be corrupted with each breath that we draw. If the parents who raised us are murderers and villains, how can that not diminish us? If the tutors who teach us are ambivalent to the death that they caused, how can that not diminish us? If our friends betray us and leave us at the mercy of the evils of the world, how can that not diminish us? And what form does that diminishment take? Poison."

Above the city of Zevarit, the pulsing light stopped, and rain began to fall. The rain was not hard, but steady and seemed to cover the entirety of the city and the surrounding area. Tess continued to speak, and the golden glow intensified to the point of being blinding. Kaitain had to shield his eyes.

"Most of those made by the Children do not feel the poison flowing through them. They are fortunate in their ignorance. But some of us feel the poison. I have felt it as long as I can remember. I didn't know what it was until just recently, but now it is unmistakable. The servants of Halicon call the poison the Blaze. The servants of Emries call the poison the Light. Those who are disciples of Aerith Seth call it the mantle. The Servants of the Creator call it the touch of the divine. But the truth is that it is all the same."

Tess levitated from where she stood at the crest of the hill and floated out into the sky above Zevarit. The rain seemed to bend around her, not a single drop touching her skin or clothing. Finally floating high above the city, a bubble of air around her, she spoke again in a voice so loud that everyone in the valley heard it clearly.

"This power that inhabits me is no different. It is poison. But it is a poison that will sweep across the whole of Creation."

The bubble around Tess dissipated, and the rain finally touched the girl. Once the rain contacted the golden glow around her hands, the light exploded into twin stars that filled the sky for several moments before fading into nothingness. It was when the light disappeared however that the real horror began. When Kaitain's vision cleared, it did not register the change to the rain that fell from the sky, at least until his eyes returned to where Tess still hovered. She should have been drenched with water, her clothes pressed to her by the weight of it. Instead, thick viscous red liquid clung to her body, smearing her hair to her face, and clinging to her in splotchy patches. Below, the blood rain fell on the buildings and people in a steady downpour. Kaitain smiled, the irony of Tess's display clear. Blood falling from the sky onto the Kingdom of Blood. It would strike fear into the hearts of every inhabitant, sapping their will to fight and making them easy for Kaitain to conquer. However, when the first screams of pain and terror rose from the city, Kaitain began to understand just how much he had underestimated the girls' intentions.

As the rain touched the people caught out in the downpour, instead of smearing onto their skin as it did with Tess, it began to smoke and then burn, eating through clothing, skin, and bone. Anyone caught in the rain dissolved into nothing in a matter of seconds, only their screams remaining as they melted away. But it was not just the people who were unmade by the sanguine downpour. As the drops of crimson rain touched the wood, stone, or metal facades of buildings, the structure began to hiss, pock, and shatter under the assault. Roofs disappeared. Walls collapsed under the weight of their unsupported structures. People who were not dissolved by the rain that fell through the now open roofs were crushed under the weight of their homes that suddenly became rickety death-traps. The blood rushed through the streets, eating the cobblestone leaving only the soil underneath. Even the men in the nearby mines were not spared from the assault. The blood rushed into the openings of the mines, down into the farthest depths, killing not only every man that it touched, but also dissolving the support beams that held the shafts open. In a matter of minutes, Zevarit had been reduced to a crater, with no human-made structure still standing, and no mortal still drawing breath in its former streets. As the clouds above the city dispersed, the blood below evaporated into nothingness. Her grizzly work done, Tess let herself descend into the bare patch of land that had once been Zevarit.

It took Kaitain several minutes to make his way from the crest of the hill down into the valley where Tess stood. Rage filled him with every step. When he finally was face to face with the girl, he unleashed his displeasure.

"What have you done! This was a place to be conquered! This was to be mine!"

No expression came to Tess's face.

"This action taught two very specific lessons Kaitain, lessons that could not be taught any other way."

Kaitain's rage did not diminish, but he would hear the girl out.

"What lessons?"

Tess motioned to the emptiness around her.

"You wanted those who oppose you to fear you. If you used force of arms, what would have been the response? If one kingdom could not have stood against you alone, they would have united. If two could not stand, they would try to find a third. The hope would be that you would exhaust your resources before they did. Conventional thinking will not make the gains that you wish to make. Now, the stories of your power will spread far and wide. Those chosen from your Imperial Guard will make sure that all of Cadaria knows that you stood upon the crest of the hill, pointed your finger, and Zevarit was swept away like the morning fog when the suns rise."

Kaitain's jaw went slack.

"But my men will have seen you floating in the air, calling down the rain of blood."

Tess smiled.

"Your men saw nothing of the kind. They saw exactly what I wanted them to see. A wave of your hand destroyed a kingdom that dared to stand against your will. Fear of your new power will rob all of your enemies of their will to fight, and you can focus your attention on those who cannot be forced to yield through fear; the dragons and the Dark Gods."

Kaitain's mind whirled. The possibilities of what he could do with Tess at his side were staggering. He could decimate the Heart of Stone. He could eviscerate all of his enemies with the snap of his fingers. He could reduce every dragon to dust. Lost in his power-hungry thoughts, he barely heard his own voice ask a question.

"And the second lesson?"

Tess put her hand on his shoulder.

"You desire to be a god, Kaitain. This was to teach you to stop thinking like a mortal. Eliminating armies and conquering kingdoms is beneath the scope of a god's appetites. You must turn instead to bending whole worlds to your will and remaking the very essence of all that you survey in the images of your deepest desires."

Kaitain's laughter resounded through the empty valley.

Unintended Consequences

Year Two of the Divine Empress and Child of the Creator Marlae Tamerlane, Creator's Calendar Year 1872

Shouts for assistance called out mere moments after Aelind's fall from Anabel's window. Neither Anabel nor Jeroch had any clear idea of how to proceed, but both knew it would not take much time for the authorities of the Heart of Stone to discover where Aelind fell from. However, neither were in much of a condition to defend against potential allegations. Jeroch moved away from the window to the door and looked out into the hall, observing the movements of the acolytes and adepts. Anabel for her part finished drying herself and then as quickly as possible dressed in one of the simple dressing gowns that was left for her and the wrapped a thick robe around herself. The scandal of the actions of the personal assistant to the High Priestess of the Church of the Creator would be lost if it was discovered that a Dark God was responsible for her death. After Anabel had finished dressing, she took hold of Jeroch's shoulder and pulled him away from the door. It took but a moment to weave a bubble of silence around them, ensuring that their voices would not carry.

"You need to leave," Anabel said quickly, keeping her voice down, despite the bubble of silence. "Stay close, but make sure you aren't seen."

Jeroch pressed a cloth bundle into her hand.

"Keep this safe. This is one of the daggers that Talisia created that are designed to steal the powers from Dark Gods and others. I'm not sure what the intention of this woman were, but it was clear that she was in league with Talisia or one of her functionaries."

Anabel frowned.

"What does this mean?"

Jeroch shook his head.

"At the very least it means that Talisia has infiltrated the Heart of Stone. So watch your back. You can't trust anyone."

Anabel nodded.

"I can trust Baeata, and I can trust the priestess Rhya. But I take your warning. Now go. I'll contact you when it is time. I'll open and close a portal quickly. When you see that, come back here."

Jeroch nodded and quickly formed a portal. Moments later he stepped through the portal which winked closed behind him. Anabel waited for several moments before moving to the door of the chambers. She heard the sound of people coming up the stairs. She centered herself, purged all emotion out of her face and posture before opening the door and stepping into the hall. Anabel became totally aware of her surroundings as she entered the hallway. To her right, several sets of footfalls quickly ascended the steps, and from the sounds, many appeared to be armed. Anabel did not run or even hurry from the doorway of her quarters, instead taking calm and deliberate steps toward the door to the private garden. While Anabel could have simply opened the door and entered Baeata's presence without permission, that could easily have been misconstrued as an attempt on the High Priestess's life. Instead Anabel stood straight and proud, knocking firmly but without any sort of urgency. As she stood, waiting to be acknowledged, the footsteps coming up the stairs became louder and quicker. By the time the door to the private garden opened revealing a partially disheveled Baeata, the oncoming individuals had reached the floor's landing and many were brandishing weapons. For her part, Baeata kept her expression calm and even, letting her eyes go past Anabel to the men before letting them settle back upon Anabel.

"What has happened?"

Anabel opened her mouth to speak, but her words were interrupted by the voice of one of the armed men who was quickly making his way down the hall.

"Are you well, High Priestess? Should we clear this floor?"

Baeata feared for the worst, but Anabel's calm face and clear eyes were a welcome reassurance. The High Priestess drew herself up and tried her best to project confidence.

"Please secure this floor, lieutenant," Baeata said, recognizing the markings on the man's uniform. "I am in an important conference at the moment with a representative of the Divine Empress Marlae Tamerlane. Stand guard by this door, and you shall be summoned for your report momentarily."

The lieutenant saluted quickly and waited as Baeata motioned Anabel to enter the garden. Anabel moved slowly and calmly, trying her best to give the impression that nothing was amiss. As soon as she was through the door, Baeata nodded to the soldier before closing the door behind her. When she turned to face Anabel, it was then that she noticed the woman's odd state of dress. Of course, it was very late at night, or early in the morning depending upon one's point of view, and so some state of odd dress was to be expected. Baeata expected that she must have looked a fright. Anabel regarded Baeata, as though the much older woman was gauging Baeata's potential reaction to whatever information that Anabel had regarding whatever had occurred.

"You should sit," Anabel said calmly.

Baeata opened her mouth to speak, but then thought the better of it. From the short time that Baeata had known Anabel, she had come to know that Anabel would not exaggerate or be melodramatic. There was simply no place for it in Anabel's way of thinking. Baeata sat down slowly on one of the low benches, expecting that Anabel would do the same. When Anabel made no motion to sit, Baeata began to sense the grave nature of the situation. Anabel shifted her weight between her feet for a moment before letting her voice hit the air. It was an expression of disquiet that was even more striking coming from a woman as practiced in courtly manner and controlled poise as Anabel. Baeata noticed immediately that Anabel's tone was serious but not grave, measured but not forced. She was the picture of control, the voice of the practiced politician and unflappable regal presence.

"Firstly," Anabel began, "I must apologize for my appearance. It defies decorum to appear before someone of your position in such a manner, and so I beg your indulgence. This is not how I honor my position as advisor to the Divine Empress or your position as the High Priestess of the Church of the Creator. But, I hope that my explanation of events will gain your forgiveness and understanding of the situation and for the hastiness of my dress."

Baeata was impressed by Anabel for a number of reasons. First and foremost was her clear adherence to diplomatic norms. Even though Anabel and Baeata had spent the majority of the night discussing the various ways in which the Church of the Creator could ally itself with the Divine Empress and her overall agenda to protect the faithful, Anabel did not attempt to trade on any of that familiarity. On top of that, while Anabel was quick to apologize for her appearance, she did not for a moment acknowledge Baeata's own improper attire. One of the key points that diplomats always needed to be aware of was the fact that they were guests in a powerful leader's house. These leaders were often vain, aloof, or boorish in their manner. Diplomats often had to absorb these affronts to common decency, accepting as normal behavior that which would be frowned upon in normal societal circles. The ends of proper political discourse required thick skin and the ability to see everything while reacting to very little. In that moment, Baeata was very glad that she never saw herself as a diplomat. She was content to be a shepherd of a disparate flock who needed someone who put their spiritual lives first.

"Now," Anabel continued, her tone remaining even, "I would ask that you wait until my tale is finished before you ask questions that I may or may not be able to answer. Do you agree?"

Baeata nodded.

"Good," Anabel answered, her tone still controlled but with slight relief. "Once our discussions broke for the evening, I retired to the quarters that you prepared for me. As I'm sure you can imagine, I was exhausted from the series of days that I have been directly involved in and was looking forward to at least two hours of uninterrupted rest. Of course, your generous offer of a bath despite the late hour was too tempting to pass up. Conducting such important negotiations while still covered in the remnants of a collapsing palace is the height of bad manners. I did not want to continue to present such an offensive presence in our continued negotiations. So, I chose to await the arrival of the bath."

Baeata considered Anabel's characterization of herself. Baeata of course had known of the circumstances of their flight from Hedorah. There had been the attack on the palace, and had been the attack by the creature called Conquest. And yet, despite the risk to their lives and the risk to the very soul of Cadaria, Anabel was concerned that she was potentially offending Baeata because she was covered in sweat and some dirt. Now there were some of lesser intelligence or understanding that would view Anabel's statements as those of vanity. But Anabel's clear characterization not only of herself and her history made seeing her as anything but a woman who respected the office of the High Priestess as well as the woman who inhabited it impossible.

"Once the bath arrived, I was quick to avail myself of the warm water."

Anabel paused for a moment. Her eyes dropped to the floor, and her next words were tense, and she clearly was struggling with them.

"As I have told you, Baeata, my brother was a great warrior on our world. And beyond my brother's own skill, he and my family were constantly surrounded with special people of great skill. So, I have had guards around me for as long as I can remember. Those guards would beat certain truths into my mind and into my reflexes. Never sit with your back to the door. Stay away from open windows. Assume there are assassins around every corner. Now I know that cannot be considered much of a way to live, but on my world, a world that was constantly at war for practically my entire adult life, it was reality."

Anabel paused, and Baeata considered her words. Though Baeata had found herself thrust into a position of power, she did not have the paranoia about her that Anabel had just described. Cadaria was not always a safe place, and over the last five years it had continued to destabilize. And even now, with worship of the Creator outlawed by the supposedly rightful leader of the Empire of Cadaria, Baeata did not feel the threat hanging over her head. She did not feel the knives at her back, nor did she feel as though she needed to look over her shoulder every moment. Baeata could not conceive of a life lived under constant threat of death.

"But as I sank into that water," Anabel continued, "I forgot many of the reflexive lessons that had been drilled into my head for so long. I sat with my back to the window."

Anabel went silent, and the fear entered Baeata's heart. Anabel had constructed her narrative very deliberately, and even before the next words came out of Anabel's mouth, Baeata knew where the story was headed.

"I almost didn't feel the assassin coming. But at the last moment I was able to throw myself out of the bath and prevent the assassin from striking. I disarmed the assassin and was attempting to capture and restrain that assassin but was unable to. In that attempt however, the assassin tried to escape and fell over the window sill, out the window, and to the ground below."

Even though she knew where the tale was going, hearing the words was still shocking and appalling. It was not just an affront to the beliefs of all those who served as members of the Church of the Creator, but it was also an affront to the sacrifice of those who fought to make the Heart of Stone a safe haven for all those who called Cadaria home, whether they believed in the worship of the Creator or not. The fact that there could be an assassin on the grounds of the Heart of Stone was not just insulting, but it made Baeata consider possibilities that should never have been possibilities.

"What I have not told you to this point," Anabel continued, "the thing that I have been working up the courage to say, is that I knew the identity of the assassin. And while I do not believe that the assassin was acting of their own volition, it does not make the betrayal any less impactful."

Baeata braced for the revelation.

"I wish, Baeata that I didn't have to speak these words. But the assassin was your aide, Aelind."

For a moment Baeata was sure that she hadn't heard Anabel correctly. She was sure that it had been a different name that had crossed her lips. Surely it had to be. Aelind was a member of the Church of the Creator. She had been raised by the Church. She had found redemption in its teachings. She had risen through the ranks by demonstrating true adherence to its tenants and its beliefs.

"Surely, you are mistaken," Baeata said, trying to direct calm into her voice. "Aelind would never be capable of what you are describing. There must be those with power who can make themselves look like others. Could it be some kind of shape-shifting assassin trying to sew division in the new alliance we are attempting to forge?"

Anabel nodded.

"It is possible. Though the best way to determine that is to send your guards to locate Aelind, and to recover the body from beneath my window. But Baeata, I must caution you on one point."

Anabel produced a parcel that appeared to be wrapped in a shirt. She held it very carefully and gingerly pulled the edges of the shirt away. Once uncovered, Baeata could see the dagger laying in Anabel's hand. The hilt and blade were both black. The whole dagger seemed to drink in light, and even the quick of the blade did not reflect any of the light that struck it. There was no ornamentation on either the hilt or the blade, and to anyone who simply glanced at the dagger would see nothing special about it. As Baeata stood looking at the blade, she could feel a palpable malice rolling from the weapon. It felt like there was a thought crawling in the back of her mind. She wanted to reach out and take hold of the weapon. She wanted to feel the firm hilt in her hand. Then her eyes drifted up from the blade to Anabel. Distrust and disdain filled Baeata's heart. Baeata's eyes retuned to the blade, but this time it did not drink in the light. There was a glow deep within the heart of the blade. It needed her to take hold of it. She needed to pick it up. She needed to plunge the dagger deep into

Anabel's heart. The next moment, Anabel covered the dagger again. Baeata could no longer feel the malice, could no longer feel the distrust. She blinked her eyes several times in an effort to clear her suddenly foggy thoughts and was immediately troubled by the dull throb behind her eyes and in the back of her head. Finally, Baeata found her voice once again.

"What is that?"

Baeata's voice was disturbed, almost on the edge of panic. Anabel slid the bundle back into the pocket of her robe. Holding the dagger in her hand, even wrapped in the shirt, felt like barely contained rage and death. The weapon wanted to be used, needed to be used. It thirsted every moment to draw blood and to make those with power suffer. The weapon was pure distilled violence and bloodlust.

"You felt it, didn't you?" Anabel asked. "You felt the blade's need to kill. Its need to taste my blood."

Baeata nodded absently, her mind still processing how her normally placid and pacifistic mind could be so easily turned to violence.

"A friend told me of this weapon. It was created by one of the Children of the Creator, and it has only one purpose. That purpose is to steal the powers from those who have been touched by either one of the Children or by divine power. More directly, it was meant to kill Dark Gods."

Even though she knew the answer to the question she was about to ask, Baeata needed to hear the words.

"And how would such a weapon find its way into the Heart of Stone?"

Anabel knew the question was coming, and she did her best to keep the emotion out of her voice. Baeata would find the answer disturbing, and it would force her to consider something even more dire than the possibility that her closest aide and confidant was an assassin.

"The only way that a weapon like this would find its way into the Heart of Stone is if it was brought here by an agent of the one who created it. In short, Talisia has at least one agent here. And where there is one, there are probably more."

Baeata fell silent for several moments. Without answering Anabel's statement, Baeata stood, smoothed her clothes, and made her way to the door. Anabel's concerned voice stopped her advance.

"Rhya may be in danger as well. Even though she does not have power, if someone tried to eliminate me, they may try to eliminate her as well."

Baeata did not turn to regard Anabel, but instead simply nodded in agreement. The supposition was a sound one. Baeata opened the door and as she expected, the soldier was still on the other side, waiting for orders. The man snapped to attention and waited for the High Priestess to address him, without turning his eyes in her direction.

"Lieutenant, I want you to find Aelind Torral and bring her here. I also want the body of the assassin who attempted to assault my honored guest brought here. Additionally, send two men that you trust to bring my guest Priestess Rhya here. Hopefully she will still be asleep, so take care."

The soldier snapped a salute and started to move, but Baeata's next words delayed him.

"And Lieutenant," Baeata said with grave seriousness in her tone, "no matter what you see, I do not want rumors flying around the Heart. This is to be kept in the strictest confidence. Do you understand?"

The solider turned.

"Yes, High Priestess."

He gave another salute, even though he knew it was not necessary, turned on his heel, and then moved quickly down the hall. He stopped at the group of soldiers at the end of the hall, gave two of the men orders and pointed toward the door to the garden, and then continued with the rest of the soldiers down the stairs. The two guards that had been tasked as protectors for the High Priestess made their way down the hall and took positions beside the door to the private garden as Baeata closed the door and returned her attention to her guest. Anabel's face was still calm, and she had moved to take a seat on the low bench near the wall. Baeata also returned to the bench where she had been seated moments before, and the two women sat in silence for several moments. Finally, Baeata broke the silence with the only thought that was in her mind.

"Lady Binosear," Baeata said, preferring to use the woman's formal name given the dire nature of the circumstances. "I am horrified and embarrassed that your life was put in danger while you were under my protection."

Anabel raised her hand, and then shook it slowly.

"Please, Baeata, its Anabel, or if you prefer, Anne. And whatever threat my life may have been under, it is no different than the threat on your life while you were in Hedorah. You may have not have felt the threat as directly, but the danger was no less real."

Baeata nodded.

"Be that as it may, Anne, you are a guess in my house, and your safety should not be in question."

Anabel smiled.

"Safety has been something I have had to be concerned with for the entirety of my life, Baeata, and I could tell you some stories that you might not believe, but I assure you are very true. On my birth world, in the kingdom that I once called my own, my palace was considered one of the most secure in the world. The stone the walls were made of was supposedly impossible to scale. Troops were stationed everywhere to ensure there would be no infiltration. But in the end, it did not prevent a betrayal from within. It did not prevent the palace from being engulfed in fire. It did not prevent severe losses."

Despite how well Baeata had taken the information about other worlds and the nature of the Dark Gods, Anabel felt it best not to introduce the fact she had died during that incursion upon the supposed safety of Trelon.

"All we can do," Anabel continued, "is be vigilant."

Baeata considered and then finally nodded.

"So, how should we proceed?"

Anne let a lighter tone life her words.

"We continue," she said finally. "We work to finalize our alliance, and we prepare for what is coming. Serentis has given us her support and the support of those who would hope to see our success. I received a missive from an ally that there is a message from the Divine Empress awaiting delivery, I need only signal for it. Of course, I would not do so without first informing you."

There was a part of Anabel that felt bad for deceiving Baeata. Of course, deception was all part of politics and negotiation. But for her part, Anabel felt that Baeata did not require knowledge of how everything worked, nor did she need to know how truly disorganized her new allies were. Among the forces that sought to protect Espre, there were so many factions, and so many competing priorities. So, Anabel needed to continue to present the face of confidence.

"Perhaps in the morning, once we have sorted out this business with Aelind, we can hear your message. I fear that I do not know if I can stand more news that I will be unable to properly understand."

Anabel felt for Baeata. But if the Church of the Creator was going to be a valuable ally, the woman would need to make difficult decisions quickly. That said, Anabel knew that everyone had a point at which they could no longer take in any information. Baeata may have felt she was at that point, but the real break would come when she had to accept the truth about Aelind. As if on cue with Anabel's thoughts, a knock came at the door. Baeata started to get up to answer, but thought the better of it. She was too tired for everything, especially the bad news that she felt was coming.

"Enter."

There was a moment of silence before the door finally creaked open. A soldier that Baeata did not immediately recognize strode confidently into the room, gave the High Priestess a quick salute, and then stood silent, waiting to be acknowledged.

"Report?"

Baeata's voice cracked slightly. The soldier paid it no mind and answered quickly and clearly.

"As commanded, I conducted a search of Aelind Torral's quarters. While she herself was not there, there were the pieces of a shattered mirror as well as this note folded on the desk."

The soldier handed Baeata the note, and waited.

"Thank you," Baeata said curtly. "Dismissed."

The soldier again saluted, turned, and let the room without another word. Once the door closed behind him, Baeata took a deep breath and then opened the note. Anabel watched as the color ran out of Baeata's cheeks. She closed her eyes for a moment, took a deep breath, and then stood. She walked past Anabel, handing her the note, and then continued into the garden, where she let her eyes float from plant to plant, not really seeing anything. Tears leaked from the corners of her eyes, and she was desperately trying to keep her emotions in check. Anabel opened the note and read the simple words there.

I'm sorry. I had no choice.

Artifacts

Year Five of the Just Emperor Kaitain "Dragonsbane" Lorien, Creator's Calendar Year 1871

When she was a girl, Midarin Rice was the ever-present bauble at all diplomatic functions that her parents attended. She had travelled the whole of the civilized world by the time that she was five. Everyone knew of the precocious yet well-behaved Princess Midarin Rice, and she was the delight at formal balls and feasts alike. However, as Midarin grew older, the world became less kind and the roads between kingdoms more dangerous. Midarin's mother worried for her daughter's safety, and by the time she was seven, caution began to win out over convenience. Despite her objections, Midarin was not included on a trip to Marcwell for the celebration of the engagement of Lord Cedric Binosear to the Lady Erika Belnosian. Despite the fact that it was probably the most important single diplomatic event for several years, the increased occurrence of attacks by bandits and the rumors of monsters lurking in the forests around Marcwell was enough to give everyone pause. Despite assurances of the Royal Guard of Brea, Midarin's mother could not be convinced that their only child would be safe making the journey to and from Marcwell. Should the worst come to pass, the continued rule of the Rice family in Brae had to be assured. And so, for the first time in her life, Midarin was left behind.

For the first day Midarin pouted and raged. She would not eat, and she would not leave her room. She was nearly inconsolable in her grief and in her rage. However, despite her best efforts to keep herself awake fueled on anger alone, she eventually fell asleep and by the time the next day had dawned, her rage had turned nearly entirely to sorrow. Again, efforts to feed her were rebuffed in the morning and the afternoon, but by the time the sun was beginning to set, her resistance was starting to wane. Despite her growing hunger, the young Midarin would still not heed the demands, entreaties, or commands of her governesses or chambermaids. However, there was one man that could get through to the impulsive young princess.

Commander Teerin Domae was a grizzled old war veteran well beyond what would have been considered his best fighting years. His gray and white beard grew unevenly and he had long since given up worrying about appearances. Teerin was nominally the captain of the Rice family personal guard, but in truth he remained on active duty for his knowledge and his tactical prowess. He was responsible for planning all of the protection details and travel routes for the family as well as maintain the guard schedules when the family was in residence in the palace. Many of the fortifications and defenses of the Palace of Brae Teerin had designed himself in an effort to make the palace one of the most heavily fortified and defensible positions ever created. For some reason, Teerin and Midarin always had a playful relationship, more than likely because unlike the governesses and chambermaids and tutors, there was no expectation between the two.

That night after all of the others had given up, Teerin brought two plates of food to the young princess's room. He sat one of the plates on the table, while the other he sat in his lap after sitting in a chair across from her bed. After taking several bites of food, the old warrior started to speak.

"You know, princess, a long time ago, this palace that you use as your playground didn't even exist. I know, from your prospective, this palace is the center of the world, but this whole area used to be farmland as far as the eye could see in all directions. The people that used to live here were farmers and horse breeders and needed as much of the land as possible for grazing and planting. It was much more peaceful than the bustling city that is here now."

The old man took another bite of food, maintaining a posture completely unfitting of the relationship between himself and his charge.

"In fact," he said wiping his chin, "there were really two separate settlements here. You see, the horsemen didn't like the farmers because they thought that the farmers were using up too much of the land and the water for their crops. The farmers didn't like the horsemen because they let their horses roam across the landing eating whatever they wanted, whenever they wanted."

The old man looked up at the little princess.

"Kind of like you, little one. You roam around this palace with no thought of what is going on around you. You play in the halls when diplomats are trying their best to impress your parents and generally make a nuisance of yourself at every state dinner and festival. You throw tantrums when you don't get your way, and our important visitors have to make nice and pretend like they don't see what is going on in front of them. And now here you sit, pouting, because you didn't get to go to the party. But the only one you're really punishing is yourself, little princess, yourself and your parents for having to deal with your temperamental ways."

Again the solider stopped to take a bite of food.

"No different than the farmers and the horsemen. Each was temperamental. Each thought they were right. Each thought they had a right to the land that the other didn't."

The old man fell silent and focused again on his plate of food. The seconds stretched to minutes and the soldier said no more, instead content to slowly and deliberately chew his food. Finally, the young girl's voice broke the silence.

"What happened between the farmers and the horse people?"

The soldier kept looking down at his plate for a long moment before looking up at the girl. With his fork he motioned toward the plate of food sitting on the table. She folded her arms and shook her head. The soldier made no motion, instead returning his attention to his plate where he slowly and deliberately ate every fork-full of food. After several exasperated exhales from the girl, she moved with obvious irritation to the table and sat in the chair in front of the plate. The soldier had strategically placed the plate so that the girl would have to face him. She sat down at the table but made no motion to pick up the cutlery. After several more moments of no response from the girl, the soldier pointed at the plate with his fork. Finally, Midarin picked up the small fork and stabbed it forcefully into a piece of the steak that had already been cut for her. She lifted the piece off the plate and held it up so that Teerin could see and then put it in her mouth. As if mocking her, the soldier put a piece of the meat in his own mouth and held it there for a moment before exaggeratedly chewing. Midarin eventually acquiesced, chewing her food and even swallowing without being prompted further. She even gathered another fork-full of food and continued to feed herself. Keeping their unspoken bargain, the soldier began to speak again.

"The largest family from the farmers met with the largest family from the horsemen and tried their best to negotiate out some kind of bargain. But the same old arguments continued to crop up. The farmers needed more water because the crops needed to be able to survive should the rains not come on time. The horsemen needed more untouched land so that their horses could feed. They tried for day after day to come to an agreement, and neither would budge from their demands or from their assertion that the land was theirs. So, it looked for the partisans of both sides that it would become a fight. But neither side really wanted a fight. As much as they wanted the land, they were not yet willing to shed blood for it."

Teerin stopped for a moment and looked at Midarin.

"If you hear nothing else I say, little one, or heed nothing else I have ever tried to teach you, heed this. The desires of men are a fickle thing. There are those who crave power. There are those that crave wealth. Many of these men will do anything they can to gain those things, including kill. But most people you will encounter simply want to live. They want to be happy, be able to provide for their families and be in a world that is quiet, peaceful, and safe. When most men are given the opportunity to avoid bloodshed while still achieving these goals, they will take it. Your parents, and good rulers like them understand this fact, and use it to make the world a better place. You should strive to be a leader like that. Protecting the peace, quiet, and safety of all those who you are responsible to rule over should always be your primary concern. Not conquest. Not amassing riches or power. Simply peace and prosperity for as many as can find it."

The old soldier fell silent for a long time. He then smiled a lopsided smile and returned to his story.

"Now, as I said, the farmers and the horsemen didn't want to fight, but they also didn't want to give up. Both groups were stubborn. They had to be to do what they did. The horsemen constantly were on the lookout for predators, illness, and ensuring that their bloodlines were able to be sustained. The farmers worried about rain and sun, cold and heat. It took fortitude to get through every day, and that fortitude could never allow them to simply give up. The next time the two leading families met, they tried again to find common ground on how to settle their conflict. They settled on a fight. Not to the death, but a simple fight between a representative from each of the families. The night before the fight was set to take place, a group of bandits set upon the horsemen's camp, intent on stealing supplies and horses so that they could strike at larger targets in the future. The farmers, who ordinarily wouldn't have been close enough to the horsemen's camp to hear the disturbance, saw what was happening and came to their defense. So, these two groups who had been arguing over the use of the land to the point they were going to fight for it, worked together to fend off the bandits and prevent any of the horses or supplies from being stolen."

Midarin smiled.

"So they became friends and lived happily ever after. Good story."

The soldier shook his head.

"It's never that simple in real life, Princess; no matter what we wish to believe. After the bandits attacked, there were a large number of both the farmers and the horsemen that wanted to return to negotiation, to find a way to share the land. But the leaders on both sides resisted. They didn't see a reason to go back to negotiating, because neither side expected the other to relent in their demands. So here is where your fairy tale comes in,

Princess. During the fight, the oldest daughter of the largest horsemen family had been saved by a son of the farmer family. The next evening, when the fight was about to take place, the young man and young woman announced to their families that in order to prevent the fight, they would marry and create a new way to peace. And so, the two families became one. The horsemen and the farmers united in their own mutual defense against raiders and bandits, and in time they found a way to use the land to everyone's best benefit."

"The end," Midarin said cheerfully.

Again, the soldier shook his head.

"For a part of the tale, yes. But it's what came after that is the part the impacts your everyday life. Just a few years into the alliance between the horsemen and the farmers there was a tragedy. The bandits who had previously attacked the horsemen, due to years of lean living, hunger, and desperation grew bolder in their attempts to take what they needed. At first, they were content to nibble at the edges of the growing community, stealing a horse here, a basket or two of harvested crops there. But these gains were not enough to sate the bandits' need. And so, with the newly acquired ill-gotten gains, the bandits launched one final desperate attack. And what do you think happened, little princess?"

Midarin put her fork down for a moment and frowned.

"I thought this was story time, not lesson time."

Teerin smiled.

"As you grow older, little one, you'll realize that all stories are lessons, and the moment you feel that you know everything is the moment that you understand the least. One day you will sit on the throne of one of the greatest kingdoms in this world, and you will be required to make difficult decisions based on how you look at the facts of what you hear. Again, what you hear in a story matters. But stories are incomplete accounts usually from one point of view. Remember that. It is just as important what you do not hear, as what you do hear."

The little girl rested her elbows on the table and cupped her chin in her hands. For a moment she pouted. She never liked this game with Teerin, but no matter how often she resisted playing, he always wore her down with his soft voice and unflappable persistence. But even as much as she did not want to play the game, it did not prevent her mind from working on the puzzle that the old soldier had put in her lap.

"Were the bandits bad men?"

Teerin shook his head.

"As I said, what makes a man bad or good is a matter of perspective, little princess. Stealing is bad, but does it make a man bad who steals to feed his starving family? Killing is bad, but does it make a man bad who kills in defense of his life? Lying is bad, but does it make a man bad who lies to make the world a better place? These are all questions that separate law from justice. Another quality of a ruler that you will learn. Law is not absolute. The definition of law isn't absolute. So, laws must be applied based on the facts and the intentions of those being judged. But in answer to your question, these men stole so that they could live."

Midarin looked down, picking up her fork again and pushing her food around the plate. She knew what Teerin was saying, at least from her seven-year-old mind.

"Why didn't the farmers and the horsemen try to share with the bandits like they did with each other?"

The smile that came to the older man's face told Midarin that she had stumbled on the lesson that Teerin was trying to teach her.

"They did try, little princess, and that is why what happened was tragic and unnecessary. But ultimately it is why we are sitting here today. While the bandits were defeated and that group would never threaten the settlement again, the young couple who had stopped the conflict between the horsemen and the farmers were killed. But from that day forward, there would be no more farmers and horsemen. The loss of that young couple united the two groups in a way that their marriage never could. In the years that followed the newly united group would build a settlement surrounded by a wide wall. The wall was to help keep out danger. The wall was to help protect what they would build from that day forward. The wall was the beginning. And once the wall was built, they called the place Brea, and it became the heart of the kingdom that would rise around it."

Midarin smiled and clapped her hands at the end of the story. The disappointment and anger had been completely banished, and she happily ate the rest of her meal, and every meal that followed until her parents' return.

* * * * * * * * * * * * *

Emerging from the command tent, Midarin dabbed the last remnants of tears from her cheeks. For the first time since the day Gwydeon was taken from her all those centuries ago, she felt whole. She no longer mourned the time lost with him when he sacrificed himself for the good of Espre. Those centuries alone had been replaced by the handful of years that they had spent together in the Dark Mirror world, happy and in love. Despite the danger, and despite the fear, the nights they had together in that place in that time were worth more than the endless days as a Dark God. She had memories of raising their son with her husband, spending time with her husband's family, and building an island of sanity in a world that was trying desperately to tear itself apart with every breath. Now, the lessons from her old teacher running through her mind, they had a chance to do it again. Two old warriors, wanting nothing more than to protect the innocent against forces they could not hope to understand, would build a beacon of light that could never be shrouded in darkness.

Gwydeon's plan was as simple as it was crazy, but much like all of his plans, it made perfect sense. They were Dark Gods, after all, and if they could not conjure the impossible, what kind of gods were they? Together the four Dark Gods walked wordlessly from the command tent toward the small crest of a hill several hundred feet in the direction of what once was the Imperial Palace of Aldere. Midarin brought the four to a halt and looked at the wide vista before them.

"This is the spot."

The four took each other's hands and Midarin began to concentrate on her memories of the past. While what they intended to do probably would not have required the four Dark Gods' powers, the speed in which they intended to accomplish their goal did. The strain would be considerable, and considering they were about to send up a flare that anyone with power would have recognized from any corner of the world, it was better that they were together. However, what Midarin also knew in her heart was that Mirana and Liara were the key. They were born with their abilities, and they had a raw and untapped potential that rivaled anything Gwydeon and Midarin could do. The more that Midarin and Gwydeon could keep the twins focused on creating and assisting the suffering, the greater the chance that should the Creator once again seek to use their abilities to do harm they would be able to offer some resistance. Midarin hoped that in the end intention mattered.

In her mind's eye, Midarin conjured a vision of the place that she used to play as a child. The wide halls, the gentle arches, and the tall windows that glistened in the morning and evening light. The lower floor constantly open to the petitions of the common man, with a massive banquet hall that could feed dignitaries from all over the world. Off the massive dining hall was an equally massive kitchen. In the heart of it all was the throne room and receiving hall that reminded the people that the person who commanded the kingdom did not see themselves as above those that they were responsible for. The upper floor was divided into two wings. The east wing was for the ruling family while the west wing was for guests. Two out-buildings sat behind the palace, out of the view of most visitors. One of the buildings was a barracks that would house the troops responsible for protecting the palace and those who took residence within, while the other building served as an armory and supply storage warehouse that was doubly fortified against weather and bombardment.

As the image continued to form in Midarin's mind, the air around the four Dark Gods began to hum with power. The ground rumbled and the sound of stone splitting could be heard for miles. The troops emerged quickly from their tents, gathering behind the Dark Gods, watching the inexplicable occurring before their very eyes. From the ground, stone columns began to emerge, bending and stretching to accommodate the new shape dictated to it by the Dark Gods. The walls of the building formed quickly, segments recessing and dividing to reveal beautiful glass beneath. Inside, the stone reconfigured into breathtaking marble and quartz with sweeping arches and polished surfaces. More buildings began to take shape in the area surrounding the palace. These images came from Gwydeon's mind. A large three story building that would become the site of an inn like the one that Gwydeon had spent so much time in when he was a boy. Other structures would be simple homes, a hospital, a stable, and a training area like the one he practically lived in back in Aradon. The building that sprung up near the palace was a concession made by both of the architects that were directing the project. During Gwydeon's travel under the guise of Wynne, he had seen the opulent churches erected in the service of the Creator. But it was in the small convents and rectories that the faith transcended the religion, the place where Gwydeon felt what such spirituality could represent. And so, Gwydeon directed some of the new construction toward the creation of a humble church. It would be a place where those fleeing persecution could feel connected to that which they believed no matter what name it took.

Finally around the perimeter of the newly constructed town, great structures erupted from the ground like the teeth of some monster that wished to swallow the new construction whole. The new stone columns stretched several feet taller than the tallest building in the new town. Once complete, each of the towers sprouted walls that stretched to meet one another forming a thirty-foot tall circle around the whole of the city. Between each of the dozen towers at the top of the wall was a six-foot-wide path that allowed troops to patrol the wall, protected on the outside of the walkway by a four-foot-tall barrier. In the eastern section of the wall, a wide arch opened forming a gate into the walled city. A secondary gate formed opposite the one in the eastern wall, creating a clear path through the city. Between the two, the soil spread apart to reveal a cobblestone street between.

As the last of the construction was completed, the rumbling stopped for a moment. However, the next moment, the rumbling began again, a furrow forming several yards from the wall of the newly-built city. The furrow itself was as wide as the walls of the city were tall, and twice as deep. This was the brain-child of Mirana and Liara who felt the underground river that flowed beneath the new city. Once they breeched the rock, the water of the underground river flowed unobstructed into the furrow, forming a sparkling crystal blue barrier around the city. Cobblestone extended from the gates of the city to the edge of the new moat, until it seemed to leap across creating a bridge. The last formation were thick iron gates which erupted like fingers from the ground and would serve as another line of protection for all those who dwelled within the city.

Finally, all of the seemingly unnatural activity ceased. Mirana and Liara nearly simultaneously dropped to their knees, completely exhausted. Gwydeon bent forward, resting his hands on his knees, feeling as though he had been running at a full sprint for hours. Midarin's head throbbed, but her joy at the success of their plan removed any of the fatigue from her body. When she turned, she saw the stunned faces of the soldiers first, and then found the astonished face of Quyhn Ravenheart. Not waiting for the others to recover, Midarin strode slowly and confidently toward Quyhn, stopping several feet in front of her. With a smile on her face, Midarin motioned in the direction of the new city.

"On our world, Gwydeon and I held the forces of darkness at bay from a place very much like this one. It was a haven for all those who were fleeing war, and the very center from which all light would radiate on that world. Cadaria is in dire need of that kind of haven now. This place will be the foundation of your new Cadaria, Quyhn, and you must rule justly and with mercy."

Quyhn was still gripped with astonishment but managed to find her voice.

"Does it have a name?"

It was Gwydeon who answered the question.

"On our world, the light truly began in one small town. We would not be here today if it wasn't for that place and the heroes who came from it. Though some of us were not strong enough to carry the weight that was placed upon us, there were those whose sacrifices will be what wins this war for those who still value life. So while Fortress Peregrim stands at the center, a monument to those who fight and die for the innocent on this world, the city itself is called Aradon, to honor those who have fought and died on every world that the Children have corrupted with their poison."

* * * * * * * * * * * * * *

In the history of Cadaria, the foundation of Fortress Peregrim in New Aradon was formally recognized as the beginning of Empress Quyhn Ravenheart Lorien's rule over the Cadarian Empire.

Year One of the Just Empress Quyhn Ravenheart Lorien,
Cadarian Calendar Year 1872

CHAPTER 113

Chapter CXIV

The Cost of Uncompromising Ideals

Year Five of the Just Emperor Kaitain "Dragonsbane" Lorien, Creator's Calendar Year 1872

It didn't take long for Korrd to find himself completely overwhelmed by the crush of dead soldiers. Gwillim, Talon, and Korrd fought back to back, keeping the oncoming enemies at bay. But it became clear mere moments after the assault began that it would only be a matter of time before they were completely overcome. If the trio still had their powers, the fight would have been progressing much differently. It would have taken merely a thought to level hundreds of the attackers at once, reducing them to ash. Fortunately for all three of the men, they were all accomplished fighters before they gained use of Emries' powers. Even as quickly as they were being overrun, the trio of warriors were inflicting an immense amount of damage. However, no matter how many of the army of the dead fell at their feet, more kept coming. Gwillim spotted a small building at the mouth of an alleyway and rallied his companions in its direction. Moving proved to be more difficult than Gwillim expected, the mass of fallen creatures making it challenging to find steady footing. Talon almost tripped several times, his foot catching on severed limbs.

As Gwillim burst through the door of the small building he thought he had made a serious tactical mistake. Inside the building were half a dozen of the walking corpses. Unlike the majority of those who they had been fighting, these were not the reanimated bodies of fallen soldiers from forgotten wars. These former people appeared to be nothing more than the inhabitants of Thorigald who had been murdered in War's attempt to pacify all resistance to Dorovar's will. Unlike War's other conscripts, these unfortunate souls were not clad in armor or brandishing the weapons of past conquerors, but instead were clutching common kitchen knives and other household implements. One former man holding a broom handle like a spear charged Gwillim as soon as he was through the door. Gwillim made quick work of the man, breaking the broom handle with the hilt of his sword before slashing clear through the man's neck and letting his head fall to the floor. Two of the other corpses charged even before Gwillim had struck down the first man, these two appearing to be women. Each were brandishing knives in each hand, stabbing, and slashing wildly with every step. By the time Gwillim moved to intercept the two former women, Talon had pushed his way into the building and found himself face to face with what had to be an eight or nine year old child. The child was gripping a small hand axe and swinging it with a might that belied his diminutive size.

Talon had been struggling with his new-found freedom from the moment he awoke after their defeat at the hands of War. For so long Talon had been going through the motions of his life, knowing that he did not have full control of his actions. He had done what he was told to do without reservation or delay. He killed who he was told to kill. How many fathers didn't go home to their families because of order that Emries gave? How many people trusted Talon because he was the harmless bard, only to find his blade in their hearts? How had it been so easy for Emries to force Talon to undo all of the good he had done in his life on Onea? That moment, faced with the little boy holding an axe, everything crystalized for Talon. War, like Emries, had perverted those who did not want to be used. Those who only wanted to live their lives and be left alone. That was what Talon had wanted all those years ago. He had no ambition beyond living in Aradon, working enough to support himself, and carousing in the tavern until he passed out. How could there be anything better? Emries had changed all that. From the moment that Aryx Terian had come to Aradon with that letter from Cedric Binosear, Talon's life had never been the same, and had been pulled completely out of his control. In a way, he was no different from the dead boy with the axe; just a mindless weapon waiting to be put in front of its next target. However, now was no time to reflect upon the unfairness of existence. Talon struck down the walking corpse and tuned to face the door just in time for Korrd to come flying through the doorway.

Korrd was only a few steps behind Gwillim and Talon but between the time that Talon entered the building and Korrd approached, several of the dead soldiers surrounded Korrd. The former Coromor brought his sword up and struck out in as many directions as he could. Only a few hours ago he could have conjured another blade out of thin air and enhanced his reflexes to make himself faster than his opponents. But this was the new normal, at least for the moment, and so Korrd had to rely on his old skills and old reflexes. Gwydeon had trained Korrd to be aware of everything that his opponents were capable of, and to use that knowledge to give any measure of advantage that he could create. Despite the fact that the corpses of the dead soldiers had few if any of their musculature left, they moved with surprising agility and struck with impressive strength. Korrd could feel their power with every block, and despite his attempts to outflank and out maneuver his opponents, they always seemed to be able to keep up. So, Korrd was contending with multiple opponents who were stronger, faster, and more agile. Despite that, he was keeping up the best he could. Gwydeon had always taught that against a superior opponent it was often the best tactic to fall back into a totally defensive shell and let the opponent make the mistake that would end his life. While that was a workable strategy against one opponent, it became increasingly difficult the more opponents that were added. After Korrd struck down one of the walking corpses, he pulled the sword out of its hand and attempted to parry attacks from all sides as he edged toward the door of the building. Striking down two of the members of the army of the dead, he made one more lunge for the door, spinning so that his back hit the doorframe. Then the long-dead soldiers came all at once. Korrd parried one strike with his weak hand, his left hand, and stabbed another through the eye with his right. Korrd just managed to move his head out of the way of the last strike, as the tip of the sword buried itself in the wooden doorframe. Korrd kicked away the corpse that he had impaled on his blade and then took off the head of the third attacker. Before the next wave came at him, Korrd pivoted using the doorframe and propelled himself through the door. As he landed on the other side of the doorway, Gwillim was finishing off the last two corpses that once probably called the building home.

Korrd got to his feet and kicked the door closed before any of the army of the dead could follow him through into the building. He knew that the door wouldn't last long under continued assault, but it would buy them the precious few seconds they needed to prepare for the next wave. Taking a quick look around the room, Korrd was at least slightly relieved that the building seemed somewhat defensible. Two of the four walls were solid, butted up against the neighboring buildings. The south facing wall was the most vulnerable with the wide front door. The west facing wall had a window in it that was in the back wall of the kitchen, but it was small and would only allow for one of the corpses to come through at a time. However, it was a vulnerable port in the wall, and if the soldiers were as strong as Korrd thought they were, it would only be a matter of time before they would pull that wall down and have open access to the inside of the house. Korrd backed up toward the corner of the northern and eastern wall, the most secure position in the house and waited, both weapons ready. Talon took up a position to Korrd's right and Gwillim fell in to his left. The banging on the door grew louder and louder, and then finally the blade of an axe broke through the center of the door. Two more strikes by the axe shattered the door, and a group of the dead soldiers surged into the room. Korrd steadied himself, held his weapons in a defensive position, and waited for the attacks to come. Unless something changed, they would not live through the next few minutes.

* * * * * * * * * * * * *

The blade of War's massive sword shot downward with surprising speed. Though Gideon was ready for the strike, at the last moment he was unsure if he was up to the task. His hands filled with the incredible power granted to him by Raenera, Gideon reached up at the last moment and caught the blade. Despite the power at his disposal, the incredibly sharp and colossal blade cut into the flesh of the palms of Gideon's hands, sending sprays of hot blood in all directions. Gideon paid the blood and the pain no mind and focused solely on his task. Even as Gideon restricted the downward thrust of War's sword, he could feel the near impossible strength behind it. Gideon knew he didn't have much time, so he began to channel all of the power that he had gathered into the sword. If War knew what was happening, it didn't show on the gargantuan creature's face. There was no emotion at all, only the constant pulsing red of its eyes. The blinding white power began to creep up the length of War's blade, at first only silhouetting the blade and then finally beginning to burst through the surface, creating cracks in the ebony and gold weapon. The cracks continued to move up the length of the sword as the seconds passed. Time seemed to slow to a crawl. The bright red energy in War's eyes flashed, and the green haze of the Chorus of Souls condensed around the blade. The battle of wills between Dorovar's power and those of Raenera had been rejoined through their proxies. This time however, Raenera was not content to lose for the furtherance of her plans. The brilliant white light that tore through War's blade pushed back the phantasmal emerald energy, pushing past the blade, past the guard, and into the hilt. From there the blinding white power flared outward, taking hold of War's gauntlets. The faded and tarnished bronze and gold color of the inlayed filigree and ornamentation of War's armor began to be slowly overcome by piercing white light. The red light of War's eyes flared brighter, and it tried to release its hold on the sword and draw away from Gideon's attack. However, despite War's attempts to withdraw, the white light kept War connected to the weapon.

The filigree glowed brighter and brighter with the power of the Child of the Creator, Raenera, until the light cracked through the hearty and thick armor. The Chorus of Souls screamed uncontrollably, and whirled around the body of War. The light crept up War's arms, and the fog of the Chorus of Souls swept in and out of War's armored form, trying to keep the light from ripping War apart from the inside out. But try as it might, the Chorus could not impede the invasive light. More and more cracks formed in the armor, and the wailing from the Chorus became sorrowful and full of pain. The fissures continued up the arms, across the shoulders and into the massive Herald's chest. All at once the patterns in War's chest erupted in light and the Chorus of Soul cried out in a uniform piercing cry of such force that is leveled three of the buildings that bordered the square. The cloud of power around War evaporated, and all that was left was the monstrous form of the Herald, burning with light. The red light in War's eyes faded and was replaced with white. Flaring brighter and brighter, the white light eventually obscured the sight of the Herald until finally there was an explosion of such force that it could be felt for dozens of miles in every direction. The bubble of white light that engulfed the Herald contained the concussive force of the explosion and prevented any further damage to the city. Moments later, the second portion of Gideon's attack revealed itself.

From the bubble of brilliant white force, dozens of individual tendrils of light lanced out in all directions. Each of the tendrils struck a member of the army of the dead. Once the brilliant white light touched one of the walking corpses, it coursed through every part of the fallen body's being, expelling the phantasmal green light from out of the creature's mouth. Once the influence of the Chorus of Souls had been removed, the corpses crumpled to the ground, no more unnatural life left in them. As each member of the army of the dead fell, two tendrils of the brilliant white power lanced out. Each of the corpses that fell caused the destruction of two more. The destruction spread exponentially until the whole of the army of dead had been returned to their former decrepit state. Its job done, the light faded away, leaving only silence behind. It took Gideon several moments to get back to his feet. Weakness pervaded his entire being, and his legs felt as though they could give way beneath him any moment. As it was, Gideon felt himself stagger backwards as soon as he was standing, and had to support himself with the side of a building. His head throbbed, his vision was blurry, and he could feel the blood running down his neck and face. Blood trickled from the corners of Gideon's eyes, his nose, and his ears. His head felt as if it was being squeezed, and though he expected the feeling to dissipate as the minutes passed, it did not abate. More than once Gideon thought he would lose consciousness, but managed to keep hold on his senses. By the time Gwillim, Talon, and Korrd emerged from the small building at the edge of the alley, Gideon had recovered most of his former stability.

The three men approached slowly, cautious of the change in conditions not only of the city, but of their old ally. Whatever Gideon had done had not only defeated the Herald but his army as well. Even at their fullest power, they had not been able to make a dent in War's defenses, whereas Gideon had been able to bring him low all by himself. When the trio was several paces from where Gideon stood, the slight man put up a hand halting their approach.

"Dat's close enough."

CHAPTER 114

Korrd and the others stopped in their tracks. Talon took an additional step forward.

"Gideon," Talon said, confusion thick in his voice, "what's going on?"

Gideon narrowed his eyes. He tried to reach out with his abilities, but was not able to focus the kind of control he needed. The fight with War took more out of him than he had expected, and the longer he was unable to focus his powers, the less he was able to trust what his former allies would say or do.

"Depends on who's askin'," Gideon said finally. "You or Emries."

Korrd raised his hands.

"I'm not sure how it happened, but our connection to Emries has been severed. We don't have any abilities anymore. If we did, we would have used them against War's army. We're free again."

Gideon frowned.

"Wish dere was some way ta know if dat's true or not, Korrd. Can't take da chance tho."

Gwillim took over.

"Look Gideon, I know we've done a lot of terrible things under Emries' control, but you have to know that wasn't us. It was Emries."

Gideon shook his head.

"Tell yerself dat if ya got ta, Gwillim. But we both know dat ain't true. Emries' touch is strong, but he can't be in control of ya every second of every day. He didn't kill most of da people ya all killed. Sure, he may have started ya all on it, but most ya did yerselves. Blame Emries all ya want, Gwillim, but da real villains here are ye three."

Korrd was quick to respond, anger thick in his voice.

"And what about you Gideon? I don't think that power came to you because you've been such a good person."

Gideon pulled himself up, standing as straight and tall as he could manage.

"Got no illusions 'bout what I am Korrd. Been ready for dis day fer a long time. Watched the world pullin' itself apart for no reason. Watched the dragons cause trouble, watched the Dark Gods cause trouble, watched the others like you just make a mess of things. Just like we did on Onea. Just like Dorovar did on Loinn. Ain't nothin' right in what we do, Korrd. Ain't never been nothin' right about us."

Korrd's jaw went slack. He couldn't believe the words that came from Gideon's mouth. Those clearly weren't his words. But it didn't really matter. Gideon was right about one thing, there was nothing right about any of this. After several moments of silence, Gideon sighed, and motioned in the direction of the ranks of white armored troops filling the streets.

"Now, as much as I like 'dis family reunion, we all 'ave work ta do. Dis one time I'm gonna let ye go."

Gwillim frowned.

"What are you talking about Gideon?"

Gideon sighed.

"Ye know what's coming, and what I 'ave to do. Don't think fer a moment dat it means ye get ta walk away. So, if I were ye, I would be headin' as far from here as ye can. And then I'd pray dat somet'ing else gets ta ye before I do."

The white clad soldiers snapped to attention.

"If ye don't leave now, my soldiers will run ye down and eliminate ye. And in yer current conditions, ye won't last a minute."

Korrd wanted to say more, wanted to argue, but there was nothing to say. Talon took hold of Korrd's sleeve and pulled him away, back towards the entrance to the city. The three fled the now empty city of Thorigald, unsure of their destination. Korrd thought that perhaps they could make for Mythryn, or maybe they would try for Rashaleb, a city already devastated by the ravages of the war. But the more he thought about it, the more he knew that was impossible. They could not run. They could not hide. After everything that they had done, there was only one choice. They would have to fight. Of course, they would have no chance against the echo warriors now, but perhaps in time they would either recover their powers or learn some way to even the odds. No, there was only one course to take, only one path left to follow. They would have to find Logan. Logan was the key. Now the trick was trying to figure out what door that key would unlock, and whether or not Korrd would like what he would find on the other side.

****

Gideon watched as his former friends fled through the streets. Perhaps it had been a mistake to let them go, and perhaps if he hadn't been so impacted by the battle with War, he would not have been so hesitant. Or perhaps Raenera would not have been willing to let them go. Either way, in a matter of days it would not matter whether Gideon had let them go or not. The host of echo warriors would spread across the whole of Espre without thought, without pity, and without remorse. Their only goal would be to kill everything in their path; destroy every vestige of life. Several moments after Korrd and the others passed from view, Gideon felt a portal open nearby. Gideon started to walk in the direction of the portal, but the first step he took failed. He felt as though he was going to pitch forward and land flat on his face. The stumble carried him forward, several unsure steps before he was able to recover his balance.

"You're not looking too good there, dad."

Gideon looked up and took in the sight of his sometime daughter. Taya Viruci was a refugee from a world that should never have existed, and a life that could never have been under any circumstances. Gideon remembered that world, that world of darkness and pain. Some would have wanted even that life that he had forged in the darkness. The wife who loved him, the child who he nurtured and taught. But those things were phantoms. Erika didn't love him, but she was a good woman with a good heart and tried to make her best of things. As for Taya, she was an unfortunate victim of a set of circumstances that needed her to be a warrior and a killer. The most unfortunate part of that existence was that when she found herself in the last days of Onea, she found herself under the protection of Aerith Seth and Bryn Aplee, two people who would only serve to intensify the skills of the killer. From a distance, Gideon had watched Taya on this world, seen the pirate that she had become, seen the murderer and thief. Taya was filled with so much rage and so much hate that it consumed her. When Gideon finally reached out to his daughter, she was skeptical, but soon was made to come around to his way of thinking. Jessica Chandara had seen to that. Taya was strong, but no match for someone as skilled in manipulating thoughts and refocusing one's emotions as Jessica. With Taya programmed to do as she was told, it was only a matter of time before she returned to Gideon.

"We all make sacrifices to the cause of justice, Taya," Gideon said, his accent gone. "And I fear that I will not be alive past the grim work that is ahead."

Taya's face showed no expression. Gideon waited for a moment and then turned his attention to the soldiers. With one wave of his hand, they saluted as one and then started marching toward the edges of the city. The order given, Gideon turned his attention back to Taya.

"Do you have something for me?"

Taya smiled. The woman turned and walked back in the direction of where she had emerged from the portal. Gideon followed slowly, his balance returning and strengthening with each step. When they rounded the corner, Gideon saw the body of the woman lying in the street. It took a moment for Gideon to recognize the woman, but from the memories of Raenera, he was able to determine her identity.

"Jillian Corven."

Taya nodded.

"She was the one you wanted me to look for. Rhain and the others learned that she was the daughter of Cedric Binosear and the Dark Seer Jehna Feris."

Gideon nodded. This was the one that Raenera had hidden the soul of the High Priestess in. The soul had been passed down the bloodline from the first Empress Liette Lorien, down to the Dark Seer, and then to her progeny. It was the legacy of the Forer clan, the legacy of the Creator's influence on the world of Espre. Now the last mystery could be solved.

"Now what do we do?"

Taya's question was an obvious one, and Gideon dreaded the answer.

"I'm going to take our guest to meet with my seer to see what we can learn from her. Hopefully we will find how this woman's burden can benefit the work ahead."

Gideon pulled the Taya into an embrace.

"You did well, Taya."

Taya snaked her arms around her father and held him tight. Gideon patted Taya on the top of her back between her shoulder blades. He pulled his hand back to pat her gently again, and the thin blade of the dagger appeared between his fingers. The strike was clean, efficient, and immediately fatal. Taya felt no pain, and did not even have time to process the betrayal. Taya's body went limp in Gideon's arms.

"But where I'm going, you cannot follow. This world is wrong, just as your world was wrong. I'm sparing you from the horror that is to come."

Madness Born, Madness Gained

Year Five of the Just Emperor Kaitain "Dragonsbane" Lorien, Creator's Calendar Year 1872

Talisia Masile was odd even amongst the other members of the Children of the Creator. Each had their own way of looking at the reality that stretched out before them, and devised ways of bending that reality to their will. Talisia was the second youngest of the Children with Pyrrus her only younger sibling. While the Creator made them each with different perspectives as to the nature of the Cosmos, He did not dictate to them the manner in which they pursued that perspective. Raenera was one who viewed everything as a calculation. The endpoint of each of those calculations, if all of the variables were properly accounted for, yielded a perfect and predictable result. And, as Raenera theorized, if one knew the perfect endpoint of every equation, then all of the variables could be mitigated or eliminated. That mitigation could take any form, as that the benefit for eliminating the variable far outweighed the short-term losses that would be encountered. In the early iterations of her worlds, this uncompromising dedication to what she called Perfect Order had little in the terms of true consequence. If the temperature had tendency to become too hot, she would destroy the world and start again. If the rains fell too infrequently in what should be the fertile land, she would start over. Time and time again these worlds were created and destroyed until Raenera had discovered the proper calculations. Distance from a star, size of the world, quantity and quality of water, weather, and vegetation. These worlds would, without outside intervention, turn for millennia without the need for monitoring. They were for all intents and purposes perfect. It was when she started to introduce life onto her worlds that Raenera's frustrations grew. Even with simple lifeforms, finding the correct balance proved challenging. Too many predators, not enough predators, those species that could become predators under the right circumstances. Life cycles, access to food, water, territory. Each of these challenges needed to be overcome to balance each new introduced species into the environment. But not only did the species need to be balanced to one another, they also needed to be balanced to the vegetation and the environment to ensure that one did not kill the other. These simple autonomic functions were soon balanced perfectly, and again the Perfect Order seemed to be attainable provided that all variables were properly accounted for. The next challenge was intelligent life. Of course, there were various types of intelligence, and various levels of what that intelligence could do. Introduction of this kind of life required much more thought, and also had much greater consequence to failure to account for all of the possible variables. Again, too many of these creatures, the whole of the world would need to be destroyed and the process started over again. The wrong balance of intelligent life to the autonomic life, and the intelligent creatures would be overrun. Wipe the slate clean and start over. If the intelligent life was not intelligent enough, they would compete with the autonomic life and unbalance the environment. Again, everything was destroyed and rebuilt. There was no telling how many millions of intelligent creatures were simply wiped away to make room for the next experiment. But eventually, Raenera found success in her calculations. That world would become known as Loinn. Raenera would set everything in motion and then simply walk away, satisfied that her example of perfection would outlast the petty attempts of her siblings. That was why Talisia took such pleasure in destroying every last vestige of Loinn and turning its inhabitants into weapons that she could use against not only her siblings but against the pompous dragons and her father the Creator. The irony and the tragedy were delicious, and it filled Talisia with pride that she was able to create such destruction with such little effort on that world. It proved her view of the Cosmos superior in her mind, but there were so many other proofs, and so many other opportunities to make things in the Cosmos bend to her will.

Pyrrus, Talisia's younger, idealistic, and foolish brother cared little for the creation of worlds. He sought to create his harmony in ways that were less concrete. He would spend hundreds of years designing stars so that they would cast their light through the whole of the Cosmos. He created a great system of wind in the void that allowed the systems of stars to touch one another. Comets and asteroids danced across this wind, depositing ice in places where water had never existed before, allowing for the random formation of what Raenera had with great irritation referred to as rogue worlds. Pieces of rock would collide in the gravity of a star, infused with some rare mineral that had been part of a comet that had drifted upon the solar wind. Then a chunk of floating ice would collide with the new planet enabling the land to become fertile. Over and over these small adjustments to the harmonious systems would create and destroy worlds, give rise to potential life. Stars would rise and fall, their gasses and volatile materials cast off into the nothingness, only to reignite as they came into contact with the remnants of a dead star. Huge stellar nurseries stretching across the vast emptiness, sending colors of light to the farthest stretches of the Cosmos as new stars flared into life and old stars winked out. Even the emptiness of space seemed to not be so empty as the tides of gasses, debris, dust, and light worked together to create a tapestry that glided between the pull of stars, planets, and other stellar bodies. Pyrrus' harmonious Cosmos intrigued Talisia. There was a randomness and a danger to everything that Pyrrus set into motion. Once Talisia collapsed one of Pyrrus' massive stars. Because the star was so large and exerted so much force upon everything around it, when it collapsed it became a massive well that seemed to draw everything to it. This dark hole in space swallowed everything, including the light and wind that passed between the stars themselves. The massive gravity well ripped planets to pieces, sucked the ignited gasses off the surface of stars, and threw comets off their trajectories until they collided with and destroyed proto-planets. Talisia grew giddy with the destruction that the one act had caused. But if Pyrrus was irritated by her intervention, he never let it show. If anything, he seemed intrigued by what the new cosmic body could mean to the harmony of the others. The path of solar winds changed, the light stretched in different directions, and though the harmonious system had been disrupted, it had not been destroyed. It simply changed shape to accommodate the new beast that shared the emptiness. It was Pyrrus' unflinching trust and optimism in the possibility of harmony in all things that enflamed Talisia the most. Raenera's Perfect Order could be upset so simply with the addition of one unaccounted for variable. However, with Pyrrus it seemed that even a massive change could be absorbed by his harmonious approach where all things were accepted, and all things would bend to accommodate all others. That was why when the opportunity presented itself, Talisia struck Pyrrus down. Perhaps that was why when she was presented with the piece of his essence, she had been so willing to be led into a trap. She hated Pyrrus but at the same time respected what he had created. It was feral, untamable, and yet at the same time utterly beautiful. Some would say that that was how Talisia saw herself. She and Pyrrus may have been two halves of the true nature of the Cosmos, but they could never coexist.

Emries was a bully. That was what Talisia enjoyed the most about him. He would do anything to get what he wanted, even if it meant subverting the will of the other Children of the Creator, or even the Creator himself. He would seize worlds from the other Children and make them his own, adding his own randomness and ill-fitting structures to them. Where Raenera strived to create worlds that bowed to a Perfect Order, Emries saw order in what Raenera would call the lack of control. He could spin webs of random occurrence to create outcomes that benefited him. This chaotic morass would spin out ideal circumstances that Emries would then nudge in the direction that he wanted. He could influence with praise, he could influence with bounty, or he could influence with fear and death. He enjoyed walking on his worlds and pushing the creatures in odd directions to see what happened. But Emries' true motivation was always clear. He did not care about the ideological war. The passion for that game faded quickly from his mind. There was no need to prove any point, Emries knew he was right. And just like his view of the Cosmos, the way to get what he wanted was to insert his chaotic will into the systems of his siblings, setting them against each other until the opportunity he waited for presented itself. Loinn had been the last step in the long game that Emries played. Once Raenera was out of the way, he set his sights on his true target. The golden throne. The world of Onea meant nothing to Emries. He had made a thousand worlds, filled them with billions of creatures, and Onea could have just as easily been one of those other worlds. But it was there that Emries chose to flaunt the one commandment that the Creator had set upon his Children.

The one trait that had always puzzled Talisia about the Creator was his pettiness and his vanity. When the Children of the Creator began to create intelligent beings that could understand the nature of life and the possibility of something beyond their existence in the dirt, the Creator decreed that upon the gaining of sufficient intelligence, a book of the Creator's laws had to be introduced to the beings of that world. The book in essence created the only possible religion, the worship of the Creator, and elevated the Creator to the highest place in the thoughts of those beings. The book of the Creator would make no mention of the Children or the reality that those beings had not in fact been made in the Creator's image. But the Creator required worship. The Creator required that his need for attention be fulfilled. And so, it became clear to Emries that this was where the Creator was vulnerable. This vanity would be where Emries could taunt the Creator into actions that would eventually lead to Emries' ascendancy. So, it was on Onea that when Emries presented the book of the Creator to the beings there, he presented himself as the Creator, subverting the praise for himself. As Emries luxuriated in the palaces that the first beings of Onea made for him, and beheld the statues made in his honor, the Servants came one by one first entreating and then demanding Emries' adherence to the Creator's law. But time and time again Emries rebuffed these advances. The Voice was turned away first, its words falling on deaf ears. Even when the Voice went to the beings of Onea and tried to convince them that they worshiped a false Creator, the beings took up stones and flung them at the divine Servant, calling it a false prophet. Next came the Will, its firm visage calling out to all that could hear that it was there to set right the course of the world. The Will toppled monuments and churches, and yet the beings there did not cower. They took up arms against the Will, and even as they died under his sword, others would continue to come as the monuments and churches were rebuilt. Eventually the Creator had no choice but to recall the Will, choosing instead to send the deadliest of his servants, the Wrath. Flaming sword in hand, the Wrath descended upon Onea with but one ordained path. The Wrath smote all that he surveyed. He leveled cities, killed beings by the thousands, ground monuments to dust, and with each massive loss, the Wrath would stand before Emries, point his sword at the Child's chest, and demand that he follow the tenants of the Creator's law. Again and again these demands were rebuffed, and Emries presided over the death aloof and unflinching in the adherence to his goals. What

Emries saw was that as the Wrath burned and killed, the next generations of beings were heartier, stronger, and more willing to fight and die for what they had. They built their cities stronger and more defensible. They became more convinced in the identity of their Creator, and dedicated themselves wholly to the worship of Emries. Again, Emries prospective on the nature of the Cosmos proved true. No matter the divisiveness that was attempted to be sewn into the fabric of that which Emries created, the pattern would always return to the path that Emries had designed. The more chaos, ruin, and randomness, the quicker that the path would reassert itself, the collective need for that destination clear.

Rebuffed yet again, the Creator would for the first time call for the direct engagement of one Child against another. Halicon was dispatched to Onea, his singular goal to bring Emries to heel and to introduce true worship of the Creator to the beings of that world. While Emries and Halicon had always had a tumultuous relationship, Talisia had little care for Halicon or the way they he chose to invoke his will upon the Cosmos. In truth, Halicon had no desire to enforce any perspective, rather he let his perspective be shaped by the Cosmos and how it expressed itself. Where Pyrrus would wander through the emptiness helping the stellar systems work together, Halicon floated in the darkest spaces, letting the Cosmos speak to him. Halicon had once said that there was a beauty in the emptiness that was impossible to see unless you surrendered yourself to it. That the Cosmos demanded nothing less than total and complete surrender to it. Halicon had been missing for millennia, a habit that he partook in quite frequently. When he finally returned to the Heavens, he brought with him something new. Like a fledgling flower that he protected from the wind with his hands, he revealed to the other Children a tiny green flame. When pressed by the Voice, Halicon said that he had found the flame floating in the darkness between everything. It was a place where no light from any of Pyrrus' stars reached. A place that was not stirred by the stellar winds, and where no matter created by the Children had ever gone. He called the place a nexus. It was Raenera who called it a Blight. In Raenera's mind, it was a random occurrence of factors that should never have been able to exist. And yet, regardless of how many times Pyrrus would attempt to bring light to every corner of the Cosmos, there would remain that pocket in which no light could touch. This Blight remained, ignorant to the will of the Children, and it was in this Blight that the little green fire had raged. Halicon called the flame the Blaze, and he spent millennia studying and communing with it. For so long, the stubborn green flame was nothing more than that. It would not give up the secrets of its existence, nor would it truly rebuff Halicon's attempts. It seemed to entice him to continue while at the same time pushing him away. Finally, after untold millennia of frustration, Halicon would learn that the flame was not a flame at all. The Blaze was a living thing, and more than that, it was intelligent. The intelligence revealed itself in different ways, never the same twice. Sometimes the flame was empathic, pushing emotions to the surface within Halicon. Other times it was omnipresent, showing visions of actions on the other Children's worlds. And then still other times the Blaze was prophetic, giving Halicon glimpses of things that had not happened yet. Long before Onea was even created, Halicon saw himself as a huge black dragon raining death down upon innocent beings. He saw the death that would be wrought in his will. Just before the Voice came to give Halicon his orders to go to Onea to stop Emries' blaspheme, the Blaze showed Halicon one more vision. The Blaze showed Halicon his own death, and what would come after. After the last vision was imparted to Halicon, the Blaze fused itself with the Child's essence, and the two became one. Halicon became a vessel for the Blaze, and it would enable him to do what needed to be done in the millennia that would follow.

Of course, all of this was hidden from the other members of the Children. They knew of this strange force that Halicon had discovered in the nothingness, but they truly paid it no mind. How could something that was floating in the spaces between ever be a match for the divine powers that inhabited the Children? A little green flame could not create worlds or snuff out the inhabitants of a planet. Halicon could have his little bauble, it mattered little. The Children were connected in a way that was unclear even to them. They could feel one another in their minds at all times, and could even share thoughts and emotions. They knew where each other were at all times, but could also hide from one another if they concentrated hard enough. However, what became a greater impediment to that constant location awareness was the ambivalence that eventually set in. The Children ceased caring where the others were, so they simply did not know. It was a form of active ignorance. But it was apparent quickly that whatever knowledge the Blaze imparted to Halicon was not subject to the connection between the Children. They could not tap into the Blaze, could not touch it, and more importantly could not hear it. This fact was on full display when Halicon made his way to Onea. For a long time Halicon watched the actions of his brother, cloaked in the powers of the Blaze, invisible to even the scheming and plotting Emries. Then, when Halicon revealed himself in his new guise as Shau-ling, flanked by his new progeny the phasia, Emries was unprepared. But in his mind Emries knew what Halicon was capable of. He waved off his brother, unimpressed by the creatures he called his children. Emries' followers had already rebuffed the Servants, what could Halicon do? The war that would follow would change the course of everything.

Talisia for her part watched the war between her siblings with little interest. She was a conniving and vicious creature who took pleasure in seeing death and destruction reign where there was once life and prosperity. She wanted nothing more than to watch everything burn. But there was little challenge in that. She was one of the most powerful beings in the whole of Creation, and so what true challenge was there in burning worlds and killing billions of simple beings? And so, Talisia turned her attention to the one race that pre-dated even the Children of the Creator.

When the Creator first moved upon the emptiness of the deep, the foundation of everything that would come after was the Heavens. The Golden Throne formed first, and from that place the Creator began to experiment with his powers. Formlessness took form, darkness became light which then became darkness. Worlds grew and died in seconds, and the Creator soon found himself bored. So, in a single burst of power, a whole universe sprang into being. Hundreds of stars, thousands of planets, life on a scale that could not truly be quantified. And so, the Creator sat, once again bored with that he had made. Then the Creator made the first of his intelligent creatures. The first, the oldest, was a being called Tarot. This dragon floated beside the Creator in the nothing, and the two spoke. They crafted language together, turned thought into word, and the words spoken made other things. Each idea that flowed between the two gave rise to whole streams of life and possibility. It was Tarot that called stars stars, called planets planets, and named space space. In fact, it was Tarot that first referred to the Creator as the Creator. It was that name that would shake the Cosmos for eternity. The Creator was fascinated and delighted by Tarot, and so he made more of the creatures that Tarot would soon name dragons. Ninety-eight more of the creatures would come into being, each different than the other. They would wander the worlds, giving names to everything that they found crawling, flying, or growing on the myriad worlds. And yet the Creator again found himself bored. So, he gathered several of the dragons and engaged them in intellectual combat. But no matter how he tried to get the now ancient creatures to move their disagreements beyond tolerance, the dragons were united by the fact that they were dragons. They were a monolith, and they were boring. The Creator let the dragons wander the worlds with impunity, and he set about to his next creation, the Children. These new creatures would give him the ideological war that he wanted.

But while the Creator had soured on his first children, Talisia respected their strength and their near immortality. Though they could reproduce, the dragons' numbers remained small. However, their power was nearly without limit, and if Talisia was going to accomplish her ultimate goal, then she would need the beasts on her side. While Emries had always talked about his desire to unseat the Creator from the throne, he was more interested in crafting his intricate patterns and watching them come to fruition. Raenera and Pyrrus had no care for the throne, and Halicon's motives were often impregnable. And so, it was left to Talisia, and she wanted the throne with every fiber of her being. From that throne she could destroy and recreate the whole of existence over and over and over again. There would be no end to the death and the fire and the destruction. For eternities to come she would be surrounded by death and life. It would be glorious. However there was one thing standing in her way, and that was the Creator. But the path to unseating the Creator began and ended with the Children. The first blow was struck with Raenera. The loss of her precious Loinn had damaged her will, and once Talisia had harvested the souls of her most ardent followers, she had exactly what she needed to empower the beast Dorovar to exact his revenge on his onetime goddess. Dorovar's grudge against the dragons would also prove useful. Talisia had easily been able to form a pact with the ancient dragon Shadowweaver. While he was initially unwilling to raise arms against his own kind, he was not hesitant in lending his power to killing angels, servants, and the other Children. Some within the ranks of the dragons resented the Children, feeling that they were cast aside in favor of the Children. Others cared little about the Children, seeing their creation as a catalyst for their freedom from the Creator's attention. Regardless, there was no loyalty that could be exploited, and when Talisia started her war, at least some of the dragons would be on her side.

Halicon and Emries' war on Onea ended exactly as Talisia had predicted. Both were damaged by the confrontation, and neither would be in a position to stop her assault on the Throne. From the moment the attack on the Heavens was launched, Talisia knew that it was doomed to failure. Barely half of the dragons that Talisia had courted appeared to fight for her, while others stood in opposition to their brothers. What Talisia had also not counted on was the interference of the so-called heroes of Onea that the Creator chose to allow to ascend to the Heavens. They fought against the dragons and the hordes of corrupted angels that Talisia had drawn to her side. But the one victory that Talisia took from her rebellion was the death of Pyrrus. That made the losses worth it. She had not taken the throne yet, but that was one more of her siblings out of the way. She had also identified at least some of the dragons that were willing to stand against her. And so, when Talisia came to Espre, she made sure that attention was directed to those dragons, and that when the time came, they would be struck down, just like the so-called heroes that tried to thwart her ascendency.

What she had not expected, what she had not seen coming, was the cunning of her brother. Pyrrus for all of his talk of harmony and coexistence had used himself against her. He knew that she could not resist the opportunity to steal his power and make it her own. And so, she had been baited. Baited by the girl with the sliver of his power that shown like a beacon in the blackest night. She had been defeated with her own power-stealing dagger, her power and her consciousness trapped in the frail form of a girl who was filled with such doubt and self-loathing that it ate at her resolve and weakened the walls of the prison meant to hold Talisia's might. Talisia pounded against the walls of the prison, the poison of her hate and desire for death seeping into the body of the girl. Whatever her ultimate goal, Talisia would not allow it to come to fruition. She would escape the prison, she would subsume the girl's will, and then she would loose her frustration and venom on her brother. Only this time, she would make sure that Pyrrus stayed dead.

* * * * * * * * * * * * *

Darrien staggered down the dusty path, the hard stone walls of the Heart of Stone rising in the distance seeming impossible far. The pounding in her head was growing worse, and she could hear the violent screams of the goddess Talisia ringing in her ears louder and louder with every step. The screams and curses made her bones ache, and each step seemed to take a lifetime. Blood leaked from the corner of her eye, and her vision blurred. Her will was beginning to fracture, and if she did not make it to Albitonin soon, her sacrifice would be for nothing. Steps devolved to shuffling. But Darrien would not fail. She could not. Even if she had to crawl the last miles on her hands and knees she would. She would not let Talisia win, no matter the pain and no matter the hardship.

Open Secrets

Year Five of the Just Emperor Kaitain "Dragonsbane" Lorien,
Creator's Calendar Year 1872

Despite their unclear and sometime tenuous hold to the term living, the remaining members of the Adhradair did still feel as though they were alive, and as such were susceptible to the entire range of emotions that they had in life. The one that filled Maedoc at the moment was trepidation. He would have argued outwardly if someone had referred to it as fear, but the more steps he took into the mouth of the massive cave, the closer that description became to the reality of the situation. The situation was preposterous for many reasons, not the least of which was that the two members of the Adhradair were following one of the architects of their betrayal on Loinn to meet with the ultimate betrayer. Stormbane the Traitor and Shadowweaver the Demon Dragon were practically curses among the Adhradair, both for what they had done to the people of Loinn, and what their interference and evil had ultimately resulted in. While some might have rightly argued that the whole of the dragon race could not be held responsible for the ultimate fate of Loinn, the same could not be said for Derelor, Stormbane, and Shadowweaver. Now though at least one of the betrayers was dead, and if Maedoc had his way, before the day had ended, he would see the end of at least one of the other two demons.

As they continued into the dank cave, the smell became the most difficult factor to content with. Sulphur seemed to roll in from every direction, creating a yellowish fog about a foot thick clinging to the floor. With every step the fog was disturbed, intensifying the smell. Both Maedoc and Luighsech wrapped themselves with the power of the Chorus of Souls in an effort to repel some of the smells and the crushing oppression of the place. The dragon leading them ambled slowly, no pattern to its steps, no rhythm, no pace. Stormbane's tail moved back and forth slowly, not with the sway of the creature's steps, but instead seeming to try to stir up more of the sulfurous fog. The dragon wanted the members of the Adhradair off-balance, easy to manipulate. But that was the nature of everything that Stormbane and Derelor did. They needed control of a situation to ensure that they got what they wanted. Even as powerful as the dragons were, and even as unassailable as the creatures seemed to be, they still used tools like manipulation and psychological warfare. The dragons were as different as humans, as subtle or as loud, and dealing with one did not mean you knew how to deal with another. Ahead of them, the cave opened into a massive cavern. And there, sitting in the center of the wide space was the Demon Dragon Shadowweaver.

Huge braziers were spread around the perimeter of the cavern, giving the space an eerie glow. Maedoc's eyes went to the barely illuminated dragon as soon as their guide Stormbane came to a halt just inside the cavern's opening. Shadowweaver was huge even by dragon standards. But despite the creature's size, it still appeared lithe and agile. Unlike some of the other larger dragons, Shadowweaver's limbs were long and lean, with elongated feet and claws. The elongated claws had all of the dexterity of a human hand, and Shadowweaver's talons were less like a bird's and more like a bear's The hooked portion at the tip of the talon did not have a prominent hook, but rather a subtle curve. The talon was no less sharp of course, glowing in the dim light with a dangerous and fatal edge. Shadowweaver's powerful tail curled up behind it, disguising its overall length, but Maedoc knew from experience that the tail was as long as Shadowweaver's entire body, including its neck and head. Unlike many other dragons however, there were no spikes or talons at the tip of Shadowweaver's tail, and even the entire final third of the dragon's tail was devoid of the row of black spikes that ran from the creature's neck, down the length of its back, and onto the tail. In life, Maedoc had seen

Shadowweaver pick up massive boulders with its tail and then drop them from great heights onto the inhabitants of unsuspecting villages. The ancient dragon believed in the tenants of creating maximum damage with minimum effort. As such, Shadowweaver believed that fear was the greatest weapon that any dragon could bring to bear.

Shadowweaver's wings were impressive in that despite their flimsy appearance, they were capable of not only holding the giant beast aloft in the skies, but also able to lift the massive creature off the ground. The dark purple nearly black membrane that stretched between the bone skeleton of the wing was translucent, and when the light caught the tissue at the right angle, they became mostly transparent. The three bony structural appendages that held the wing together were tipped on the end with an eight-foot-long black spike that while not as sharp as talons would have been able to impale a man with little thought. The same could be said for the six-foot spike that protruded from the front tip of each wing, a weapon that Maedoc had seen used to brutal and lethal effectiveness more times than he cared to remember. But it was Shadowweaver's head that brought back the most painful and fear-inducing memories for the former inhabitants of Loinn.

At the top of Shadowweaver's neck were two appendages, stretching to either side of the base of the creature's jaw. These looked like miniature wings, with long bone structures that mimicked those of its wings. When Maedoc had first seen them, he compared them to fish fins. This proved to be an accurate assessment after the first time Maedoc saw the huge dragon erupt from one of Loinn's oceans. Not many of the dragons that Maedoc had encountered could navigate water as easily as the air or vice versa, but Shadowweaver seemed to have no limitations as to where he could go or what he could do. Two massive demonic horns curled backwards from the top of Shadowweaver's head, and those horns along with the dark red eyes had been the features that had helped Shadowweaver earn its nickname as the Demon Dragon. The rest of the dragon's head was long and lean just like the rest of its body, the flat snout ending with a four-foot hook of bone on the very top of the nose. Long nostril slits constantly produced a purple smoke that those unfortunate enough to be in the dragon's presence for a long period of time said sapped the strength and will of the dragon's opponents.

As Maedoc and Luighsech approached, they were partially shocked to see Shadowweaver sitting back on its back feet, with an angelic warrior clutched in one of its front feet. With the massive claws of the other foot, Shadowweaver slowly plucked each individual feather from the angel's wings. Maedoc couldn't tell from a cursory inspection whether or not the angel was still alive. In addition to the angel clutched in Shadowweaver's claws, a pile of angelic warriors was gathered beneath the dragon. The disdain for his enemies clear, Shadowweaver was not content to simply kill, he wanted to humiliate, subjugate, and destroy all vestiges of those that dared to stand against him.

"What have you brought me, Stormbane?"

Shadowweaver's voice was smooth. Many dragons spoke with a pronounced hiss or some kind of impediment to either their cadence or their syntax and grammar. Shadowweaver spoke very cleanly and clearly with no impediment and should someone hear the voice without seeing the creature, it might have been mistaken it for a human voice. Shadowweaver was considered one of the most intelligent dragons and had made it a point of studying every opponent that he had ever fought to such an exacting degree that he could predict their movements and their tactics with an unerring and eerie proficiency.

"These are two of Dorovar's Adhradair come to avail themselves of your council and to discuss the terms of an arrangement with their leader."

Shadowweaver stopped plucking the feathers from the angel's wings for a moment, looked at Stormbane and then at the two humans, before going back to plucking feathers.

"And what interest should I have in talking with these ghosts?"

Luighsech took a step forward, and despite the sulfur smell, spoke with as full-throated voice as he could manage.

"Stormbane made it clear that you were willing to discuss terms with us. Or has Stormbane proved himself to be a traitor once again?"

Shadowweaver held up a single feather and looked down his long snout at Luighsech.

"I have always found it curious that you people have chosen to dub Stormbane a traitor. It seems that you ascribe meaning to that word that is misplaced in this regard."

Maedoc moved forward a step, his blood beginning to boil.

"Stormbane made a deal, one that was supposed to benefit the people of Loinn. That deal led to the death of our people and the death of our world."

Shadowweaver let the feather fall and watched as it slowly fluttered toward the ground. Once the feather passed beyond the border of the sulfur cloud, Shadowweaver spoke again.

"Again, I believe your prejudice comes from a misunderstanding of the facts of the situation that you are describing. While you may have believed that the deal you made with Stormbane was to benefit your world or your people, that was never the case. Stormbane was negotiating on behalf of the dragons, not on behalf of the people of Loinn. It was your responsibility as the protectors of your world to ensure that your people were well represented in the negotiations. If anyone is responsible for the downfall of your world, it is Dorovar alone. He was the one negotiating with Stormbane, and as I understand it, that was not his role to fill. Your Adhradair had their own negotiator did they not?"

Maedoc was forced to concede that point. There were many times that Dorovar exceeded his role within the Adhradair, always claiming to be following the visions given to him by the goddess Raenera. If Drust had been the one negotiating with Stormbane, perhaps the deal would have been less one sided in favor of the dragons.

"So in truth," Shadowweaver continued, "it was not Stormbane who was the traitor, but rather the inept negotiations done on behalf your people by Dorovar."

Shadowweaver snorted a cloud of purple smoke into the air.

"All this time you have carried a grudge against Stormbane because of your own foolishness and pride. Of course, Stormbane was going to insure that dragons benefited the most from our deal with your people. To do otherwise would have been stupid and pointless."

Shadowweaver lowered his head so that he could glare down the length of his nose at the two members of the Adhradair.

"So let me be clear," the dragon snarled. "If this is to be a negotiation, be aware that I am working on behalf of the dragons, and my intent is to see that all dragons will benefit from any agreement and I could care less if you or your master feel slighted. And I am not above killing the two of you if I feel that you are not dealing honestly with me. Do we have an understanding?"

When neither member of the Adhradair made answer within the first few seconds after Shadowweaver's pronouncement, the massive dragon returned to his former posture and returned to plucking feathers from the angel.

"Good. Now, what accord do you wish to discuss?"

The two Adhradair looked at each other for a moment and then it was Luighsech who spoke.

"We come seeking information as to the location of the soul of the High Priestess Genovefa. We are to understand from Stormbane that you would be willing to discuss terms for an accord with Dorovar in return for this information."

Shadowweaver stopped once again, rubbing a feather between his claws.

"Still hunting that pretty bauble are we?"

Maedoc tried to restrain his fury, but the subtle tone of disrespect in the dragon's voice was too much for the proud man to ignore.

"Pretty bauble? Is that how you see the imprisoned soul of our great and beloved leader? You may not care for our world, for our people, or for our religion, but do not denigrate our High Priestess. She was stolen from us by Talisia's treachery. Stolen from us by Emries' betrayal, and stolen from us due to our own failure. The atonement of the Adhradair will not be complete until the souls of all of our imprisoned brethren are released and the High Priestess is returned to us."

Again, the dragon snorted.

"You're even more foolish than I thought you were."

The dragon paused for a moment.

"And so we are clear, that is an insult, as I did not believe my opinion of you Adhradair could be any lower."

Maedoc's fists clenched so tightly that the sound of his knuckles cracking echoed through the cavern.

"But soon," Shadowweaver continued, "you too will realize the enormity of your own stupidity."

As Shadowweaver pulled the last feather out of the angel's wing, he crushed the body of the angel in his grip and let the crumpled course fall to the ground. The next moment, Shadowweaver scooped up another angel body and squeezed it until the wings pushed outward from the creature's back. After considering the corpse for a moment, Shadowweaver returned to plucking feathers.

"I do not have much time for this banter. I am preparing to launch an attack on my enemies. So let us make this short. You have been operating all this time under the assumption that Talisia is responsible for stealing the soul of your High Priestess in the same way that she stole your souls. And so, you see her imprisoned somewhere, trapped in lifeless steel in the same way that you were. But that assumption, that dangerous assumption that has driven you and the rest of your order to hunt down and murder anyone who might have that information is tantamount to your lack of understanding of the politics of the Children of the Creator and the lengths they are willing to go to advance their own agendas."

Shadowweaver pulled two feathers from the angel's wing and held them up looking down his long snout for several moments as though considering the meaning of their existence.

"I was alive long before the Children. Once they were born, I watched them. Saw their pettiness. Saw their greed. They had a lust for power unlike any creature that came before or after, almost as much as the Creator himself. Though the Creator is all-powerful, he lusts for more. Though he is all-knowing, he needs more. Though he is all seeing, he knows there are things outside of his vision. For all his limitless being, he is limited by being unable to understand why he cannot understand. The Children are the same. They flaunt their power. They flaunt their intelligence. They scheme and fight against one another like dogs in the street, and yet they pretend that they are noble and that their ends are noble."

Shadowweaver let one of the feathers fall, and then looked past the other to the members of the Adhradair.

"So why do you think that Talisia would give a damn about your High Priestess unless she wished to use the soul for a greater purpose."

Luighsech frowned.

"Does it matter what the purpose is? Talisia imprisoned us…."

Shadowweaver's snort cut off Luighsech's words.

"You should care very much what the purpose is, fool. Because as you continue to make these assumptions about the aims of your betters, just as you make failed assumptions about the dragons, you will continue to fall and fail as you have done since your return to the land of the living."

Maedoc's words were intended to mock Shadowweaver's supposed superior intelligence, but the words came out more genuine than he desired.

"So what are these aims that we should be paying attention to, dragon?"

Shadowweaver let another feather fall.

"I tell you this, not because I feel the information is owed to you, or from any sense of responsibility for what happened to your world. In fact, your knowing this information will have little in the way of impact on what is to come. Your Dorovar is a fool and has always been a fool. That is why it was so easy for Talisia and Emries to manipulate him. Despite Raenera's supposed Perfect Order, there was still something inside of Dorovar that could be exploited. Dorovar wanted to be more than he was. In a society predicated on everyone accepting their role, the role that the goddess dictated for them, someone willing to question that role was the fundamental danger. Raenera thought that she had bred out all of the inquisitiveness of your people. Thought she had left you completely docile and accepting. But perhaps there was just enough ambition left in your flock of sheep that one of you would eventually start asking questions that you shouldn't."

Again, the dragon paused, its next words taking on a much more sinister tone.

"Had Raenera been a better architect, or had she been less concerned with making a perfect system that would continue to function without her attention or intervention, she might have been able to predict what was coming. If the Perfect Order had indeed been perfect, then Dorovar would have immediately seen through Talisia's falsehoods. The so-called visions and prophecies would have been ignored as petty attempts to test his faith. But Dorovar wanted to believe. He did half of Talisia's work for her. She barely had to nudge Dorovar in the right direction. He undermined you; he undermined your High Priestess; he undermined your perfect order. At every step he usurped the roles that were intended for other members of the Adhradair. Do you think that a coincidence?"

The words were like a vice gripping Luighsech's heart.

"Dorovar became your prophet," Shadowweaver continued, "taking the role from your High Priestess. He entered talks with Derelor and Stormbane, taking the role from your negotiator, and then in the end, when your world was on the edge of its fall, he tried to caution the rest of you from taking the power from Talisia, usurping the role of your protectors. But he had so undermined your trust in his words that all you could see was the fate awaiting your people. You never would have seen the danger. Your roles were to protect, and you would do that to the bitter end, because you could not see beyond what you were meant to be."

Again, Shadowweaver plucked a feather from the angel in his clutches.

"Talisia used your doubt and loss of faith in Dorovar to tie your souls to her wicked purpose and to her even wickeder sense of irony. Your world destroyed, you were safely tucked away in the Heavens waiting for your return to this world, while Dorovar floated in the vast nothing. But do not think for a moment that that was not exactly where Talisia wanted him to be. Talisia wanted him cut off from the Perfect Order. Wanted him cut off from those that betrayed him. Dorovar thinks that your souls were used to forge a prison that sealed measures of his power away. But again, you are deluded and far too unintelligent to see the truth of it all."

Another feather fell, and Shadowweaver plucked two more.

"The Sacred Weapons weren't the seals on the Vault of Terrors. They were keys. As each one was broken the locks on the Vault of Terrors weakened. Eventually enough of the power that held the Vault outside of this world was eroded away and Dorovar was able to break through. But the real prison that Talisia concocted was far more sinister."

The two feathers fell simultaneously.

"Do you think that the names of the weapons that you were imprisoned in were some kind of artistic flourish?"

Shadowweaver ripped a clump of feathers from the angel's wing and let one fall with each of the names of the Sacred Weapons.

"Dorovar floated in the nothingness, and Talisia needed him to be a weapon. Needed him to turn his back on the Perfect Order and everything that made him part of the Adhradair. So, your souls were the fuel and the catalyst to rob from Dorovar everything that made him human. Wisdom, Faith, Temperance, Tenacity, Discipline, Harmony, Patience, Valor, Courage, Perseverance, Spirit, Strength. Even Gravity. All of these were pieces of Dorovar's being that needed to be taken from him in order for him to fulfill Talisia's design. No wisdom to see beyond his own desires. No faith in the Perfect Order or in Raenera. No temperance in his application of death and pain. No tenacity to resist his urges and his wants. No discipline in his anger or his rage. No harmony within himself or with his former allies. No patience to watch things come to pass on their own. No valor in action, always willing to take the lowest road with the most damage to the innocent. No courage of conviction or belief. No perseverance against the ravages of time or isolation that would keep his mind whole. No spirit, only thinking of the moment and not what would come after his goals were realized. No strength to resist the madness that grew within him. No gravity to keep him rooted to everything that made him what he was. Talisia used you to strip away all of the essence of the man Dorovar, and left only the monster Dorovar. The thing that Raenera feared and hated. The perfect embodiment of disorder."

Maedoc was able to find his voice as the last of the feathers fell.

"And the High Priestess?"

Shadowweaver snorted again.

"Oh, the High Priestess was not stolen by Talisia. That was denied to her. It was Raenera who took the soul of your High Priestess, and it is Raenera who denies you yet again what you feel that you are owed from your long service and even longer captivity."

Both Maedoc and Luighsech's eyes went wide.

"Where is the soul?" Maedoc implored.

Shadowweaver snorted once again.

"Oh, I have no intention of telling you that."

The next moment, Stormbane's jaws came snapping down on Maedoc. The strike threw Luighsech several feet across the cavern, but was enough to rip Maedoc in half despite his thick armor. Stormbane spat out the upper half of Maedoc's body, and with one clawed foot reached out and pinned Luighsech to the floor. Shadowweaver shifted slightly so that he could stare down at Luighsech.

"I had no intention of sharing information with Dorovar, but I wanted him to know the depths of his failure and the depths to which he has been betrayed by his own goals and desires. There is no future in a cosmos ruled by that child, and when I have finished crushing my enemies it the Heart of Stone, I will come for Dorovar to finish what we started on your world."

Shadowweaver reared up so that his head nearly touched the ceiling of the massive cavern.

"I leave you alive so that you may return to Dorovar and tell him of his failure. Tell him that I have the information that he wants, though it will gain him nothing. Tell him that I am coming for him, and I shall revel in ripping his heart from his chest and tearing his body into pieces so small that they will be envious of the dust that floats in the nothingness. Go, while I am still feeling magnanimous."

Stormbane released Luighsech, and the moment the man got to his feet, he vanished from view. Shadowweaver snorted again and retuned to idly plucking feathers from the angel's wing. Stormbane turned back to Shadowweaver.

"Do you think it was wise to tell that being where you intend to strike? Do you not think that Dorovar will come for you there?"

Shadowweaver lifted a feather and pointed it at Stormbane.

"I'm counting on it."

CHAPTER 114

Chapter CXV

Debating Chaos

Year Five of the Just Emperor Kaitain "Dragonsbane" Lorien, Creator's Calendar Year 1872

Cedric Binosear sat on the ground, his back to a tree, looking up at the stars. He wasn't sure how many hours had passed since he had plunged the dagger into Emries' heart and watched the life go out of his impossibly blue eyes. He could not help staring up at the sky and reflecting on everything that had come before. All the lies. All the death. All the suffering. For what? Part of Cedric had hoped that once he had gained Emries' knowledge, there would be answers to those questions. All that Cedric found were more questions, and more emptiness. It must have been close to midnight when the rustling came from the trees to Cedric's left. The visitor made sure that he was heard to avoid a conflict.

"Hello Pyrrus."

Cedric knew the moment Wolf Ranthall had appeared nearby. That was the first and most striking piece of information that Cedric was able to glean from Emries. The Children of the Creator all knew where each other were at all times, at least to a certain degree. With effort they could mask their movements or their presence for a time, but the moment they utilized their abilities it was like a giant bonfire being lit. Some, like Raenera, had become adept at minimizing their use of power to prevent the divination of her exact location, while others like Emries and Talisia cared little if their siblings knew where they were. The Children of the Creator were as dismissive of each other as they were single-mindedly focused on besting the others in their ideological conflict. It was personal without being personal, and it was as all-consuming as it was ultimately futile. It seemed that deep down each and every one of them knew that there would be no winner to their conflict, and that the conflict itself had become a kind of self-fulfilling prophecy. They existed to be in conflict, they existed because of the conflict, and they could not live or be allowed to live without. They were as trapped in their cycle as the very creatures that fought their war by proxy.

Wolf Ranthall sat opposite Cedric, leaning against a tree himself, picking up a small stick and rubbing it between his fingers until flames danced across the dry bark. A pile of leaves collected of their own accord between the two men, and when Wolf threw the flaming twig into the tinder, the small campfire sparked to life.

"Underwhelming, isn't it?"

Cedric knew instantly what Wolf was talking about. Where was the great fountain of knowledge, or the cosmic realizations of such massive proportion that they would shake the mortal to his very core? All Cedric felt was the power eating at his soul, trying to hollow him out with every second that passed. That, and rage.

"That's as apt a word as any."

Silence held between the two men for a long time. Wolf picked at the fire with another stick while Cedric continued to stare up at the stars, trying to find meaning in their movements. Finally, Cedric looked across at the other man and sighed.

"I suppose we should have a conversation about what comes next."

Wolf nodded.

"I would have thought that was obvious."

Cedric cocked an eyebrow.

"You've had your connection to the divine a lot longer than I have, Wolf. I'm just a guy who finally got his revenge after thousands of years and found that it wasn't worth all of the trouble that it took to get here. I was hoping for some kind of clarity. Some kind of map to show me what to do next to keep this from ever happening again. And all I have is this feeling of hopelessness. All I have is this realization that it was all for nothing."

Wolf nodded.

"We held the Children of the Creator up as this impossible thing. They had power to create and destroy worlds. They could make whole races or snuff them out with a thought. And yet for some reason, we could stand against them. My father actually fought Emries. You stood against Halicon. How is that even possible if they are so powerful and we are nothing?"

The comment made Cedric's blood boil, not because it was inflammatory, but because it was true. At least until you factored in the one part that no one did when they looked at the Children.

"Because we didn't understand the Creator."

There was another rustle to the west of where the two men sat, but neither paid it much notice, even when a new voice joined the conversation.

"I have lived longer than the two of you combined and I still feel as though I will never understand all that I must."

Bryn Seth emerged from the darkness, her form-fitting black outfit seemed to deflect all attempts for dirt and dew to cling to the sheer fabric. She stood regarding the two men seated on the ground for a moment and shook her head.

"Really?"

With a wave of her hand, roots sprung up from the ground and fashioned themselves into a high-backed chair. Once the chair had finished forming, Bryn sat slowly, the dimension of the chair tailoring themselves to her. Cedric looked first at Bryn, then the chair, and then at Wolf before shaking his head and chuckling to himself.

"I'll never understand that."

Bryn cocked an eyebrow.

"Understand what?"

Cedric pointed at the chair.

"That. You didn't even hesitate; you just made a chair. I don't think that I would have even considered that. I have the powers of one the Children of the Creator and I'm sitting here on the ground while you, who have had your powers from the moment you drew breath just create a chair."

"Isn't that the whole point of all of this?" Wolf interjected. "This whole war just seems to revolve around the respect for and application of power; from the Creator to the Children to the phasia, to us the lowly humans."

Bryn sighed.

"After a fashion I suppose. But in truth it's about the Creator and what he does and doesn't understand about his own existence."

As if suddenly realizing, Cedric turned back to Bryn.

"Why are you here?"

Realizing that his words and tone may have been misconstrued, Cedric continued.

"I understand why Wolf is here, but I don't understand why you would come here, or how you would even know to come here at all. Clearly you knew I would be here."

Bryn shook her head.

"Here the two of you sit, two of the most powerful beings in Creation, trying to discern the motivations of the Creator, and yet you are completely oblivious to the obvious. You are just as dim as your father."

Even before the shock could register on Cedric's face, Bryn turned her venom to Wolf.

"And you are as reckless as yours."

A golden flash sparkled in Wolf's eyes.

"Be careful with that tongue of yours, sister. One day someone might snatch it out."

Whatever reaction Wolf was expecting, it certainly wasn't the laughter that came from the eldest daughter of Halicon.

"How quickly we fall into old patterns," Bryn said shaking her head. "And I am just as much to blame as the two of you. I was bred to be a killer; all I know how to do is attack. Cedric is an idealist like Aerith, trying to find the right answer to a question that has no right answers, and Wolf, a volatile mixture of phasia, human, and god with a penchant for doing things his own way. But that is the lesson we have all learned in this war. As long as we do what is expected, we will lose."

Wolf hung his head. Bryn was right. Cedric took the opportunity the awkward silence afforded to stand.

"So Aerith sent you."

Bryn scowled.

"No one sends me anywhere."

Sensing that her brand of playfulness was not going to be of use in this conversation, Bryn sighed, shook her head, and refocused her gaze on Cedric.

"Aerith, Rhain, and Logan felt that felt that it would be better if I approached you than any of them. Rhain for obvious reasons, your father because of your strained relationship, and Logan, frankly because he is needed elsewhere."

Cedric smiled lightly.

"I've always appreciate your candor, Bryn."

"So Rhain told you where to find Cedric," Wolf said, answering Cedric's earlier question. "To what purpose?"

Bryn's answer and tone were matter-of-fact.

"To figure out what to do next, same as the two of you."

Cedric crossed his arms and could not keep the frown from turning his lips.

"To your point Bryn, how can we possibly know what we are supposed to do next if we can't understand why the Creator is doing what He is doing. Does He want to destroy everything and start over? Does He want us to stop him? How do we know that everything we are doing and have done are not part of a plan that he has been pushing from the beginning? How do we know that he has not foreseen this very conversation and knows everything that we are going to do and say? So, then what is the point of making plans at all? If the Creator knows how we are going to fight him, then we have no chance of winning."

Bryn started to counter Cedric's words, but it was Wolf's voice that rang out first.

"The Creator is not that much different from the Children, or from us in the grand scheme of things, and I think that is why we are at this cross-roads. If we take dogma out of the equation, then we are left with a set of facts that we all believed to be immutable. The Creator is the origin of all things. The Creator knows all. The Creator has crafted a grand plan and design by which all things must come to pass."

Bryn saw the direction of Wolf's thoughts and answered.

"But we know that two of those facts are untrue."

Bryn's words pulled Cedric partially from his hopelessness and he turned his quizzical gaze in her direction.

"We do?"

Bryn smiled and nodded.

"The Creator is not the origin of all things. That much we know for certain. The Creator was actually made by the Cosmos, or at the very least came into being at the same time as the Cosmos. We also know that the Cosmos is where Aerith's power comes from, and the Creator doesn't know why or what the limits of Aerith's abilities are, which is why He has been so interested in Aerith's children. That very fact means that the Creator does not in fact know all."

Wolf continued from that point.

"So, if those two facts are not in-fact facts, then we can infer that the third so-called immutable truth is not true either. The Creator does not have a grand plan and design by which all things must come to pass. He may be able to predict or influence most events, but there are a least a few things that he cannot foresee."

Cedric nodded.

"But He tries to mitigate those things through the use of his Servants, and by influencing events surrounding the ones he cannot directly control."

"And by gathering as much knowledge as he can," Bryn added. "The Children were a method by which the Creator was attempting to learn about himself and his connection to the Cosmos. He knows he can't do that in a vacuum. If he unmakes everything, that just means he'll have to start over. New Children, new Servants, new worlds, new lower races. The cycle will start all over again."

Cedric glowered.

"So why doesn't He? It's not as though it will change anything for Him. He is the Creator after all. Does time have any meaning for Him at all? He didn't get his answers this time around, so He can just start over. Who's to say he hasn't done this a hundred times already?"

Bryn's stomach lurched. She had not entertained that possibility, even when she was having her conception of reality destroyed in the Heavens at the words of the woman she had known as Liette.

"I don't think the Creator has done this before. There would be more method, less waste and less risk. There certainly wouldn't be a Dorovar, and there may not even be an Aerith. The more iterations the Creator would make, the fewer things would be left to random chance. We saw it with the Children. Experiment, fail, refine, experiment again. It all led here to Espre. It all led to the final experiment. Whatever it may be."

Bryn scowled again.

"It's Aerith."

Cedric started to speak, but Bryn raised her hand. She was chewing on the words in her mind, trying to make them make more sense than they had mere minutes prior when they were being bandied about by her husband and their daughter. Wolf's presence made the subject matter more troublesome, but no less necessary. Finally swallowing the last of her trepidation, Bryn let her voice hit the still air once again.

"Aerith's powers come from the Cosmos, and the Creator desperately wants to understand the Cosmos and His place in it. So, the Creator has engineered a sequence of events by which he will be able to somehow, we think, absorb Aerith's powers. That's why you were allowed to kill Emries and absorb his powers, Cedric. The Creator has targeted all of Aerith's children and put his own children on a collision course with them. The plan will put the powers of the Children of the Creator in each of Aerith's five children. Gideon already has Raenera's powers, you have Emries', Rhain has Halicon's. Talisia's powers are on their way to Anabel, and we believe Ayden will be coming after Wolf to take Pyrrus' powers. Once Aerith's five children are in position, the Creator will…"

"Use Tess to reshape reality so that He can siphon off Aerith's powers and either absorb or subjugate the Cosmos," Cedric interrupted.

Wolf let a low whistle break the stunned silence that followed Cedric's words.

"That's quite a plan. Too bad it has a few flaws."

Wolf didn't bother to look at either of his companions. He kept his eyes trained on the fire as he began to speak. His voice was low and slow, measuring each word to assure that he was understood.

"Aerith's ties to his children are tenuous at best. Even more so now. Cedric isn't from this reality. Ayden has been the vessel of one of the Servants, and we know that no one is the same once that power has inhabited a mortal form. Even if Ayden does succeed in taking Pyrrus' power, that's not all he's getting."

Wolf paused for a second, closing his eyes.

"I spent time in the Vault of Terrors, studying all of the things that Dorovar studied, and I came to the same conclusion that Dorovar did. Power can be stolen. This isn't new. Other races on other worlds that the Children oversaw also came to this conclusion. Power is a transient thing. Sometimes it's a living thing that allows itself to be used like the Blaze. Sometimes it's the very essence of life that can be tapped into and moved from one place to another, or from one form to another, like Jeroch did in the Black Tower, or like what my father did when he transitioned from humanity to whatever he is now.

"When power is itself, unadulterated, it doesn't matter the shell it inhabits. But when you start mixing power with other power, the results can be curious at best. Take Dorovar for example. The gifts from the dragons combined with the gifts from Emries and Talisia, as well of the touch of Raenera created an immortal that can command the souls of the dead. He mixed his own power with a member of the phasia and got Jerah. He mixed his power with that he stole from Raenera and got his other Heralds. There is no issue with Cedric, because he was touched by Emries and was made into the Coromor. His power is his power. He's never attempted to touch Aerith's power through his own blood, and probably wouldn't know how to do it if he wanted to. Dorovar and I both learned of that ability in the Vault. My father happened to stumble on it, seemingly by accident, though I think now it wasn't an accident at all."

Here Wolf paused again.

"Things were not so easy with me. I had no powers from my birth because Emries wanted to make sure he chose someone he could control. But Basille did the unthinkable and gave me his string and his connection to the Blaze. Like my father would become, I was not completely human, and I wasn't completely a member of the phasia. I was somewhere in between, unsure how to create harmony between my soul and the powers of the phasia. Then, when I ascended, I was touched by the powers of the divine, and became ostensibly a god. So added to the part of me that was phasia, was part divine."

Wolf stopped for a moment, as though a new thought came to him.

"There were a few of us in the group from Onea that ascended. Gwydeon and Midarin had no powers, so no problem there. Pike was the Pike from the Dark Mirror, and Halicon had removed his tie to Emries. Aryx was a mixture of Emries, Halicon, and the divine, always at war with himself. Diana and Lissa both were a mix of Emries and divine power. Neither Aerith, nor Bryn, nor Taya ascended. Erika and Jerrard ascended, and Jerrard was half-phasia, so similar to myself in that regard."

Wolf's tone shifted. From contemplative and half-rambling, he became sorrowful and heavy.

"Aryx and Diana sacrificed themselves, passing their powers to Orren Eldrath and Felicia Lorien, two mortals with no touch of the divine. Felicia got Nightwing and Diana's memories, but no tie to Emries or divine power. Aryx passed his knowledge and the remnant of his primal string as a member of the phasia, but nothing more. No tie to the divine, no mixture of power. Erika and Jerrard were murdered. My wife killed herself in an attempt to kill Talisia. So that just leaves me as the sole mixing pot of powers."

There was another short pause, but when Wolf spoke again, the sorrow had disappeared from his voice.

"So after being brought here to Espre, Basille was able to reunite with the other half of his powers in Draven, and Pyrrus became the glue that held us all together. But in becoming that bridge between Basille and Draven and Wolf, the four of us were changed. Our powers changed. I'm not sure they can ever be separated again. Perhaps that too is intentional. Perhaps I'm the backup if something happens to my father."

Wolf could not help but feel Bryn's quizzical gaze.

"Do you think it's an accident that it was Logan who just happened to figure out he could reach through his blood and touch the powers of Emries in Korrd and the powers of Pyrrus in me? My father still has a role to play in all of this, and I have a funny feeling that if something goes wrong with Ayden, the Creator has a way of putting either Logan or myself into a different role. After all, haven't you noticed that there are a few more Ranthalls running around lately than there should be?"

The jaw-drop moment that Bryn had been waiting for finally came.

"It hasn't been very subtle actually," Wolf continued. "My father doesn't like to look at things that way, but practicality was never his strong suit. My grandfather Arin, my father Logan, my uncle Korrd, my half-sister Isabella, my cousin Gwillim, my newly discovered cousin Rhionna, and myself, not to mention my daughters. Six Ranthalls to make the plan work, with a few spares just in case. It's pretty genius if you think about it. But then again, we are talking about the Creator."

Bryn couldn't find the words to speak. Fortunately for her, Cedric asked the question that was inflaming her mind.

"So, how do we stop this? Can we stop this? Is there anything to stop? It seems like Emries, Talisia, and Raenera invested a lot into finding a way to unseat the Creator, but is there enough of any of their plans to make a difference? I've been with Tess; I know what she's capable of. She's just unstable enough to believe anything she's told, and if the Spirit or the Voice manipulate her in just the right way, it won't matter who tries to stand in her way; she'll simply snap her fingers and wipe them out of existence."

Bryn finally found her voice.

"I have a better question. Even if there is a way to unseat the Creator, what then? Does everything just end anyway? Does someone even have the opportunity, as Dorovar suspects, to replace the Creator? And what do we do about Dorovar? At the rate he's collecting powers, he may beat us to the punch. It gives the Creator now three paths to getting what he wants."

Wolf nodded.

"Like you said, Cedric, mitigate those things He cannot foresee through the use of his Servants, and influence events surrounding the ones He cannot directly control."

Cedric frowned.

"There is only one path that I see. We have to kill Tess before any one of the three groups has all of the Children's powers."

Wolf sighed.

"And now she's far more dangerous because Cedric has trained her to at least somewhat control her abilities, more than a match for any of us."

A thought his Bryn's mind like a thunderbolt.

"So, if the powers of the Children can be stolen, can the powers of the Dragon's Tear?"

Legends

Year One of the Just Empress Quyhn Ravenheart Lorien, Cadarian Calendar Year 1872

"You know what we forgot?" Midarin said standing in the doorway of one of the suites at the far end of the west wing of the newly constructed Fortress Peregrim. "Furniture."

The new palace was beautiful inside and out, but as Midarin stood looking at the empty room, she could not help but find the humor in the moment. She felt Gwydeon come up behind her and wrap his arms around her waist.

"Fortunately for you, the man you love is a pretty fair carpenter."

Midarin did her best to keep the smile from curling her lips.

"Good. So when is he getting here?"

Gwydeon spun her around quickly and kissed her hard. For a moment, he had forgotten all of the terrible things that were coming and was just in love with his wife. Nothing else but her mattered, and no matter what was coming nothing would stand between them ever again. Playfully she pushed him away, which just made him pull her closer once again. There was a gentle titter of laughter behind them and both turned to see

Mirana and Liara standing in the hall behind them. It had been Liara who laughed, unable to control herself in the emotion of the moment. The twin girls had missed so many years of their parents' love, and they benefited from being close to the strong emotions that Gwydeon and Midarin held for one another.

"Rhionna dispatched several groups of the soldiers to the forests nearby to harvest some wood," Mirana said quickly. "I'm sure once we have some materials we can help put together some basic amenities."

Gwydeon looked at the girls and then at his wife.

"Maybe we should go help them."

Midarin put her hand on his arm as he started to pull away.

"They just saw us pull a whole city out of the ground. We should let them take some ownership of this place. If we do everything for them, they might start to resent us."

Gwydeon nodded and kissed her lightly on the forehead. He turned back to the twins and took two steps in their direction.

"Where's Quyhn?"

Liara finally recovered from her barely stifled laughter.

"Exploring her rooms in the east wing. I think she's a little overwhelmed."

Gwydeon nodded.

"I think I'll go check in on her. Why don't you two help supervise the resource gathering. I'm sure that Midarin is going to want to look over the towers and the parapets to map out the defensible positions for the archers. After I check on Quyhn, I'll meet with Rhionna to finalize the patrols and the defense positions on the ground."

Midarin sighed gently.

"If you want me to work, you better make sure there is a comfortable bed waiting for me when I get back. A queen does have her standards after all."

Gwydeon chuckled to himself.

"Apparently not if you married a carpenter," Mirana teased.

Midarin whirled around, the look on her face incredulous. Liara broke out into laughter, unable to control herself. Gwydeon gave Mirana a withering look for just a moment before letting the broad smile spread onto his face. Caught in the emotion of the moment, Gwydeon reached out and pulled both of the girls into his arms. He held them for a long moment before kissing each on the top of the head and walking past them out of the west wing. Midarin watched him walk away and then watched as the looks on the faces of the girls changed from momentary surprise to quiet contentment. Midarin felt for the girls. They were trapped in the middle in the same way that Camille was. The difference was of course that Camille still had her mother and father to depend on. The girls had lost their mother and it was still uncertain what had happened to their father. They were Ranthalls and had a great extended family, including their newly revealed cousin Rhionna. But the problem with the Ranthall family, as Midarin had experienced up close, was that they were always in the middle of the worst of it, whether they wanted to be or not. Logan, Korrd, Wolf, none of them had a choice once Emries and Aerith Seth had their hooks into the family. The twins hadn't escaped either, pulled into the dirty end of the war by benefit of their divine birth. Gwydeon had taken their inclusion into his crusade personally. For their part, Gwydeon viewed the two girls as innocents, no different than the humans caught up in the war. Finally, Midarin walked over to the girls and patted them each on the shoulder.

"Family is family," Midarin said finally. "And we always take care of family."

For Midarin's part, she could not look at the girls without thinking of her own daughter, lost somewhere in the wilderness, trapped between doing what she knew was right and doing what the Creator forced her to do. In her heart, Midarin hoped that that Camille would find her way back to them.

"Now," Midarin said willing the tears from her eyes. "let's get to work."

* * * * * * * * * * * * *

Quyhn could not help but feel impossibly alone as she looked out the pristine new window of the large suite on the far side of the west wing of the palace. She was still trying to come to terms with the battle than had taken place only hours before. So many had died, and for what? But that was true across the whole of Cadaria. Between Kaitain's wars on the dragons and his fomenting of civil war between the kingdoms, thousands were dead and thousands more were slated to die. Then there was Dorovar and his Heralds. They had destroyed the whole of Rashaleb, murdering an untold number of innocent people. And now for all Quyhn knew, they were rampaging across the rest of Cadaria, destroying everything in their path in the name of their perverse master. What hope did she stand of stopping that? What difference could she really make? She was just a little girl who was raised in an isolated world of her parents' construction. Her father never intended for her to be part of the greater world. As far as he was concerned, her entire world existed within the walls of the Academy of Arcane Arts. There she would be loved, there she would learn, there she would teach, and most importantly there she would be safe.

"Overwhelming, isn't it?"

Gwydeon's voice made her jump for just a moment, but she did her best not to let it show. Rhionna would have chided her for not being aware of her surroundings. She had been so focused on her own thoughts that she did not feel Gwydeon come up behind her. The man had a feline grace, and while she would not have heard his footfalls, she should have been able to feel that she was not alone. Gwydeon had done nothing to hide his approach, and were she paying attention, she could have felt him.

"Which part?"

She meant the comment as a joke, but as soon as the words left her lips, she knew that the humor had not translated into her words. Gwydeon walked to stand beside her looking down on the fledgling city.

"If you'll forgive my saying so, I think I know what you're feeling."

Quyhn looked sidelong at Gwydeon for just a moment before motioning for him to continue.

"When I was a boy, I looked up to these great men that I thought were the most heroic men that could ever live. I was in awe of the stories I heard about them, and I wanted nothing more than to follow in their footsteps and be a hero someday too. My father in my eyes was anything but. Don't misunderstand me. I had great respect for my father, but his ambition began and ended where he was. He had the life that he wanted. He was a father, he was a respected member of his community, and he helped people with his trade. I think that perhaps our fathers were not so different in that way."

Quyhn's expression was one of surprise.

"How so?"

Gwydeon moved past Quyhn and sat on the low wide sill that stretched beneath the window.

"I spent a lot of time in the world, and I heard a lot about your father. Everything I heard about him was that he was a good man and his whole life had been dedicated to helping humanity better itself. I actually met your father once. He was on one of his scouting trips looking for those with the potential to join the Academy."

Quyhn smiled.

"I remember those trips. Mother never liked them. She thought that they were beneath his position, and that Fiona Ebonsight was better suited for the task. Mother thought that father was too kind-hearted and spent too much time testing those children who did not have any aptitude in order to keep the people happy. So many trips, he would be gone for twice as long as he should have, and come back with no candidates. But father would always say that it was equally important to let the people know what the Academy was doing for them, not just what it was trying to take from them."

Gwydeon nodded.

"That is what I remember. I was working as a carpenter at the time in this little village in the middle of nowhere. I'm not even sure it appeared on most maps. Those were the kind of towns that I felt the most comfortable in, because they reminded me of where I came from. But when Alistair appeared, it was as though he were walking through the streets of Aldere. Everyone was the most important person that he talked to. It didn't matter how long it took, he spoke to every parent, tested every child, was gracious and understanding to everyone equally. He was a good man. But there was more than that. He took great pains in ensuring that everyone understood the good work that their sons or daughters could do at the academy. Research into healing the sick, new methods for planting and harvesting, ways to avoid drought and disease. I truly believe that he would have made a better world for everyone if he had been given the chance."

Quyhn's eyes were sullen, and yet Gwydeon could see the pride there.

"My father wanted the same things. A better world. He didn't have the talents that your father had, but my father was a blacksmith, and a very talented one. There was never a farmer who could not shoe his horses because they did not have the money to pay. My father understood that people could fall on hard times, and there was no reason to make it worse if you could make it better. And I'll tell you, when my father's storage shed caught fire after a freak lightning storm, all of those farmers, all of those people who had been touched by his generosity were the first ones to lend a hand putting out the fire and then building a new shed. And while my father didn't have to, he paid each of them for their time and for the materials they brought to the job. He always taught me that generosity was not for what it could gain you later. It was what we should all strive for."

Quyhn nodded absently.

"Did you want to be a Master in the Academy?"

Quyhn's eyes went wide as though she could not believe the question. Of course she wanted to follow in her father's and mother's footsteps. Of course she wanted to be a Master in the Academy of Arcane Arts. Of course she wanted to continue the Ravenheart legacy. But then she realized suddenly where she was standing. She was being treated like the Empress of Cadaria, even if it was a role she had neither earned nor deserved. How far she was from where she once thought herself. Gwydeon didn't wait for her answer. It seemed that his intention was to frame her thoughts.

"As much as I admired my father, I didn't want to be my father. But I also wasn't foolish enough to think that I would be like those great men that I idolized in my youth. I wanted to be good enough with the sword to catch on with the Lion's Mane, which was the most important army on the whole of my world. I trained every day with that goal in mind. I was going to be a soldier. Then do you know what happened?"

Quyhn leaned against the doorframe.

"A war?"

Gwydeon smiled.

"I fell in love."

Quyhn also could not help but smile.

"And you've been with Midarin all this time?"

Gwydeon didn't realize what a blow Quyhn's words were until he saw shock come to her face. He covered the momentary pain with a forced smile.

"No. Her name was Gabrielle. And we were madly in love. I was ready to give up my dream of being a soldier for her, and I thought about my father. What dreams must my father have had before he met my mother? What dreams kept him awake into the late hours? And in the moment that I knew I loved Gabrielle; I knew that I could be happy not being a soldier. I could be happy being a blacksmith in a little farming town in the middle of nowhere."

Quyhn was fascinated. Even though she had been traveling with four members of the Dark Gods for several days, she still could not see them as human. But this disarmed Gwydeon, this mortal, dreaming Gwydeon thrust home the point. They were really no different than the Cadarians. How could they have been so wrong about the Dark Gods for so long? Was their power so great and so terrifying that it was impossible to see anything other than what they could do? And then it hit Quyhn. She understood what Gwydeon was trying to say. How must those of the Academy have looked to those who had never met someone who could bend the arcane nature of their world to their will? And then they would meet her father, and suddenly they would see not the power, but the person. How must the Emperor and the Knights of the Flashing Blade have looked to the commoners, and yet there were those like Gregor Quicksilver and Hannah Ironheart who were the soul of the group, human and relatable. Standing in this palace, above the world as far as she was concerned, she had begun to separate herself from the little girl who dreamed of what she would do when she grew.

"So what happened?"

Gwydeon swallowed. It was still hard to talk about even after all the time had passed, but if he was going to make the point to Quyhn that he wanted to make, she needed to hear it. He saw so much of himself in the young woman, so much that he wished she had not had to go through. But he knew that she would be stronger for it so long as she continued to believe that there was a path forward and did not find herself crushed by the circumstances.

"There was an accident, and she died. And for a long time, I felt like a part of me died too. I had been so ready to give up my dream for her, and once she was gone, the dream seemed so hollow. I wasn't sure if I wanted to be a soldier. I wasn't sure if I wanted to be a blacksmith. I wasn't sure if I wanted to stay or go. I was lost. But my good and dear friends were there. They pushed me. They helped me to remember who I was. And while the dream was not the same, it was still there. I trained harder. And then my destiny found me."

Quyhn could see parallels now. Gwydeon and his loss, not knowing how to move on. Quyhn with her loss, unsure if her dreams still had merit.

"And my destiny was something that I never could have dreamed of. A great quest, powerful allies, powerful enemies, things beyond description around every turn. Standing shoulder to shoulder with legends as I fought against creatures with the powers of gods. Fighting gods themselves."

Quyhn saw herself in Gwydeon's words. Adopted by the Emperor, folded into a rebellion, meeting and allying with Dark Gods, fighting against angels and the Servants of the Creator. It was absurd, and yet somehow Gwydeon made it seem less mad.

"And of course, I had to face the greatest challenge of my life. One I could never have dreamed of."

Quyhn was so enraptured with his tale she could not imagine what this man who had seen so much and fought against the unimaginable would consider to be the greatest challenge of his life.

"What was it?" Quyhn urged.

Gwydeon's broad smile was disarming.

"A spoiled stubborn princess."

Quyhn could not suppress her laughter.

"But don't tell her I called her that," Gwydeon continued. "She does have a bit of a temper."

Quyhn's mood was much lighter, and she felt so much of the weight lifted off her shoulders. All she had seen was the responsibility. The cost. Now, she began to see the opportunity and the place where destiny could take her.

"You have your own strong-willed woman to deal with, Quyhn, but remember that love can never be a weakness, it can only make you stronger. Provided of course that you remember the key thing."

Quyhn felt her cheeks color with embarrassment, but also felt relief that whatever secret she and Rhionna thought they were keeping for appearance sake, it was obvious to at least one other person.

"And what's that?"

Gwydeon got up from where he sat and walked over to her. He put a hand on the girl's shoulder for a moment and leaned down to whisper in her ear.

"There's nothing wrong with saying you're wrong when you know you're right. It can make things go smoother."

Quyhn knew he meant it as a joke despite his dry and wry tone. When he stood and moved past her, he let his voice hit the air once more.

"Especially when you know they can slit your throat in the night."

Quyhn's laughter rolled through the empty room. For the first time in a long time, she did not feel out of place. She did not feel like the little fish in the impossibly big pond, or the pawn on someone else's board. She was exactly where she was supposed to be, and she would make the most of the opportunities that destiny continued to put in her path.

* * * * * * * * * * * * *

It was the end of a long day, and as Gwydeon returned to the chambers that had been designated for he and Midarin, he could feel his muscles aching. Even despite the powers of a Dark God, manual labor still made him feel alive. The other benefit of taking up a hammer and a saw alongside the soldiers was that they at least for a few hours stopped seeing Gwydeon as a Dark God, and saw him instead as just another soldier. The men had lost several great leaders the previous night, and so they would benefit from seeing Gwydeon among them. The burial of their comrades had been hard, and lighting of the funeral pyres had been harder, but building beds and tables gave a feeling of ownership to the soldiers of their new home. By the end of the night, the men were telling stories, laughing, and were able to forget for just a few moments the horror of the night before. There would be more losses to come but these men would be ready to do what needed to be done to defend Quyhn and all the other innocents that would come to see refuge in this new place.

Gwydeon was relieved to see the large bedframe standing in the center of the room. Of course, mattresses would be a long way off, but sleeping on firm wood was better than cold stone. At least that was the theory. The cushions from the inside of the carriage had been cannibalized for Quyhn's bed, and Gwydeon did not begrudge that. The girl deserved to get a good night's sleep. Besides, Gwydeon and Midarin had slept in much rougher conditions over the years. He was surprised that Midarin was already laying atop the thick blanket that would serve as their mattress for the foreseeable future. She had spent much of her day working with the army to ensure the security of the grounds, and Gwydeon had also seen her whipping the archers into shape. She had become quite the military leader since their days on Onea. Some of that was of course out of necessity, but she also had quite the knack for the tactical aspect of ranged combat. Just another thing that Gwydeon loved about her. He laughed to himself as he unfastened his sword-belt. He had an attraction to lethal women it seemed.

Gwydeon stood his swords in the corner of the room and then pulled his shirt over his head. Hanging the shirt on the bedpost, he crawled onto the blanket and snuggled up next to his wife. It felt good to hold her in his arms, and as he closed his eyes and felt her push back against him, he could feel peace descend upon his mind. For the moment, they were safe. For the moment, they were home.

* * * * * * * * * * * * *

The hour was late, and moonlight shone through the wide window that looked into Gwydeon and Midarin's room. In the corner of the room, the moonlight glinted off of the golden hilt of the cruel curved sword that Gwydeon had taken from the assassin who had stalked Feyd and Felicia Lorien. The glow on the hilt of the blade intensified, and the whole of the hilt became illuminated with an eerie blue light. The light faded away, and suddenly there was another figure in the room. This creature, clad in black from head to toe, only its brilliant white eyes shining in the moonlight, took hold of the hilt of the sword and silently pulled it free from the scabbard. The blade glinted in the moonlight, and as the figure made its way silently across the chamber, it raised the blade high above its head. Standing beside the bed, the assassin measured its victims. Just before the assassin brought the blade of the sword down upon the sleeping forms, there was a crash behind him. The sound of breaking glass woke both Midarin and Gwydeon, the latter holding his wife close to him and throwing the both of them onto the floor, shielding her with his own body. His wings flashed outward the next moment, creating a barrier between whatever threat had invaded their room and themselves. Midarin pushed away from Gwydeon, rolling across the floor for a moment before popping up to a knee and conjuring a bow and arrow from the nothingness. Gwydeon had not moved from his protective position, but when he saw his wife's face, he knew that something was not right. His wings beat once, propelling him upward onto his feet, where he whirled, creating a blade in each of his hands.

Standing on the far side of the bed was the assassin clad in black, the sword already fallen from its hands, broken in two and laying impotent on the bed. The assassin's head was missing, presumably on the floor, and a spray of blood splatted across the wall. Beside the assassin, gleaming crystalline blade in her hand was Camille Sandar, her wings still extended from where she had swooped through the window to come to their parents' aid. Camille smiled and lowered her sword as the assassin's body slumped to the ground and then disappeared into a plume of black smoke.

"Nice place," Camille said folding her wings back. "Did you save me a room?"

Keeper No More

Year Five of the Just Emperor Kaitain "Dragonsbane" Lorien, Creator's Calendar Year 1872

Tess Annis sat on the crest of the hill looking down on the plain that had once been the thriving city of Zevarit. Perhaps she had been too literal raining blood down on the Kingdom of Blood, but she could easily be forgiven for her theatricality if the act had served its purpose. As soon as Kaitain had returned to the ranks of his troops, a huge cheer had gone up from the soldiers of the Imperial Army, and they had moved into the new clearing to set up camp. The next morning would see them march in the direction of Celidar, the next target on Kaitain's march of destruction. Though Tess had tried to dissuade him from worrying about conquering cities and kingdoms, Kaitain still could not escape the mortal thinking that had brought him to this point. He was a lost soul bent on acquiring what could never be his. It was sad really, but Kaitain was a means to an end. It was an end that Tess could never have found with her family, or with Emries, or with Cedric Binosear. This was a path that she was meant to follow alone. And she would follow it until there was nothing left.

Kaitain had been nearly giddy as he relayed his orders to his men. Two members of the Imperial Guard were dispatched to each of the remaining kingdoms with orders to relay what they had seen become of

Zevarit. Some of the kingdoms would not be swayed by the words of the soldiers, while others would dismiss it as propaganda. However, there would be those of the masses, those of lower intelligence, easily swayed ones who had been terrorized by the near constant state of war of the last few years. They would spread the information, and the fear would spread. When the Imperial Guard appeared where they fear preceded them, resistance would wane, and obstructions would melt away. In addition, those who were craven and seeking the protection of the Imperial Guard would be more than happy to inform upon those cells of the Church of the Creator who were still operating, or were taking refuge in the homes of collaborating faithful. These people would be destroyed for their arrogance and their ignorance, leaving only those who were willing to be ruled, and those who would do anything to serve their most feared and powerful emperor. As Tess watched the ants move below her, she felt that she was no longer alone on the crest of the hill. It would have taken just a trickle of power for Tess to reach out and touch the mind of the person who approached and learn their identity. But there was really no need to waste power. The person behind Tess could have only one identity.

"Are you planning to try to assassinate me, Alise?"

Alise had stopped approaching some time ago, and was simply standing and looking at the girl who had caused such destruction. Yes, the girl had disguised her role in the destruction of Zevarit for the rank-and-file troops of the Imperial Guard, but Alise had seen everything that had transpired. Either Tess had allowed her to see, or her unnatural nature made it possible for Alise to perceive it. Regardless of the method, what Alise had seen was utterly terrifying.

"Could I, if I wanted to?"

Tess considered for a moment. It was an interesting question. With the abilities she had at her disposal, the training from both Cedric and Emries, plus the years spent amongst her extended family of the Dark Gods, was there any creature that could realistically stand against her? With the power to shape reality with a thought, could she even be killed?

"It's an interesting thought," Tess said finally, "I'm almost curious."

Alise felt a chill pass through her. The girl's demeanor coupled with her powers were terrifying, even to the cold heart of the emperor's personal assassin. Clearly Tess wasn't human, and clearly she was something so volatile and destructive that she could not be contained. If Kaitain thought he was in control of the girl, her was sadly mistaken.

"You have a question?" Tess said, still looking out on the location of her handiwork.

Alise steeled herself. One of her primary responsibilities, perhaps her only true duty, was the protection of the life of the emperor. She would remove every obstacle in his path, and ensure that there could never be a threat upon him. But this girl defied that responsibility. Defied even the possibility of preventing her from acting should she choose to turn her gaze against Kaitain's will. Alise was galled by the untenable position she found herself in.

"What are your intentions?"

Tess considered for a moment, and turned to face Alise. The moment the woman's face came into view, Alise had to prevent herself from taking a step back and shrinking away in fear. Tess's eyes glowed a brilliant gold and the few lines and cracks in her young-looking face also glowed a brilliant gold. Alise felt as though the girl's power was beginning to leak from her; that she was increasingly unable to contain that power within her mortal body.

"You worry for the fate of your father."

Alise's expression remained detached and emotionless.

"I have a responsibility to the Emperor to protect him from all threats."

Tess smiled an eerie smile. Alise felt immediately that the smile was full of madness and malice. Something within Tess seemed to be on the edge of snapping. Perhaps the fact that she had the ability to warp and reshape reality was breaking her own hold on any reality.

"And you wish to know if I am a threat to your Emperor."

The wording struck Alise, but was not surprising. Of course, someone with the kind of power that Tess had at her disposal would not recognize Kaitain's authority. That was honestly all the answer that Alise required, but Tess gave her more a moment later, and it did nothing but fill Alise with concern and trepidation.

"My father was a man of appetites like your emperor. He had power, more power than Kaitain, but he was very mortal in the manner in which he exercised that power. He liked drink, and he liked the company of women. It would not be unrealistic to say that, like Kaitain, he enjoyed the company of those women who did not want to be his company the most. My father was a brutal man, and that brutality expressed itself through manipulation and murder."

Tess cocked her head to one side.

"How many mistresses have you disposed of for your father?"

Alise kept her face cold as stone. She was not going to give Tess any leverage that she could use, but that moment Alise felt as though it did not matter if she controlled her emotions or not. If this girl could reshape reality, she must have been able to read thoughts or sense emotions. Maybe she could even hear the change of the pace of the beat of Alise's heart, or sense the tension in her muscles or the slight raggedness in her breathing. Of course, Alise realized that the question was rhetorical, so she waited for Tess to continue her explanation.

"Your Kaitain has barely had twenty-five years of life, and perhaps a quarter of that inflict any real damage through his callousness and desires. My father has had almost two thousand years to break, destroy, and humiliate anything in his path. My sister thought that she was hiding my father's misdeeds from me, but I knew. Like you, my sister Darrien had been co-opted by my father to help make his misdeeds disappear. With her partner Alderin, they kidnapped, murdered, and disposed of women, children, troublesome royals, farmers, and other mortals. All to protect a man who deserved no protection from his evil desires."

Tess smiled again.

"So I know something about powerful evil men."

Alise flinched. The girl's words were unnerving and were starting to break the assassin's practiced resolve.

"My mother knows something about evil men too. That was why she chose my father. She saw the brutality. She saw the lust. She saw a man who continued to think of himself as a hero no matter what vile and reprehensible deeds he perpetrated. He was a man who thought he had banished his demons and had earned himself immunity from repercussion. It was that seed of darkness that my mother was drawn to. Remember, my dear assassin, that it is not the light within us that matters; it is how far the darkness extends from the depths of our soul that determines what we are."

Tess paused for a moment.

"But I will share with you a secret. Everyone is deceived. Those who have been chasing me, training me, desiring me; they believe that I am something I'm not. I believed it as well for a time. But I know the truth now. I feel it deep in my soul the way that you feel the unnatural power that made you deep in yours. It was believed that the Child of the Creator Raenera chose my father in an attempt to create a powerful weapon against those who had betrayed her. But that is not what I am. My father may have believed it was Raenera, but most likely my father was too drunk to know the difference. In truth, it was Talisia, the other daughter of the Creator who used my father to create a weapon. Fitting don't you think that a man who used women without care or compunction would be used by a woman to create a weapon that could destroy him. It's too bad that I didn't get a chance to visit justice upon my father. But that matters little. My path is clear."

Alise could not help but take a step backwards. Fear radiated through her with every heartbeat. What the girl represented was beyond terrifying. Tess blinked her eyes once, and then turned back to face the remnants of the destruction that she wrought.

"Your worry is not with me, Alise Modrall. Your worry is that your emperor ceases to be useful before my path is complete. His purpose is only to ensure that what I have seen in my visions comes to pass. Nothing more, nothing less. Should he fail in that task, I will have no choice but to leave him behind. How that manifests itself is completely up to him. But I would care little to leave him broken if it came to that."

There was a slight pause, and then Tess turned her head slightly back in Alise's direction.

"And there is nothing that you will be able to do to stop me."

At that moment, Alise was conflicted. It was clear that Tess was a threat to Kaitain, but it was also clear that Kaitain's fate mattered little to the girl. She could destroy him with a thought, she could tear him limb from limb in a matter of seconds. But she did not desire to do so, at least not yet. Regardless of that, even if Alise did want to act against Tess, could she realistically do so? Would not Tess simply rip her apart as well? Maybe that was the better course. However, if Alise struck at Tess and forced Tess to destroy her, would then Kaitain see the danger that the girl represented and take some unwise action against her? So, by attempting to fulfill her duty, Alise could actually be causing the very course of events that she was seeking to prevent. Kaitain's instability coupled with Tess's made the situation impossible.

"It's an interesting dilemma you find yourself in, assassin," Tess said finally. "However, your moral quandary will have to wait. There is an army approaching from the south. Tell your father that I believe his brother has come calling."

* * * * * * * * * * * * *

The remnants of the Army of Steel marched at the vanguard of mass of commoners who had formed into an angry and vengeful mob. The Army of Steel had been in disarray since the disappearance of the kingdom's representative to the Knights of the Flashing Blade, Tolon Morr. Jerrard had tried his best to keep the army together, but military tactics was not his forte, and he did not have many within his circle of trust that held sway in the army. Feyd Lorien's attempts to rally the troops had been more successful, but the strength of the army had been reduced by nearly half of its former number. The advantage that the group that marched upon Zevarit had however was the fact that Feyd, with the help of his new patron, Emries, had been able to inflame the hearts of the people of Celidar by blaming the death of their beloved lord and lady on agents of Kaitain Lorien. During the whole of their lives, Feyd had never considered the enmity that he felt for his brother as hate. Yes, the two brothers had never seen eye to eye, and yes, Kaitain always felt that he was in competition with his younger brother. But there should have been no competition. Kaitain was the older brother. He was the next in line to sit on the throne of Cadaria. He could have anything that he wanted, be whatever he wanted with no repercussion. But that was not enough. It wasn't enough that Kaitain could have everything. He wanted to make sure that his brother had nothing. If Feyd was loved, Kaitain needed to be loved more. If Feyd was popular, Kaitain needed to be more popular. Kaitain would never be happy, he could never be whole, so long as Feyd existed. However, once Feyd had left the imperial province of Aldere, and had taken residence in Lordhill, much of the competition had faded into the background. It could not last however. As soon as Kaitain became the emperor, Feyd returned to the forefront of his mind. Feyd would always be a threat to his brother's sense of himself, his sense of his own worth. That was why Kaitain sent assassins to murder Feyd following Kaitain's coronation. That, Feyd could forgive. What Feyd could never forgive was the attempt on Feyd's daughter's life. Felicia was no threat to Kaitain. There should have been no enmity there. Kaitain's cruelty knew no bounds. So Feyd had no choice but to take any action necessary to eliminate the threat that Kaitain represented. The threat to himself, the threat to his family, the threat to the world.

As the Army of Celidar crossed over a rise that overlooked the city of Zevarit, the people were shocked to see that the city simply was not there. They should have been able to see the larger buildings of the city even at this distance, but there was simply nothing there. What the mass of people from Celidar did see however were the advancing ranks of the Imperial Guard. Feyd knew at that moment, that this was the test of the fervor of the people. There had been enough rage to mobilize the people and get them to march into Zevarit. Now though was there enough to keep the mob together faced with the organized and well-equipped Imperial Army bearing down upon them. Riding at the vanguard of the Imperial Army were three individuals. Feyd immediately recognized two of them. The first, his brother Kaitain, rode confidently, tall and straight, sans the vicious mask that he had once worn following the disfigurement that was caused by the assassination attempt during his wedding. One of the women to his side Feyd did not recognize. The other woman, however, he did know, and it was her appearance that made his blood boil. The woman was one of the assassins that had chased Feyd and Felicia from Aldere. She had been the one that would have ended their lives had it not been for the interference of the man who had called himself Wynne. Of course, Feyd had known that the assassin was in the service of Kaitain but seeing her riding at his side was an insult that could never be allowed to stand.

The command group rode further ahead of the Imperial Army, and Feyd started to ride out to meet them. However, there was rumbling within the ranks of the mob. Several at the back ranks had already broken and started to run in the opposite direction, back toward Celidar. There were shouts and rallying cries, but no amount of motivation was going to keep the cowards with the faithful. Feyd ordered his army to hold, thinking that perhaps the trained soldiers at the vanguard of his force would be able to help keep the commoners in line. A hand signal from Kaitain also halted the advance of the Imperial Army, and for several long moments the two brothers looked at each other across the field that was about to become a battleground. Feyd knew that he had a slight advantage in terrain, but the relative lack of experience in his troops would negate most of that advantage. If this did indeed come down to a battle, the likelihood that the forces of Celidar would be victorious was slim at best. After several moments, Kaitain began to slowly move toward the center of the battlefield, trailed by his two companions. Feyd wasted no time in joining his brother there. Their horses standing nearly nose to nose, the two brothers stared at one another. Kaitain's malicious smile was meant to unnerve his brother, but it did not touch Feyd's resolve. Kaitain could intimidate others, but he could not intimidate Feyd.

"It seems my brother has assembled a little army behind him. Did you come to finally admit that you serve the rightful Emperor of Cadaria, and to swear your fealty to me and to my quest to reunite our homeland?"

Feyd sighed and shook his head.

"Have you become so delusional, brother, that you see threats and enemies where they do not exist?"

Kaitain frowned.

"So I should not see a bitter usurper who curses the fact that he was born second as an enemy and a threat?"

Feyd grimaced and snarled.

"I have never been jealous of your position, Kaitain. I have never wished that I was the older brother. You were destined to be the emperor, but that was never enough for you. You needed to be the most popular, the most loved, the most admired, the most feared. You needed everyone fawning at your feet. And the fact that one person loved me more than you, the fact that one person admired me more than you offended you so much that there was no alternative in your mind other than my death. How many times have you wished my death? How many times have you plotted it? How many times in our lives did you declare that you wished that I was never born? If there is any jealousy brother, it was yours."

Kaitain's laughter was tinged with madness.

"And you call me delusional. Was it not you, brother, who tried to sickeningly ingratiate yourself with all of those who wished my downfall? Have you not always sought the adulation of the people and wished to elevate your status in the eyes of the people? You have always fancied yourself a man of the people, a commoner in royal dress. You're nothing but a pretender."

The banter fell silent and Kaitain looked beyond Feyd to the troops allied behind him.

"Is this rabble your army? It seems as though you are having difficulty keeping them together. What lies did you tell them to get them to follow you?"

Feyd shook his head.

"I didn't need to lie, Kaitain. Look at what you've done. Wars against the dragons and the Dark Gods that you knew you could not win. The murder of Alistair Ravenheart. The attempted assassinations of myself and my daughter. Dissolving the Knights of the Flashing Blade. Declaring war on your own people by outlawing the worship of the Creator and seeking the dissolution of the Church of the Creator. You have become the greatest danger to the people of the Cadarian Empire, and those who stand here with me are only the first of many. The whole of the Empire will stand against you."

Kaitain's laughter echoed across the field. He swept his hand back in the direction of the obliterated city of Zevarit.

"Do you see the fate of those who stand against me, Feyd? Zevarit thought that they could follow the lead of Gregor Quicksilver and ignore the will of the rightful Emperor of Cadaria. They harbored the criminals of the Church of the Creator, and so they had to be made an example of. I snapped my fingers and erased them from this world. There will be no more resistance to my rule. Those who refuse to bow will be destroyed, and in the world that will be reborn in the shadow of my beneficence, new glimmering cities will be erected with shrines and monuments to me. This world will continue to exist because I deem it thus."

Kaitain turned his attention back to the troops behind Feyd.

"These people will meet the same fate as those of Zevarit if they will not bend their knee to me. They will kneel and bow and offer praise to me. I am the God Emperor of Cadaria. I am the God Emperor of Espre. All that moves upon this world are mine to command, and there is no one that can stand against me. Not dragons, not Dark Gods, not even the Creator. I am the light, I am the will, and I am the breath of life for this world. But just as I can be magnanimous to those who offer me the proper praise, my malevolence will be visited upon all those who dare to raise arms against me. I will destroy them, their families, their homes, their cities. I shall wipe every trace of them and all they know from the face of the world."

Feyd could not believe what he was hearing.

"You're mad."

Kaitain shook his head.

"Is it mad to want to build a better world? Is it mad to demand worship from those who owe you such? Do you call the Creator mad for demanding the supplication of his faithful? Do you call the priests and priestess of the Church of the Creator mad for calling for tithes and sacrifices in the Creator's name? I shall be treated as the god I am. There is no other course."

Feyd pointed a single finger toward Kaitain's chest.

"You are not a god, Kaitain, you are an ill man who has lost grip on his sanity. In the world you describe there will be no room for anyone other than you. You will eliminate your enemies, and then you will eliminate those allied with your enemies. Then you will eliminate the friends and families of your enemies. You will eliminate their acquaintances and their neighbors. Then the neighbors of their neighbors and the acquaintances of their acquaintances. Soon you will be the only one left. Walking alone, comforted only by your madness."

Kaitain shook his head.

"Your ignorance is astounding, and is only eclipsed by your short-sightedness. This is not the only world, Feyd, and if the people of this world are unworthy of my godly love, I shall simply go to another. As my wise advisor recently reminded me, eliminating armies and conquering kingdoms is beneath the scope of a god's appetites. I must turn instead to bending whole worlds to my will and remaking the very essence of all that I survey into the images of my deepest desires. The whole of Creation shall love me, and if they do not, they shall meet the same fate as Zevarit."

Feyd's stunned look was all that he could manage. There were no words, and despite how he tried to find them, there was nothing that could be said in the face of the insanity that he faced. Kaitain did not wait for a response from Feyd. There was only one thing left to say.

"So, brother," Kaitain said coldly, "do you and your army yield to the will of the God Emperor, or will you be swept away as Zevarit was?"

Feyd reached for the sword at his hip.

"I'll never yield to you."

The next moment, Feyd exploded into a fountain of blood that sprayed in all directions. The horse spooked and fled, and the unbelievable display cause several of the members of Feyd's army to break and run. Tess pointed in the direction of a half dozen of the soldiers in the front rank of the army, and each of them exploded as Feyd had. The army's morale was broken and they ran. Tess turned to face Kaitain and was momentarily puzzled by the irritation on his face.

"That was boring," Tess said finally. "We have better things to do."

Tess turned her horse and headed south towards Celidar. There was something there that waited for her, she could feel it, and there was little time to waste. Kaitain watched as the girl rode away, and then after a moment began laughing again. Alise Modrall was left, watching, wondering, unsure what her next act should be. For the moment however she decided to fall in behind the emperor, signaling for the Imperial Army to follow. What lay ahead was uncertain, and that made it all the more frightening.

CHAPTER 115

Chapter CXVI

Entr'acte

Year Two of the Divine Empress and Child of the Creator Marlae Tamerlane, Creator's Calendar Year 1872

There is an inherent problem with organizations that have been around for hundreds if not thousands of years. More often than not, the person who serves as the genesis for the organization either does not intend to create such a monolith, or if that person does intend to create something that will last long beyond themselves, they cannot comprehend how future events may or may not shape that organization. Even in young organizations, mythologies begin to form. Despite texts, teachings, or strictures, rumors eventually fester into fact, and as time presses forward, those pseudo-facts sometimes become more powerful than the teachings. As Logan Ranthall sat looking out upon the vast horizon before him, he reflected on the folly of some of his own decisions and lack of decisions in the formation of the Order of the Flickering Flame. The one that was most prescient to his mind was the practice of the initiates scaling the Peaks of Patience and sitting contemplating on the teachings of the Order.

It began innocently enough. In the early days of the Order, Logan was still coming to terms with his rebirth and his purpose upon Espre. By this time, he had already found Kamen, and had begun the work of helping refugees and disillusioned soldiers from the Foundation Wars find a new path. At the same time, he was feeding information to Sabrina the best he could so that she could coordinate the hunting of their old allies and enemies from Onea. But Logan was a conflicted man. He had been one of the first to reconcile his two former lives into one memory, and in doing so had much to try to figure out. He knew that his son Wolf would be somewhere on Espre, and at the same time he mourned for not one but two lost wives, and a lost child who never had a chance to have a life. He contended with the betrayals that he suffered at the hands of Emries, and considered the great lie that was the Creator and his parasitic church. Someone confronting these existential issues could not always separate the demands of the living world from the demands of the inner world. So, when Logan felt overwhelmed and needed to purge some of his lingering doubts and internal conflicts, he would climb to the top of the Peaks of Patience and sit, working through issues that could not be explained in words, until he was able to return to the good work being done in the Order. But his trips to the top of the Peaks of Patience did not go unnoticed. Curious newcomers would ask the veterans who had been with the Order since the beginning, and they would be told that Logan was simply clearing his mind so that he could continue to do the good work of the Order. Over time, the practice took on a more spiritual persona for the fledgling members of the Order. They saw Logan's sojourns as a kind of spiritual cleansing. Logan remembered the first day when he saw another member of the Order make the trip to the top of the Peaks. At first, he didn't know what to make of the man's actions. He had known the former soldier for quite some time, and he was a man of conviction who had rededicated himself from an instrument of death to an instrument of peace. When the former soldier returned from his meditation, Logan had asked him what he was doing. The man said simply that he was trying to align the weaknesses of the man that he was with the strengths of the man that he was trying to be. Over the weeks and months that followed, more of the original members of the Order would make the journey to the top of the Peaks of Patience to find that alignment between the past and the present. The practice would soon become tradition, the tradition would become dogma, and what began as a man trying to find himself upon the seas of uncertainty would become the path by which others would leave that uncertainty behind to embrace a new life.

But in times of uncertainty, Logan reverted to form. He would find solitude in a place where he could not be disturbed and try to find a path forward. Now, not unlike many of the times that led him to the top of the Peaks of Patience, Logan needed to reconcile many disparate voices in his head, and many different conflicts in his heart. The Peaks of Patience may have been gone, but there were other places in Cadaria where the troubled mind could find peace. In the Kingdom of Ice, Rashaleb, there was a mountain known as the Needle of Heaven. It was the highest peak in the whole of Cadaria and was considered to be unscalable by human means. Some of the rock faces of the peak itself were nearly vertical, some even formed inverted angles that defied logic. Add to that the fact that the composition of the peak was predominantly snow, ice, and impregnable rock; inhospitable barely began to describe the nature of the Needle of Heaven. To Logan Ranthall however, none of those obstacles were of any concern. Even the whipping wind and the thin air were nothing more than momentary annoyances as Logan sat at the very tip of the Needle of Heaven, his feet dangling out into the nothingness. The wind whipped, frost and snow were cast about around him, but Logan payed none of it any mind. He was at peace, and he could now focus on doing the work that needed to be done so that he could move forward. And there was much to consider.

From the moment that Rhain told Logan about Jillian and her role in what was coming, his stomach was in knots, and his heart felt as though it was in his throat. Rhain had been able to put the pieces together from information that had been gathered by Saurn, Jeroch, Bryn, and had been relayed by Logan himself. Once the mystery of Jillian's parentage became clear, the rest of was matter of fitting the right pieces in the right places. Not only that, Jerah, through her rescue of Logan and Bryn, had provided some missing pieces. Even though Jerah had been cut off from the Brotherhood of Phasia because of the influence of Dorovar and the Chorus of Souls, Jerah had imparted a skeleton key of sorts into the Chorus when she healed Logan. Thus, Rhain was able to nibble around the edges of Dorovar's knowledge to find some information about what Dorovar needed with Jillian and why she was so important to what was coming. All of the information proved too much for Logan, and instead of staying to work through the knowledge with Rhain, Logan had immediately created a portal and brought himself to the one place left in the world that he could think.

Logan wasn't sure how long he sat, his mind turning over all of the things that had happened over the past few days. It seemed like several lifetimes had been squeezed into the space of two weeks, and there was still so much more ahead. There was a feeling that an ending was coming. Whether it was The end or just an end was still in doubt, but what actions that Logan and others would take in the next few hours and days would have a great deal of influence upon those eventualities. Soon though, Logan realized that he was thinking through the same paths over and over again without making progress. He was stuck, and there was only one way that he could get unstuck.

Clearing his mind, Logan let his thoughts float beyond his physical self. Many hours Logan and Kamen would sit together, exploring the capabilities of the Blaze, learning the bounds of the physical world. Alone, Logan would continue those explorations, finding how the powers of Aerith Seth could work with the Blaze to expand into the realm of the unseen. When he was a boy on Onea, Logan's father would tell him stories about the Other Side, when he would ask where his mother had gone. Arin Ranthall would tell his son that his mother's soul was in a place called the Other Side, a place where the forces of the Light still struggled against the forces of the Shadow in an attempt to protect the world of the living. As childhood stories went, it was comforting. However, after Emries' betrayal, and Logan began to learn more about the nature of the conflict between the Children of the Creator, the truth about the Other Side gnawed at his mind more and more. Logan knew that the Other Side existed, he had seen evidence of it when an army of the dead came to protect Logan and his companions during their journey to Marcwell. But the reality of the place's existence and the truth of its nature were not the same. So, once Logan had begun to explore his powers, he made it his mission to uncover the truth of the Other Side.

It took a great deal of time and effort before Logan finally made contact, and what was waiting for him was not what he had expected at all. The first person that returned his attempts at contact was his mother Victoria. What she told him made his soul ache. The Other Side was not a place where the forces of Light were fighting the good fight against the forces of the Shadow. Instead, it was a prison where the souls of those who were useful to the Children of the Creator and the Creator Himself were kept in case of future usefulness. It was a pocket of reality between the living world and the nothingness beyond, very much like the place that Bryn had discovered adjacent to the Heavens where the being known as Liette was imprisoned. The more Logan learned about the Creator, the more he disliked the divine dictator. The Creator seemed fascinated by prisons. Whether it was the Other Side, or the Tomb, or even the Vault of Terror. These were places that potentially useful things were tucked away, saved ostensibly for eternity. In the Tomb, Liette and other creatures like her presumably waited until the Creator deemed that their purpose was required once more. The Vault of Terrors was designed to lock away dangerous things, but perhaps it was also a place where those dangerous things could be used to make other dangerous things, like Dorovar, even more dangerous. And then there was the Other Side. This was not just a waiting area where the souls of those useful to the Creator and the Children were kept. It was also an active warzone where potential conflicts played out on a daily basis. The Other Side was a place where beings from different worlds who never could have met would be forced into conflict with one another. The ideological war was fought in this place too, perhaps more brutally than it was fought in the world of the living.

Over the many years, Logan became more adept at communicating with the Other Side. It required complete concentration, and he could only hold the connection for a short amount of time, but each of those conversations proved both fruitful and comforting. What was disconcerting, at least until Logan met Marlae Tamerlane, was the fact that he had not been able to find Elwyne on the Other Side. He had not been able to find Cairyn either, but now that he knew she was alive on Espre, that made sense too. Now, as Logan concentrated and extended his mind into the place where the souls of the lost fought endlessly at the whim of the Creator, he looked for one that he knew would be there. After only a matter of moments, the person that he sought appeared in the mists before him, and Logan was struck by how much easier it was to make the connection this time.

"Your habits have changed little, Phoenix."

Kamen's hulking figure was no less imposing even mostly insubstantial. But in the years that Logan spent with the gentle giant, he would never be afraid of the man who had become even more of a brother than Logan's own brother. There was no better council, no more contemplative mind, and no deeper feeling creature that Logan knew than Kamen.

"I still find no better place to think than these quiet places, Kamen. So you'll have to forgive me a little predictability."

Kamen's expression remained impassive.

"Perhaps if the places you chose to find your solace were more accessible to those of my size, there would be less apprehension in my heart, Phoenix."

Logan could not suppress his laugh. Many times Logan had tried in vain to convince Kamen to join him at the heights of the Peak of Patience. Kamen's resistance came in the form of questioning whether or not there were suitable places for him to sit comfortably.

"What troubles your mind, Phoenix?" Kamen asked finally.

Logan stayed silent for a long moment before speaking.

"The pieces are starting to fall into place, finally, Kamen, and it seems like the Creator has gotten what he wanted. Tess has been turned into a weapon that will be used to unmake the world, and the only way to stop her may damn us all and cost a good woman her life. I don't know what I'm supposed to do. I'm so tired of watching my friends die."

Kamen considered very briefly before speaking.

"Death is an inevitable consequence of this war. As we have spoken about on many occasions, brother, there is a difference between senseless death and purposeful death. To our minds, the crimes and sacrifices perpetrated by the Creator and the Children are senseless deaths. However, from their perspective, these deaths are purposeful, at least if you believe their words and their actions. But what purpose can the death of the entirety of reality serve? Is the mere process of starting over enough? Would the Creator truly learn from this reality's demise, or would he make the same mistakes in the next one? Perhaps it is only the deaths and sacrifices that we do not learn from that we should truly concern ourselves with."

Logan frowned.

"That's not what I wanted to hear."

Kamen demurred.

"Of course not. You came here hoping to find an answer you could live with, Phoenix. But first, as you taught me all those years ago when you found me wandering in the wilderness, you must accept that there are no answers that you can live with, but there are answers you can survive."

Logan smiled.

"It's very irritating when you quote me to me."

Another voice added itself to the conversation the next moment.

"It's only irritating Logan, because you know he's right."

Rael appeared beside Kamen, looking incredibly small next to their massive brother.

"It still doesn't tell me what to do."

The third voice was not unexpected.

"Your issue is not that you do not know what to do, Logan, it is simply that you are trying to live with doing it."

Trece appeared next to Rael, and Logan found himself looking at the three other pieces of his shared soul. He would never be able to reconcile the sacrifice that they had made for him. The only thing he could do was try to make the best decisions so that their sacrifice was not made in vain.

"And so, Phoenix," Kamen said finally, "what must you do that you do not believe you can live with?"

Logan frowned.

"Raenera understood what was coming. In her way, she perhaps even more than Halicon saw the direction that the war between the Children was going. The death of Pyrrus was the last straw. She had stood by and watched as Loinn was torn apart by the dragons and Talisia and Emries, and while that failure stung her, it was watching as her beloved brother was cut down while the Creator did nothing that set her course.

"In the final moments of Loinn's destruction, Raenera commanded her High Priestess to sacrifice herself in an effort to remain pure. We know this from Jerah. In the same way that Talisia harvested the souls of Dorovar's fellows and had them placed into the Sacred Weapons on this world, Raenera took the soul of the High Priestess and fused it into a receptacle on this world. Dorovar has been hunting relentlessly for that soul, thinking it is the key to merging all of the Children's powers together and giving him what he needs to defeat the Creator. But in the same way that Raenera intended to use the High Priestess's soul to undo Talisia's schemes, she had crafted a way to use the Creator's own power against him. Rhain believes that Raenera found Liette in the Tomb and learned of her connection to the mortals of Espre. The Creator in an effort to exert direct control over the direction of this world had fused a small sliver of the Spirit into the bloodline of the first Empress of Cadaria, thus creating the Seers. As the Creator needed to exert more control, Seers became more powerful, and when the Creator sensed it was time to bring all of this to an end, he crystallized as much of the Seers' power as he could into the body of Jehna Feris, the so-called Dark Seer. This was the thing that Raenera had been waiting for. She appeared to Jehna Feris, co-opted her body, infused some of her own power into the woman and set out to seduce the one man whose power would create the very thing she wished to create. Jehna and Cedric's offspring became Jillian Corven, a living combination of divine power, the power of two of the Children of the Creator, the soul of the High Priestess of Raenera, as well as the blood of Aerith Seth."

Rael nodded along with Logan's explanation.

"And she is the one who is to defeat the Dragon's Tear?"

Logan shook his head.

"No, you don't understand. Jillian is the Dragon's Tear."

The shocked expression on Trece's face was mirrored by the other two former members of the phasia.

"Then what is Tess Annis?"

Logan shook his head.

"The best I can understand it, she's incomplete. She's an experiment, but one that's completely unstable. I know that everyone believes that Tess is Raenera's child with Pike, but that isn't the case. Talisia created Tess with the help of Emries and Pike's easily manipulated desires. Emries knew that Pike could be tempted and driven exactly where they needed him to be. So, he found his way into Talisia's grasp. The woman who gave birth to Tess was also gifted with the bloodline of a Seer, but her powers had not yet emerged. It was diluted and imperfect. It seems that Talisia and Emries imparted too much of their own powers into the woman, and so the balance in Tess is off. Of course she can do some terrifying things because of her connection to the divine, but just like the powers of the Children are going to burn through their mortal hosts, the divine power is going to rip Tess apart eventually with disastrous consequences because she doesn't have Aerith's blood to hold her together. And when she over-exerts, or when she is finally brought down, all of that untapped power that is growing inside of her will be released, explosively."

Kamen's tone was concerned, but reserved.

"How explosively?"

Logan grimaced.

"It will make what happened to Loinn look like a campfire."

"Then what must you do, Phoenix?"

The ache inside Logan intensified. If he were to say the words that were in his mind, it would make them real. He knew what Rhain wanted him to do. He knew what he needed to do. And perhaps Jerah had known what he needed to do as well. Everything seemed to be leading him to the next confrontation. The next point of conflict. The next sacrifice for the greater good. But now, as much as he didn't want to admit it, perhaps his allies had sacrificed themselves so that he could be able to sacrifice himself another day.

"Talisia discovered a way to make weapons that would steal the powers of others. Thanks to Wolf and thanks to Jerah, now Rhain knows how to do it. She intends to keep that information pretty quiet, but she has basically told me how to do it. Right now, I have that information segregated from Aerith. I don't want him to know how to do this yet. I'm a little concerned what he would do with the knowledge."

Trece cocked her head.

"Strange words coming from his most trusted ally."

Logan smiled.

"I'm his most trusted ally because I know he can't be trusted with certain information. Aerith would want to use the information for what he would consider the greater good. There are times though when Aerith can mistake expediency for good. There will be a time when Aerith will need to know how to do this, or maybe one of the other trusted members of his inner circle. But for now, it needs to stay with me and me alone. And I'm going to need every bit of the knowledge that I've gained from every source if I'm going to kill Tess."

Kamen folded his arms over his chest, an uncharacteristic posture for the giant.

"Phoenix," he started slowly, "I have a great deal of respect for what you have accomplished. Your single-mindedness and tendency for self-sacrifice have been hallmarks of your ability to succeed where others would have failed. Whether it was your transcendence into a member of the phasia through my powers, or it was your fight against the creature Death, or your former ally in the guise of Conquest, you were willing to die if it meant victory. However, in those moments you believed that what you were doing was necessary. I do not feel that same conviction within you now."

"And if you aren't convinced that you will succeed," Rael continued, "then you will fail."

Logan remained silent for several moments before reaching into his pocket and pulling out the gift that Rhain had given him before he fled her presence to find the answers he needed. It had been the thing that Aerith had given Sabrina in an effort to save her life. It was the mask of the Wrath, and Logan knew that if he used it properly, he could contain Tess's power within himself and survive long enough to do what needed to be done.

"My concern isn't Tess," he said finally. "Even if she nearly kills me in the attempt, I'm pretty sure that I'll be able to steal her powers before she finishes the job. It's what comes after that I'm unsure about. Rhain doesn't know what to do next, and I don't either. What happens if I let Jillian plunge a power-stealing dagger into my heart and complete the powers of the Dragon's Tear? Does that mean the Creator wins? What if I kill Jillian and take the powers of the Dragon's Tear for myself? Then what? Do I just let the power destroy me? Do I let one of the others eliminate me? Do I use the power to destroy the Creator? What does it look like after the two pieces are together? And am I really ready to sacrifice Jillian or myself if I don't know what happens after?"

Logan fell silent for a moment and was about to continue when he felt a presence growing beneath him. Moments later a form broke through the clouds and the mist, a massive form that blocked out the light of the suns when it fully revealed itself. The dragon looked like a patchwork of multiple creatures sewn together. Its long serpent-like neck and tail were brilliant gold with purple bands that circled at uneven intervals. The dragon's legs too were gold, but with a larger amount of purple splattered across them, like the uncaring application of paint. But the creature's body and wings were all a dark mottled green that seemed to suck in the light. Down the length of the neck, the creatures back, and tail were long black feather-looking protrusions which whipped around in the breeze and seemed to help the dragon keep its balance amid the gusts of wind. The head of the dragon appeared to be made completely of bone with no scale or skin stretched across it. The faded yellow bone was studded with sharp spikey protrusions that gleams with razor-sharp edges. Unlike other dragons whose appearances lived in Logan's memories, the shape of this creature's head was more bird-like, far more compact with a shortened snout that looked more like a beak. Long matte black talons emerged from each claw, as well as from the tip of each wing. Effortlessly the dragon hovered in front of Logan. Locking its dark blue eyes on the human, the dragon spoke. Its voice was akin to the sound of hard-falling rain.

"You serve the Heretic. You are the Logan."

Logan wasn't sure from the intonation of the words whether the dragon was making a statement or asking a question.

"I am Logan."

The dragon hissed in response.

"Shadowweaver say you die. You die."

CHAPTER 116

Chapter CXVII

Spirit's Fading Light

Year Two of the Divine Empress and Child of the Creator Marlae Tamerlane, Creator's Calendar Year 1872

Hannah's mouth went dry. The situation had clearly become untenable, and regardless of how she chose to proceed, the chances of what could be called a success were practically non-existent. If she tried to attack the man in the dark armor, he could snap Kiara's neck and evade Hannah's attack before Hannah could get close. If Hannah turned her attention back to the woman who called her Redissa, Kiara would be sacrificed. Yes, Hannah could clearly outfight Redissa, but that would matter little if the act would put Kiara's life in danger. Not that it was truly an option, but Hannah could not run either because it would also sacrifice Kiara. There seemed to be only one clear course of action, and even that had no guarantee of saving Kiara's life. Regardless of the slim chance of success, Hannah knew what had to be done.

Hannah put her hands up for a moment, letting the twin crystalline blades disappear. A moment later, she let one hand fall to where Spirit hung at her side.

"I will surrender Spirit, but I have to be guaranteed of Kiara's safety before you may take the weapon from me."

The man in black armor stared back blankly at Hannah. The wind lifted his hair away from his armored shoulders and his blue eyes were a whirling turbulent storm of barely contained rage. The man's eyes shifted for a moment in Redissa's direction and then settled back on Hannah.

"Place the Sacred Weapon on the ground and then step away. Once I am convinced you do intend to relinquish the weapon, I will release the girl."

Hannah considered for a moment and then formulated a plan. She withdrew Spirit from where it hung on her belt and then held it in both of her hands for several moments before bending at the knees and lowering herself to the ground. Her eyes continued to move between Redissa and the man clad in black armor, not content that the warriors would not attempt some type of ambush while she was in a poorly defensible position. After a moment, when neither member of the Adhradair made a move, Hannah let the Sacred Weapon fall from her grasp and lay upon the muddy and still-bloody ground. Again, very slowly and deliberately Hannah rose back to her feet. Neither Redissa nor the man in black let their eyes leave the former Knight of the Flashing Blade, and once Hannah was back to her feet, the man in black armor pointed at Hannah.

"Back."

Hannah nodded and took three large steps backwards. She knew that with her increased reflexes and agility she was still well within range to recover the weapon before either member of the Adhradair. Now was the moment of truth. Would the Adhradair call her bluff, or would they make good on their promise to release Kiara. Either way, Hannah was ready for what would come next, and had gathered her power slowly to ensure that the phantoms did not feel what was coming until it was too late. The man in black armor relaxed his grip on Kiara's neck. In her own mocking manner, still feeling Aerith's thoughts at the edge of her mind, Hannah pointed her finger in the direction of the man in black armor.

"Back."

A sneer came to the lips of the man in black, and he took one step backwards. It was not a large step, and truthfully a lunge forward would allow him to reacquire his hold on Kiara. But Hannah did not intend to give him the chance for that to happen. The next three actions came nearly simultaneously, but it taxed Hannah considerably to use that much power in that short of an amount of time. She was learning more about the powers at her disposal, but she was still not practiced. If anything, she worried that attempting such a complex application of power might endanger both herself and Kiara. But again, Hannah comforted herself with the thought that it was the only way.

Hannah let a burst of wind travel the distance between herself and the man in black armor the moment before he had completed his backwards step. The wind served two purposes, the first was to push the man further away from Kiara and the second was to maneuver Kiara into the position that Hannah needed her in. Kiara was pushed a foot further away from the man in black armor, and the moment that her momentum stopped, the portal appeared beneath her feet. With the complex application of power that Hannah was attempting, she could not send Kiara far, so the other end of the portal opened in the building where the acolytes of the Academy of Arcane Arts had taken refuge only minutes before. If she had been more practiced with her powers, she could have perhaps sent Kiara all the way to the Heart of Stone, but for now this would have to do. The next application of power required the most control out of all three. A burst of wind while partially focused did not require much thought or control. The portal required more control, but again not a considerable amount because she was sending Kiara to a place close by that she knew the layout off. There was no chance of the portal opening several feet into the floor or in the middle of a stone wall. The third application of power, also a portal, had to be precise and exact for two reasons. The first of which was that the destination of the portal was an exact location with no margin of error. Second was the fact that Hannah was attempting to move the Sacred Weapon through a portal. She had never tried that before, and she didn't know how the powerful item would react to such a tactic. But the portal opened underneath Spirit, the mace dropped through, and when the other portal appeared above Hannah's outstretched hand, the Sacred Weapon dropped through right into her grasp. Hannah brought the impressive War Mace into a familiar defensive stance, feeling its power running through her once again. For the first time in a long time, Hannah could feel the connection to Spirit. The Sacred Weapon hummed in her hand, and Hannah could almost feel the approval rolling from it.

"Coward!"

The man in black armor's voice rolled like thunder through the still air. He started to charge at Hannah but Redissa's voice restrained him.

"Haricos! Enough."

Haricos stopped in his tracks, but it did not stop him from letting a blade composed of the phantasmal energy of the Chorus of Souls appear in his right hand. Redissa pointed at Hannah with the tip of her sword.

"Impressive, Hannah, but it will avail you nothing. By refusing to surrender Spirit willingly, you have left us no choice but to destroy you."

Hannah set her feet and waited for the attack to come. With Spirit held firmly in one hand, Hannah let a crystalline blade form in the other. She held the weapon blade down, letting the flat of the blade rest against her forearm. The blade that she created was slightly longer than a dagger but would barely be considered a short sword. She intended to use it more as a shield than a weapon, a tactic that would give her more options. Options when you were outnumbered were your best friends. Even with Aerith's studies of fighting with two weapons, the odds were not even. Aerith had become accustomed to being the strongest warrior on the field, and as such he could confidently take on two or three opponents at once. However what Aerith was not adept at was taking on multiple opponents who could wield the type of abilities that the erstwhile members of the Adhradair could.

Haricos was the first one to charge, the blade of phantasmal green power lashing out fast and precise. The strike was meant to cleave Hannah's head from her body, but Hannah was up to the task, blocking the blow with the long dagger, and then swinging around the head of Spirit as hard as she could. The strike caught Haricos on the shoulder, shattering the plate of armor there and exposing the pale skin beneath. The strike didn't break his skin, but the force of the blow caused him to stagger back for a moment. However, rather than press her advantage, Hannah turned her attention to Redissa who was starting her charge. However, instead of coming straight in, Redissa stopped several feet away and let more tendrils of the power of the Chorus of Souls lance out. Hannah caught the tendrils on the haft of Spirit and threw the long dagger in Redissa's direction. Redissa tried to get her blade up to deflect the incoming attack, and was able to push the flight of the dagger far enough off course that it glanced off the shoulder of her armor. But Hannah's attack had not been intended to cause damage, it had only been a delaying tactic. From her off hand came a stream of water that further soaked the soil underneath Redissa's feet. Redissa's heavy armored feet sunk into the mud, and though it wouldn't have delayed the woman for long, it did give Hannah a few seconds to concentrate on Haricos. The large man had recovered from the break to his armor, and dashed in again with his sword raised. This time instead of attempting to block the strike, Hannah sidestepped, and then brought the head of Spirit down on Haricos's arm. Again, the armor shattered beneath the strength of the otherworldly weapon, but this time instead of sparing the flesh beneath, the attack broke the skin, drew blood, and shattered the bones in Haricos' arm.

Once the blood touched the head of the Sacred Weapon, a green glow erupted from the center of the weapon. The glow covered the surface of the weapon, and there was a shudder that ran through Hannah's body. She was trying her best to keep hold of the haft of the weapon, but as the seconds passed, it grew more and more difficult. After a moment, the war mace developed a crack that bisected the head. A wail came from the Chorus of Souls and a secondary wail came from somewhere inside of the Sacred Weapon. It took several moments, but the two wails began to harmonize. When they became as one, the weapon shattered with a brilliant flash of light and a wave of power that sent both Hannah and Haricos flying. Redissa was forced to a knee despite her distance from the explosion. Once the light from the explosion had dissipated and her ears had stopped ringing, Hannah got back to her feet and was greeted by the sight of a new person in the clearing.

The woman standing where Spirit exploded was slight of build and perhaps only about five feet in height. When she turned to face Hannah, the former High Priestess wondered if perhaps calling her a woman was being generous. Her features were of a girl on the edge of womanhood; soft, clean, and delicate. Long dark hair cascaded around her face and her dark eyes flashed with a wisdom that belied her physical age. She was dressed simply, more like a farmer than a warrior, but on her back was strapped a sword that was easily as tall as she was. How the girl would have had enough strength to wield a blade that size was beyond explanation. She locked eyes with Hannah for only a moment, the expression on her face devoid of all emotion. She then turned to face first Haricos and then Redissa. By this time Redissa had gotten back to her feet.

"Ninian! Sister, you are free!"

Ninian nodded in Redissa's direction.

"You have accomplished your task, Redissa," the girl's young voice answered. "Return with Haricos to Dorovar, and I shall follow you. I am eager to see our friends once more."

Haricos, who had also returned to his feet snarled.

"First we will finish this troublesome woman. Against the three of us, she stands no chance of survival."

Ninian turned, and Hannah could see the slight frown turn the girl's lips.

"No, Haricos. You have succeeded in your task, I am free. There is no need to continue your assault on this woman."

Haricos took a step forward, and raised his sword.

"This woman has insulted the Adhradair, stood in opposition of our will, and has allied herself with our sworn enemies. She does not deserve the mercy you are so quick to show her. This is the woman who has been your jailer for years, do you not wish to exact a measure of revenge against one who used you in the service of the false Creator and his perverted agenda?"

Ninian put her hands on her hips and looked more like a petulant teenager than a member of the group who was responsible for protecting a world.

"She was not my jailer, Haricos, and any ill will I might hold for her is tempered by the knowledge that during her time in possession of the Sacred Weapon, her only intention was to do good. Do you remember what that felt like Haricos? Do you remember what it felt like to live by a code and do what you could for the betterment of your people?"

Redissa freed herself from the mud that Hannah had trapped her in and approached slowly, her weapon still clutched in her hand.

"You always were naïve, Ninian," Redissa cooed. "This is not our world, and these people do not value life the way that we do. They are quick to war on one another, prey on one another, and exploit one another for their own personal gain. They do not understand the beauty of the Perfect Order that we presided over on Loinn. These people are not worth your pity or your love. They are all the enemy, and they will all be wiped away by Dorovar's ambition."

Ninian's head turned back to regard Redissa, and then she slightly shook her head and spoke.

"I was not one of you, Redissa. I was not one of you who spent your time in the cities and in the Grand Temple or the Tower of the Goddess. Like Luighsech and Zaraven I was out amongst the people. Zaraven tended to the creatures of the wilderness, Luighsech tended to the wilderness itself, and I made sure that the people lived in harmony with nature and ethically and intelligently maintained their farms and the food that they produced for the people of our world. But I was the youngest of the Adhradair, the youngest by far. And perhaps because I had not spent as much time in the Perfect Order, I have a different view on it than you do. I do not see the necessity to kill, and I certainly don't see why we should kill to further ambition. Does not the Perfect Order teach the darkness of ambition? Does not the Perfect Order warn us of the danger of putting ourselves ahead of the needs of the collective?"

Haricos' voice was filled with irritation.

"You are not a priestess. You were not taught the way that Redissa, or Seisyll, or the High Priestess were taught. It is not your place to interpret the scriptures to one who learned at the foot of the High Priestess and was educated by the words of the goddess."

Redissa continued.

"The Perfect Order taught that it must prevail. Beyond the will of the people, beyond the generations, beyond even the life of the world that we called home. There can only be the Perfect Order. That is Dorovar's only ambition, and in the absence of the High Priestess, Dorovar is our leader. He is the one that kept the faith when the rest of us fell. Even you, Ninian. You were eager to take Talisia's offering of power to take the fight to the dragons. Your thirst for blood was as out of control as ours. And as far as the collective, the people of Loinn are gone. The only collective that remains is the Adhradair. Your allegiance is to that body, Ninian, and to none other. We are the Perfect Order, and we shall see it reborn from the ashes of the Creator's design."

Haricos advanced a pace.

"Now, prove your fealty to the Adhradair and end this woman."

Ninian turned to face Hannah. For the first time Hannah took in the few pieces of armor that the woman wore over her common clothing. Over her simple shirt she wore a vest of what looked like dragon scale. On one shoulder was the upper jaw of a dragon's head, complete with its snout and eyes and upper skull. The eyes had been replaced with small jewels that must have been rubies or a similar red precious stone. Dragon scale covered grieves guarded both shins, and similar bracers protected her forearms. Apparently, the young woman had been quite adept at hunting dragons on her world, and Hannah immediately understood that this woman was not one to be trifled with.

"My fealty is not something that needs to be proven, Haricos," Ninian answered coldly.

The woman reached back over her shoulder and withdrew the massive blade from the sheathe on her back. It would have been impossible for her to wield it with one hand, and it appeared that the blade was designed more to be wielded from horseback. The final third of the blade was wider than the other two-thirds, making it unwieldy on foot, but on horseback it would be a perfect weapon to strike down troops or any other creature. Hannah imagined Ninian on the back of a horse charging toward a dragon and letting her massive blade slice through the dragon's armor as though it were paper. With the powers granted by Talisia, it's something that she could have easily done.

"I fought against the dragons just like you did Haricos. But I was defending our people. You were trying to get revenge for some slight that you did not even understand. That is what you and the others from the temple forgot at the end. You forgot the people. You forgot our world. All you cared about was the killing. You needed to kill dragons. You needed to redeem yourselves for your failures. But in the end you couldn't, could you?"

Redissa took another step closer, the frustration beginning to show on her face.

"It's not that simple, Ninian. The dragons invaded our world. They started indiscriminately killing our people. They would not listen to reason. We had to strike back."

Ninian lifted the impossibly large blade and pointed it at Redissa.

"You are the one who doesn't understand, Redissa. You weren't there. You didn't see the fear in the eyes of the farmers every day as the dragons encroached closed and closer in on their lands. The farmers feared for their livestock. They feared for their families. It was only out of fear that the first farmer struck at the dragon. He didn't mean to kill it, he only meant to drive it off. But what happened next was not the fault of the farmer, or even the dragons. It was your fault. Your fault and the fault of the other members of the Adhradair who made no attempt to follow the tenants of the Perfect Order. Did you send Drust to try to work out a truce with the dragon? Did you send Seisyll to speak on behalf of the High Priestess? No. You sent Zaraven. And you all knew what Zaraven would do. He saw the dragons as just another predator that he need to control. So all he did was inflame the situation by hunting more dragons and mounting the losses on both sides. The Grand Temple abandoned the people. And now you want me to abandon their memory by blindly following Dorovar's will."

Ninian brought the sword back to her body, wrapping the other hand around the hilt.

"I can't do that."

Hannah by this time had made her way to her feet, and with a gentle nod from Ninian, Hannah let two crystalline swords form in her hands. Hannah faced Haricos. Despite the damage that she had done to his arm, he was still clearly the most able warrior of the two. Ninian could deal with Redissa. The betrayal proved to be too much for Haricos, and he was the first to charge in. Hannah counter-charged, hoping to protect Ninian's flank as well as cut off Haricos' angles of attack. It was clear that Haricos was not ready for Hannah's tactic, and he stopped short, slashing hard at Hannah's chest. However, the angle was odd, and Hannah was able to sidestep the blow. This time when Hannah brought her weapon down, the blade of her sword bit into Haricos' exposed flesh. Though he had spent the time of his tete-a-tete with Ninian knitting the bones in his arm, it did nothing to mend his arm. Hannah would make sure he didn't get a second chance. The crystalline blade passed clean through flesh and bone, severing Haricos' left arm at the mid-point of the forearm. The hand dropped to the ground, the sword disappearing instantly. There was a wail from the Chorus of Souls, and Haricos continued his charge undeterred. Another sword appeared in his right hand, and he ducked in bringing a slash across Hannah's chest. Hannah was too close to attempt to block or parry the attack, and as she sidestepped, she realized she wasn't going to be fast enough. And while a normal weapon would have simply scraped across the chest plate of her armor, this weapon, formed purely of the energy of the Chorus of Souls, passed through the metal and cut a deep furrow across her diaphragm. Fortunately, the back step at the last moment had prevented the strike from penetrating farther and damaging her internal organs, but she could feel a torrent of hot blood flowing down her stomach. Hannah didn't have time to waste on healing the wound, so she shut out the pain and focused on ending the battle quickly. The next two strikes were hard, precise, and impossible to defend against. The first slash of her right hand blade feinted high and then moved low. Haricos was in the wrong position to block, and the blade chopped at the inside of his right knee, shattering the armor there and crippling him. The sudden loss of balance caused Haricos to pitch forward. Hannah spun under the wild slash meant as a counterattack and then brought her left hand blade up and then down as hard as she could manage. Her aim was true and the blade caught Haricos on the back of the neck, taking his head clean from his body.

Ninian did not waste the opportunity afforded to her and charged Redissa. She used her massive sword more like a spear, running forward with the tip of the blade pointed at Redissa's heart. Redissa brought her own blade down in an attempt to parry the blow, but was unprepared for the strength of her slight opponent. Though the blade was discouraged from plunging into her heart, it was only pushed down and away, slicing through the armor at her hip and drawing a massive font of blood spurting in all directions. Ninian continued her charge, burying her shoulder into the flank of the larger woman attempting to take her off her feet. Unfortunately, the tactic failed, and Ninian found herself drawn too close to Redissa. The larger woman slammed the butt of her sword into Ninian's chest, attempting to knock the wind out of her, and then continued the strike upward, the haft striking squarely under Ninian's chin, shattering it. The smaller woman fell back, releasing the hilt of her sword and letting it fall to the ground. Blood poured from her mouth along with broken teeth. But Ninian was not out of the fight. With a single thought she pulled upon the Chorus of Souls and summoned her massive blade back to her hands. Redissa seemed completely unprepared for the tactic, and by the time she knew what had happened, Ninian charged forward again. This time Redissa was unable to redirect the strike and the tip of the blade struck true at Redissa's left shoulder, where the arm met the torso. The massive head of the blade ripped through the connective tissue there, shearing Redissa's arm off at the shoulder. Again, Redissa was equal to the pain that wracked her body, dropping her sword from her right hand, grabbing Ninian by the back of her neck and bringing her armored knee and shin up into the stomach of the smaller woman. Ribs cracked under the force of the blow, and more blood was forced from Ninian's mouth. Another hard knee strike shattered more ribs and punctured internal organs. Redissa pulled Ninian back by the back of her neck, releasing the hold for only a moment so that she could grab her slight opponent by the throat. Redissa pulled Ninian close so that she could look the woman in the eye as she squeezed Ninian's throat shut. Even as Ninian heard the cartilage in her throat crack and pop under the strain and her vision begin to darken, she summoned the last bit of power that she could manage to create twin daggers. The first dagger came up cutting the underside of Redissa's wrist, freeing Ninian from her former ally's grasp, while the other dagger plunged deep into Redissa's neck, severing the vital structures there. Redissa was dead before she hit the ground, and though Ninian had won the battle she knew that she was not far behind her former ally in meeting death. The Chorus of Souls had abandoned her, and as the seconds passed, she could feel herself beginning to fade. It was just as her vision began to fail that Hannah Ironheart appeared at the smaller woman's side. Ninian tried to force a smile but with her jaw shattered, she was sure that the gesture looked horrifying. She wanted to speak, she wanted so much to impart knowledge to Hannah about Dorovar. But there was no time. Ninian clutched Hannah's hand and focused all of her power to communicate one thought.

Thank you for saving me.

Relations

Year One of the Just Empress Quyhn Ravenheart Lorien, Cadarian Calendar Year 1872

Gwydeon stood in stunned silence, barely cognoscente enough to pull back his wings and let the blade disappear from his hand. His wife proved to be much faster, sprinting across the room and wrapping their daughter in a tight embrace before the last words had left the young woman's mouth. Gwydeon finally approached the mother and daughter after a few moments and wrapped his arms around both of them. It was only a matter of moments before both Mirana and Liara were in the doorway, and when Gwydeon saw them, he stepped away from Midarin and Camille, and let the two girls rush into the room. Midarin pulled away from her daughter and the girls quickly took her place. The three divine children held their embrace for a long time, and then when both pulled back they had tears in their eyes. They both had so many questions, but restrained all of them, not wanting to completely intrude on the moment. Camille understood the sentiment all too well.

"We can talk in the morning," Camille said finally. "We have a lot to talk about."

The girls both nodded and each hugged both Midarin and Gwydeon before returning to their room down the hall. Camille looked first at her parents and then to the shattered window.

"Sorry about that."

Gwydeon laughed.

"Only my daughter would crash through a window to save her parents from an assassin and then apologize for breaking a pane or two of glass."

Midarin pulled her daughter by the elbow away from the broken glass on the floor to the other side of the bed. The two sat on the edge of the wooden frame while Gwydeon leaned against the wall with his arms crossed. Midarin leaned against the footboard of the bed so that she could face Camille, while Camille tried to keep herself angled so that she could shift her gaze between both her parents without having to turn her head. There was silence that held between the three for several moments. Neither Gwydeon nor Midarin wanted to press Camille for information. Of course, when Camille started to speak, her first words were clearly influenced by who her parents were.

"Not even a day in your new palace and you've already got assassins after you?"

Gwydeon smiled and nodded.

"I took that sword off of an assassin who was trying to murder Feyd and Felicia Lorien. That was before we got to Celidar. Seems like a hundred years ago now, but we really haven't had a moment's peace since then. However that blade was enchanted, it waited for the perfect moment to strike. Those Shadow Guild agents are a lot more resourceful than I gave them credit for. I'm sure that girl with the claws that I fought is still out there somewhere too."

Midarin couldn't resist the opportunity.

"Does every woman who meets you try to kill you?"

Gwydeon's cheeks colored.

"More than I like to think about."

Both Midarin and Camille laughed at the comment, and the silence descended again. Only this time when Camille spoke, the words were far more serious.

"I know you were probably worried with me disappearing like that, but it really wasn't my idea."

Gwydeon beat Midarin to a response.

"It wasn't your fault," he said as supportively as he could, "Mirana and Liara explained it to us. Aerith tried to warn us, and I didn't listen. I should have warned you. Maybe if I would have told you what Aerith told me…"

Gwydeon's voice trailed off, he wasn't sure where he was going with his words, wasn't even sure if what he was saying was making sense. In the end, would mere words have stopped the Creator from taking control of their daughter? Would mere words have kept Him from abducting Camille right under their noses? Moreover, if it had delayed the act, perhaps he would have sent the Spirit earlier. On the other hand, maybe he would have sent two or three of the Servants. Futility was never something that set well with Gwydeon. He had been fighting against it all his life. It was futile to challenge the phasia. It was futile to challenge Shau-ling. It was futile to challenge Emries. It was futile to challenge the Creator. All that had been around him for the majority of his life was futility. Nevertheless, that futility had saved many lives, at least in theory.

"Why does the Creator want you and the girls?"

Midarin's question was the most salient, and it also stopped Gwydeon from rambling on unnecessarily. Camille considered for a moment and then gave the best answer she could make her mind make sense of.

"The Servants aren't working. I'm not sure why, but they are limited somehow and not able to get done what the Creator wants done."

Gwydeon nodded.

"It does seem like Aerith and his friends are making sport of them. I don't know what happened to the Spirit, but we shouldn't have been able to defeat her so easily."

Midarin chimed in.

"And that's at least the third vessel that the Spirit has been in, that we know of."

Camille thought about the comments of her parents and tried to align her thoughts and the thoughts that were merged with her mind while under the control of the Creator.

"I could feel some of the Creator's thoughts in my mind, but it was hard to make sense of them. I guess a lot of it would be what you would call intention rather than thought. Or maybe intent is a better word. There was a need within the Creator to kill Cedric Binosear. That need was so all-encompassing that it crowded out everything. It was like this huge sponge in my head that drank in all of my thoughts and crowded out everything that wasn't what the Creator wanted me to do. I don't know exactly where I was, or what I was doing, all I know is that I was going to go kill Cedric Binosear, and that nothing else mattered but his death."

Midarin had multiple questions, and trading glances with Gwydeon, it was clear that he had questions too.

"I wish I understood why you," Midarin questioned. It must have been the nervous mother in her, but she could not get the thought to leave her mind no matter how she tried to justify it.

"I think Aerith put it best. The Creator sees any divine creature as His to use as he sees fit. So whatever fight is going on between the Creator, the Children, Aerith, and Dorovar has escalated to the point that the Creator feels he needs to use the weapons he has. And if the Creator sent you after Cedric Binosear, I can only see one intent. He's trying to hurt Aerith."

Midarin sighed.

"And we get caught in the middle yet again. Aerith with Logan, Emries with Korrd. Aerith with Sabrina, Emries with Nathaniel. And now it's wrapped itself around our daughter and tried to turn her into another puppet."

Gwydeon uncrossed his arms and motioned for Midarin to calm herself. Naturally this was a very emotional situation, and all of this brought up terrible memories of what happened to their son Nathaniel. Gwydeon took the opportunity to move from where he stood and knelt in front of his daughter. He took both of her hands in his and gave her his best comforting smile.

"How did you get away? Did you break the hold or did the Creator let you go? Will he come for you again?"

Camille smiled.

"I think I'm safe. In fact, I know I'm safe. But I'm also very tired. Can we finish this in the morning?"

Gwydeon laughed and nodded quickly.

"Of course, Camille, of course. There are several rooms in this wing, and they're all ours. I think the one next to the twins' room has a bedframe in it. I'm afraid we don't have much in the way of a mattress to offer. There should be another of the thick blankets on the bed itself. Hopefully that will get you through the night."

Camille nodded and Gwydeon helped her get back to her feet. They embraced once more, and just as Camille stepped back from Gwydeon, Midarin was there to wrap her arms around her daughter. Camille slowly pulled away from her mother and left her parents alone in their room. Midarin sat back on the edge of the bed and Gwydeon sat down beside her. Midarin kept staring out of the door to the suite in the direction that Camille had gone, her heart still racing. Gwydeon put his arm around Midarin and pulled her close.

"She's home," Gwydeon said before kissing her lightly on the cheek. "She's home."

Midarin surrendered to her husband's embrace, and the two sat together like that for a long time, just holding one another.

* * * * * * * * * * * * *

Midarin woke to the sounds of laughter in the hallway. She looked over to Gwydeon and saw that he was still sleeping, his arm draped over her. She moved his arm gently and slid off of the bed. After kissing Gwydeon lightly on the cheek, Midarin made her way into the hall in the direction of the laughter. It took only a moment to find the source. Mirana, Liara, Quyhn, and Camille were sitting on the large bed in Mirana and Liara's room, laughing. When Midarin appeared in the doorway Camille looked up.

"And so my dear, sweet, mother, who just got dumped onto the floor by this drunk solder ducks behind the bar, grabs the bow that she kept stashed there, and sends an arrow right between the guy's legs into the chair behind him."

The laughter continued, and Midarin immediately recognized the story. She stifled a smile and tried to give her best stern look.

"Lies, all lies."

Camille's eyebrows arched.

"Or maybe I could tell the story about the time…."

Midarin cut her off.

"Or maybe I could tell the story about how you used to amuse yourself by flying around naked when you were a little girl."

Camille's cheeks immediately flushed with scarlet.

"Alright, alright, you win."

Quyhn stood and smoothed her dress.

"I apologize, Midarin, I didn't mean to disturb your rest. After all you and your husband have done for us in the last few days, you deserve all the rest you can get."

"It's alright," Midarin responded quickly. "Sleep is a luxury, and we'll take what we can get when we can get it. Was there something you needed from us?"

Quyhn nodded.

"The soldiers that Rhionna and Gwydeon had assigned to patrol the border were approached by a small group of petitioners who wished to gain admittance for an audience. Before I met with them, I wanted to speak with you. Do you have a moment to speak in private?"

Midarin nodded and moved out of the doorway. Once Quyhn moved passed Midarin, the much older woman looked back into the room, frowned at her daughter, shook her head, and then followed Quyhn down the hall that eventually ended in a small landing under a wide window. Midarin sat on the windowsill and waited as Quyhn did the same. Quyhn folded her hands in her lap, and Midarin could tell that the woman was trying very hard not to fidget.

"How can I help you, Quyhn?"

"It is tradition in the Cadarian Empire for the reigning Emperor or Empress to have an advisor in diplomatic and courtly matters. With Dominique on her mission to the western kingdoms and Connor and Gabrielle dead, you are the only one that I know of with extensive courtly experience that I would trust to be my advisor."

Midarin started to answer, but Quyhn continued.

"Now if you don't want to do it because you don't want an official position in the government, I understand. It can be informal; it can be whatever you want."

Midarin held her tongue, moved by the urgency and concern in the young woman's voice.

"Honestly, Midarin, this scares me to death. I was never trained to be a diplomat or a leader. I was brought up well of course, I know how to behave at court, how to speak and not speak, but that's not the same as being an Empress. Gwydeon said that you were a princess and a queen, so you know what it's like to be in the halls of power, and you've run kingdoms before. I'm just asking that you help me not make a complete fool out of myself on my first day."

Midarin smiled.

"I'd be happy to help you, Quyhn. That's why we're here. Gwydeon and I are happy to act as your advisors, and to make sure that you do right by your people. And let me tell you what lesson number one is."

Midarin reached over and touched Quyhn's chest right above her heart.

"No matter what I say, no matter what Gwydeon says, no matter what any of us around you say, your best councilor and your best advisor is right here. I've watched you, Quyhn, and you have a good heart. You were taught to value people, value who they are. There is no better attribute for a ruler to have than to know that the people that you rule over and are responsible for are more than just numbers. They are real people with real lives, real concerns, real dreams, real fears, and a need to know that they are respected. If you can do that, you will be a great leader."

Quyhn smiled.

"Thank you, Midarin. That means a lot."

Midarin stood.

"Now, let me fetch my lazy snoring husband and we'll meet you downstairs. Hopefully our guests will forgive our less than courtly appearance. We didn't exactly have time to prioritize baths or acquiring changes of clothes."

Quyhn smiled. She had managed to pack a few things but knew that she was in the minority in that regard. Honestly, she hadn't really given much thought to the clothing that the Dark Gods wore. Did they change clothes? Could they just snap their fingers and suddenly they were clean? She would have to remember to ask Mirana and Liara about that later. When she rose, Midarin followed suit and the two women walked back down the hall toward the wide staircase. Midarin ducked into her room to find Gwydeon already sitting on the edge of the bed.

"Snoring I don't mind," he said smiling, "but lazy?"

* * * * * * * * * * * * *

The central feature of the throne room of the newly erected Fortress Peregrim was the throne that sat upon a low dais at the far end of the large room. With little in the way of ornamentation and décor in the throne room, the throne drew extra attention. Mirana and Liara had made it their special project on the first full day in the palace. They believed that Quyhn deserved a symbol fitting her new station, something that would help people accept her as the new Empress of Cadaria. The throne was carved from a combination of stone and wood, merging together seamlessly. The base of the throne seemed to grow out of the dais, and carved into the stone base were the sigils of each of the thirteen Great Kingdoms woven together to create an intricate tapestry. The back and arms of the throne were wood, reinforced by stone. The wood was warm with a rosy golden color that helped to accentuate the natural patterning in the wood. Sprouting from the back of the throne were massive stone wings that resembled angel's wings and were patterned after Gwydeon and Camille's. Carved into the backrest of the throne was the symbol of the Ravenheart house, a raven whose wings were flared out so that the bird looked as though it were in the shape of a heart.

When the doors to the throne room opened, Quyhn was seated on the edge of the throne trying not to look uncomfortable. Standing over her right shoulder was Midarin and standing over her left was Rhionna. To each side of the dais were a pair of chair which any visitor would assume were reserved for the Empress's advisors. In one set were Mirana and Liara while in the other set were Gwydeon and Camille. It was a motley looking crew, all looking as though they had just come from the road, with the exception of Quyhn who comparatively looked courtly. Four soldiers escorted the group of travels into the throne room, each of which was clad in a traveler's cloak. Quyhn was just about to address the petitioners when Liara broke all norms of protocol and sprinted across the room. She threw her arms around one of the figures, causing the person's cloak hood to fall back. Camille and Mirana both got to their feet quickly, and Midarin leaned down to whisper in Quyhn's ear. Quyhn nodded and let her voice hit the air.

"Welcome to Fortress Peregrim. The Empress of Cadaria welcomes the Queen of Mythryn, Sadrina Annis."

Sadrina freed herself from Liara's grasp with a smile and nodded in the direction of her companions. Each pulled their hoods down, revealing their faces. Gwydeon and Midarin both reacted to one of Sadrina's companions with shock and surprise.

"Cairyn Binosear?"

Gwydeon's voice was a mixture of confusion and surprise. Sadrina was the first member of the petitioners to speak.

"Thank you for the warm welcome. We were not sure what to expect when we came across this new fortress, but now that I see the advisors that you have at your disposal, it makes much more sense. I have seen up close what the Dark Gods can do. If you would permit me to introduce my companions. This is Cairyn Binosear, the Dark Seer Jehna Feris, and an advisor to the Divine Empress Marlae Tamerlane, Isabella Ranthall."

There were several mixed reactions that came from all members of Quyhn's retinue, but Quyhn seemed to be unaffected by the identities of the visitors. Naturally she recognized the names of Jehna Feris and the last name Ranthall, but she would not let her composure be upset regardless of her personal feelings. This would be the first test of her claim on her new position, and she would not disappoint those who put their faith in her.

"You are most welcome, Queen Sadrina, as are the rest of your companions. To what do we owe the honor of your visit?"

Sadrina regarded Quyhn for a moment. She wasn't sure what to make of the girl. It was clear that she was trying to retain some control over the situation, more control than her own courtly companions had over themselves. It was impressive, if perhaps a little misplaced. Regardless, Sadrina also knew how to play the courtly games. But it was Cairyn that spoke up first.

CHAPTER 117

"I understand that you were not expecting us, and I'm sure that more than one of us even being here is a surprise to both yourselves and those who are advising you. But I assure you, we are here on a matter of great urgency. I'll let my daughter, Isabella, tell you the rest."

Gwydeon and Midarin exchanged glances. They quickly put together the girl's identity from their memories of the Dark Mirror world. It was a world where Logan Ranthall and Cairyn Binosear were lovers, and Cairyn had been rumored to be pregnant with Logan's child. Of course, Trelon fell and the war descended into madness before anyone knew for sure, but clearly the rumors had been true and this young woman was proof. As soon as the youngest member of the petitioners stepped forward, Midarin was immediately struck by the girl's resemblance to not only Logan, but Cairyn's mother Anabel Binosear. Her slight build and intelligent eyes were an eerie reminder of the powerful woman who had once been considered the finest leader of any kingdom on Onea. But there was something in the girl's bearing, the way she held herself, that could only come from one place. She was a Ranthall, that much was certain. When the young woman spoke, her voice was clear and proud.

"Two emissaries from the Divine Empress Marlae Tamerlane, by way of Rhain Seth, were dispatched to make contact with the Lordhill Rebellion. One was Taya Viruci and the other was Jillian Corven. We greatly need to speak to Jillian and to secure her safety."

Gwydeon took a step forward from his seat and looked in Quyhn's direction. Courtly matters were not his forte, but he tried to remember his place.

"Empress Ravenheart, if I may?"

Quyhn nodded almost absently. She was confused. So many names were rolling through her mind and she felt as though she should have known some of them. The young woman Isabella as well as Sadrina Annis had spoken of Marlae Tamerlane. Of course, that could only have been Marlae Lorien using a different name. Out of the corner of her eye she had seen Gwydeon tense at the name Tamerlane, so clearly it meant something to him. She would have to remember to ask him about it later. The name Ranthall was also clear. That was the last name of not only Mirana and

Liara, but also the name of Rhionna's father. The concepts of coincidence and random were quickly losing their meaning.

"I know of Jillian Corven, and we both know Taya Viruci very well. Neither have been here. Why did Rhain send them?"

Isabella sighed, the frustration plain on her face.

"Rhain was concerned that the elements of the fight against the Creator were too spread out and being eliminated too quickly by our enemies," she said matter-of-factly. "So emissaries were sent in order to help coordinate our offensive. There is a lot that has happened, and while Rhain was not requesting your aid directly, she did want you to know what may have been coming your way."

Gwydeon nodded.

"Considering how dismissive her father was of our efforts, I'm happy know that Rhain is not following his advice."

Isabella frowned.

"I can't speak for Rhain's father. All I can speak to is the mission I was sent on, and her desire to ensure that there is still a Cadaria for Marlae Tamerlane to rule."

Quyhn let her irritation pass through her without appearing on her face. It would have been considered a little rude to talk about another presumptive ruler of Cadaria in Quyhn's presence, in her own throne room no less, but Quyhn had to let that go. She knew that she didn't have a better claim on the throne than Marlae. Quyhn really had no choice but to forgive the breech of decorum.

"It seems," Quyhn said finally, "that we have multiple avenues that we must explore."

The Dark Seer, Jehna Feris stepped forward.

"Forgive me, Quyhn Ravenheart," she said coldly, "but nothing is of more import than discovering the fate of Jillian Corven. There will be no

Cadaria, no Espre, no Creation if she is allowed to fall into the hands of the enemies of life."

Midarin added her voice to the proceedings for the first time.

"Maybe we can all accomplish something here. Clearly, we do not have the information about Jillian Corven that you are looking for, but equally as clear is that Taya Viruci did not accomplish her mission to brief us on the nature of the war and what is coming. I would suggest that perhaps some of you should stay with us and let us know what is happening with the war, and then perhaps one or two of us could accompany the rest of your party to assist with the search for Jillian."

Gwydeon continued Midarin's thought.

"Since she isn't here, Rhain should be able to figure out where Taya went."

Isabella's frown could be felt across the room.

"I don't think…"

Cairyn put her hand on her daughter's shoulder.

"I think that sounds like a very good idea, Gwydeon. After all, as Isabella said, our two main interests are ensuring the safety of Jillian Corven as well as coordinating our efforts against the enemies of life. Isabella is as knowledgeable about the nature of the war as any of us, so she and I can stay here and make sure you have all the information you need. Gwydeon, if you would like to accompany Jehna and Sadrina to meet with Rhain, I'm sure she would welcome your input."

Gwydeon looked first at Midarin and then at Quyhn. Both women nodded.

"Alright," he said finally. "Camille and I will go to meet with Rhain. I'm sure the recent actions by the Creator will be of interest to Rhain as well."

Camille nodded her ascent. Midarin saw the continued irritation on Isabella's face.

"At least, Isabella, this will give you an opportunity to spend some time with your nieces."

Isabella's eyes went wide, and Cairyn could not help but laugh.

Shadows and Supplicants

Year Two of the Divine Empress and Child of the Creator
Marlae Tamerlane, Creator's Calendar Year 1872

The hours passed slowly for the whole of the Heart of Stone following the assassination attempt on Anabel Binosear. Guards recovered the body of the assassin and returned it to the private garden of the High Priestess where it was positively identified as the body of her aide Aelind Torral. The body was ordered burned and disposed of quietly without alerting the rest of the leadership of the Church of the Creator. Any information about the betrayal would be highly compartmentalized. If anyone asked, Aelind had been sent on a sensitive mission for the High Priestess. There would be no record of the assassination attempt, no record of the strange disturbance. If the activity were discovered, the lieutenant and his men were ordered to classify their actions as a security drill design to ensure the protection of the High Priestess from a kidnapping attempt. Given the amount of political unrest in the world concerning the Church of the Creator, that would be a prudent act in anyone's view. However, there were additional changes that would bring into focus the gravity of the situation facing the faithful. Guards would be posted at the door of the High Priestess's quarters as well as the door to the private garden. Guards would additionally be posted outside of the guest quarters occupied by the emissary of the Divine Empress, in an effort to prevent a possible political incident. However, it was the relocation of the priestess Rhya from simple quarters that befitted her rank and station to guest quarters near the Divine Empress's emissary. Even though it was at the direct orders of the High Priestess, there were some within the leadership of the Church of the Creator that took a dim view of such elevation, and there were many that planned to lodge an official protest. But those petitions would wait. The High Priestess had decreed a day of rest and contemplation to pray for the souls of those who had been persecuted by the mad emperor Kaitain Lorien. Also, the decree was meant to help stem some of the confusion and misinformation that had been circling the Heart.

Though Baeata had been in consultation with Anabel since her return to the Heart of Stone, once that consultation broke temporarily prior to Aelind's treachery, she was faced with the fallout from Rhya's proclamations on the behalf of a suddenly very alive Hannah Ironheart, as well as the mass of dragons who now guarded the Heart of Stone. Stacks of missives sat on her simple desk, and every one followed the same pattern. Leadership of the Church wanted Rhya either censured or excommunicated. Some even went so far as to demand her execution for blaspheme of the highest order. There were others in the leadership that demanded that Baeata step down from her position as the High Priestess of the Church of the Creator, as she was not the rightful holder of that position with Hannah Ironheart revealed as still alive. While the Heart of Stone was a fortress designed to never fall to a siege from without, it was not immune to threats from within.

After the identity of the would-be assassin had been confirmed to Baeata's satisfaction, Anabel and Baeata spoke only a few more moments before Anabel returned to her quarters. The next day would see a great deal of activity, both publicly and privately. Upon returning to her suite, Anabel found that new buckets of hot water had been brought to her room, and that there was a parcel sitting on the bed. Unwrapping the parcel, Anabel laughed to herself. She had considered the possibility of chancing a trip back to her home in Hedorah to recover several changes of clothes. It appeared, however, that Jeroch had had the same idea. The parcel contained several dresses as well as common clothes and undergarments. There was a momentary flutter of irritation at Jeroch's audacity, but then she tempered it with the fact that it was a generous act, and he did save her life. Strange thoughts considering that Jeroch and her family had only been the deadliest of enemies for her entire lifetime. There was a time that he would have just let Aelind kill her and not given it a second thought.

Following the well-needed bath, it took Anabel only a matter of moments to get comfortable on the soft bed and fall asleep. She knew that the guards would come for her following the morning prayers and supplications, and following the High Priestess's recitation of the orders to the faith. Baeata had expected her to appear at an address for the faithful, and Anabel had agreed, not letting show her discomfort with the request. Regardless of her personal feelings about the worship of the Creator, she was the representative of Marlae Tamerlane, and that required adherence to protocol. Anabel awoke long before the guards came to fetch her, and was dressed and waiting when the knock came at the door. Anabel followed the two guards wordlessly through the winding corridors of the Heart of Stone until they reached a narrow set of steps that led up to the dais that overlooked the wide open grounds where supplicants gathered to hear the prayers of the High Priestess. There Baeata stood, her hands behind her back, dressed in a fine robe befitting her position. Behind her stood the priestess Rhya, dressed in the simple black robe of her position. Anabel felt slightly out of place in her light blue dress, but it certainly was not out of the norms for someone of her position. Anabel moved slowly up the stairs, purging whatever trepidation was still in her heart. Baeata regarded her for a moment, and with a wave of her hand, Anabel took up position behind Baeata. Her guests where they were meant to be, Baeata let her voice ring out to the gathered worshipers below.

"People of the Church of the Creator and followers of the one true faith, there have been startling changes regarding our faith and regarding our standing in the Cadarian Empire and upon this world. I understand that these changes have been concerning to many, confusing to others, and has filled others with worry that the foundation of the Church is not as strong as it once was. But I am here to address several of these rumors, and all of your concerns. The first and most important of these rumors is the disposition of Lady Hannah Ironheart, our High Priestess, our representative member of the now-defunct Knights of the Flashing Blade, and our Patron Saint of Perseverance and Fortitude. What has been kept as the most closely guarded secret of the Church is the fact that the reports of the demise of Hannah Ironheart were a fiction devised by the High Priestess in conjunction with our allies in the court of the woman who is now known as the Divine Empress Marlae Tamerlane."

Baeata let her words pass through the ranks of the faithful for several moments before letting her voice rise once again. A part of her felt guilty for the deception. While it was clear that there was a plan behind Hannah Ironheart's flight from the Heart of Stone and falsification of her own demise, the circumstances around it were a mystery to everyone. But it was necessary for the faithful to believe that the Church was involved in the plan, at least at some level, in order to maintain the illusion that the Church was all things for all people. Baeata was in an impossible situation now that the truth of Hannah's resurrection had become public knowledge. It called into question her very legitimacy as the High Priestess, and made any arrangement she made with Marlae Tamerlane suspect at best. Baeata had to be seen as working with the sanction of Hannah Ironheart, and thus with the full force of the Church of the Creator behind her.

"Hannah Ironheart uncovered rogue elements within the Cadarian Empire that were preparing to advocate for the destruction of the Church of the Creator and to remove its eternal sanction as the sole guidance for the faithful upon this world. These elements have corrupted Kaitain Lorien to the point that he believes he is a god and seeks to unseat the Creator."

There were gasps and boos from the assemblage below, and Baeata let them fester and linger for several moments before speaking again. The next piece of information would be the most troublesome of anything that Baeata was going to say. She had read the accounts of Rhya's speech once she had come to the Heart of Stone. The decree that cast doubt on the angels that guarded the Heart, and the fate of Hannah Ironheart. Baeata had not gotten much sleep in the hours before this address, pondering how she was going to get them out of the mess they were in without compromising their faith, her position, and without sounding like a complete mad woman. She thought she had found a compromise, a way that told the truth and protected the sanctity of the Church and the faith in the same breath. She only hoped that it was as convincing to the supplicants as it was in her mind.

"Kaitain Lorien, through dark means and through alliance with a creature of dire origin, has found a manner in which to corrupt even angelic warriors to do his bidding. This is the betrayal that priestess Rhya spoke of in her message from Lady Hannah Ironheart, and this is the reason that she had been pursuing, in secret, to ally herself with those who could protect us from this rogue element. Hannah Ironheart has forged a pact with a group of dragons who hold our beliefs in high regard. They believe in the sanctity of our lives, and do not agree with the war being fought against humans. I have been in consultation with the representative of these dragons, one named Serentis. They will defend us from those evil elements who want nothing more than to see the Heart of Stone reduced to rubble."

At the moment, Baeata was not sure that her lie had landed in the way that she wished. However, a moment later she knew that it had.

"Long live Lady Ironheart! Long live High Priestess Catrinel!"

The cheer continued over the next few moments, mounting in intensity until it resounded through the whole of the courtyard. A more vain leader might have let the cheer go on until it died out organically, but Baeata was not one for fawning or self-glorification. Instead, she held her hands up until the cheering died down. She spoke again, feeling some natural lightness in her words.

"Before I introduce the woman to my right, I have one piece of information that I must share. My personal aide, Aelind Torral has been dispatched on a mission of utmost importance to the Church. However, I shall not be without assistance in the days ahead. To reward her for her faith and adherence to the tenants of the Church of the Creator and faithful service to the High Priestess, Priestess Rhya Ammal will be elevated to the position of my personal aide."

Rhya took a single step forward, bowed to Baeata and then stepped back. Baeata nodded in her direction and then spoke once more to the assemblage.

"Now, I would like to introduce the High Councilor to the Divine Empress, Marlae Tamerlane, Lady Anabel Binosear."

Anabel took a step forward, drawing level with Baeata, careful not to step beyond where the High Priestess stood. Anabel could not allow for there to be any perception that the High Priestess was in any way being disrespected. She steadied herself for a moment and then let her voice catch the air. Her tone was regal, practiced, and confident.

"First and foremost, I would like to thank the High Priestess Baeata Catrinel for allowing me the opportunity to address the faithful of the Church of the Creator. Your dedication and devotion to your faith is inspiring and humbling. The Divine Empress wishes me to express the gratitude that she has for the people of Albitonin and the people of the Heart of Stone for their faith in her, and as such she will not violate that faith. Her first goal is to ensure the protection of the faithful and the continuation of the Church of the Creator. Once the madman Kaitain Lorien has been defeated, the unjust decrees that have terrorized people for following the tenants of the Church shall be rescinded and banished from the minds of the good thinking people of this Empire."

Anabel paused for a moment and then concluded.

"The Divine Empress has worked closely with Lady Hannah Ironheart in assembling forces that will defeat Kaitain Lorien and return stability to the Cadarian Empire. Those alliances are broad, strong, and unified in their desire to see peace return to Cadaria, and for all of its inhabitants, regardless of who they supported in this pointless war. This will be an Empire of peace, of faith, and of hope under the watchful and compassionate rule of the Divine Empress Marlae Tamerlane."

A cry went up from below.

"Long live the Divine Empress!"

Anabel stepped away and watched as Baeata encouraged the cheer from below. Despite the partial truth of the words, Anabel's stomach turned. She never liked misleading the people, but she knew that the common people would never accept the truth. The mob was dangerous. Anabel understood that keeping the mob happy was more important than keeping the mob informed. In these cases, it seemed that truth was never the best option. Now that the mob had been fed their measure of half-truths and placating rhetoric, the real work could be done without their watchful and disruptive attention.

****

Baeata had many obligations to fulfill following her address to the faithful, and as her dutiful new aide, Rhya was at her side. Many of the objections to both Baeata and Rhya were miraculously smoothed away, and the leadership of the Church of the Creator showed near unanimous approval. However, the one outstanding issue for all of them was the fact that the Divine Empress of Cadaria had yet to announce the Heart of Stone as her imperial palace. Such a move would shatter the two millennia history of a neutral imperial province, and would shift the power of the Empire to one of a religious state. Many within the Church of the Creator had wanted to move the Cadarian Empire to a more theocratic régime, and now seemed the perfect opportunity for that dream to become a reality. The Divine Empress had in fact been given her title by the Creator himself, what other sanction was needed that the Heart of Stone should not only be the heart of the Church of the Creator, but also the heart of the Empire of Cadaria. Baeata agreed to bring the matter to the attention of the Divine Empress's High Councilor, and that allowed Baeata to escape the meeting with the church leadership with as non-committal a commitment as possible. Feeling exhausted, Baeata returned to the private garden and found Anabel waiting for her.

"That was a very good performance," Anabel said as soon as the door was closed behind Baeata and Rhya. "I have to say I was impressed."

Baeata demurred as she sat across from Anabel.

"Public speaking was never something that I wanted to do. My talents were always more in the realm of ecumenical research and the translation and illumination of religious texts. When I came to the Church of the Creator, that is what I thought I would be. I did not feel that I was made to stand before the people and give them the teachings. I think it was because I did not feel myself worthy. Hannah Ironheart took special interest in me, and at every turn forced me to stand before the people. I think perhaps she took it as a bit of a joke in naming me as her personal aide, but now I understand that Hannah saw things the way that they are, not the way that people present them to be. That was her true gift. She was always able to see through to the soul of people and help them to find where they needed to be."

Anabel nodded.

"Now, Baeata, are you ready to meet with the emissary from the High Priestess?"

Baeata smiled.

"Always to the task at hand," she said her tone light. "Very well."

Anabel stood and after a moment a swirling blue portal appeared in the center of the garden. The use of such things still fascinated Baeata, but she could see the advantage and the utility. For Anabel's part, she hated portals. She hated using them, and she hated forming them even more. They were taxing and required a great deal of concentration and connection between memory and intention. Anabel just never found that she had aptitude for it. Fortunately for Anabel, she was not creating a portal that stretched across hundreds of miles. Instead, she was creating a portal that only spanned a few feet. Jeroch had been waiting in her quarters for just this moment, and fortunately even Anabel was able to create a portal that spanned that distance. When Jeroch stepped from the portal, Baeata stood and acknowledged him with a nod.

"Sir Vallic," Baeata began, "I was unaware that you had become a member of Empress Tamerlane's advisors."

Jeroch could not help but smile. Though he had been working in secret under pseudonyms as different members of Knights of the Flashing Blade for hundreds of years, he had still not invested fully in those identities. So to hear, now, someone that would be an ally call him by the name of one of those assumed identities was jarring and unexpected. It would not be the last such occurrence, but it would make it easy to explain how he continued to crop up in unexpected places. Fortunately for Jeroch, it was Anabel that tackled the issue of Jeroch's identity.

"Baeata, you have been thrust into a world that you were not ready to see. You have had to accept the existence of Dark Gods, and those who would be called Dark Gods. Whether it was my advising the Divine Empress, or the fact that Isabella was the daughter of a member of the Dark Gods. You have had to question your expectations about the world, both fairly and unfairly. To that end, you will need to accept one more thing you may not have believed you had to accept. This man that stands before you is not Sir Vallic Ultiv of the Kingdom of Steam, member of the Knights of the Flashing Blade. He is in fact Jeroch Yetre, the Lord Shadow of the Brotherhood of Phasia, late of the world of Onea. He is ostensibly what you would refer to as a Dark God."

Jeroch bowed low to the High Priestess, honoring her position far more than he would of as a member of the Brotherhood. Baeata to her credit did not let any surprise show in her face. She instead simply chuckled and shook her head.

"I suppose I should not be surprised," Baeata said finally. "We as a people were arrogant in our presumptions about the Dark Gods. We thought you were just these powerful creatures that lived on your island separate from us. That you were only interested in your own world until such time as you decided to descend upon us as a plague."

Baeata shook her head once more and could not help but laugh.

"To think that all this time the Cadarians felt themselves equal to the Dark Gods or to the dragons. That we were predators circling each other simply waiting for an opportunity to strike. We were just paper tigers, dancing around the flame waiting to be engulfed by it. It was just a matter of time before we found a leader irresponsible enough to draw us into that flame. And now we are all lesser for it."

Both Jeroch and Anabel kept their countenances unresponsive and unemotional. It was not an easy position that Baeata was in, and the fact that she was even willing to listen to what Anabel and Jeroch had to say was a tribute to the woman's wisdom and dedication to her position as spiritual leader to the people of Cadaria.

"I wish that I could disagree with you, High Priestess," Jeroch said after a moment, "but given the place that I am from and the purpose that I was bred for, I have little respect for you Cadarians."

Anabel felt the condemnation far more than Baeata did, but it was Jeroch's next words that surprised Anabel all the more.

"But as a member of your Knights of the Flashing Blade, I have worked side by side with some of what were considered the best and brightest of your people. I can say with all honesty and sincerity that I encountered no finer being than I encountered in Hannah Ironheart. And the woman that she considered to be her protégé and successor is due every bit of that respect. It will be an honor to fight the battle that is to come with you."

Baeata smiled. Anabel was sure that Baeata did not understand the level of compliment that she had just received, and in the end, it didn't really matter. What mattered was that the road ahead would be more difficult than anyone could imagine, and the difference between surviving and being wiped from existence was the kind of trust that could only be built with this kind of understanding and respect.

"What I'm about to tell you," Jeroch began, "would shock the best and brightest of you, and considering the fact that you are the spiritual leader of this world, I'm sure you will find this as hard to take as Hannah Ironheart did."

Jeroch paused, and Anabel found herself smiling inwardly. There were those who would call the pause dramatic or perhaps pregnant. Anabel however knew that there was no drama within Jeroch, he just simply did not have the capacity for it.

"We are not fighting for the fate of the people of Cadaria, nor are we fighting for the people of Espre. We aren't even fighting for all of the beings on all of the worlds in Creation. We are fighting for the very definition of what it means to be alive."

Jeroch paused one more moment to stabilize himself more than giving Baeata a chance to adjust to his words. What he was feeling was not easy for Jeroch. He was bred to be a killer. He was forged with a will to see before him the lifeless bodies of all of his enemies. To now have strayed so far from that path, to see all life as his own kind, and to be willing to fight and die for them was beyond any capacity for understanding. What he was and what he was meant to be no longer held any similarity to one another but given the option he would never be a destroyer. The time for that was past.

"I just lost my brother," Jeroch said after a moment. "He was one of the wisest beings that I have ever met. He fought and he lived and he believed in the better nature of all of those who were alive. That is what I believe that your Church thinks of the Creator. You believe that the Creator is filled with love, and compassion and respect for the beings of all of his worlds. But Baeata, he does not care for you. He does not care for me. He does not care for the dragons, or the angels, or the Servants, or even the Children of the Creator. He cares for nothing and no one. My brother Kamen cared for everyone. He, along with Logan Ranthall, dedicated their lives to helping the people of this world no matter where they came from or what they had done. They took people who had been born and bred to be killers and made them into carpenters and healers. They took men who had grown selfish in their desires, desiring only glory and turned them into farmers and smiths whose lives were expressed in what they did for others. Is that not what the Church demands of its people? So is that not what the Church should demand of its Creator?"

Baeata found herself unconsciously nodding.

"There is something coming," Jeroch said finally. "A force of darkness the likes of which has never been seen on this world, even going back to the Founding Wars. This place, this fortress, will be the site of perhaps the most important battle in the history of Creation and we have little time to prepare."

Baeata opened her mouth to speak, but was cut off.

"Jeroch is right, Baeata," a woman's voice said from behind her. "And if we are not ready for what is coming, then all light will go out in the Cosmos."

The four people turned to regard the new voice and all were shocked to see the grave countenance of Hannah Ironheart staring back at them.

Fading Light

Year Two of the Divine Empress and Child of the Creator Marlae Tamerlane, Creator's Calendar Year 1872

For a moment, Logan wondered if he shouldn't feel flattered. As the patchwork form of the dragon floated before him, there was a grinding sound coming up on Logan from his right. A form like a giant segmented worm with feathered wings was wriggling its way up the face of the neighboring mountain. When it reached the peak, the creature lashed its lower body around the mountain's peak and drew itself up using its brown wings as a kind of airfoil to give the creature buoyancy in the wind that whipped around the mountains. At the tip of the massive worm was a head that did not look like it belonged on the creature's body. Two massive black horns emerged from either side of the creature's head and connecting the two horns was a plate of bone several feet thick. On top of the plate of bone extended a tuft of feathers like the fin on the back of a fish. It was clear that between the feathery fin on the back of the dragon's head combined with the wings on the dragon's body, the massive beast could float through the air like a snake on the sand. The dragon's head looked more like a skull then a proper head, all of the skin and muscle appeared as though they had been stripped away. The rest of the head looked like that of a venomous serpent with two long fangs emerging from the upper jaw. Thin, nearly translucent musculature held the upper and lower jaws together. Like with the upper jaw, the lower jaw ended with two fangs, except there were closer together and looked as though they fit between the upper fangs when the creature's mouth was closed. Rearing up, the dragon stared at Logan and hissed its voice onto the wind.

"What you see before you, human, is Nidavallir the Never-ending. I am the beginning and the end, the giver and the taker of life. There are none among the dragons like me, and there never will be again. Shadowweaver has decreed that you must die. I came here to destroy you, but Shadowweaver felt that you were too dangerous to tackle alone. So, he sent this miserable pile of puss, Aquallor the Falling Death to assist in your destruction. A pathetic waste for one little human, but what Shadowweaver decrees, so shall we do."

The hovering dragon that the coiled serpent referred to as Aquallor charged in the next moment, its beak-like jaws opening wide to strike. Like a crane the neck was compressed when it flew in Logan's direction, but when it stuck the neck extended and it increased the speed at which the dragon was able to attack its target. The snapping motion was meant to envelop Logan in a single strike. But the old cunning warrior had other plans. He had seen others do what he was about to attempt, but it was a maneuver that he never thought he would have to attempt himself. It was not the same fighting on the peaks of mountains as it was fighting on firm land. A moment before the dragon's strike would have taken Logan firmly into the dragon's gaping maw, Logan pushed off the tip of the mountain peak and filled himself with the power of the Blaze. In his mind, he thought of the wings that Gwydeon Sandar had been given as the Brother of Angels. Of course, were he a more imaginative man in the use of his powers, he could have simply floated on the currents of air using the powers of the Blaze as a buoy. However, Logan knew that the more abstract the use of power, the more difficult it was to maintain in the back of the mind when fighting got heavy and concentration was strained to the limit. So, Logan opted for the more impractical yet easier to maintain use of power. Brilliant green feathered wings made of pure Blaze fire sprouted from Logan's back as he pushed off into the air. The sensation was odd, and it took Logan a handful of seconds to understand how his balance was altered while in mid-air. But Logan was a quick study, and even before Aquallor's snapping jaws closed where Logan had been standing a moment earlier, Logan felt that he could be as competent in battle in the air as he had been on the land.

The snapping jaws sped in, and Logan only cleared the dragon's head by a few inches. He took a moment to let his foot touch down on the top of the creature's head and then pushed off again, letting the Blaze wings catch the air. He dove down the length of the dragon's neck, letting two blades of diamond appear in his hands. Logan knew that the hides of the dragons were incredibly tough, and they would likely resist most attempts to penetrate. As Logan approached the bottom of the dragon's neck, Aquallor started to bank away, pulling its head back to protect the vulnerable structures of the neck. Logan was able to bank harder than the dragon, his turn tighter, putting him ahead of where Aquallor was trying to escape to. One hard diamond blade punctured the dragon's neck on the left side just above the front shoulder. The cut was not very deep as Logan's momentum was pulling him away from the dragon, however it was deep enough to send a gout of dark red blood exploding outward in a forceful plume. Aquallor continued to bank away and Logan tucked his wings behind him into a forceful dive. The dive carried Logan down the length of the dragon's body, past its soft belly to its back legs. Both legs were tucked under the dragon to help it with the bank. Though the dragon was rapidly pulling out of Logan's reach, the former Chosen One reached out with the tip of one of the diamond blades and dragged it across the bottom of one of the dragon's rear claws. The dragon shrieked and thrashed in the direction of the troublesome human with its tail. Logan thought he was clear of the dragon's strike but had underestimated the length of the dragon's tail and the power that it was able to generate down the whole length, including the seemingly thin tip. The tip clipped Logan on the hip sending him spinning out of control through the air in the direction of Nidavallir.

The instant the strike connected, Logan knew that his hip had been shattered. Even before the pain hit, the powers of the Blaze were already hard at work repairing the damage. Though the aerial battle would require less from his legs, Logan knew that he would still need full control of his appendages in order to make quick turns and stay ahead of the dragons. Despite the fact that the creatures were huge, they were incredibly agile in the air. Logan's unfamiliarity with the intricacies of flight and aerial combat put him at a distinct disadvantage, one that he would have to overcome quickly if he stood a chance against both of the monstrous beasts. As Logan tumbled into range, Nidavallir's jaws snapped outward, thick fangs aiming to impale Logan. At the last moment, Logan's wings beat against the wind and the man tumbled away from the strike. One of the fangs caught the back of the Logan's shirt, ripping it free from the man's body. The beat of Logan's wings carried Logan into a roll towards the back of Nidavallir's head. Reflexively Logan struck out with one of his swords as he tumbled away from the massive coiled beast. The blade of the sword dug deeply into the thick black horn on the left side of Nidavallir's head. Logan did not have enough leverage or speed to pull his blade free, and it remained lodged half-way through the thick cruel-looking horn. By the time Logan came out of his unintentional roll, the damage to his hip had been nearly completely repaired. However, the damage was not something that Logan could ignore. These dragons were incredibly powerful and if Logan was not careful, the dragons would be able to do him in with a single strike. The longer the battle went on, the more that it favored the dragons. Logan would have to come up with something quickly or the two would overwhelm him.

With his free hand, Logan summoned a ball of fire that he then threw toward Nidavallir's eyes. Logan didn't intend for the strike to do any damage, but instead to buy himself a few moments to take the fight to Aquallor. As far as Logan was concerned, Aquallor was the more troublesome of the adversaries at least at the moment. Blinding Nidavallir let Logan focus all of his attention on Aquallor who had righted himself from his bank and was coming around to bring its focus back to Logan. Aquallor's jaws opened once again, but instead of attempting to snap Logan in half, the dragon let loose a stream of superheated water from deep within its gullet. Logan banked and rolled away from the gout of boiling water, but even as it passed, he could feel the heat against his skin, and several of the drops of water landed on Logan's arm. The skin blistered immediately under the heat of the dragon's attack. Logan paid the attack no mind and following the roll continued his dive directly toward the head of the dragon.

Aquallor proved to be faster than Logan had anticipated and the stream of superheated water chased Logan across the sky attempting to anticipate his motions. Aquallor managed to train his sights on Logan and the stream cut across Logan's path. There was nothing that Logan could do to avoid the strike, so he plunged headlong in to the stream of boiling water. Knowing that the water was going to strike his skin once more, Logan summoned more of the powers of the Blaze and wrapped himself in a cocoon of the potent green flame. Even with the protection of the Blaze, Logan could fell the scalding heat and pressure of the dragon's breath pressing in on him. Sweat rolled down his face and he knew that he would only have seconds before the shield of Blaze fire failed. Aquallor felt the imminent threat upon him and redoubled the intensity of his attack, increasing the volume and the pressure of the boiling water that burst from his jaws. The increased pressure was almost enough to push Logan away from his intended strike, but at the last moment he veered to his left and let the cocoon of Blaze fire fail. The expulsion of the Blaze energy pushed Logan free of the dragon's breath just feet from the tip of the dragon's beak-like snout. Too late to prevent what was about to occur, Aquallor tried to roll out of the way of the impending attack. The blade of Logan's diamond sword struck the right side of Aquallor's mouth, breaking teeth and rending flesh until the tip of the blade cut through the bottom part of the dragon's jaw. Aquallor roared in pain as the jawbone was cut free from the joint and the lower half of the dragon's mouth hung obscenely open.

Aquallor flapped his wings madly, trying to put some distance between himself and the troublesome human. Logan continued his dive, the blade of his diamond sword cutting down Aquallor's right flank, until he finally buried the whole length of the blade into the dragon's right rear hip. The beat of Aquallor's wings then became too much to fight against, and Logan found himself tumbling through the air, nearly out of control. It was then that twin bolts of lightning burst from Nidavallir's mouth and lanced across the distance. While the first missed wildly, the second came so close to Logan that it actually singed the front of his shirt. The burn continued to the skin of his chest, and caused nearly enough pain to force the consciousness from his mind. But Logan was not ready to relent. His attack had caused significant damage to Aquallor, and though the dragon was not out of the fight, he certainly could not be counted as fighting at full strength. Logan hoped that by disabling the creature's jaw that the massive beast had been robbed of at least two of its most powerful weapons, its breath and its bite. Logan also hoped that the wounds to its neck and hip would slow if not significantly hamper the dragon's ability to nimbly navigate through the air. That left Nidavallir as the chief threat, and so Logan turned his attention fully to the beast.

Two more streaks of lightning came from Nidavallir's massive jaws, but these two strikes were not nearly as close to Logan as the original two. Feeling itself in a vulnerable position by being stationary, Nidavallir let go of the mountain tip and let its wings beat hard against the perturbed air. It took but one beat of its insubstantial looking wings to lift the massive girth of the dragon from the mountain peak, and freed of its hold on the surface, it slithered through the air with the grace of a fish in the water of a calm lake. Had the situation been different, Logan might have taken the time to marvel at the massive creature's grace. However, as the massive creature was intent on killing Logan, he kept his mind trained on his enemy. Quicker than should have been possible, Nidavallir was upon him, jaws snapping at his head. Unlike Aquallor, Nidavallir did not have claws to strike with, but the whole of the dragon's body could have been considered a deadly weapon. Logan dove down below the dragon in an attempt to dodge the attack, but Nidavallir was ready for the evasive maneuver by its opponent. Beating its wings hard, Nidavallir pulled up, bringing the tip of its segmented body up to smash firmly into Logan's chest. The strike forced all of the air out of Logan's lungs, and dazed him for a moment. The moment was enough to give Nidavallir the time it needed for its true attack. The tail coiled itself around Logan's body and began to squeeze. The tail pulled Logan up so that he was at eye level with the dragon. Nidavallir hissed and Logan could feel the crackle of electricity crawling over his skin with every word.

"You are every bit as troublesome as Shadowweaver said you would be. Perhaps I should feed you to Aquallor for what you did to his jaw. I'll have to rip you apart first to make sure the pieces are small enough."

The dragon's hissing laughter hit the air as the tail squeezed tighter around Logan's body. It was the jibe however that Logan had been waiting for. Logan wanted the beasts to feel confident, wanted them to believe that they would be victorious. Logan did not have a lot of experience fighting dragons and did not know the full breadth of their capabilities. Could they feel the power that he was gathering inside himself? Were they able to know that so much of the powerful flames were pulsing through his body that it threatened to leak from his pours? Nidavallir pulled Logan up, its jaws widening, prepared for a fatal strike with its massive fangs. At the last possible moment, the blinding, searing green flame burst in all directions from Logan's body. The Blaze fire burned the dragon's tail, burned its snout, scorched its fangs, and blackened its scales. Pain rocketed through Nidavallir's body, and it was forced to release Logan from its grasp. It took several moments for Logan to force the air back into his lungs, but he didn't have the luxury of waiting too long to continue his counterattack. A second diamond blade appeared in Logan's hand and he dove toward Nidavallir. The tip of the first blade dug into the dragon's flesh just behind its lower jaw. Logan's momentum would only allow the sword to create a two-foot-long gash in Nidavallir's hide. But blood poured from the wound just the same. Logan used the momentum of his dive to continue down the segmented length of the dragon, as he could, Logan drove the tip of his blade into the body of the dragon, drawing more blood and creating more damage. More and more cuts were opened in Nidavallir's body, and by the time Logan had reached the tip of the massive dragon's tail, he was drenched in the creature's blood.

While the speed of Logan's dive had enabled him to inflict massive damage upon Nidavallir, it did not allow him an opportunity to slow his descent enough to prevent collision with the mountain face below. Had he tried to slow down before clearing the dragon's tail, Nidavallir might have had an opportunity to seize him once more. Logan protected himself as best he could the moment he saw the collision before him, but regardless of his preparations, the impact shocked his body to such a degree that he could hear bones break. The small crater that Logan's body created upon impact was immediately filled by the ice and snow dislodged by the impact. Despite his injuries, Logan pulled himself free of the ice and snow that threatened to entomb him just in time to see the formerly elegant floating mass of Nidavallir begin to sag in the air like a rapidly deflating balloon. The dragon screamed and howled into the air, lightning flashing from its blood-filled maw, until its cries went silent. The massive beast faltered and it crumpled on the wind like a dried leaf. Logan watched the dragon fall and chanced a few moments to let the powers within him to heal the significant injuries that had already been inflicted upon him. But that moment almost cost Logan dearly.

CHAPTER 117

Logan had not forgotten about Aquallor, but his focus had nearly fully shifted to Nidavallir and the potential lethality of that beast's attacks. Now that Nidavallir had been defeated, Aquallor charged forward, its intent to finish off the troublesome human as quickly as possible. Logan didn't see the strike until it was almost too late. A black talon flashed in and would have ripped Logan in half had his finely honed sense of danger not triggered him to throw himself from the crater. Talons ripped through the just vacated space, and Aquallor lingered for only a moment before turning and launching itself in the direction that Logan had fallen. With many of his bones still broken or at the very least still slowly mending, Logan was not maneuverable or able to handle the pressure of rapid turns. His chest ached pulling the thinner air in and out with multiple cracked ribs and a fractured sternum. Logan's left arm still hung limply, and he tried to prioritize healing that wound, knowing he would need to fend off any attacks that came from the wounded dragon.

Below the peaks of the mountains, a bank of clouds filled with near freezing water vapor ringed around the whole of the mountain range. Logan burst into the cloud bank, and as soon as he breeched the boundary, he released the wings of Blaze fire and reached out his diamond blade. The tip of the blade dug into the mountain face, arresting Logan's fall, but at the same time sending reverberating shocks through his damaged body. Nevertheless, the tactic accomplished its aim. As Logan's momentum was broken, he saw the gold and purple body of Aquallor flash through the thick white clouds still hurtling in the direction that Logan had been falling only moments before.

Logan pulled himself around the perimeter of the mountain peak, taking time that the cover provided to heal more of the injuries that he had sustained during the fighting. He hoped that Aquallor did not have any ability to heal itself as well. Fighting one of the phasia or one of Dorovar's creatures, Logan never would have taken this much time. Giving the opponent the opportunity to recover would only serve to unnecessarily prolong the battle and perhaps even give the opponent an undue advantage. There was too much however about the dragons that Logan did not know. He would do what he thought was right tactically given the circumstances. After what seemed like far too many seconds, the strength in Logan's arm returned and the damage to his ribs and sternum had healed. The bruising remained, and it would make breathing painful, but a least the labor behind the breaths had been removed. With feeling finally back in his hand, Logan conjured another diamond blade and dug it into the rock face. Using the two weapons, Logan quickly scaled the mountain peak until he emerged through the clouds. Just as Logan emerged, before him, on the other side of the mountain peak, Aquallor's head poked through. When the dragon caught just a glimpse of the human, it let loose another stream of scalding water.

The tactic proved to be as damaging to Aquallor as it was to Logan. With its shattered jaw, some of the stream of water was not redirected forward and instead flowed down the neck of the dragon, causing the armored scales of its neck to become pocked and seriously damaged. Logan for his part was able to erect a shield of Blaze fire in front of him that took the brunt of the assault, however some of the boiling water still found its way around the shield and scorched Logan's exposed skin. Logan left the shield in place, but released his swords, falling back towards the cloud barrier. As if anticipating the tactic, Aquallor arrested the flow of boiling water and dove in the direction that Logan was falling. Confident that the dragon would take the bait and attempt to beat Logan to the cloud barrier, Logan let the Blaze wings form again at his back and pulled up hard several feet before the clouds. The maneuver took an immense amount of effort, and Logan's chest seized under the stress. His repaired ribs threatened to break again, and his lungs and heart felt as though they were being squeezed in a vice. However, this was the tactical advantage that Logan had been waiting for.

Aquallor passed below him and Logan released the Blaze wings and let himself fall. Once more swords made of pure diamond appeared in each hand. Aquallor tried to pull up from the dive and reacquire sight of the human, but by the time he realized that Logan had not passed through the clouds, it was too late. When Logan fell upon Aquallor, the first blade quickly was buried just to the left of the creature's spine. Using the first blade as an anchor, Logan took aim at the base of Aquallor's right wing. With a single hard slash, the wing was cut free cleanly. Another cry of pain erupted from Aquallor, and all of his buoyancy was robbed from him in an instant. Though he floundered through the air, Aquallor did not relent in his attempts to kill Logan. Aquallor's tail snapped back and forth, trying to dislodge the meddlesome human, but Logan dodged each of the attempts even as he sought to reposition himself on the creature's back for another blow. As they fell, Aquallor was attempting to use his one remaining wing to steer himself toward the mountain face. After several attempts, the dragon was successful in the maneuver, bringing him close enough to the mountain that he could dig two sets of talons into the rock. The whiplash effect made it impossible for Logan to keep hold of the sword protruding from Aquallor's back and he fell away, just barely able to avoid the dragon's tail whipping wildly behind it.

Again, Logan's Blaze wings formed, now becoming almost a reflex, and he arrested his fall and charged where the dragon hung. This would be the end of the fight, one way or another. Two more diamond swords formed in Logan's hands, and Logan's target was Aquallor's neck. Logan's first strike missed, the sword burying itself half-way into the mountain face, but the second strike was on target. He brought his sword slashing down on the back of Aquallor's neck, bringing a massive gout of blood spraying in all directions. The cut was not complete, the blade sticking in one of Aquallor's impossibly thick vertebrae. What the strike did do however, was buy Logan enough time for another strike. The next diamond sword followed the path of the first, breaking through the whole of the dragon's neck, separating it from the rest of the body. Logan hung tight to the hilt of the sword still embedded in the rock face, and watched as the broken pieces of the dragon fell into the obscured mountain range below. For several long moments, Logan simply hung there, taking in long slow breaths.

Once again making use of the wings of Blaze energy, Logan floated back to the tip of the mountain peak where he had been meditating earlier and settled back down into a seated position. While fighting dragons was difficult, it did not compare to the fights that he had been through with Death and Conquest. Wounds were inevitable in combat, but these wounds at the very least would quickly heal. As Logan sat looking out over the vista that stretched before him he saw a flash of brilliant crimson light coming from the direction of Zevarit. Even at this great distance, Logan could feel the amount of power that had been wielded. There could be no other source for the power. It had to be Tess Annis. Logan would sit and continue to meditate until he had fully recovered all of his strength. He would need everything at his disposal if he was going to survive his next confrontation. Logan found that he was no longer looking beyond the next moment. Tess was his destiny. If that destiny killed him, then perhaps everything he had been fighting for had been a lie yet again.

CHAPTER 117

Chapter CXVIII

Lives Lived, Choices Made

Year Two of the Divine Empress and Child of the Creator Marlae Tamerlane, Creator's Calendar Year 1872

Marlae woke in a cold sweat. The simple dressing gown that Rhain had given Marlae to wear was soaked through, as were the bedsheet and the pillowcase. As she sat up, she brushed back the hair that was matted to her face and forehead. As she turned and put her feet on the cool floor, she closed her eyes again and took a deep breath. Her mind had been troubled by racing dreams throughout her slumber, but none of them left enough of an impression to be remembered. The cold floor felt good on her feet, and after a gentle stretch, Marlae pushed her way onto her feet. Despite what must have been a deep sleep, she did not feel rested. She padded her way gingerly over to the wardrobe, and caught sight of herself in the mirror. With the thin dressing gown clinging indecently to her body and her hair a mass of tangles, Marlae looked a fright. Her mind flashed back to a time when she would have simply snapped her fingers and a dozen servants would have sprang to work. In a matter of minutes her hair would have been combed, her clothes laid out, and a bath drawn with perfumed soaps and oils. Of course, at the time, Marlae did not pay any of this any mind. It was just the reality of her position. Marlae had taken all of that for granted; if anything, she would have complained about the slow response of the servants, the temperature of the water, or the indelicacy of her hair being pulled as it was brushed. Standing there looking at herself in the mirror she was happy that those days were behind her, and at the same time hoped she would never have to be in the position to take others for granted ever again.

Marlae sat at the small dressing table and for a moment found it odd. These were supposed to be the chambers of the Grand Master of the Shadow Guild, and yet there were very feminine touches to the space. Then again, Marlae thought that a man of such power must have had the need for female company from time to time, perhaps these trappings were a concession to those appetites. Or perhaps it was possible that once she had commandeered the quarters for herself, Rhain saw fit to make changes of her own. Either way, as Marlae sat down on the cushioned stool she was happy for the opportunity to make herself look more presentable. As she sat and picked up the pearl-handled brush and ran it through her hair the first time, her mind projected to a different place in time. She wondered about the life she could have, not the life of dream and unreality.

If she had been less realistic about her situation, her desires would have been easy to describe. Regardless of what lay ahead, she would be the Divine Empress of Cadaria, sitting on a new throne in the reconstructed Imperial Palace at Aldere with her beloved Rhain at her side. Marlae would preside over a kingdom of conscience with a new order of the Knights of the Flashing Blade formed to return the stability and honor to the Cadarian Empire. Hannah Ironheart would be her spiritual advisor, Anabel Binosear as her Chancellor and the Voice of the Empress, and Leonora Wastri as the backbone of the new Knights. Isabella Ranthall would act as Grand Master of the new Shadow Guild, one that was less militant and more focused on information gathering. Marlae would also forge a new working relationship with the Academy of Arcane Arts, ensuring there would never be another breakdown in communication or diplomatic relations. Everyone would have to have a voice in the new Cadarian Empire, or it would never survive. However, she knew that those thoughts were nothing but a dream that could never be realized. There would likely never be a Cadarian Empire again, and if there was, it would not be helmed by the Lorien family, or anyone who once was a member of that family. The Lorien name would be cursed forever, and though she had left it behind by virtue of her selection as the vessel of the Creator's authority on Espre, the poison was still in her blood. She hoped that there were enough good deeds that she could do that would erase her arrogance, her carelessness, or her destructive past.

It was then that the truth of her desires manifested in the back of her mind. She had been born to a position of power, bred to walk those halls every day. Marlae had become numb to the trappings of what she had and knew only desire for what she could take. There would have never been enough power, never enough status, never enough of anything. Her appetites would have grown and grown until they consumed the whole of the world. But now that her eyes had been opened to the potential horror of that future, her stomach turned at the thought of it. Marlae found herself sickened by power, repulsed by its trappings, and exhausted by the constant want of more and the never-ending fight to defend what was had. Now her thoughts turned only to a small farmhouse in a little town that did not appear on most maps. A life lived quietly. A life she could be proud of. Her fear now of course was that she would have to live that life without the woman that she loved. Rhain's love would never be lost to her, but something inside continued to scream out that Rhain did not have a future after the war. Regardless, Marlae had set her mind to a singular truth. She no longer wanted to be an Empress. She no longer wanted an empire. All she wanted was to spend what time she could with Rhain before she was lost forever.

Her hair back in some semblance of order, Marlae stood and moved to the wardrobe. Pulling the doors open, she saw an array of dresses, and instantly knew that she had been right about Rhain's alterations to the quarters. She took hold of one of the black dresses that hung on the far end of the wardrobe and brought the garment to her face. It smelled like Rhain, and Marlae could feel her pulse quicken. As she ran her fingers across several of the other dresses, she noticed some that were smaller. Clearly, they were too small for Rhain, but they would have been almost the right size for Marlae. The smile on her face widened as she pulled out a light blue dress. As Marlae held the dress up to herself and looked in the mirror, she saw another person. Not in a literal sense, but in a figurative one. The dress was simple, and it reminded her of something that her new namesake Elwyne Tamerlane would wear. It took only a minute to strip off the dressing gown and pull the simple dress over her head. The fabric felt cool against her skin and light as the air. There was a simple cloth tie at the waist that she tied loosely, and a clasp at the back of her neck that she was able to fasten with little effort. The buttons in the back however would require assistance, but at least the dress wouldn't fall of her if she went looking for Rhain. Marlae looked back in the direction of the bed and considered sitting to pull her boots on. She thought better of it, and as she was enjoying the feel of the cool floor on her feet, she made her way to the door, still barefoot, and opened it slowly.

Once the door was open and she stepped out into the other room, her heart caught in her throat. Rhain was slumped in a high-backed chair, and against the far wall were the remnants of a shattered chair. When Marlae's eyes went from the shattered chair back to Rhain, she was unsure if the red-haired woman was breathing or not. Fortunately, Marlae saw Rhain's chest rise and fall. The breath was shallow, but at least it was a breath. Marlae moved quickly over to Rhain's side and knelt beside the chair. Taking Rhain's hand into her own, she held it gently and stroked Rhain's arm with her other hand. For several moments she knelt like that and Rhain didn't react for a long time, but finally Marlae felt Rhain squeeze her hand. By the time Marlae looked up, Rhain was looking down at her smiling.

"I didn't know how long you were going to sleep."

Marlae smiled.

"It seems like I missed a lot."

Marlae quickly looked in the direction of the shattered chair. Rhain's eyes followed Marlae's and she let a small chuckle escape her lips.

"Family reunion."

Marlae nodded. With a wave of her hand in the direction of one of the other high-backed chairs in the room, the chair slid across the floor and stopped in front of Rhain. Taking the suggestion, Marlae stood slowly and then sat on the edge of the chair, Rhain's hand still clutched in hers.

"I assume your experiment was successful?"

Rhain nodded. That next moment an internal conflict raged inside of Rhain. Did she chance telling Marlae the risk that Rhain had taken with her life, or what it had ultimately cost? Would Marlae see that the benefits had outweighed the cost? Would she see that the information they gained and the potential leverage that was created could mean the difference between winning and losing the war? Looking in her eyes, all Rhain thought Marlae would see were the few days that she had left with the woman that she loved. Just as Rhain began to open her mouth to speak, a jolt of pain shot through her. Her chest seized and she had trouble catching her breath. With every moment, the pain in her chest increased until it felt like a great vice was tightening around her heart. The edges of her vision went red and then finally black. Just before she lost consciousness, a series of pictures shot through her mind, and she could feel the tears streaming down her face.

****

Rhain woke with a start. For several minutes she didn't know where she was. When she opened her eyes, she could not see anything and panic began to set in. Her other senses started to take over. She was laying on a bed, that much was for certain, and given the luxury of the mattress, it was most likely her bed in the Grand Master's quarters in the Shadow Guild. Reaching out with her other senses, she could hear two sets of heartbeats. One was quick and erratic while the other was even and controlled, with no variation. That could only mean that one of the people was a member of the phasia, and it didn't take long for Rhain to realize that it was her mother Bryn. Bryn must have arrived moments after Rhain had lost consciousness. Between she and Marlae, the two had carried Rhain to her bed and now stood vigil until she regained consciousness. Weakness wracked her body, and she knew where it came from. The part of her that was so intimately connected to the Blaze had felt that pain before, many times. The pain was from a connection to the Blaze being forcibly severed. Halicon had felt that pain many times during the war with Emries on Onea. It was another secret that Halicon had kept from his progeny. Each time one of the phasia was killed, Halicon was filled with such searing and all-consuming pain that it nearly robbed him of consciousness. There was no mistaking that pain. There was no mistaking that searing agony that gripped her heart so tight she thought it would never beat again. One of their own had been taken from them, only this time, the lost would not be returning. There was not another generation, not another world, not another chance to make right the things that went wrong. No penance, no redemption. There was only these next few days, these next few hours. So pain could not be the thing that prevented Rhain from seeing it through, no matter how personal, and no matter how intense. She had to persevere, because if she didn't untold numbers would suffer greater pain than what she felt.

After several moments of riding the wave of the weakness and pain, Rhain began to feel some of her strength return. Her vision was still cloudy, and her head still felt thick and heavy, but she forced herself up to a seated position. The first attempt was a failure, and as she tried to sit up, there was a spasm in the muscles of her stomach, and she fell back onto the pillow. The second attempt was more successful, and Rhain found that she only had to grip the edge of the bed to give her the leverage she needed for the final few inches. Once upright, Rhain let her blurry eyesight pass between the two other women in the room. Seated across from the bed by the door was Rhain's mother, the Lady Fox, Bryn. As expected, the woman did not look relieved or even happy at her daughter's recovery. She looked irritated. Rhain could almost guess at her mother's thoughts without peeking into her mind. All she would have seen was weakness. Bryn could not tolerate weakness in any form. It was her anathema. And for her daughter, let alone the Mistress of the Blaze to show such weakness was untenable. However, in the woman's eyes Rhain also found the slightest glimpse of concern. When Rhain turned her attention to the woman who sat on the edge of the bed however, the tapestry of emotion was almost too complex to decipher. But unlike with her mother, Rhain did not have the ability to look into Marlae's mind to figure everything out. Clearly Marlae was worried, scared, relieved, confused, and myriad other things. It was her smile however that told the real story. She was simply happy that Rhain was alive and awake. As Marlae moved up the bed to sit closer to Rhain, it was Bryn who first spoke.

"You gave us a bit of a scare, dear," she said calmly. "By us of course, I mean your friend the Empress."

A sly smile came to Bryn's lips, and it was that moment that Rhain knew she was going to be alright. Marlae took hold of Rhain's hand.

"What happened? You were fine and then all of a sudden you were on the floor. If your mother hadn't arrived when she did, I don't know if I would have been able to get you into bed."

Rhain felt the sly comment roll across her mother's mind, but a stern glance from Rhain cut it off before the indelicate words could be spoken. Bryn nodded at the unspoken request for decency, and waited for Rhain's explanation.

"Taya is dead."

Silence held for a long time between the three women. While Marlae did not know the woman very well, it was clear that there was a connection between Taya and Rhain. They had been through a lot together, and the loss of a close ally was something that few could afford given the circumstances. Bryn on the other hand knew Taya very well. In another reality, Taya was Bryn's only grandchild, the daughter of her first child, Gideon Viruci. Taya had lived with Aerith and Bryn in their early days on Espre before Ayden and Rhain were born. Eventually Taya needed to find a place and an identity of her own outside of her grandparents, but Taya still remained close and visited often. Once she began her life of piracy, Taya would often bring supplies to Aerith and Bryn as well as news of the outside world. When Rhain was born, Taya became immediately invested in her new aunt. Rhain always found it amusing that she was Taya's aunt, but that was in name only. Rhain had never seen the woman as anything other than a big sister that she could learn from. The loss was profound for both women, and Rhain could not picture a world where she could no longer depend on the council of the woman who had been there for her entire life. It was the first true loss the family had suffered in this war, and it would not be the last.

"How?"

Bryn's voice didn't crack, but it betrayed the emotion that she felt. There was sorrow there, but mostly there was anger. Rhain steeled herself for the storm that would come once she answered her mother's simple question. Rhain cleared her throat and tried to keep her tone even when she spoke. Adding her own emotion to the powder keg that she was about to ignite would benefit no one.

"I sent Taya and Jillian to rendezvous with the Lordhill Rebellion that was moving on the remains of Aldere. We needed to gather as much information as we could, and we needed to ensure that Gwydeon and Midarin knew that we had not abandoned them."

Bryn's eyebrow arched.

"Gwydeon?"

Rhain started to say something, but Bryn held her hand up.

"That was what your father meant."

Rhain's confused gaze was met by her mother's half smile.

"Your father has always thought that people find their place in war. Not everyone is cut out to be a soldier, or a strategist, or a leader. But there are some people who have a gift that cannot be quantified. Gwydeon Sandar is one of those men. He inspires those around him to do the impossible. He, like Logan Ranthall, can make people believe. On the Dark Mirror, Gwydeon surrounded himself with farmers, survivors, and a handful of trained warriors and repelled siege after siege by superior phasia forces. Time and time again we were turned away, and it only emboldened those that fought for Gwydeon and Midarin. Aerith told me that he needed to remind Gwydeon of who he was. It's not Gwydeon's role to fight the Children, or the Servants, or Dorovar, or the Heralds. He had to keep the people of this world believing that it is not the end. They have to believe there is still a fight that can be won. So, of course, Gwydeon would be with rebels who were trying to pick up the pieces of a shattered empire."

Rhain nodded in understanding, and continued her part of the tale.

"Taya and Jillian were supposed to help if they could, but not to put Jillian in any danger. Taya took the opportunity instead to take what she knew about Jillian and turn her over to Gideon."

Rhain felt Bryn's scowl.

"Gideon? Why would Taya take Jillian to Gideon?"

Rhain felt the sadness creep into her voice.

"Taya knows who Jillian's parents are. It makes sense that Taya would take Jillian to Gideon since he is now the vessel for Raenera's power. It all has to be part of Raenera's endgame. After we were able to uncover the truth of Jillian's parentage, she became too valuable to leave in our control."

Rhain's voice fell silent. When she spoke again, her voice was unsteady and uncertain.

"I should have seen it coming."

Bryn shook her head.

"There was no way you could have, Rhain, not even with your connection to Taya. No matter what she means to you or I, she was Gideon's daughter. Who knows how long they have been in contact. Taya learned in a world where a lack of loyalty meant death. Gideon and Taya kept each other alive for so long in that hell, I don't know that anything could have separated them. Not even you, not even me. With her pirate network, she was probably feeding Gideon information for years."

Rhain nodded. The supposition was a sound one, which made the next part of the tale that much more tragic and painful.

"Once Taya delivered Jillian to Gideon…"

Rhain's voice trailed off, she didn't know if she could say the next words. It was almost too terrible to contemplate let alone give voice to. But ultimately, she knew she had to say the words. The deed was too real, and so to try to ignore it was a crime in itself.

"Gideon killed her."

A single tear fell from Rhain's eye as she spoke the words, the pain still so real inside her. Marlae gasped and brought her hand to her mouth, shocked by the words. Bryn did not react at all. Her features were stern, controlled, and seemingly ambivalent. She stood, smoothed her dress, and finally let a frown curl her lips.

"Raenera killed her."

Rhain started to speak, but a single raised finger from Bryn stopped her.

"Gideon, our Gideon, would never sacrifice his own daughter for any purpose, just as Aerith would never sacrifice you, or Gideon, or Ayden, or Cedric, or Anabel. This family does not make those trades. Not for any price or prize. Raenera is in control of Gideon now. And whatever Raenera has planned required Jillian and also required that Taya could never communicate what she knew to anyone else."

Bryn looked down at the ground and then back to Rhain.

"After talking to Cedric and Wolf, I have a better understanding of what you and Gideon must be going through. That voice crawling around in the back of your mind. Those plans within plans that have been brewing since the dawn of Creation. You're able to control it in part because a part of Sabrina is with Halicon, and Halicon wants to you make the choices that are going to benefit us all. Pyrrus wants harmony for us all, and Wolf is able to make all of the voices he's dealing with work together, even Draven and Basille. I fear Cedric may soon become like Gideon. Emries was powerful and evil. That malice will run through Cedric like a poison until there is nothing left of Cedric and only Emries will remain. Raenera planned for far too long to let something as trivial as the free-will of her host stand in her way."

Rhain nodded. Her mother's words were well reasoned, as usual. Marlae let her glance move between Rhain and her mother, and she felt very out of place. She was doing her best to follow the names and the ideas that were being traded between the two, but she knew that it was beyond her at the moment.

"What can we do?"

Marlae chose to hazard a question since she had nothing of value to offer. She could try to comfort Rhain at some point in the future when things were not so raw, and also when her mother was no longer hovering. Bryn looked at Marlae and shook her head. Then she let her eyes fall on Rhain.

"Who did you send to Albitonin?"

Rhain looked at her mother blankly for a moment.

"You sent ambassadors and emissaries to the different factions in order to ensure you had support for the war that your father and Logan are fighting. Who did you send to Albitonin. Who is going to meet with Anabel?"

Rhain nodded, finally understanding the question.

"Jeroch."

Bryn nodded.

"Very logical. Given their history, the one person that Anabel would least expect to see but the one that she would be most likely to trust. And given the fact that she would not accept any other members of the family, other than perhaps you, it seems the only prudent choice. Though now I fear that I have no choice but to pay her a visit myself."

Rhain's eyes went wide.

"Do you think that's wise?"

Bryn wished that she would have projected more confidence into her voice.

"It may not be," Bryn responded, "but Anabel deserves to know what's coming."

Bryn turned and walked through the bedroom door back into the sitting room. She closed the door behind her, and Rhain knew the next moment that she had created a portal. Rhain could not help but chuckle to herself and smile. Marlae smiled with her.

"What is it?"

Rhain lifted Marlae's hand and kissed the back of it softly.

"Just my mother being my mother. She is not much for small talk when there are things to be done."

Marlae was happy to be alone with Rhain once again, but there was one nagging question in her mind.

"Your mother has a history with Anabel?"

Rhain chuckled to herself again and then nodded softly.

"As my mother said," Bryn said finally. "We're all family. Anabel is my sister, but not my mother's daughter. The Seth family is more than a little complicated."

On Being Bait

Year Two of the Divine Empress and Child of the Creator Marlae Tamerlane, Creator's Calendar Year 1872

When Aerith awoke, his head pounded and his eyes hurt, but beyond that there was no other pain. The wave of energy from the death of the woman who called herself Drust was potent and was enough to render Aerith unconscious for a few moments but not powerful enough to do any real damage. However, as he got back to his feet, he began to wonder whether or not he may have underestimated the power of the blow. Sitting on the ground, he felt no lingering effects, but the moment he tried to get to his feet was when he began to feel the impact. Finding his balance was harder than it should have been, and he constantly felt like he was on a ship in the worst conditions he could imagine. But after a few well-placed applications of power, Aerith started to feel more like himself again. The issue was, when he tried to release those flows or power, the unsteadiness and nausea returned. He would need to maintain the power, at least for a time in order to ensure that the effects were gone. Whatever that power was that the Adhradair possessed, it was potent stuff. Looking around, he was the only member of the group who had made it back to their feet. He looked around for the Black Snag first, uncertain if it had survived its close contact with the power of the Chorus of Souls. Aerith found the creature dazed, leaning against a rock. Once it realized that Aerith was standing over it, the Snag sent a wave of emotion that conveyed confusion and disorientation. While he felt for the creature's discomfort, Aerith was just happy that his old friend was still alive. Aerith left the Snag to recover and moved over to where Arin Ranthall still lay.

Arin looked to be in pretty bad shape from the large puddle of blood that he lay in. There was a nasty gash on the side of his head, but Aerith could see the flows of power beginning to knit through it. In a matter of minutes, it would only be a scar. Aerith put his hand on the old soldier's shoulder and channeled some additional strength into him. From what Aerith could tell the serious wounds had already been dealt with, and it would just be a matter of time before Arin was back to fighting shape. Aerith considered going to Saurn next, but when he saw the woman's body farther away, Aerith knew that she was clearly the priority. Laying on her back, Felicia Lorien looked like a broken doll. Shards of metal that had once been pieces of the creature known as Nightwing were strewn all around her, including the two bladed wings that had been torn into multiple pieces and scattered to the winds. Both of her legs were clearly broken. Her left was snapped just above the ankle. One bone protruded from the ankle side while the other protruded from the knee side. It was a vicious wound. The other leg was broken just below the hip and hung like a deflated balloon barely attached to her body. But those were by far the least severe of her injuries. When he was a boy, Aerith had seen old barrels split open by sledgehammers in an effort to quickly destroy them. Felicia's chest looked like one of those old barrels that had been broken open. Bones protruded from several points on her chest with blood oozing in all directions. Her breathing was ragged and uneven, and Aerith was shocked that the young woman was capable of breathing at all. Taking a moment and centering himself, Aerith laid his hand on the woman's arm and concentrated.

Aerith was not an adept healer. He never had the patience for it. He understood it innately which was how he was able to apply his powers to knit his own wounds. But that was practically reflexive. Healing someone else was an active application of power and required a level of precision and control that Aerith did not often have the patience for. However, in this case he found he had no choice, and if he didn't do something both Felicia and Orren were likely to die. First, Aerith had to visualize the damage to

Felicia's body. Her chest was the most problematic area, so he would need to start there. In his mind he pictured each individual rib that had burst through her skin. One by one he envisioned the rib pulling itself back through her skin and setting itself back in place. Once there, it would meld with the other broken piece of itself and seal itself closed. Then above the newly mended bone the muscle and skin would pull themselves back together, the flow of blood restored to the now healthy tissue. That visual locked into his mind, Aerith set on about his work.

When the first rib pulled itself back through her skin, Felicia let out a low moan of pain. The intensity of the moan increased as the bone slowly and stubbornly was put back where it belonged. Once the skin, muscle, and bone were fused back the way they were supposed to be, the moaning ebbed. When Aerith moved to the next rib however, the moan became a shriek of pain and Felicia's eyes shot open. Diverging from his work for a moment, Aerith pressed calming flows of sleep and numbness into Felicia's mind. It took only another moment for Felicia to drift away into unconsciousness, and for Aerith to return to his grisly work. One by one each of the dozen broken ribs were pushed back into position, and the skin and muscle knitted. Once her damaged chest had been dealt with, Aerith proceeded to work on her injured legs, again pushing the bone back through the skin and mending everything back the way that it was. Unfortunately, Nightwing was a lost cause. In order to resurrect that creature, the power of the Blaze was required in a quantity reserved for Halicon. Whether Rhain wanted to attempt such a feat would be up to her, but without access to the special metal that made up Nightwing's skin, it was highly unlikely that such a task was possible. Felicia would have to be content just being Felicia again.

With the young princess's injuries treated, Aerith turned his attention to Orren Eldrath. The expenditure of energy coupled with the constant drain that was keeping him upright against the aftereffects of the wave of power from the Chorus of Souls was starting to become a serious drain on Aerith's reserves. He felt tired and realized that he shouldn't have felt tired. The potency of the Chorus of Souls was something that would need to be contended with, and he understood now why it had taken Logan so long to recover following his altercation with Conquest as well as why Aerith had lost track of the man for so long. Exposure to that much concentrated power had to have incredible lingering effects.

Though Orren's condition was not as grave as Felicia's, his injuries were still serious. There were several pieces of the Nightwing armor embedded in Orren's skin, and one of his arms as well as one of his legs was broken. The breaks were not as severe as Felicia's but there was considerable internal bleeding. Because of the nature of the metal, it took more power than it should have to dislodge the fragments. The metal was designed to absorb power as a defensive measure, so it resisted Aerith's attempts at every turn. Eventually, Aerith found that his efforts were successful and all of the shards of Nightwing's armor were finally removed from Orren's wounds. The broken bones were simple enough matters, and after a few minutes all the medical and stabilizing work was done.

Walking away from where Orren still lay, the dizziness returned to Aerith's perception, and he was forced to sit back down on the ground. All of his strength was gone, and he could not catch his breath or stop his hands from shaking. He closed his eyes for a moment, and then found that he could not open them again. His mind was trying to push him into unconsciousness again, and no matter how hard he resisted, the blackness continued to gain ground. It was a hand on his shoulder that pulled him back from the abyss, and when he opened his eyes, he saw Arin Ranthall looking down at him. Arin looked better, but still looked as though he was not back to full strength. Arin squeezed Aerith's shoulder once, and then moved to sit in front of Aerith about five feet away. Once he was on the ground, he took one long sigh and then forced a smile.

"I suppose if you're here, things are bad."

Aerith smiled and nodded.

"As you can see, our enemies have gotten to be a bit more challenging than we expected."

Arin nodded.

"They do seem quite insistent."

Arin looked over to where Orren and Felicia still lay.

"They fought well. Not exactly practiced or polished, but they have heart."

"Good," Aerith said after a moment, "they're going to need it."

Arin smiled.

"You know who they remind me of?"

Aerith cocked and eyebrow and then shook his head.

"Victoria and I, back in the war."

Arin was a holdover from a more innocent time in the war; a time when the battle lines were clearer and there were really only two sides. The people fighting alongside Cedric Binosear were the good guys and the creatures they were fighting were the bad guys. Arin left a little farm town with nothing but his sword and a group of friends and family and signed on to the most important war in the history of the world. They just wanted to do their part and felt moved not to be heroes but to protect the lives of the family they left behind. Aerith was glad that he was out of the war by this time. Cedric Binosear and his people were powerful fighters, strong of character, and completely ignorant as to who and why they were fighting. Those were the hardest opponents to shake. The idealists. Fanatics were troublesome because they never knew when to quit, but idealists would go beyond their own abilities so long as they believed they were right. When Aerith fought as part of Bryn's army, the people who fought for him fought out of fear and fought out of some sense of obligation. It was no different than those who fought for Kaitain Lorien. They fought because they were expected to fight, but they were not going to push themselves to the brink for an evil man like Kaitain. Not like those who fought for Cedric. Those who fought for him, loved him. They were willing to die for him because they believed in him.

"I wish I could have met your wife," Aerith said finally.

Arin nodded.

"She was a good strong woman. A fighter."

By this time, Saurn had made it back to his feet. The man garbed in violet and gold robes took great pains dusting himself off before moving to join the two seated men. Saurn of course did not sit, instead opting to fold his hands behind his back and loom over the other two. He was still after all a member of the Brotherhood of Phasia, and was superior to these humans no matter how much power they may have gained over the years.

"Cedric was a fine man who fought a discreet war. Had Jeroch not been so arrogant, perhaps things would have been far different."

Aerith could not help but laugh.

"You never change, do you, Saurn? You still think that there was something that you could have done all those millennia ago to make things turn out different. All your plans within plans. And how did that serve you here? You've kept your finger on the scales in the Cadarian Empire since the day it formed. The Academy of Arcane Arts, the Shadow Guild, the Knights of the Flashing Blade. All your ideas. And just look how quickly they were destroyed once Talisia and Emries decided that they were tired of the way things were going."

Saurn's expression did not change.

"And would you have preferred that I allow things to grow wildly out of control? That I just sit and watch as the whole world fell under the sway of the fanatics and the agents of the Creator? Would you have preferred that there were no checks on the power that the Church represented? Can you imagine how this empire would have come into focus should ten generations of rulers be beholden to the Church? A Holy Emperor whose only focus was spreading the dominance of the Creator's law to every corner of the world. How would the Dark Gods have handled that? How would you, Aerith? Just think what would have happened if the Emperor of Cadaria would have sent an expeditionary force to the Pritan Islands and discovered your little hideaway. What would you have done then? Would you have been forced to kill them all until they stopped coming? Would the Dark Gods have been forced to descend upon the Empire of Cadaria en masse? Then where would this war be? I helped to decentralize power until such time as one of the greater powers made their move. It was a necessity, just as your division of power was."

Aerith wished that he did not agree with Saurn's assessment of the situation, but he could not find flaw in the phase's analysis. Saurn after all was one of the most intelligent beings that Aerith had ever encountered, and his capacity to foresee the path that events might take was unparalleled. It had been Saurn who had identified how special Aerith would be, and while he underestimated the type of impact Aerith would have on the war, he had still been right. With Saurn it was always about changing the landscape to ensure that events unfolded as he wanted. Where beings like the Creator and the Children made changes on the large-scale to mold the future into a desired shape, Saurn preferred to work small. He had seen the power of one man or woman turn the tide of history too often to ignore it. The trick was making sure that the right people were in the right place at the right time to be ready to make the impact that most benefited Saurn's plans. Sometimes those plans played out over a matter of weeks, but Saurn had the patience for plans that played out over years, decades, and even centuries.

"But we are not here to debate the merits of the actions that I have taken over these last millennia, nor are we here to talk about yours. We are here because no matter our interventions or lack thereof, the time of this world is coming to an end, and those that must be in their places for the final act of all that is are being called."

Aerith chuckled.

"You have a dizzying way with words, Saurn."

Arin frowned.

"I'm glad you understood that."

There was a slight groan from the direction of where Orren Eldrath lay. Aerith looked over to see that the former Knight of the Flashing Blade had pulled himself to a seated position. It took several attempts for him to find his feet long enough to take two staggering steps in the direction of the trio. When he was close enough Orren crumpled to the ground in what could be considered a partially controlled fall. It was clear the man was not worried about appearances, nor did he care to let his compatriots know how much pain he still was in.

"I didn't understand much of it," Orren said drawing his knees up to lean upon them, "but what I did understand, I didn't like."

Orren looked back and forth between the three men.

"So what is this about the world ending?"

Aerith looked at the Knight of the Flashing Blade and smiled.

"You're Orren Eldrath, right? We haven't been introduced, but I think you have a pretty good idea of who I am."

Aerith was right. As soon as Orren had laid eyes on the man he knew exactly who he was, at least a facet of it.

"You're Aryx's son, right?"

Aerith smiled at the characterization.

"You know, that may be the first time anyone has ever used that as the first way to describe me."

Arin chuckled.

"That I believe."

Aerith gave Arin a withering gaze but then joined in the laughter. Orren observed this with puzzlement and confusion. These men were just talking about the foundation of the Cadarian Empire, the Creator, the Dark Gods, and now the potential destruction of the world, and they were sitting and laughing about how someone was identified. It would have been disturbing if it wasn't so odd. It was Saurn who broke the levity.

"How you continue to find humor in the most trivial things boggles the mind. We may very well all be dead in a matter of days, and you sit like…."

"Humans."

Aerith's word was serious and his tone harsh.

"That's what we are fighting for, Saurn," Aerith continued. "I know you were never human and don't understand what that means, but it's what all of this is about. The innocent, the powerless. Whether they were on Onea, or Espre, or Loinn, or one of the hundreds of other worlds that the Children destroyed. Those people deserved to live; they deserved a chance to find peace for themselves. The Creator and the Children don't care about them. They only care about this petty disagreement about how everything should work. And when the Creator is bored, he knocks everything over and starts again. And now we have Dorovar who thinks he has a better way. But he's no different. Just kill everything and start over with a different set of laws. Something born out of so much death cannot be the way forward. Not with the Creator on the Throne, or Dorovar. The madness has to end."

Saurn's frown was filled with malice, not sadness.

"I may not be human, Aerith Seth, but now neither are you. And though I may have been born from the mind of one the Children of the Creator, that does not place me above the fate of this world. No matter who wins this ideological war, I lose as well. That is why we must all work together to stop the genocidal aims of our enemies."

Aerith was about to compliment Saurn, but the ancient phase pointed an accusatory finger at the old soldier.

"But just as the Creator and Dorovar cannot be allowed to sit on the Golden Throne and dictate the future of this and every other world, neither can you. You would be just as dangerous with that power, regardless of your intention to do good with it."

Aerith found the energy to stand, and after dusting himself off, he put his hands on his hips.

"You're right, Saurn."

For a moment, Saurn seemed taken aback by the concession.

"I have no business sitting on the Golden Throne, and I have no intention of it. I was made to be a monster, Saurn, and you have just as much of a hand in that as anyone. You tried to use me, just like Bryn, just like Ellis, just like Halicon, just like everyone who crossed my path in those days. And you know what it made me, it made me an efficient killer. It made me into every bit the monster that you wanted me to be. But Halicon made you to be a monster too. An unrepentant killer just like the rest of the phasia. Yes, you can all feel. Yes, you all have emotions, but I have lived with my wife for so long, I can feel the hunger in her. She needs to kill. For her it's like breathing. No, I can't sit on the Golden Throne, and neither can any of the phasia, or any of those touched by Emries or Raenera. Not my kids, not any of us."

Aerith stopped for a moment, trying to keep the rage and the pain within him at bay.

"But we're a long way from worrying about who does deserve to be on that throne," Aerith said finally. "The Creator is still holding all the cards, and Dorovar seems to be making a lot of gains. And now that I've felt for myself what that Chorus of Souls can do, we have a serious problem."

Orren rubbed the back of his head.

"How so?"

Aerith pointed at Saurn.

"When the phasia were created they were tied to the Blaze, Halicon's power. They were limited in how they could access that power and no matter how many of the phasia there were, that limit didn't change. It wasn't as though when one member of the phasia died, the rest suddenly got more powerful. Unfortunately, it seems like that's exactly what happens with the Adhradair. The less of them there are it appears that the Chorus of Souls become more potent for the ones that remain."

Arin caught on to Aerith's thinking.

"So are we doing Dorovar a favor by eliminating the Adhradair?"

Aerith shrugged.

"I'm not sure, but it feels like that may be the case."

Orren finally felt like he was putting the pieces together.

"So, what, Dorovar is using the Adhradair to free their confederates from the Sacred Weapons, hoping that some of them will be killed in the process, because he needs all of them to die in order to make the Chorus of Souls the most potent for him to use?"

Aerith nodded.

"It seems like that is what is happening."

Saurn's sneer was palpable.

"It's ingenious in its simplicity, and it seems exactly like the kind of thing Talisia would envision. Making Dorovar sacrifice his confederates in order to achieve his full power."

By this time Felicia was making her way to her feet and moving to join the rest of the group. Like Saurn Felicia did not sit, more due to the pain that was still wracking her legs than for any purpose of her position as a princess of the empire.

"So what do we do?"

Aerith found himself immediately liking Felicia. She was a woman of action, not interested in the finer points of strategy or logistics. She was a hunter, a predator, and all she wanted was to know who she needed to kill. After a moment, it was Saurn who interjected.

"Rhain sent me to fetch Orren and Felicia. There is something big coming, and she wants to make sure that all of those who are fighting to protect this world are unified in their action."

Saurn paused for a moment and then turned his attention to Aerith.

"I assume you had something to do with that."

Aerith shrugged again.

"I was just doing what I thought was best. Hannah made her agreement with the dragons, and we set them on the path to fight a battle in the skies above Albitonin. I have a feeling Talisia's people are going to be there as well, along with whatever Raenera has up her sleeve. That is where we need to marshal our forces. So when you go back to Rhain, tell her she needs to send everything she's got there."

Saurn nodded.

"How long?"

Aerith looked up into the sky and thought for a moment.

"A day, two at the most."

Saurn nodded.

"Then we should be on our way. What will you do?"

Aerith looked first to Arin and then back to Saurn.

"We can't afford to have Dorovar or his people interfering in that battle. Our job, Arin's and mine, will be to keep Dorovar distracted as long as we can. Maybe if we're lucky we can draw some of the Creator's attention too."

Saurn nodded and wasted no time in creating a portal back to the stronghold of the Shadow Guild. Orren and Felicia said their goodbyes and followed Saurn through. After watching them go, Aerith reached into the pocket of his cloak and pulled the Sacred Weapon Discipline from it. Aerith stuck the blade into the ground at Arin's feet.

"Take that to the Academy of Arcane Arts in Jelan. There's no one left there, so if they come for you, there's no chance of anyone getting hurt. I'll go to Hedorah. Seems like a good enough battlefield considering the circumstances. If they come for you, hold them off the best you can, but don't put yourself at risk."

Arin nodded. He continued to sit as Aerith collected the Black Snag and opened a portal to Hedorah. Arin took his time processing all of the information he had had to absorb over the past few days. As Aerith had said, the losses were mounting and they were running out of time. Finally, Arin got to his feet and took hold of the sword known as Discipline. The weapon felt cold and angry in his hand. Just as he was about to open a portal, he saw motion out of the corner of his eye. Walking toward him was the priestess Lya. Arin shook his head and could not help but laugh.

"I thought I told you to use the stone at the first hint of trouble. To just run. To get away."

Lya frowned and started to speak, but Arin cut her off.

"Never mind. I suppose I'm not going to be able to get rid of you, am I?"

Lya smiled and shook her head.

"Alright, but if you're going to follow me, from now on, you need to do exactly what I tell you, when I tell you, or we're both liable to end up dead."

If the woman was shocked or concerned, it did not register on her face.

"Congratulations," Arin said finally. "You are now officially bait."

Returning Home

Year Two of the Divine Empress and Child of the Creator
Marlae Tamerlane, Creator's Calendar Year 1872

Hannah Ironheart moved across the room and stood opposite the other four people in the private garden. Hannah remembered the first time when she was allowed in the private garden. Her predecessor as High Priestess was a woman named Rochelle Davin. Rochelle was a woman who fiercely respected her privacy, and when she was meditating or praying in the private garden, she did not want to be disturbed under any circumstances. When Rochelle was in the private garden, it was Hannah's responsibility to sit outside with her back to the door, contemplating the lessons of the Creator. One day as she was sitting and contemplating, three of the soldiers ran up the stairs from below. They demanded to be allowed to see the High Priestess. Apparently, there was a fire in the kitchens, and it was in danger of spreading. They wanted to evacuate the High Priestess from that wing until such time as the fire had been contained. Hannah told the soldiers that the High Priestess was not to be disturbed, and that she trusted the acolytes and initiates in their ability to address the fire. That there would be no need to evacuate. The soldiers persisted, attempting to push past Hannah and force the door. Hannah stood and blocked the doorway with her body, continuing to profess the fact that there was no need to disturb the High Priestess. Just as the soldiers were about to pull

Hannah out of the way, the door opened and the High Priestess emerged. She admonished the soldiers for their presumption and reiterated Hannah's assurances that the acolytes and initiates could address any issues and should any drastic action be truly necessary it would become apparent. The High Priestess also admonished the soldiers that their efforts would be of better use in attempt to fight the fire than to needlessly fret over the High Priestess. If anything became necessary, the High Priestess's aide would be more than capable of seeing to her health and safety. She dismissed the soldiers and closed the door behind her before the soldiers could voice any concerns. The soldiers left keeping whatever objections they had to themselves, and Hannah returned to her position guarding the door.

Several minutes after the soldiers were dismissed, the door opened behind Hannah once more. The High Priestess said nothing but summoned Hannah inside. Hannah followed dutifully, closing the door behind her. Rochelle moved to the center of the garden, sat and closed her eyes. When Hannah did not move from the doorway, Rochelle opened her eyes once more and then indicated the place across from her on the ground. Hannah was unsure how long they sat there. But when the High Priestess finally spoke, she told Hannah that an initiate could guard the door from that point forward, and that Hannah would join her in her daily contemplations. From that day forward, Hannah was in the private garden every day that she was in the Heart of Stone, and it was one of her favorite places in the world. She inwardly wished however that she had returned under different circumstances.

"This is Kiara Aren," Hannah said after a moment. "Kiara was supporting Jillian Corven in her dragon hunting efforts and has since found her way into my service despite the dangerous path that I am walking."

After being introduced, Kiara walked to Hannah's side, standing behind a step to Hannah's right. Hannah then turned her attention to the other people in the garden.

"Baeata, it is very good to see you again. I think you have done as good of a job as anyone could have given the circumstances. Neither Kaitain Lorien nor your allies have done anything to help make your job easier and wrangling the wills of the leadership of the Church is trying at the best of times. I'm proud of how you have performed, and you have proven to be a credit to you name and the faith that I placed in you as my chosen successor."

Baeata smiled and bowed slightly. It was a breach of protocol technically for the High Priestess of the Church of the Creator to bow to anyone, but given the circumstances, it was completely understandable and forgivable.

"Of course I know you Jeroch Yetre. My memories of you are split across two lives. My memories of you know the enigmatic but ultimately altruistic Vallic Ultiv. Of course, Aerith Seth's memories of you are completely different. Aerith Seth remembers you as an unrepentant killer who leveled whole cities and reveled in the death you caused."

Jeroch's expression did not change.

"Being called an unrepentant killed by Aerith Seth is not exactly what I would call a pointed critique. There are few creatures besides the dragons who is a more efficient killer than Aerith Seth."

Hannah nodded. She was not interested in getting into a debate with Jeroch about the finer points of the ancient feud between the two men.

"Unfortunately, Jeroch, what we are going to need in the days to follow is the efficient killer that almost brought a world to its knees."

Jeroch crossed his arms and considered for a moment. Hannah was right, and he hoped that whatever skills and tenacity that Aerith Seth had imparted into the pious woman would help them carry the days ahead.

"Priestess Rhya of course I know through the memories of both Arin Ranthall and Aerith Seth. I would like to apologize to you Rhya on behalf of my confederates. It was unkind the manner in which they used you to deliver a message. The outcome was one that was necessary, but you should have had more of a say in the manner in which that outcome was attained."

Rhya nodded and bowed more formally in Hannah's direction.

"One more thing," Hannah said after a moment. "Your sister Lya is well. She is still with Arin Ranthall and continues to fight the good fight on behalf of the Church."

Rhya bowed again, a small smile coming to her face. She welcomed the news and was humbled that Lady Hannah Ironheart would take the time to worry about the fate of Rhya's sister.

"And of course, Lady Anabel Binosear…."

Anabel raised her hand and shook her head.

"We understand you are acquainted with all of us through Aerith Seth," Anne said with a hint of irritation in her voice. "Shall we proceed to the dire news that you bring us?"

Jeroch could feel the tension in Anabel. If the woman had a weakness, it was her connection to her father. Anabel had no respect for Aerith Seth, had no respect for what he stood for, and did not even consider him to be her father. Hannah for her part did not press the issue and returned to the tactical nightmare that waited for them.

"Aerith fears that he may have painted himself into a corner. In his zeal to create a trap for our enemies, he may have constructed it too well, without considering all of the options. Regardless of that, the battle is coming here, and it promises to be the deciding conflict of our time."

Hannah paused and let her words sink in. Baeata considered Hannah's words, and then asked the only question that mattered.

"What information can you give us about what is coming?"

Hannah nodded.

"As you no doubt know now, Aerith and I have forged an alliance with one faction of the dragons of Espre. The dragons that now protect the Heart of Stone and Albitonin are loyal to Mariti Brightblade. Some of the most powerful of their number are part of this group. However, the Demon Dragon Shadowweaver and those loyal to him have taken losses at the hands of Mariti Brightblade, Aerith, and myself, and they have vowed vengeance. They will be coming here in force. Mariti is rallying her allies and is on her way here as we speak. We expect that within a day the battle will take place over our heads, in the seas to our west, across the mountain range, and in the plains all around us. The potential for destruction is catastrophic."

Baeata's face twisted.

"The people!"

Anabel nodded.

"Our first priority should be to send the people somewhere safe as we did in Hedorah. We cannot in good conscience allow anyone to be sacrifice needlessly."

Hannah agreed.

"The base of operations of the Order of the Flickering Flame is considered a safe place," the former High Priestess said after a moment. "The surviving members of the Academy of Arcane Arts as well as the Masters have helped the members of the Order there set up a post to treat the injured and shelter the displaced of this war. We should make ready to move the people of Albitonin to Menoris as quickly as possible."

Baeata's cheeks filled with color.

"Would those heretics actually accept the people of the Church of the Creator and share their resources?"

Anabel tried to keep her tone even and calm.

"Baeata, it was one of those heretics that saved your life in Hedorah. Whatever your personal feelings about the beliefs at the core of the Order, I can tell you that they would never deny someone in need, regardless of what they believed in. The Order has existed for two thousand years because it was always willing to help those who came to the Order find a better path for their lives, even if that path did not continue their association with the Order. They will not turn away the people of Albitonin in their hour of need, this much I can assure you."

Baeata acquiesced.

"Very well, Anabel, I have no reason to doubt your assertion."

Baeata paused for a moment, a perplexed look coming to her face.

"How could we possibly move so many people so quickly?"

Hannah motioned in Kiara's direction.

"I have trained Kiara in how to utilize the portal stones that Aerith created. There are several that are keyed to the Order of the Flickering Flame's base. This way we can move the people without alerting our enemies to our aims."

Jeroch nodded approvingly.

"Aerith has taught you well, Hannah. If we used as much power as would be required to open multiple portals from here to Oradrim, it would draw a great deal of attention. Perhaps our enemies would think that we were fleeing, or worse would think that we were summoning reinforcements. It might entice them to attack before we were ready. With Aerith's stones, the process will be slower, but at least we will be safe for a time."

Hannah continued the thought.

"If we contain our muster locations to indoors, places where the people will not be seen actively entering a portal, we would gain even more advantage. We don't know if there is a dragon circling high out of our sight watching troop movements, or perhaps a warrior angel that is keeping tabs on our progress. Either way, any advantage we can create we should."

Baeata stood.

"I should address our people."

After a moment, Hannah nodded.

"Would the people be disturbed by your taking over the mid-day supplication?"

Baeata considered for a moment.

"It would be unusual, but it would not be disturbing. Mid-day supplication has become a formality, and only on holy occasions does a member of the Church leadership even attend. It is usually only a matter of personal adherence to the teachings. However, in light of the announcements that were made this morning, I believe the people would be comforted by my appearance to reaffirm their faith."

Hannah smiled.

"Good. Then perhaps you should move the supplication to the Grand Temple. Spreading the word that all would be welcome to pray for our deliverance from danger in the presence of the High Priestess would guarantee larger attendance. There you will be able to announce the evacuation."

Baeata turned to Rhya.

"Go and see to the announcement, Rhya. It may ruffle some feathers, but that will matter little once I make the announcement."

Rhya bowed first to Baeata and then to Hannah before turning and leaving. At that moment both Hannah and Baeata felt conflicted. Baeata began to speak but Hannah cut her off, addressing the unspoken concern.

"I am not returning to Albitonin or to the Heart of Stone, Baeata. This is not my place any longer. And my place is certainly not as the High Priestess of the Church of the Creator. When this battle is over, if I survive, I will rejoin the efforts against the larger threats to this world. But the Heart of Stone will still need someone at the center of the Church. We will still need a voice that the people will trust to lead them through the coming darkness. You are the High Priestess of the Church of the Creator, Baeata. You have nothing to fear from me."

Baeata's smile came to her lips for a fraction of a second, and then she bowed far deeper than would have been permissible for someone of her rank. When she straightened again, she spoke.

"I should go and prepare for the supplication and to address our people."

Hannah spoke once more as Baeata turned to leave.

"I would ask one small favor of the High Priestess."

This time Baeata's smile was wide and genuine.

"If it is in my power to give," Baeata said warmly, "I would gladly."

Again, Hannah indicated in the direction of Kiara.

"Kiara was an acolyte in the Church before a difference of opinion and misunderstand brought her training to a halt. However, I believe the work that she has done to save lives and protect the innocent has more than erased any perceived transgressions. As she will be acting as my surrogate in the evacuation of the people, it would be of benefit if she did so with a recognized position within the Church. Would you be willing to grant her pardon and a position as a priestess within the Church?"

Baeata considered for a moment. It was a breach of etiquette of course, but it was not outside of the realm of possibility. Under the current circumstances, it would most likely not even be noticed. Of course, should they survive what was coming, there would likely be some formality necessary. But again, that was a long way away from where they stood. Finally, Baeata nodded her ascent.

"Come with me, Kiara," she said after a moment, "we need to get you changed into proper vestments. I don't think any prospective priestess could do better than a personal recommendation from the High Priestess and a member of the Knights of the Flashing Blade."

Kiara bowed first to Baeata and then smiled in Hannah's direction, unable to find any words for the privilege that had just been bestowed upon her. She never thought that she would be back in the bosom of the Church once again, nor did she believe it was possible that she would ever attain the rank of priestess. It was too far-fetched given her past. But now here she was, standing in the Heart of Stone beside the High Priestess and one of the greatest heroes that the Kingdom of Stone ever produced. Time seemed to have a strange way to smooth over past sins. Baeata once again nodded in the direction of Hannah and then Anne and led Kiara out of the garden. Once the door closed behind her, the three supposed allies were left alone.

"Now that the tender ears are out of the room," Jeroch said finally, "how bad is it?"

Hannah took the opportunity to sit down on one of the benches. It seemed like she had been on her feet forever, and there were only a few opportunities to rest.

"Bad."

That was the only word that Hannah could come up with. So much had happened, and much more to those who shared Aerith's mantle than to herself alone.

"Obviously you all know that we lost Hedorah, on top of that the Academy of Arcane Arts is off the board. Aerith made sure of that. Talisia had one of her agents infiltrated into the highest ranks, pulling the strings to ensure that when the time came they would fall to her will."

Anabel shook her head.

"I suppose we should not be surprised. Talisia had one of her agents embedded in Hedorah as well, so did Emries."

Jeroch continued.

"They were placed in the Imperial Court as well. It seems like the only place they didn't have a foothold is the Order of the Flickering Flame."

Hannah arched an eyebrow.

"What about the Heart of Stone?"

Anabel frowned.

"Talisia had at least one assassin stationed here as well. Aelind Torral, Baeata's aide."

Hannah's face did not register her disappointment for several moment, but then she sighed and shook her head. Of course it made sense. Talisia had her fingers in every crack and crevice that were open to her.

"Talisia also had an agent within the Dark Gods, Hannah. Even they were not immune to her treachery."

Anabel seemed visibly shocked by the news, and she turned to face Jeroch.

"Who?"

Jeroch signed.

"Lissa Terian. According to Rhain, she was coopted while the Dark Gods were still in the Heavens. She was the ones who brought the souls of Dorovar's Adhradair to this world to be imprisoned in the Sacred Weapons."

Anabel frowned.

"And how does Rhain know that?"

"Wolf Ranthall," he said finally. "Wolf has inherited Pyrrus' power, and Rhain has Halicon's. They communicate somehow, at least in pieces. I'm not really sure how it all works. But then again, I'm not sure we're meant to."

Hannah was the next to interject.

"The Adhradair are actively hunting the rest of the Sacred Weapons, and from what I can tell, most of them have been destroyed by this point. I know that Aerith still has two, but more than that I don't know. With the dissolution of the Knights of the Flashing Blade, it's very difficult to know. What I do know however is that at least six members of the Adhradair have been defeated. I also know that at least three of the Heralds have been accounted for."

Anabel's tone was hopeful when she spoke.

"Does that mean you know about Logan?"

Hannah smiled and nodded.

"He's alive. He defeated Conquest but it was at great cost. Unfortunately, he's cut himself off from the rest of us. I'm not sure what he's doing, but he doesn't want any of us following or interfering."

Jeroch scoffed.

"Knowing Ranthall, whatever he's doing is extremely dangerous and reckless."

Hannah frowned.

"Be that as it may, Jeroch, Logan is the reason that two of the Heralds were defeated. Arin Ranthall was behind the defeat of a third. You may not agree with his methods, but you can't argue with his results."

Rage came into Jeroch's eyes.

"I can argue with the results, Hannah, because I know the cost, better than you. Yes, what Ranthall did was necessary, and yes what he did was heroic, but his deeds cost us the lives of three of our siblings. Kamen, Rael, and Trece sacrificed themselves to enable Ranthall's victory over Conquest, a villain of Ranthall's own making."

Anabel was quick to interject.

"Logan was as responsible for Pike as you were, as Taron was. We don't have time for grudges and we don't have time to be divided, not with what is coming."

Anabel turned her attention back to Hannah.

"Can you tells us exactly what is coming?"

Hannah shook her head.

"Exactly, no. From the information Mariti has been able to provide, she believes she has between two and three dozen of the elder dragons behind her as well as between one hundred and one hundred and fifty of the younger ones. The bad part is that Shadowweaver may have as many if not more behind him. Whatever the number, the fighting will be intense and horrible."

Anabel frowned.

"And is that the only support we can expect?"

Jeroch shook his head.

"No. I'm staying. Hopefully Rhain will dispatch Saurn, Orren Eldrath, Felicia Lorien, Leonora Wastri, and Alderin Terian once they return to Bellnoc. Any of that number, combined with the dragons, and whatever other forces we can muster will at least assist us going forward."

Anabel nodded.

"I don't suppose Aerith will be bringing any reinforcements to the festivities."

Hannah shook her head.

"No. Aerith is going to use this opportunity to attempt to further destabilize Dorovar and his schemes. He also is hoping to draw some of the Creator's attention away from the Heart. Should the Creator decide that it is in his best interests to strike at all of his enemies in one place, this would be that place. Can you imagine the chaos if suddenly in the middle of the fight a couple of the Servants and a host of warrior angels simply appeared? I'm afraid the most you get is me, and perhaps a few hundred of our little friends, the Snags."

Jeroch's lips twisted.

"I hate those things."

Hannah took a deep breath and laid out the last bit of bad news.

"Unfortunately, we don't know what Raenera is doing. We don't know what Talisia's agents are doing. We don't even know what Kaitain is doing. I'm not worried about the threat that Kaitain represents, at least not as far as the Heart of Stone is concerned, but I am very concerned about the havoc that Raenera and Talisia's agents could inflict should they learn of an opportunity to press a perceived advantage. Whatever happens once the battle is joined, we have to be prepared for all of the things we don't know far more than the things we do."

Sisters and Sovereigns

Year One of the Just Empress Quyhn Ravenheart Lorien, Cadarian Calendar Year 1872

Isabella Ranthall stood at the end of the hallway looking out one of the wide windows down onto the bustling new city. Fortifications were being erected, troops were on patrol, and it seemed as though there were also common people from the surrounding area that were turning up to see what the new city was all about. At the farthest edges of her vision, she could see wagons moving in the direction of New Aradon, the place that defied time. Standing in the palace, Isabella felt utterly alone. Though she was happy to be reunited with her mother, she longed to return to Marlae Tamerlane and the court of the Divine Empress. While she understood the need to ensure that all allies of the Divine Empress needed to be aware of the aims of the war, that was the place for a diplomat. Her mother, Cairyn, could have easily accomplished it on her own. Isabella needed to either be with Marlae or on the front lines fighting the enemy. Though where she truly wanted to be was at the side of her father, the father she barely knew, and the father who seemed to always be in the thick of the fight, trying to make a difference. She heard the footfalls behind her, but did not turn. There was no danger to be found in this fortress, and despite the discomfort, Isabella was an able woman more than capable of handling herself in a fight should it come to it.

"You look so much like your sister."

The words shocked Isabella so much that she turned. Isabella knew the identity of the woman on sight, from the stories of her mother and her grandmother. However, the words, most assuredly meant to be kind, only served to remind Isabella of her place. She was a woman out of time. A woman that by all rights should not have existed. Isabella was an accident of two wars, a person that could only have come to be through the intervention and interference of divine beings. The Creator had made it possible for the Dark Mirror world to exist, and it had been the Creator that had allowed refugees from that world to find a home on this one. But unlike most of the refugees from the Dark Mirror reality, Isabella did not have an echo that existed in what was colloquially referred to as the Light Reality. The place where things progressed as they should have been, not how they might have been. Isabella had grappled with her own existence and identity for a long time when she came of age. Was she just a cosmic mistake? A cosmic joke? Was she intended to be leverage against her father, or perhaps a weapon to use against him? It was clear the only reason that the Creator allowed her existence was because of the importance of her father. For a long time, Isabella had resented her father. But then, she met Sabrina.

Isabella knew Sabrina the moment she laid eyes on her half-sister. They shared physical characteristics, though Sabrina was slighter of build than Isabella. Their eyes and facial structure were nearly mirror images of each other, though the power that raged in Sabrina's eyes could not be ignored. It was Sabrina who told the most overwhelming stories about the man who was Isabella's father. The stories of his heroism, of his sacrifice, and of his dedication to ensuring the safety of everyone who walked on every world. For a time, Isabella wanted to run off and join the Order of the Flickering Flame, to serve at her father's side in that Order, but Sabrina required a sacrifice of Isabella. Isabella was meant to protect her grandmother Anabel Binosear, and to keep her eyes and ears open for all information that she could pass back to her mother and grandmother. Sabrina had said that there would be a time when she would be needed for a greater purpose; a greater purpose that Sabrina had planned for her. Isabella would know the day that that greater purpose began on the day she met her father. Isabella now felt the call of that destiny. Though she would never lay eyes upon Sabrina again, she felt that the path before her was now unavoidable, wherever that path would ultimately lead.

"Thank you," Isabella's voice was small.

Midarin immediately felt that her words did not find the tone that she intended. Midarin had a great deal of respect for Sabrina Binosear and the entire Binosear family. They had all sacrificed much for the good of multiple worlds, and Sabrina herself had been the catalyst that had allowed the war against the Creator to have a possibility for success.

"I thought you would be spending time with your nieces."

Isabella considered for a moment. Of course, she knew she had a greater extended family and while she was eager to accept her father and even her uncle, the thought of these nieces bothered her immensely.

"Midarin," Isabella began, feeling some of the strength return to her voice, "both my mother and my grandmother have told me stories about you."

Midarin smiled.

"I'm sure quite a few were colorful."

Isabella nodded.

"Yes, but the one constant was that you were a woman who respected forthrightness and honesty. A woman who did not shy away from hard truths, and would be one of the first to speak them when necessary."

"You sound so much like your grandmother," Midarin said after a moment. "I assume she is the one who trained you in courtly manner."

Isabella nodded and turned back toward the window.

"Would it be too much to ask if I could take you into my confidence?"

Midarin moved up to stand beside Isabella looking out the window.

"Anything you say to me, Isabella, will go no further. I won't even share it with Gwydeon."

Isabella nodded and continued to look out the window for several long moments in silence. She was conflicted about the words that she wanted to speak. If she put the feelings in her heart into words, they would suddenly become real. However, she could no longer carry these burdens around if she was going to be of any use in the days to come.

"I know that my mother thinks that I should try to have a relationship with my nieces, but I just can't get the thought out of my head that by acknowledging them, I somehow make myself less."

Midarin saw the young woman's face reflected in the glass. There was pain in her eyes, a pain that had clearly been there for a long time. But Midarin kept her council until Isabella asked for it. She wanted to hear Isabella out, to fully understand.

"There's a part of me that knows I shouldn't be. My grandmother never hid from me the other life that my father had. The woman that my father married, the son that they had. That son then had two daughters, granddaughters that my father had never met, just as he had never met me until now. But what my grandmother tried to teach me was to not resent the man for the decisions that he made that were necessary for the betterment of everything that followed. My grandmother did not know her real father, did not have a relationship with him regardless of his long life. She resented him, and resented the fact that he had a relationship with my mother, though under an assumed identity. Sabrina also encouraged me to forgive my father and to forgive my family."

Again, Isabella paused. The next words would be the hardest to speak, the hardest to feel, and were the ultimate cause of her internal conflict.

"I suppose that most of this wasn't real to me until Marlae came to Hedorah. When I got to meet her, I got to meet also the piece of her that was tied to Elwyne Tamerlane. It was yet another cruel joke perpetuated by the Creator. Pulling Elwyne's soul back from the beyond and tying it to a woman whose reputation was one of arrogance, usury, and decadence. For my part however, I learned that perhaps the life that I resented, the life that my father had, was the better life, and somehow that made me even more of a mistake."

Isabella fell silent, and Midarin knew that there would be no more coming from the woman. Midarin did not turn to face the young woman, instead choosing to speak to the glass in front of her.

"You may not believe this, Isabella," Midarin began, "but for a long time I felt that my life was a lie as well. I did everything in my power to destroy the life that I had, and to become something that I wasn't. Like your mother, I was raised in court with expectations that I knew I could not fill. That was where the similarity between us ended. We liked to think that we had a little rivalry, as all of the princesses of our generation did, competing for the attention of the men who would come to woo us and to secure alliances. It's hard to live in a place and time when your gender was a commodity through which your family advanced. Of course, your mother was in a much better position than I was. Her kingdom was ruled by women, and so any alliance that was made with her would not diminish who she was. No such guarantee was waiting for me. I would have been married off to the best suitor, the one that offered money or protection, and my identity would be sacrificed for the supposed good of the people. Really I would have been sacrificed for the good of my parents."

Midarin paused to let her words sink in.

"So I rebelled. I seduced a man that I shouldn't have. Ran wild. I gave up the person that I was to prevent losing the person that I was."

Midarin could see Isabella's frown in her reflection.

"I know it doesn't make sense, but closing that door gave me so much. If I hadn't been exiled from my home, I never would have met your father or my husband. I never would have been in the position to aid the people of your reality as a beacon of hope in the darkness. And I never would have been here speaking to you."

Now Midarin turned to Isabella.

"I knew Elwyne Tamerlane, and I was lucky to call her my friend. I know your father, and I am proud to say that he is as much my family as my husband and my daughter. And I can say this without any hesitation whatsoever. Elwyne would have understood your conflict and would have been humbled by it. In that place, that dark hole that we somehow found a way to survive, finding light was a blessing. Both Logan and your mother had lost so much, and the fact that they found one another and were able to make something beautiful shine between them could never be a mistake."

Midarin put her hand on Isabella's shoulder.

"Never be afraid of who you are," Midarin said finally, seeing the tears begin to run down Isabella's face. "You have a family that is only waiting to love you. No matter what happens in the days to come, there is one truth that you will have to let into your heart. You are a Ranthall, and while that carries with it a great deal of tragedy and responsibility; it also carries with it bonds that will never be broken. Not by time, not by distance, not by blood, and not even by death. I love your father, and so I love you."

Midarin wrapped her arms around the woman as tears continued to fall from her eyes. At that moment, and perhaps for the first time in her life, all of the doubt inside Isabella melted away, and she felt that she was exactly where she needed to be.

* * * * * * * * * * * * * *

In another time, the meeting of three queens would have been something to write about. It would have been a gathering attended by only the most influential of lords and ladies and would have been the diplomatic event of a lifetime. There would have been gold and jewels, finery of all kinds, feasts and drink, and a great many lies told. But that reality was a long way from the sparse throne room of the newly constructed Fortress Peregrim, where the three women sat on common chairs in front of the dais that held the now-empty throne. Quyhn had opted to sit with those women who could easily have been considered her betters, Rhionna standing behind her trying not to look threatening and imposing. It was Midarin who began the proceedings, the woman who had been a queen, but had long since given up her crown. The woman who should have been a ruler, but had given up that opportunity to preserve a political necessity.

"After our meeting with Aerith Seth, Gwydeon was convinced that our place in this war was to ensure the protection of those who could not protect themselves from forces they could not hope to understand. And I know that it may not make sense to either of you, but even though

Gwydeon and I have great abilities at our disposal, those abilities are better served in this capacity, and not on the front lines with our old allies and enemies."

Quyhn took up the conversation.

"And we are grateful for the protection that Midarin and Gwydeon have offered. Considering the losses that we suffered at the hands of the Spirit and the angelic host, I don't think that any of the people who are fleeing the war would have any other place to hide."

Cairyn nodded solemnly.

"I've been in dark places during this war, but none darker than as an agent within the Hand of Chaos. Trying to gather intelligence on Talisia's movements had been a challenge, but at least I was able to ferret out that the Hand of Chaos was in coordination with Kaitain Lorien and had assisted in the abduction of Sadrina Annis. The act led to the destruction of the Citadel of the Dark Gods, the abduction and eventual death of Lissa Terian, and the crippling of the Hand of Chaos's leadership. But this war has had a terrible cost. I've seen what Kaitain Lorien's rampage has done, and I have to commend you on trying to create a safe haven here. But, we do have a bit of a dilemma."

That moment, the doors to the throne room opened and Isabella entered. She took a place behind her mother and waited for her opportunity to speak.

"The Binosear family has continued the war that we had no desire to fight. My mother wanted no part of her brother's war, wanted no part of this war, but felt compelled to fight when my own daughter shamed us into doing what was right. Sabrina I think was the best of us. Though I wish that both of my girls where here today."

Isabella put her hand on Cairyn's shoulder.

"As to our dilemma," Cairyn said finally, "I'll let Isabella elaborate. It seems as there is but one throne, and many people who are attempting to claim it. And when the innocent are fleeing the ravages of war, they need to know who is protecting them."

Isabella felt all eyes shift to her, and immediately felt badly for the way she had spoken to Quyhn upon her arrival. They were all in untenable positions and trying to do their best to find a way through. When Isabella spoke, her voice began low and uncertain, but increased in strength as she let the words fall from her lips.

"On behalf of the Creator, Marlae Tamerlane was declared the Divine Empress of Cadaria. Of course, that was a ploy by the Creator to sew division. It was a transparent maneuver, made no less transparent by the dispatching of two of the old gods to advise the Divine Empress in the execution of her role. What may not have been accounted for however was the fact that the soul of Elwyne Tamerlane would have such a profound effect on the soul of the former Marlae Lorien and turn her away from the direct control of the Creator's envoys. That's how my grandmother came to be in Marlae's service, and that's why we find ourselves here today."

Cairyn took up the negotiation.

"Marlae's claim to the throne is just as tenuous as yours, Quyhn, but for different reasons. Everyone here and most right-thinking people agree that Kaitain Lorien has gone mad, and that he is unfit for the throne. However, when his leadership was still recognized, he accused his daughter of treason and removed her from the position as the Voice of the Emperor and heir to the throne of Cadaria. Further complicating the issue was the fact that the emperor's new wife was not considered to be fit for her position. And though you were named as a ward of the empire following your father's death, Quyhn, and then subsequently elevated to the position of Voice of the Emperor and designated heir, there will be those that will never accept you as the Empress of Cadaria."

Midarin spared Quyhn the need to immediately respond.

"And so we have four claimants to the throne, and none that all of the people will follow. But those that will could cause problems for the others."

Quyhn felt the strength inside her grow that moment.

"I can't worry about those who follow Kaitain Lorien. Whether it is due to fear, or to obligation, or to greed, or to evil, their loyalty to him has been bought and paid for with blood and treachery. They will follow him to the ends of the world and will only ever be the enemies of those who wish to save the lives of the innocent. And while my dear friend Dominique could be considered a claimant to the throne, she has made it clear that she does not see herself as worthy of the position, nor is it a position that she desires. But the issue that she may cause is that she intends to use whatever good will that she garnered as the Empress of Cadaria to increase support on my claim for the throne. The people who accept her may be pushed to support me. However, those that reject her could be pushed into the hands of Kaitain, should they think she was part of the attempt to assassinate him, or to Marlae, should they be the faithful of the Church of the Creator. Those who are faithful to the Church will be more likely to follow Marlae considering that I have forged a public alliance with members of the Dark Gods."

Cairyn nodded. She was impressed with the young woman's bearing. She was taking the situation far better than she had any right to. Cairyn found it interesting that the fate of the empire would fall to two young women who were polar opposites, but both desired the same outcome. They wanted peace and prosperity to emerge from the shadow of cruelty.

"I'm not so sure that all of the members of the Church of the Creator will fall so quickly behind Marlae, even if she's calling herself the Divine Empress. Hannah Ironheart is still on the field."

Isabella frowned.

"My grandmother is in Albitonin negotiating with High Priestess Baeata Catrinel. But Baeata was clear on one thing. She did not have the full support of the Church yet. There were still many who were unclear as to the fate of Hannah Ironheart and awaited her return to her rightful place. If Hannah does return to Albitonin, it could destroy the potential alliance between Marlae and the Heart of Stone. Or worse, it could cause a civil war among the faithful."

Quyhn looked up at Isabella.

"Isabella, I'm going to assume that Marlae would not be willing to entertain the idea of abandoning her claim on the throne of Cadaria."

At first Isabella started to respond, and then she realized that the question was rhetorical. Quyhn was just working out ideas in her head, trying to find a solution to a problem that had no solution. Quyhn had been publicly declared as the rightful ruler of Cadaria by Dominique, and that was something that could not be ignored or dishonored.

"Midarin," Quyhn continued after a moment, "what would be the consequence of my recognizing Marlae Tamerlane as the rightful Empress of Cadaria?"

Midarin considered for a moment.

"Assuming of course that Hannah Ironheart does not fracture the faithful of the Church of the Creator, it would give them cover to seek refuge here without worrying about incurring the wrath of the Creator. It would at least in theory unify the sides. But there would be a number of issues to contend with. The first of which of course is the work being done by Dominique. We would have to get word to her of the alliance and insure that she is not working against us. Secondly, and perhaps most importantly, Marlae would have to recognize your station as the Voice of the Empress and Heir to the Throne of Cadaria. That would give you the veil of legitimacy to act in her stead, and would also give sanction to everything you have done to this point."

Midarin turned her attention to Isabella.

"Do you think that Marlae would agree to that condition, if it cleared her path to the throne?"

Isabella considered for a moment, but it was Cairyn who answered.

"I suppose should the offer be put to her in such terms, she would agree. It strikes me that Marlae desires to prevent a war, not start another one."

Quyhn nodded.

"Then it seems our course of action is clear. Someone must take the offer to Marlae, and someone must communicate the situation to Dominique. But I fear that Dominique would only trust the information from two people. I cannot leave here, so that means that Midarin, you must carry the message."

Midarin frowned.

"And of course, Gwydeon picked the wrong time to go off gallivanting yet again. I don't like the idea of leaving Quyhn defenseless. The girls have power, but they aren't practiced. Rhionna has power, but she doesn't know how to use it. If the Creator were attempt to strike at us again, I'm afraid they wouldn't be able to stand against the onslaught."

Cairyn interjected.

"I'll take the offer to Marlae, and I'll send back Gwydeon. He'll understand I'm sure the necessity of his return. In the meantime, Isabella will stay here. She is trained in the use of her abilities and can serve as a measure of defense until such time as both you and your husband are able to return. Perhaps she can also take the opportunity to teach her family members some things that will enable them to be more self-sufficient when the time comes."

Cairyn craned her neck to look up at her daughter.

"Do you think you're up to it, Isabella? Or would you rather take the message to Marlae?"

Isabella recognized the fact that her mother was giving her an opportunity to escape the necessity of dealing with her extended family. Cairyn understood Isabella's conflict. She had her own when it came to Logan's family. But being a Binosear necessitated accepting that blood had a way of making things messy. Finally, Isabella nodded.

"I'll stay and support Quyhn until Gwydeon and Midarin's return."

Quyhn smiled.

"Thank you Isabella. Now, if you and Rhionna wouldn't mind. I have some things I would like to discuss with Cairyn and Midarin privately before they depart."

Quyhn nodded to Rhionna and she and Isabella moved out the door that led to the staircase to the upper floor. No doubt they would quickly run into Mirana and Liara who were lingering somewhere close. After the two had left the room, Midarin turned her attention back to Quyhn.

"What did you need to say to us that you couldn't say in front of Rhionna or Isabella?"

Quyhn smiled.

"Nothing. But if I didn't force Isabella and Rhionna to speak, I doubt they ever would."

Cairyn felt a blush come to her cheeks for a moment.

"Don't be so eager to force Ranthalls together, Quyhn. Trouble finds them wherever they go, and the more of them there are, the more trouble will come."

* * * * * * * * * * * * *

Rhionna and Isabella walked wordlessly in the direction of the stairs that led to the upper floor. Mirana and Liara were waiting at the foot of the stairs, and Rhionna could tell by the look on Liara's face that something was wrong. The younger of the two sisters was very intuitive, and seemed to know things that no one else should have known.

"What's wrong, Liara?"

Rhionna's voice was confident and smooth. It was clear to Isabella that she was a practiced soldier and knew when the time was to show emotion and when the time was to understand the terrain.

"Isabella?"

Isabella nodded.

"We need to talk to you about your father."

Isabella felt her blood run cold.

"He needs your help badly, and I don't know if you can wait until Gwydeon gets back."

Chapter CXIX

Prophets and Priestesses

Year Five of the Just Emperor Kaitain "Dragonsbane" Lorien,
Creator's Calendar Year 1872

When Jillian awoke and opened her eyes, she saw nothing but black. For several long moments, Jillian wondered if she had been blinded by whatever Taya had done to her. However, once she brought her hands up in front of her face and could see them clearly, she realized that her eyes were not the problem. After several moments she found enough strength to sit up, and once she did, she was almost sorry that she made the attempt. The blackness was all around her, a great void that stretched in all directions for as far as the eye could see. She felt as though she was sitting on something solid, but when she looked down, there was nothing. A strong sense of vertigo set in, and she had to close her eyes to keep from vomiting. When her stomach calmed and she felt that she could open her eyes again, she hoped that the blackness would be gone and that it would have been all part of a bad dream. Perhaps she was still sleeping and the betrayal at the hands of someone who was supposed to be her protector had never come to pass. But then the void captured her vision once more, and she felt her heart sink.

After several moments, Jillian started to lose her sense of orientation. Up and down had no meaning, and though whatever she sat upon was solid, she continued to lose that sense of being anchored. Her mind wandered and when it did, she began to feel as though she were drifting on a great sea that had no end. As much as Jillian wanted to try to stand, there was no purpose in it, and so she continued to sit, feeling as though she were losing control more and more as the moments passed. Once again, she squeezed her eyes closed, but this time there was no solace. Her stomach began to lurch again, and the feeling of dizziness and lack of control was almost doubled. However, when she tried to force her eyes back open, she failed. Fear rocketed through her body, and she rubbed her eyes with the back of her hands trying to force them to open once more. Finally, her eyelids obeyed her will, and they opened to the void once more. This time though, her field of vision was not completely dominated by the void. At the very edge of her sight, there was a speck. At that distance it was impossible to call it more than that. It was so far in fact that it was impossible to assign a color to it. The speck was just there in the nothingness, no sense of where it was in relation to where she was. With no sense of scale and no objects to help determine distance, all Jillian could tell for certain was the speck was out of the reach of her outstretched hand. Now though, Jillian had a reason to get to her feet, and it helped to steel her sense against the oppressive and disorienting void.

After several failed attempts to get her legs to cooperate with her mind, Jillian was able to force her way to her feet. She spent so much time however concentrating on the process of standing that she had not noticed until she was back on her feet that the speck in the distance had grown in size. It was still just a speck at the edge of her vision, but it was larger. Maybe it was longer? Or was it wider? With no frame of reference to how she herself was oriented, it was impossible to determine. But the speck was large enough now that her mind could begin to assign a color to the object. It was a reddish gold. Or perhaps it was two colors, red and gold, and the size and distance simply made her eyes conflate the two. Jillian took a tentative step in the direction of the speck, but as she stepped, she expected the invisible floor to continue in front of her. When her foot touched where the floor should have been, there was nothing there. Jillian almost fell forward, but fortunately she had not committed enough momentum in the forward motion to send her tumbling into the nothingness. Her concentration and focus shifted totally to regaining her balance on the invisible floor beneath her, and while she was able to return to some semblance of balance, she had once again lost track of the speck in the distance. When Jillian looked up again the speck had once again grown larger, and had started to take on a definite shape.

As the moments passed the speck grew closer and closer, and Jillian began to tell that the object was not a speck of dust or anything of the kind. It was definitely a person. As the person continued to move forward, Jillian began to be able to make out more details. Where once the red and gold colors had melded together to make one blurry color, as the person grew larger in her vision, the colors clearly separated. Whoever the person was had long red hair and was wearing some kind of clothing that was made from golden fabric. Or perhaps it was armor? The person was still too far away to tell for sure. Jillian felt her hand go unconsciously to her side. It was then for the first time that she realized that her sword was no longer on her hip. Scaleripper had been with her for so long, part of her for so long, that the feeling of it not being with her was alien and disturbing. Her resolve was shaken by the realization, and the lack of the weight of the weapon at her side became magnified. That moment Jillian felt as though she had been robbed of a limb. Again, Jillian was forced to steel her resolve against the disturbing sensations, focusing all of her attention on the oncoming form.

The being continued to grow larger and larger, but the more Jillian watched, the more she began to lose track of time. How far away must the form had been to take so long to cover the distance. Jillian tried to mark time with her heartbeats, but there seemed to be no correlation between the number of beats and the relative size and clarity of the person who approached. Either the person's pace was so erratic that it was impossible to mark it with time, or time had no meaning in the void and she was only driving herself to distraction trying to make sense of the senseless. Finally, Jillian surrendered her senses to the will of the void. She no longer worried about up or down; no longer worried about time. She just stood, not even waiting, not even expecting. She quieted her mind the best that she could. In that moment, Jillian's thoughts turned to Logan and to Kamen. The two seemingly opposites whose views of the world were in perfect alignment. Logan, the agitator, the wanderer, the instigator, the philosopher, and the emotional being. Kamen, the gentle giant, the contemplative, the slow-spoken and formal. Yet at the same time they were so alike, as though the two together would form a perfect being. But it was the philosophy of the flickering flame that came to Jillian's mind. She saw the candle flame in her mind. The flame that knew it could be much more but was content to be what it was, to do what needed to be done in that form so that it could go on to be what it needed to be next. The ultimate expression of surrender to the self. Accepting yet dreaming, content yet yearning, dedicated yet transient. Focusing on the flickering flame in her mind helped to calm Jillian's nerves. She no longer felt the vertigo that threatened to twist her mind and her stomach. She no longer felt the desire to reach for the sword that was not there. The flame helped her surrender to the moment, surrender to the void, but not lose herself in the process. When Jillian's eyes returned to the oncoming form, she realized that its pace had stabilized, and more of the being was coming into focus.

It quickly became clear that the form approaching was that of a woman. The gate and the manner in which she moved made it obvious. As Jillian had surmised previously, she had long wavy red hair that cascaded over her shoulders and down her back. From Jillian's angle she could not see how long the woman's hair was, but something inside of Jillian guessed that it stretched at least to the middle of her back if not farther. The details of the gold dress that the woman wore also came into better relief as the moments passed. What Jillian had once mistaken as one piece of clothing from a distance was revealed in fact to be two layered atop one another. The first, the one that was most prominent was the golden cloak that sat upon her shoulders and moved elegantly around her with every step. The cloak itself did not appear to be made of a heavy material, but the color was so brilliant that it gave the garment a solid and substantial feel. Perhaps if there had been some kind of external light or shadow it would have been easier to gain perspective as to the material, but Jillian had to guess it was some kind of silk or similar fabric. The golden color was brilliant and overwhelming, completely drowning out the crimson dress that was wrapped around the woman's form.

As far as Jillian could tell, the deep red dress stretched from the woman's throat all the way to above her knee, but despite how it clung to her form, it moved easily and did not appear to be restrictive in any way. The closer the woman came, the more details of the dress that Jillian could make out. The dress, while at a distance appeared to be solid crimson, was not in fact. Sewn throughout the incredibly beautiful dress were shapes that resembled leaves and flowers. The color of the ornamentation of the dress matched that of the golden cloak, and sparkled and shimmered with every step. The woman's arms were bare, as were her legs beyond the hem of the dress. She wore no boots or shoes, nor did she wear gloves of any kind. The only adornment on her arms or legs was a band of gold that wrapped around the top of the bicep of each arm. At first Jillian thought the piece of jewelry was a single solid piece. However as the woman approached it became clear that the band was in fact three distinct circlets of gold with slight separation between each of the circlets. Clearly, the three bands were part of one piece, snaking around her arm snuggly enough that they did not shift with her movements. In addition to the circles of gold around her arms, there was a distinct piece of jewelry on her head. Because of the woman's hair it made it difficult to pick out the details of the circlet. It had a design like a vine with small branches that reached down onto her forehead. The central spines of the vine that made up the body of the circlet met in the center of her forehead in a white jewel. From the bottom of the jewel there was thin vine that hung all the way down to a spot between the woman's eyebrows, almost reaching the top of the bridge of her nose.

What Jillian found strange was that despite being able to make out the details of the dress, the jewelry, even the circlet that she wore on her head, Jillian had been unable to make out any of the woman's features with the exception of her hair. When Jillian looked down again at the approaching woman's feet, she noticed something strange. With every step there was motion around the woman's feet. At first Jillian could not make out exactly what it was, but finally the detail of the motion became clear. As each foot touched down on the void, ripples emerged around her feet as though she was stepping onto the surface of a pool of water. The ripples did not extend infinitely, and seemed to be contained to only a foot or so around where each step landed. When the woman was no more than a few feet from where Jillian stood, she stopped. It was then that whatever had obscured the woman's facial features disappeared, and Jillian felt her breath catch in her throat and her heart begin to beat wildly.

That moment Jillian felt as though she were looking into a mirror. From the shape of her nose, the shape of her mouth, the way the corners of her eyes had a slight upturn to them. The arch of the bone above her eye and the width of the bridge of her nose. Even the subtle point of her chin coupled with the shallow divot between her nose and her upper lip. Her pale skin with a near constant slight flush in her cheeks that accentuated her high cheekbones. The only difference that became readily apparent to Jillian was their eyes. While Jillian's eyes were a brilliant green, the strange woman's eyes were a golden brown. The two women stood silent for several long moments regarding one another. Finally, the strange woman spoke, and when she did the sound was like the voice Jillian heard in her head when she was trying to work through her own thoughts.

"Peculiar, is it not?"

The words hit Jillian's ear like silk. While the voice was familiar, the tone and the manner were not. The woman's voice was soft yet powerful, and her tone was stilted and formal. The words did not linger on the air, but had gravity to them that was undeniable. At first, Jillian was too stunned to speak. She was still trying to process the similarity between the two women. Again, the thought came to her mind that she must have been dreaming.

"I assure you, Jillian," the woman's voice came again, "this is not a dream."

A sudden rush of fear ran through Jillian. How was this woman able to read her thoughts? Was she able to influence Jillian's actions? Did she know everything that Jillian knew? The woman held her hands up gently and smiled softly.

"Fret not," the woman's voice was soothing and calm. "I assure you that I mean you no harm, and in fact I would be unable to harm you even should that be my intent. Should I attempt to harm you, I would accomplish nothing more than harming myself."

Jillian was confused, but she nodded anyway. The woman's voice was comforting even if her diction put Jillian on edge. At heart, Jillian was a simple woman, born in a simple village to a simple life. But that simple life had been destroyed. And yet, there was still something within Jillian that clung to those simple origins. She did not feel comfortable around those of supposed superior breeding. There was something about the way they spoke that always put Jillian on edge. On top of that, Jillian had no patience for those who used four words when the same thing could be said in one, and also had no time for those who had been taught practically since birth to lie with a smile on their faces. And of course, for those who were able there was a difference between lying and tailoring information to fit the necessities of the moment.

"Your suspicion is understandable given the uncertainty of your current circumstances, Jillian, and I shall try as I can to allay that suspicion and help you to understand exactly what your situation truly is. You have pieces and nothing more. I would like for you to understand everything, at least as far as I understand it."

Jillian again nodded, her words feeling unfit for the moment. Of course, the only question that kept coming to her mind was perhaps the least important, but it tumbled out of her mouth before she realized she was speaking.

"Who are you?"

The woman in red and gold smiled.

"That is a fair place to start, and I apologize for my lack of manners in not introducing myself at the outset of our encounter. My name in life, was Genovefa. I was the High Priestess of the Perfect Order of the Goddess Raenera, and the advisor of the protectors of the world of Loinn known as the Adhradair."

Jillian took the words in stride. She had been exposed to others who had come from worlds other than her own, and those who claimed to have died. In fact, Logan was from another world, and also had died at least once. Kamen as well. Again, the woman's next words seized upon Jillian's unspoken thoughts.

"I suppose in a way there are similarities between myself and Logan Ranthall or man known as Kamen. But were I to pinpoint exactly where there is divergence between Logan and myself is the fact that Logan had choices in the manner in which he lived his life and what he made of himself. I unfortunately did not, and I am unclear as to whether or not Creation is better for that fact."

Jillian was puzzled and it showed on her face. Genovefa's smile faded slightly, and she tried hard to explain her previous words.

"On my world," Genovefa began, "my path was set from the moment of my birth. On the day of my birth, the High Priestess at the time waited at the Grand Temple for my parents to arrive. Moments after my birth, I was wrapped in plain swaddling and carried by my parents to the steps of the Great Temple. The High Priestess opened the Book of the Goddess and found the names of my parents and spoke the name that the Goddess had decreed for me. I was pronounced by the High Priestess to be from that moment forward, Genovefa. And then standing there on the steps the High Priestess announced that I would be the next High Priestess. I was barely minutes old and the whole of my future was laid out for me. Everything that I would ever need to learn. Who I would marry. How I would spend every day of my life. All set from that moment. How much would everything that you know be different if Logan Ranthall had come from a world like mine? Perhaps he never would have become anything other than a farmer. Perhaps he never would have stood against the Children of the Creator. Perhaps he never would have come to this world, and perhaps he never would have met you. In some ways, you are giving me an opportunity to see how my life could have been had I not been born upon that world."

Jillian was horrified. As much as she longed for the simple life that was taken from her, she could not conceive of a world where she wouldn't have the choice of who she wanted to be, who she would love. Genovefa's smile relayed that she understood exactly what Jillian was feeling.

"Suffice it to say, however," Genovefa continued, "that the Book of the Goddess did not dictate my life, nor did it dictate my end."

The woman's smile faded, and her gaze became serious and somber.

"I implore you Jillian, there is much to my tale, and until you hear it all, you will not understand. But your story does not begin as you think it does. It does not begin on this world. It does not begin in that small cabin in the arms of the woman you believed to be your mother. No, your story actually begins on my world, on the day our world fell."

The former High Priestess let the words sink in for a moment before continuing.

"The final days of the siege of my world were chaotic and completely out of any measure of control. My days were spent in the Grand Temple, praying to the goddess for guidance, protected by my greatest advisor and friend Seisyll. The rest of the Adhradair were beyond my council. They had been swayed by the pretty words of Talisia and Emries and had taken the powers offered so that they could take the fight to the dragons who were tearing our world apart and slaughtering the innocent. Though I advised against that course of action, and I pleaded for patience and faith in the will of the goddess. But the Adhradair did not heed my caution, and took the power, thinking that somehow the ends would justify the means in the eyes of the goddess. Even Seisyll took the power, though her rationale was that I needed to be protected at all costs, and if the price was her soul, she was willing to pay it."

There was a pause, and then Genovefa continued, her voice grave.

"But no matter of power gifted to the Adhradair would do anything beyond hasten the path to the destruction of our world. And in fact, in the end, that is what happened. The war between the Adhradair and the dragons tore our world apart, creating disasters and death on a scale that could not be imagined. The night before our world passed beyond the point of saving, the goddess Raenera appeared to me. It was not in a dream, and it was not in the guise of a mortal woman. No, it was in her true form, a form so alien that I do not believe I have the words to describe its beauty and horror. She touched my head and told me to have no fear. Raenera told me that Loinn would not survive, but not to lose faith in the teachings of the Perfect Order. The goddess told me that I was still needed to serve the will of the goddess and to preserve the Perfect Order. The Adhradair believed that they were getting revenge upon the dragons for their treachery, but the treachery was not the dragons' but was in fact perpetrated by Talisia. Talisia used the dragons just as surely as she had used the Adhradair. The incursion of the dragons forced the Adhradair to accept powers they were never intended to have, and thus made them vulnerable to what would come after. As each of the Adhradair met their fate, Talisia captured their souls for the nefarious purpose she had planned upon this world. In order to ensure that Talisia would not succeed in her plan, my soul needed to remain in the hands of the goddess. And so, in the end, on the spot where I was given my name, I plunged a dagger given to me by the goddess into my own chest. I surrendered my soul to my goddess, and trusted in her plan."

Genovefa fell silent, closed her eyes for only a moment, and then continued her tale.

"My journey was a long one to this world. I roamed in a place like this for a long time, alone. But soon I found myself in the company of others. They could not see me, and they could not hear me, but at least I no longer felt alone. Eventually, one of those who found this space with me could see me. She could speak to me, and I could speak to her. Her name was Jehna Feris."

Jillian's eyes lit up at the name.

"It was in my conversations with Jehna that I understood what had occurred. Raenera in an effort to hide my soul had bound it to a bloodline that was susceptible to divine influence. As the Creator intended to keep his thumb on the scales of this world, he imbued one bloodline with a direct connection to the Spirit of the Creator, enabling those of that bloodline to know what the Creator wished them to know, and to help influence the direction of the world. You know them as seers. I learned so much from Jehna. And it was then that my purpose was revealed."

Genovefa put her hand on Jillian's shoulder.

"My purpose, Jillian, was you. The goddess appeared to me once more, and on that day, I saw Jehna for the last time. In this place she appeared, but she could no longer hear me. But in her arms, she clutched a little baby girl. You. It was then that Raenera appeared. She said to me that you were the path to the ultimate expression of her love. That you would be the catalyst that could help save all of us from the Creator's wrath. That the power that inhabits you is drawn from the power of multiple worlds and multiple realities, and through that you can make the world however you wish. You need only accept that potential. I have been waiting here in your mind, waiting for you to be ready to hear me. But just as you were on the verge of hearing my voice in your mind, you were blocked from me. I could not see you. I could not hear you. You never came to this place from that point forward."

For a moment Jillian's thoughts were filled with the revelation of her strange birth and the fact that this woman, Genovefa had also lived in the mind of her mother. But it was the description of being blocked from Genovefa's voice that took Jillian's attention. There was only one thing that could have been the cause of that obstruction.

"Scaleripper," Jillian said absently.

Jillian reached up and put her hand on Genovefa's.

"When my mother was taken and the village destroyed, I wanted nothing more than to destroy the dragons responsible. Scaleripper found its way to me just as I was old enough to learn how to use it, and learn how to fight. I assume that's the time when you would have been able to speak to me. Scaleripper and I were never separated from that moment forward. It was always with me. Now I don't think it's with me anymore. I think that maybe I dropped it when Taya ambushed me."

Genovefa's face was hopeful.

"Where did that weapon come from?"

Jillian thought.

"There was a bard. He used to travel around to all the towns, but he took a special interest in me because I was an orphan and because my home had been destroyed. He said that it reminded him of his own town and all of the friends that he had seen killed, and the orphans left behind. I remember his stories about the dragons and the Dark Gods, and about beings of light and darkness. He would sing for hours and never seemed to tire. One day he said that he was going away and that I would probably not see him again. He said he had a gift for me, to help me find a way to get back what was taken. He gave me Scaleripper."

Jillian's voice trailed off. The man's blond hair stuck in her mind, but she could not remember his name. She remembered his kind face and his singing, but not much else. Finally, Jillian shook herself away from her thoughts and returned her attention to Genovefa.

"How do I use this power?"

Genovefa smiled.

"I shall teach you," she said finally. "But I must give you this warning. This power is not to be trifled with. It is the power to change the fabric of reality, and to shape reality to your thoughts. This is not a power that humans were intended to have. But like the Dark Gods, and like the Adhradair, these abilities are necessities of the time. These abilities, while nearly without limit, are dangerous not only to those who dwell inside this reality, but also to you. They are dangerous because these powers are not yours, you are only fated to borrow them for a time."

Jillian could not keep the confusion from coming into her eyes.

"If they're not mine, whose are they?"

Genovefa smiled wider and put her hand on Jillian's stomach.

"They are your child's. The future of us all."

Angels and Architects

Year Two of the Divine Empress and Child of the Creator Marlae Tamerlane, Creator's Calendar Year 1872

Rhain was still recovering with Marlae by her side when she felt the first portal open in the common room on the other side of the compound. The second portal formed moments later in largely the same place. It seemed like her emissaries were returning, but already she could sense that something was wrong. After several moments, Rhain leaned over, stroked Marlae's hair and then kissed her on the cheek.

"We have guests."

Marlae nodded and quickly made her way to the side of the bed to help Rhain to her feet. Rhain was still feeling the effects of Taya's death, which didn't make much sense. Halicon's memories did not contain anything that remotely echoed this feeling, and he had lost dozens of phasia during his time on Onea. The only thing that seemed to make sense was the fact that Taya was killed by a possessor of the powers of a Child of the Creator. Of course, on Onea, Emries had been the cause of Logan Ranthall's death after he had become a member of the Brotherhood, but even that had not felt like this. Perhaps Raenera had found a way to damage Halicon through his subordinates. It would help to put further context to Taya's death. Though her mother had been at least partially right, Rhain felt that there was more to Taya's death than just preventing information getting back to the other members of the Brotherhood. If Raenera had indeed found a way to inflict damage through the death of the phasia, that would be her way of dissuading Rhain from taking direct action in an effort to interdict against Raenera's plans. The phasia were now a vulnerability, and Rhain had to seriously consider how they were to be used. Already Halicon's powers were causing serious damage to Rhain's body, and a few more losses like Taya's might be the final straw.

With Rhain leaning heavily on Marlae for support, the two women made their way out of the quarters of the Grand Master down the narrow hallway to the common room that often served as a meeting room and briefing room for the members of the Shadow Guild. When Rhain arrived, she was shocked to see more than a few faces, and disappointed that others were not there. Saurn and Orren Eldrath stood together on one side of the room in quiet discussion while Gwydeon Sandar, Camille Sandar, Felicia Lorien, and Sadrina Annis stood together in another corner. There was concern for a moment that Camille was there, but as the two women locked eyes, it became clear to Rhain that something was different about the woman. Marlae helped Rhain to a chair and stood beside her as the others moved to closer positions.

"What has happened?"

Saurn's voice was not one of concern, but he was clearly aware that there were limitations on Rhain and the manner in which she was able to contain Halicon's abilities. The Blaze was eating through her at a rapid pace, regardless of her ties to Aerith Seth, and it would only be a matter of time before the Blaze would need a new master or mistress. Once upon a time Saurn would have done everything that he could to hasten that coming, but now, he was more concerned with the potential ramifications for those forces arrayed against Dorovar and the Creator.

"What I'm about to say, I believe has something to do with why Gwydeon and Camille are here," Rhain began, putting as much strength into her voice as she could manage. "I have sent emissaries to each of the factions that are fighting on the same side of this war in an effort to rally everyone to the common interest against the common enemy without unnecessary risk or unnecessary duplication of effort. Jeroch was sent to the Heart of Stone in Albitonin to meet with Anabel Binosear and the resistance forming there. Saurn was sent to bring Orren Eldrath and Felicia Lorien back into the fold. Leonora Wastri was dispatched to find Alderin Terian, and Isabella Ranthall was sent to connect with her mother Cairyn Binosear. The last group sent was Taya Viruci and Jillian Corven. Their responsibility was to make contact with the Lordhill Rebellion and to inform them of the progress in the other areas of the war, as well as to render assistance if necessary. Unfortunately, as I now know, Taya and Jillian never made it to that rendezvous."

Rhain steadied herself and tried to make her voice as dispassionate as possible.

"The short version of the events are these. Gideon Viruci is now the vessel of the powers of the Child of the Creator Raenera. Taya has been relaying information for an unknown period of time to her father to further Raenera's agenda. It is unclear the type of information that was relayed or the manner in which Raenera intended to use it. However, what I do believe is that some of that information has enabled Raenera to concoct a method to attack me directly through the phasia. I come to this realization because once Taya delivered Jillian to Gideon, he murdered her."

There were strong reactions all around the room, none stronger than from Gwydeon. The winged man began to protest, but Rhain held up a hand to restrain him.

"I know what you're going to say, Gwydeon. My mother said the very same thing. Gideon would never consciously harm Taya, and any action that he took against her must have been at the direction of Raenera. While in part I agree with this assessment, there are two points that cannot be ignored. Gideon, as well as all of his knowledge and abilities are lost to us, co-opted by a hostile Raenera who has her own designs on this war. It increases the number of enemies that we must fight, and also adds a large unknown to the conflict. The second point is the one that concerns me most. If Raenera has found a way to use the death of a member of the Brotherhood as a weapon against me, I am placed in an awkward position. Can I in good faith send the phasia into dangerous situations knowing that it may lead to my own death, and therefore weaken our position? But by the same token, can I rob the conflict of some of our most powerful assets in order to save myself? I have no clear answer to this quandary, and I would rely upon you, my friends and allies to help me determine how to proceed."

Gwydeon took a step forward and set his eyes on Rhain. She could feel his mind working, the famous tactical insight formulating some kind of strategy.

"How many of the Brotherhood, or at least the extended version of it, are still alive?"

Rhain's look was sullen.

"Including yourself, Gwydeon, the number is small. Alderin Terian, Leonora Wastri, Saurn, Jeroch, my mother, Logan, and of course Caris, though I don't know how we count her. I would have counted Nightwing within that number, but it's clear that its powers have been lost to us."

Saurn's eyebrow arched.

"Ranthall still lives?"

Rhain smiled and nodded.

"I discovered it shortly after you left. He and my mother returned from Hedorah together. The creature known as Conquest has been destroyed, and though the effort was costly, it has solidified Logan's control over the Blaze and has made him a formidable weapon. But his path is not ours. I cannot hold him back from what he must do now."

Saurn frowned.

"And that is?"

Rhain shook her head.

"I'm sorry Saurn. I know that I implored that we all work together and have no secrets from one another, but this one I have no choice but to keep. Should even the idea of it leak out into the ether, the task is doomed to fail, and if Logan fails, nothing we do from this point forward matters."

Gwydeon laughed.

"Sounds just like something Logan would jump at."

Saurn rounded on Gwydeon.

"You may put utter faith in your old friend, Gwydeon Sandar, but the man that we now must put our faith in is not the man you once knew. Day after day he becomes more like his patron Aerith Seth. He is reckless and he is unaware of the limits of his abilities. And while yes, he may have been able to defeat Conquest, he did so only because three of the Brotherhood were sacrificed to his vanity. While Jeroch and I agree on very little, I do agree in this instance that the cost was too high to pay."

Rhain's voice cut through the squabble.

"Enough! What Logan did was done with my sanction and was necessary. Kamen knew that it was coming, as did Rael and Trece. And regardless of whether or not you agree with my decision, it is done. And it gets us no closer to finding a resolution for our quandary. Do I continue to commit the phasia to the front lines, or do I hold them in reserve until such time as they are in dire need?"

Gwydeon scratched his chin.

"Logan is going to do what he is going to do; he'll always be in harm's way. And I don't suspect that you will have any better chance controlling your mother than Aerith does."

Rhain chuckled and shook her head.

"Saurn," Gwydeon continued, "as much as I respect your abilities as a member of the phasia, your skills and disposition have always lent themselves to a more clandestine bent. Your gift for strategy and underhanded tactics are best kept with Rhain in a planning and preparation capacity. Of course if you disagree?"

Saurn shook his head. Though he had little use for mortals in general, Saurn had to give grudging respect to Gwydeon Sandar for his ability to quickly and astutely size up situations.

"I agree that my talents would best be used coordinating information and intelligence for the war effort here."

Gwydeon nodded.

"I'll be returning to our defenses in New Aradon."

The name of the city brought looks from all of the people in the room. Some out of confusion, others out of exasperation.

"Yes, I know, but it was fitting given the circumstances," Gwydeon demurred. "Regardless, I made a promise to stay out of the ugly parts of the war and devote my time and energy to protecting the innocent from the fallout. We created a stronghold that I can defend with Wolf's daughters and with Midarin. We've already had to fend off an attack from the Spirit and a host of angels which cost us a lot of good people. We need to be ready in case they come again."

Rhain frowned. The fact that the Creator thought Gwydeon was important enough to attack was troubling. Then what Gwydeon said struck a chord in Rhain's heart.

"The Creator came after Wolf's children."

Gwydeon nodded.

"He came after Camille too, and managed to take control of her. He sent Camille after Cedric."

Rhain nodded.

"That makes sense. The Creator has actively been targeting our family. And he wanted to get to Cedric before he had a chance to do what he has done."

Saurn's perturbed voice hit the air once more. He did not like being the last to know things.

"And what has Cedric done this time to complicate our lives?"

Rhain steeled herself for the fallout of her next words.

"Cedric has killed Emries and taken his powers."

The explosion that Rhain expected never came. There was just a quiet acceptance. Though it was Gwydeon's words that best summed up the situation.

"While I appreciate the poetic justice, this all feels like a setup. Gideon with Raenera's powers, Cedric with Emries', you with Halicon's. Anyone seeing a pattern?"

"Aerith Seth."

Saurn's pronunciation of the ancient man's name made it sound like a curse. Rhain waved off the myriad questions and turned her attention back to Camille.

"We'll get back to my father in a moment. Camille, how were you freed from the Creator's control?"

Camille looked first at her farther and then back at Rhain.

"Jerah. She stopped me from killing Cedric and then somehow cut my tie to the Creator. I'm not sure how she did it, but my abilities are different now. More like the rest of the Dark Gods', and less like my father's."

Rhain considered for a moment.

"So through Dorovar, Jerah has learned how to strip the divine power from beings. That could prove to be useful if Caris ever decides to return to the fold. Do you know where she went?"

Camille shook her head.

"All I know is that after she did whatever she did, she dropped me through a portal close to Aldere. I don't even know how long I was unconscious before I found my way back to my parents. It had to have been the better part of two days."

"Unfortunately," Rhain added, "Dorovar's influence keeps Jerah shielded from me. I wonder how long Dorovar will allow her to continue to operate as a rogue agent."

Orren finally added his voice to the proceedings.

"I think Aerith may have figured out an answer for that."

Rhain acknowledged the man with a wave of her hand. All eyes turned to him, and instantly Orren felt self-conscious. The conversation being had was way beyond him, and he was still coming to terms with the fact that a Child of the Creator had tried to kill him not long ago. There was too much running through his mind, and if he tried to make sense of it all he felt his head would explode. So, he tried to focus on the moment and only the moment. The rest would have to take care of itself later.

"Aerith believes that Dorovar has to eliminate all of his Adhradair in order for the Chorus of Souls to be potent enough to harm the Creator. If that is the case, maybe he doesn't want to do the deed himself. Maybe that's why he needs Jerah."

Saurn nodded.

"It is just devious enough to be plausible."

Rhain also nodded. The supposition made a great amount of sense. Jerah could eliminate all of the Adhradair and then Dorovar could simply snap his fingers and rid himself of Jerah. She was the ultimate disposable tool that could assist Dorovar in alleviating any crisis of conscience when it came to executing his former fellows. If of course the man had any measure of conscience left after executing billions to fuel his path to the Golden Throne.

"Could perhaps Jerah be going to remove the divine influence from these other children?"

Marlae's question was well-timed and astute. Gwydeon frowned. He had not considered it because he had just been made aware of the circumstances behind Camille's freedom. Of course, the thought immediately concerned him.

"If Jerah does go to the fortress, I'm not sure how the girls or Midarin will react. Plus, with Isabella there, it could turn into a fight, and that would not do anyone any good. I should get back, just in case."

Rhain held up her hand.

"Please remain a few moments, Gwydeon. I find your council invaluable, and I have a favor I wish to ask of you. In light of what else I know to be happening, and due to the fact that Alderin and Leonora have not returned, it is important that we have a firm understanding of what to do next. My mother and Jeroch are both in Albitonin with Anabel Binosear and a mass of dragons that are loyal to my father and Hannah Ironheart. Another contingent of dragons is on their way to Albitonin, one that at one time was loyal to Talisia Masile."

Felicia added her voice to the deliberations.

"That's why Aerith wanted us to get back here as quickly as possible. He thinks the battle at the Heart of Stone will happen in no more than two days, maybe sooner. He wanted to make sure you had all the reinforcements you could manage to send along to assist with the defense."

"He also thinks that whatever Raenera is going to do is going to have an impact there as well," Orren added. "The way Aerith made it sound, it's going to be one hell of a fight."

Rhain narrowed her eyes suspiciously.

"And just what is my father going to do?"

Saurn frowned.

"For once, it appears that Aerith is going to follow the more logical and tactical path. With Dorovar hunting the Sacred Weapons, Aerith did not want to take the chance of the Adhradair interfering with the battle in Albitonin. He and Arin Ranthall are going to make targets of themselves in an effort to keep Dorovar busy. He also hoped that perhaps the Creator would take interest in what he was doing and thin out the potential combatants in Albitonin."

Rhain could feel the wheels turning in Gwydeon's mind.

"I appreciate what Aerith is trying to do, but I don't think it's tactically the right plan."

Felicia was not a novice when it came to military tactics, but she did not see the point that Gwydeon was trying to make.

"Why wouldn't less opponents be a better circumstance?"

Gwydeon frowned.

"As usual, our side has made decisions based on incomplete information and flawed assumptions. I don't blame Aerith for what he's trying to accomplish. But he doesn't know about Raenera's ability to hurt Rhain, he doesn't know about Jerah being able to remove connections to divinity, and he doesn't know about Gideon or the Creator's attempt to acquire Mirana and Liara."

Saurn felt the pieces click into place in his mind.

"And so you feel that rather than prioritizing removing combatants from the battlefield, we should concentrate on adding as many as possible."

Gwydeon nodded.

"I don't know how many dragons will be fighting on Aerith and Hannah's side, but for some reason I don't like their chances of holding off both Raenera's forces and the enemy dragons. Even if the enemy dragons are divided between Raenera and the Heart, it may still be too much. But if we added the angelic host and the Adhradair to the mix, Anabel and the others could be more strategic in their attacks, and they could also hold Jeroch and Bryn in reserve to minimize the risk to Rhain."

Marlae followed the logic, but some of the details were fuzzy. She was just beginning to pick up some of the finer points of strategy from Terrance Aldora and from Isabella Ranthall, but there was still so much she could not see. Once upon a time one of her tutors had tried to teach her chess. He told her that it was the greatest way to expand her mind to be able to process the possibilities. That the pieces on the board were not the game, but the way the opponent moved the pieces. Marlae had the man executed for being boring. Of course, he had been right, and it was yet another shameful mark on her history that she needed to make up for. One of far too many to count.

"And how do we make sure that those other two forces join the battle?"

Here is where Rhain could tell that Gwydeon was uncomfortable.

"We have to accentuate our opportunity and minimize our risk."

Rhain could feel Gwydeon's tension. He didn't want to say what was in his mind, didn't trust that he was thinking logically.

"We need to send Mirana and Liara to the Heart of Stone, and we have to make sure there is a Sacred Weapon there before the dragons arrive. Once there is a Sacred Weapon and a mass of dragons for Dorovar to kill, he'll be sure to send forces."

The look on Camille's face was incredulous.

"You'd actually put the girls at risk? After all you've said about protecting them and making sure that they're safe?"

Gwydeon frowned.

"If I felt there was any other way, Camille, I would take it. But there isn't. There's only this. We have this chance, this one chance, to really hurt our enemies and to give us a chance for a victory we could never imagine. We've suffered too many loses, lost too many friends, and all we've managed are a series of holding actions that get more costly with each engagement. We succeeded in eliminating the Children, at least in one form, but their schemes continue, and their danger has not lessened. The phasia are nearly gone, the strength of the Dark Gods is waning, and we again have to put our faith in the plans of men who know they have to walk their paths alone."

Several heads turned at once, and Felicia, Gwydeon, and Camille all let weapons form in their hands as a portal burst into existence in the far corner of the room. When Cairyn Binosear stepped through, she immediately put her hands up against the arrayed weaponry.

"You should knock first," Gwydeon said finally, releasing the weapon from his hand.

Neither Orren nor Felicia could prevent themselves from laughing, and even Camille smiled at her father's dry humor. Cairyn was quick to move toward Gwydeon, pat him lightly on the side of the face, and then turn to Rhain.

"Isabella stayed behind to defend Quyhn and the city until Gwydeon's return. I've come with an offer from Quyhn Ravenheart that will settle any dispute as to the disposition of the throne of Cadaria. It's a good offer and should help us to assuage any internal conflicts among the innocent and refugees. Unfortunately, to make sure the terms of this accord are properly communicated to the people, Midarin has gone to meet with Dominique Lorien."

Camille pulled on her father's sleeve and whispered something in his ear. Gwydeon nodded.

"Camille just reminded me that Chelsea Zarova when we last saw her still had her husband's Sacred Weapon. She is acting as Dominique's personal protector. They're on their way to Albitonin by way of Iltorp with Alderin Terian."

Rhain sighed.

"Which means Leonora Wastri is now with them, and if nothing changes, it puts two more of the Brotherhood in harm's way in Albitonin."

Rhain shifted her gaze to Camille.

"Camille, I need you to go to meet with your mother. You can accompany Chelsea and Dominique to Albitonin. If Dominique wishes to come here, then so be it, but Chelsea must continue to Albitonin, or she must give you the Sacred Weapon to take there. Nothing I can do now will prevent Alderin from continuing to Albitonin, but Leonora must come back here."

Rhain fell silent for a moment.

"What is it, Rhain?" Gwydeon said finally.

"Something Wolf didn't want me to know. But he couldn't hide it from me forever. Camille, tell Alderin that Darrien is on her way to Albitonin. He'll be sure to go with you then."

Camille nodded.

"And when you get to Albitonin, try to convince my mother and Jeroch to come back here. I don't expect that Bryn will listen, but if you explain the situation to Jeroch I'm sure he'll relent."

Gwydeon put his hand on his daughter's shoulder.

"I'll send the girls through to meet you once I let Quyhn know the situation."

Gwydeon formed a portal and started to walk through. Rhain's voice restrained him for a moment.

"I would tell you to send Isabella back, but I have a feeling she may have her own plans. There's too much of her father in her."

Gwydeon stepped through the portal and let it close instantly behind him. Rhain then turned her attention to Orren and Felicia.

"Orren, Felicia, I need you to go to Albitonin to help with the defense. I can't tell you what you're walking into, but it's going to be unlike anything you've ever faced before. I'll understand if you don't want to take part."

Orren looked at Felicia, there was a quick unspoken conversation, and both nodded.

"We'll go."

Rhain concentrated for a moment and a portal opened.

"Jeroch will have felt that. I'll give him a moment to understand what is happening."

Rhain waited, keeping her thoughts focused on the portal.

"Go. And remember, explain to Jeroch exactly what is happening."

Orren and Felicia both nodded and stepped through the portal one after the other.

When the portal closed, Rhain turned her attention to Camille.

"Are you ready?"

Camille nodded and then the portal opened. After Camille stepped through the portal closed, and Rhain slumped into the chair. Portals shouldn't have taken that much out of her, but every expenditure of energy was getting harder and harder. She could have let Saurn open the portals, but Jeroch and Leonora needed to feel that it was coming from Rhain. Trying her best to regain her energy she forced a smile and turned her attention to Cairyn.

"So, what is this accord?"

Destiny of Our Own Making

Year Five of the Just Emperor Kaitain "Dragonsbane" Lorien, Creator's Calendar Year 1872

Dorovar stood looking out into the nothingness, feeling changes upon the wind. Things were happening across the face of Espre and the Heavens above, but those events were outside of Dorovar's perception. Despite all of the power that Dorovar had amassed, despite the enormity of information that Dorovar had absorbed over the many millennia he was floating between worlds and then trapped in the Vault of Terrors, there was still so much outside of himself. When Dorovar joined with the Chorus of Souls, he believed that he would instantly gain access to all of the knowledge of all of the souls within the Chorus. However, the Chorus proved that the greed that tortured the souls of these beings in life also gripped their souls in death. They would not give up their secrets easily or quickly. Though the Chorus seemed to be indifferent when it came to lending its power to Dorovar, it took much longer for the ancient man to learn how to commune with the souls. At first, all the Chorus of Souls represented was a collection of echoes of life and death. Dorovar could not parse the individual identities within the Chorus, but he could feel the mass of death that held them in their place. He could feel how each of the souls died, perhaps not the exact details, but a general impression. Was the death natural or unnatural? Was it murder? Was it peaceful? Was the soul ready to depart or was it clinging to the mortal world with every breath and beyond? It was an overwhelming mass of emotion, and Dorovar who was not practiced with understanding and processing emotions would have to shut himself off from the cacophony for long periods of time just to prepare himself for the next interaction.

In the early days with the Chorus of Souls, Dorovar did not even bother to open himself up to the emotions of the Chorus for more than a few moments at a time. He did not see the relevance. The dead were the dead. He could use their power to lay waste to the worlds of the Children and that was all that mattered. So long as he accomplished his aims, what did it matter how the poor and wretched dead ended their lives? The fact that they would not part with their secrets meant that Dorovar only needed to see them as a tool and nothing more. But as the numbers of the Chorus of Souls grew, Dorovar could feel a change inside the mass. They wanted to speak to him; wanted to impart their stories and their wisdom. But Dorovar was too blind, too angry, too filled with his need for revenge to listen. Yes, the Chorus had come to him in his moments of desolation and depression, feeling as though he would pointlessly destroy for the rest of eternity, but the power that the Chorus represented had rekindled something within Dorovar, something that could not be denied. Though he would no longer be able to be motivated by hate and rage, he did still have hate within his heart. He hated the Creator. He hated the hypocrisy of Creation. And most of all, he hated himself. Dorovar could not separate himself from the actions that had taken place on Loinn, and for many millennia that self-loathing had taken the form of wanton destruction. Like the petulant child lashing out at his parents by destroying, so too did Dorovar visit his impotent rage on the absentee father and mother who had made him what he was.

The devastation of Loinn was Dorovar's responsibility, and it was also Dorovar's fault. But part of him still did not understand why. Yes, Talisia had disguised herself as Raenera in order to trick Dorovar into allowing the dragons to come to Loinn. What was it though that allowed Dorovar to be tricked by Talisia? In the Perfect Order, everyone had their place. The words of the Goddess Raenera were transmitted through the High Priestess and no one else. So why did the Goddess appear to Dorovar, and why did Dorovar accept that? If Dorovar had truly been a custodian of the Perfect

Order, as the Adhradair were intended to be, then why did he not simply dismiss the visions out of hand? Why did he not go to High Priestess Genovefa with the visions when they first appeared? Why did he keep the revelation to himself? It occurred to Dorovar that something within him must have been broken. He was not a perfect member of the Perfect Order as the Adhradair were intended to be. Something was malformed within him. But whose responsibility was that? If Dorovar was made wrong, it could only have been at the hands of Raenera. But the Goddess could not be wrong. Therefore, the Goddess intended him to be the way that he was. It was circular logic based on a faulty assumption. Dorovar was unable at that time to make the distinction between the Perfect Order and the Goddess Raenera. But all this time away from Loinn, all this time away from the mistake that he made, he now had a better understanding of why he did what he did.

In truth, there were two Perfect Orders. There was the perfect order that was the religion of Loinn and the Adhradair. It was the teachings of the Goddess; it was the ceremony and the trappings. But that was not the real Perfect Order. The real Perfect Order was the book of names, the strict adherence to roles, the enforcement of those roles, and the harmony that the Order represents. No war, no conflict, no question. The tragedy of what happened on Loinn was the fact that worship of the Goddess would eventually create a circumstance that conflicted with the central tenants of the Perfect Order. Dorovar became trapped. The Goddess had appeared to him, told him to meet with the dragons and give them sanctuary. The Goddess was the ultimate direction for the Adhradair, and so Dorovar did not see the purpose of discussing the content of his visions with the High Priestess or any other member of the Adhradair. He needed only to inform them once the deed was done. And that was what he did. Now, the Adhradair should not have had a choice in what happened next, neither should the people of Loinn. The words of the Goddess superseded everything, and so the Adhradair should have simply accepted Dorovar's words, as should have the people. The Adhradair however, who had not seen the vision from the Goddess fell back on the teachings of the Perfect Order. The Adhradair had a prophet, that was the High Priestess. The Adhradair had a negotiator, and that should have been the person who met with the dragons. The Adhradair had an emissary, and that should have been the person who took the message of the agreement with the dragons to the people. And so, despite the fact that the orders came directly from the Goddess, in Dorovar's mind, the rest of the Adhradair and the populace could not internalize those words. The conflict was untenable, unexpected, and ultimately fatal to the entirety of the world.

Again, in reflection, Dorovar should have questioned the visions, should have discussed with the High Priestess, should have involved Drust and Seisyll. But the belief in the Goddess prevented the belief in the Perfect Order. And that was what Dorovar was trying to rectify. Without conflicting directives, the Perfect Order could succeed on the grand scale of Creation. Though Dorovar would sit on the Golden Throne, he would not intervene. The Perfect Order would simply move on, untouched, unmoved, and unmolested. That was the true power of the Perfect Order. I needed no intervention, and had Raenera been a true goddess, she would have understood that.

These thoughts led Dorovar back to the Chorus of Souls. He had used the Chorus in the same way that Raenera had used the Adhradair. They were merely tools to execute her will. But that could not be what they were in the best expressions of themselves or the Perfect Order. The Chorus of Souls also could not simply be a tool if the Perfect Order was going to rearrange Creation in the manner in which Dorovar intended. Despite the discomfort that communing with the Chorus of Souls caused, Dorovar forced himself to remain open. At first all that was communicated from the Chorus was pain, anguish, and anger. The pain was so intense in fact that Dorovar almost aborted his attempt and closed himself off once again. Dorovar pushed through the pain that filled him, feeling the touch of it through his heart and through his own pain. It was then that Dorovar truly understood. It wasn't just that Dorovar was trying to understand the Chorus of Souls, the Chorus of Souls was trying to understand Dorovar as well. That was why all that Dorovar felt was pain when he touched the Chorus. That was the way the tortured souls there felt that they could communicate. They felt the pain brewing and building inside of Dorovar. They felt his conflict. That created a bridge by which they could communicate. The Chorus taught Dorovar to move beyond his pain and to find the peace that the Perfect Order had once created within him. Once Dorovar had rediscovered his center, he would spend long hours communing with the Chorus of Souls, learning all that he could. In the first long sessions of commune with the Chorus, the souls that would come forward were the ones that knew Dorovar by name. Many of the souls Dorovar knew from Loinn came to him, telling stories about their deaths, their violent horrible deaths at the hands of dragons or burning in the fires of their world as it tore itself apart. It was through these communal sessions that Dorovar learned of the fate of the Adhradair. They had not been taken into the Chorus of Souls, and so Dorovar feared what they were to be used for by the enemies of Loinn; be it the dragons, Talisia, Emries, or Raenera herself.

As time passed, more voices began to emerge from the Chorus. The first that were to appear were always the angry souls, those that felt their time was cut short by unfair circumstances. Some were those that were killed by Dorovar, but others were killed by others of their own kind, disease, accident, other forms of violence. But beneath those angry voices were more content voices, those that had accomplished great things in their lives. Those that died in their bed at an advanced age surrounded by their families. It was those souls, some from the departed generations that preceded him on Loinn, that restored his faith in the Perfect Order. There was a Creation that could be made that would allow all beings to die that peaceful death. There could be a Creation where there was no murder, no vice, no disease, and no unfulfilled legacies. That was what the Perfect Order promised, and it was why Dorovar had to ascend to the Golden Throne and prevent the perpetuation of the usury and violence that permeated the Creator's domain.

Dorovar continued to commune with the Chorus of Souls, until there was suddenly a new surge of rage and confusion that filled the Chorus. A mass of new souls was added to the Chorus from Espre, and they were loud and violent. For several long minutes, Dorovar could not make sense of the cacophony. Finally, one person's voice came through. It was the voice of a boy. He had lived in the city of Thorigald. At first Dorovar felt his lips curl into a smile, but as the soul told its story, the smile turned to a sneer. The boy had immediately gone into hiding when the Herald War marched through the city. The song of the Chorus of Souls had taken his parents, inflaming them to kill their neighbors and then one another. But the boy's innocence had protected him from the initial call of the Chorus. But it was what the boy saw after the majority of the city's populace had been killed that turned Dorovar's stomach. The boy was hiding under the porch of his little house, watching the corpse army spread through the city. Suddenly there was a new army in the streets; an army clad in brilliant white armor with no faces. The faceless army cut down the corpses that served War, and then cut down the few citizens that had not been converted by War's touch. This faceless army spread from the city center of Thorigald, killing all in its path. War too had fallen to this army, but the perpetrator of that crime had been touched by the hand of Raenera herself. Even though Dorovar had struck down the demon that had haunted his memory, her schemes and her power remained.

Dorovar did not have time to linger on thoughts of Raenera as thoughts from another mass of fallen souls crowded out the dead from Thorigald. The burst of confusion was almost too much for Dorovar to stand, and for the first time in centuries he considered shutting himself off from the Chorus. However again a child's voice came through. This child had looked up into the sky and seen an angel. At least it was something he thought was an angel. The woman shone like a star in the sky, all radiance and light until water began to fall from the sky. As the water touched the floating woman it turned into blood. The blood melted the buildings, the people, the streets; everything it touched. In a matter of minutes, the whole of the city of Zevarit had been wiped from the face of Espre. Dorovar saw the face of the woman through the Chorus of Souls and felt the shudder through him. It was the face of the woman in the dream. The woman who meant the end of all things, the blood raining from the sky, the mad emperor dreaming of godhood. It was all coming to pass. Kaitain had touched the Dragon's Tear and unleashed its power upon Zevarit. It was a small use of that power, and it paled in comparison to what Dorovar had done with the Chorus of Souls. However, Kaitain was a small man with a lack of true vision. That was the reason that Dorovar told Kaitain how to find the Dragon's Tear. It was not to further Kaitain's agenda, it was to further Dorovar's. The Tear needed to understand her potential; to understand just what her powers would accomplish. The Tear would learn from these small-minded deeds that Kaitain would unleash her own, and then would grow beyond him. Soon the Tear would begin reshaping reality unbidden by Kaitain's lack of vision. That would be when she would be ready for Dorovar's guidance. That is when she would welcome him with open arms. Because of the breadth of power that the Dragon's Tear represented, it would not have the ability to see exactly how its power could be best used. Dorovar would teach the Tear of the Perfect Order, the way that Creation should be organized, and the Tear would thank Dorovar.

"Dorovar?"

At first the voice did not register to Dorovar's memory. He was so lost in communing with the Chorus of Souls that his mind could not properly process his own thoughts. Slowly Dorovar pulled himself away from the angry new voices of the Chorus and let his own memory reclaim his mind. The voice had been that of his old ally Luighsech. Dorovar turned and regarded the man and immediately took note of the pain and anguish in his eyes.

"Maedoc is gone."

Dorovar nodded. He had felt the moment when each of the Adhradair had met their end. He felt the power of the Chorus of Souls grow and his own power increase exponentially with each loss. However, the Adhradair did not need to know that their status was nothing more than fodder for the greater war effort.

"Explain."

Luighsech frowned.

"We followed the traitor Stormbane to meet with Shadowweaver as agreed. However, Shadowweaver never had any intention of giving us the information we required about the High Priestess's soul. The meeting was nothing more than a ploy to ensure I delivered his ultimatum to you. Shadowweaver said that he will be coming for you, and that the only way he would reveal the information about the High Priestess's soul would be when he was ripping you limb from limb and mocking your failure."

Dorovar let the insult pass. He would not lower himself to the level of the base filth that Shadowweaver represented. It was not clear if Shadowweaver even had the information about the disposition of the High Priestess's soul. Perhaps it had all been a ploy.

"Shadowweaver and his followers are planning an assault on Albitonin. I would assume that Shadowweaver allowed me to leave alive to give you that information. He is hoping to bait you into the conflict."

Dorovar nodded absently.

"Our losses are mounting, Dorovar," Coriden's voice came. "I was unable to free the soul of Judoc from the sacred weapon, and I assume that Maedoc has been lost to us."

Luighsech nodded, and Dorovar frowned.

"Seisyll betrayed us, attempting to kill me following her release. And Ninian, though she was freed from captivity, turned on her allies and assisted Hannah Ironheart in battle. Haricos, Redissa, and Ninian all met their ends in that battle. Drust fell at the hands of Aerith Seth, after Zaraven had been killed by Arin Ranthall. The enemies of the Perfect Order have been efficient in stopping our task, leaving but the three of us."

Dorovar could hear Coriden's knuckles crack as he balled his fists in rage.

"We will take revenge for our fallen brothers and sisters. We shall release those who are still in bondage and we will make them all pay for ever daring to stand against the Adhradair. The Perfect Order must live again, and the only way it can is if Aerith Seth and his pathetic followers are brought to heel for their affronts."

Dorovar suppressed his smile. He had hoped that Coriden's zeal for the task had not been diminished by his failure. Now however, the path was narrowed, and Dorovar needed to make sure that the tasks he appointed to his remaining followers would best serve the goals of the Perfect Order as well as the goals of the new Creation that Dorovar sought to build.

"Brennus' soul has been put into the keeping of Arin Ranthall, and he has taken it to the former Academy of Arcane Arts in Jelan," Dorovar began. "Aerith Seth has attempted to separate us from where the great war is taking place. Shadowweaver is baiting me to Albitonin, and it seems that our enemies are attempting to do the same. Aerith Seth himself has taken

Vercin's soul to Hedorah where Conquest was cut down. Unless I miss my guess, Judoc's soul is on the way to the Heart of Stone, right in the middle of the conflagration that is about to happen."

Dorovar could feel the hate roll from Coriden.

"I shall not repeat my failure. I am going to free Judoc."

Dorovar shook his head.

"While I appreciate your zeal, Coriden, we must think and we must use what our enemies think is a sound strategy against them. Shadowweaver wants me in Albitonin, wants me to insert myself in that conflict. I have no intention of disappointing him. How surprised is that ancient lizard going to be when the battle ends and his heart has been ripped from his body and is beating in my hands. I can end the dragons in one engagement, and I do not intend to miss that opportunity."

Coriden was incredulous, but Dorovar's words made firm sense.

"Arin Ranthall is a soldier, but he is not the challenge that the dragons posed on Loinn. Luighsech, he should be easy prey for you. No matter what happens, you must free Brennus from the Sacred Weapon. But do not underestimate the soldier. He is crafty, and he is a follower of Aerith Seth."

Luighsech nodded and immediately faded from view.

"Coriden, you will take the fight directly to Aerith Seth. He will be the most difficult opponent that you have ever faced. He has lifetimes of battle experience under his belt, and he is resourceful and brilliant. But what he does not know is that Drust injured him far worse than he can imagine. Even now the power of the Chorus of Souls is eating its way through him, robbing him of his abilities, taking from him everything that makes him special. Goad him, make him use his powers. Let the Chorus of Souls drain him of every drop and then rip him apart. Bring Vercin back to us. Make our family whole once more."

The dusky man bowed and was gone the next moment. Dorovar was left alone with his thoughts. If Luighsech and Coriden did not succeed in breaking the Sacred Weapons, Dorovar was unsure whether or not he could act directly against them. The fight in Albitonin would be the test. The Sacred Weapons were a prison, and they were proof against the touch of Dorovar. Perhaps Dorovar could not break them himself. Perhaps if the last of his freed Adhradair fell before the last of the Sacred Weapons was broken, his only hope would be Jerah. Jerah however had already proven to be unreliable. She followed her own path, took her own initiative, and aided and fought whoever she wished. Perhaps it was time to put Jerah's intentions to the test. The man Logan Ranthall needed to be dealt with. He was not a high priority because he did not carry one of the Sacred Weapons. But he was a troublesome thorn in Dorovar's side. Already the man had cost Dorovar the services of Death and Conquest. Jerah had a relationship with the man from the time that she was the Lady Wolf, Caris of the Brotherhood of Phasia. Now, Jerah would either destroy Logan Ranthall, or she would meet her end at Dorovar's hands. Jerah could serve only one master, and that master would and could never be herself.

Again, Dorovar turned his attention to the stars above, and then looked beyond in the direction of Albitonin. He could feel it now. He could feel the patterns on the wind, driving everything in that direction. It was as though the very essence of fate was winding itself around the Heart of Stone. The dragons, Dorovar's ancient enemies would be there. A prison of one of his Adhradair would be there, which meant that servants of Aerith Seth or the corrupt Emperor Kaitain would be there. The Heart of Stone was the home of the worship of the Creator, and so it would only be a matter of time before the angelic host would descend to protect that most holy place. Then there was the faceless army to the north in Thorigald. From the angry and sorrowful words of the Chorus of Souls, it was clear that that plague was sweeping through the countryside, killing everything that it came across. Soon enough the faceless army's path of destruction would lead it to the Heart of Stone. It was no coincidence the timing of these events. The Heart of Stone was the beginning of the end of the Creator. The side that reigned victorious over that place would be the true inheritor of the Golden Throne.

There could be but one victor. There could be but one true vision for Creation. Dorovar would stand over the broken bodies of his enemies atop the shattered walls of the Heart of Stone. None would be left to stand against him. All that would be left would be to realize the full potential of the Chorus of Souls through the destruction of the last of the Adhradair. The Chorus would sing Dorovar into the Heavens, and the Creator would fall. Creation would answer to a new vision, a new Perfect Order which would banish suffering, banish loss, and banish hardship forever.

Epilogue

The View Through Broken Windows

The Heavens, Time Immemorial

The palace of the Creator lay silent, and the Golden Throne did not hum with power. Ayden Seth had been summoned back to the Heavens following the attempted murder of his mother Bryn, an act that he knew was a test of his loyalty. He also knew that ultimately the gesture was futile. Whether Bryn lived or died was not a matter of great import. She was nothing more than an irritant. Her greatest power undoubtedly was her uncanny ability to support and to inflame her husband, the irascible Aerith Seth. What had become abundantly clear however was that Aerith Seth had become a problem that could no longer be ignored, and Ayden was spoiling for an opportunity to strike at the heart of the problem. The problem facing Ayden however was that he could not take action against Aerith without clear sanction from the Creator. There were rules for members of the Servants. Even should Ayden try to take the fight to his father, the Creator could summon Ayden back before he would be able to do any real damage. At best he could be summoned back, at worst he could be destroyed outright. Servants were disposable to a point, and if one host of a Servant was unwilling to follow the commands of the Throne, then they could be replaced.

Ayden could feel a change in the palace. Power was beginning to swell around the throne and two dozen angelic warriors appeared, one in front of each of the pillars that served as the perimeter of the throne room. Light pulsed in the Golden Throne faster and faster until it was a near constant glow. A low hum began as the pulsing solidified, and finally the white haze began to rise from the Golden Throne denoting the presence of the Creator.

"All Moves As It Should," the Creator's voice reverberated through the whole of the Heavens, "Soon The Whole Of Creation Shall Be As It Was Always Intended To Be."

The throne fell silent, and Ayden watched as an unassuming looking man in a white robe appeared at the side of the Throne. His short dark hair and blue eyes immediately triggered Ayden's memories, and while his first intention was to form a weapon and attack, he was restrained by the power of the Golden Throne. After a moment the rage inside of Ayden faded, and he looked into the deep blue eyes and noticed there was something different about the man. He was not substantial as Ayden or the warrior angels were; he seemed more like an apparition. To test his thought, Ayden reached out and his hand passed through the body of the former Child of the Creator.

"Emries is gone," the apparition said softly in Emries' voice, "but the aspect of the Creator remains. All of the Children have served their purpose, their power manifesting upon the world of Espre like a plague. It will spread, corrupting and killing, ruining and burning, pushing those who fancy themselves as the definers of fate to even more desperate acts. Even now they place themselves in the positions ordained for them, thinking that they are the architects of their own futures. They are but expressions of the will of the Creator, and once the last of the pieces are in position, the suns shall set for Espre for the last time. The world will know only darkness, and the Creator shall absorb into himself the knowledge and totality of power that has been denied to him for far too long."

The apparition of Raenera appeared next, her gold and green eyes sparkling with every word, and her voice chilling.

"Order has failed. Destruction has failed. Balance has failed. Harmony has failed. Discord has failed. The Children have seen their plans eclipsed by that which they created. And yet, their purpose was not to prevail. Their purpose was to create expressions of their desires and their dogma that would last far beyond their usefulness to the Throne. The ultimate expression of the power and their vision was not to be found in the creation or the sustenance of the lifeforms that were seeded upon the worlds. The ultimate expression of their ideology was to be found in how efficiently they could destroy that which they created."

Next to appear was Talisia.

"Even dedication to destruction could not fully express the necessity of the act. Killing, burning, devastation, these are nothing but natural forces expressed in an unnatural way. Beings killing other beings, even in the worlds of so-called order, was unavoidable, and thus uninteresting. Beings killing other beings, to the point that the whole of a world was destroyed was likewise unavoidable, and thus uninteresting. But killing other beings to the point that the whole of creation was destroyed, that was the very essence of what the Creator needed to understand. The Creator, the essence of everything that came after, had to know whether all of Creation, all of his will, could truly be undone by that which he created."

The voice of Pyrrus preceded the appearance of the Child's apparition.

"At the beginning there was the Creator, but the Creator was aware that he was not alone. And so, the Creator began to wonder whether or not he was alone. Was he but one of several Creators? Was he a facet of a greater being that even he was not powerful enough to understand? So, the Creator had to understand himself. Had to understand the limits of his power. But knowing everything of his domain and of his own mind could not allow for growth, could not allow for adaption, could not allow for true understanding. The Creator simply was, the Creator simply knew. What change was possible? How could there be anything beyond when he knew that there was nothing beyond? But what if what he knew was incomplete? He knew all, but there were pieces of knowledge denied to him? Was that even possible?"

Halicon appeared before Pyrrus was even finished speaking, his grim countenance mirrored by the black robe that he wore.

"So the Creator sat with these questions for an untold amount of time. Pondering his own existence, with no direction to take his thoughts. He was eternal, he was beyond any understanding, and as he pondered, he began to realize he was beyond his own. It left but one avenue open to him, one line of inquiry that could be expressed. Entropy. It was the only true path. If the Creator was truly alone, if the Creator was truly the Creator, he could not be destroyed. Creation could not be unmade. His path would always be true, and his understanding would always be infinite. But the Creator could not simply unmake himself. If he did not believe it could be done, it could not be done. And there was no way for him to convince himself that he could be undone. And so, he pondered. Could he create a plan that would test the limits of his own inevitability? Could he forge a path that he himself could not walk?"

Talisia took up the tale once more.

"After pondering the quandary for untold millennia, the Creator set upon a course. If he could not create expressions in his own mind, his mind that knew only certainty, then he would create beings who were not inevitable, that did not have certainty, and could attempt to know their unknown. And so, the Creator made the first dragon. That dragon was the Elder Dragon Tarot. For untold millennia, the Creator and Tarot spoke. The Creator would pose questions to Tarot, testing its knowledge and testing its ability to see beyond what it knew. But Tarot was limited. Like the Creator, Tarot knew. Tarot knew the Creator and knew what the Creator wanted Tarot to know. There was no growth there, at least no true growth. Could growth exist where there was true knowledge? That question still plagued the Creator. And his first attempt to answer it was met with the same answer. There could be no answer. Tarot was not all knowing, but there was no essential difference between Tarot and the Creator except for how much Tarot knew. Tarot could not see the patterns before it, could not see the potential of its own life, but at that point in Creation there was no such thing as potential. Things simply were, or were not. There was nothing in between."

Emries' voice came once more.

"So the Creator wondered if distance was a factor. Because Tarot knew, did it inhibit understanding? And so more beings were required. More dragons were created, but they were not allowed to have direct contact with the Creator. They still knew that the Creator existed, but they were taught by Tarot instead of by the Creator. And yet as the Creator watched, he could see no change in the dragons. They were as they were made. They learned what they could be taught, and that was all they were. They were limited. The Creator began to believe that he too was limited. Could that even be possible? The Creator who knew all, could see all, was all; could that in itself be a limitation? And so, the Creator began to wonder if the finite nature of knowledge was the issue. Perhaps if there was more to know, then the dragons would express the learning of that knowledge differently. Perhaps as they learned, the Creator would learn."

Raenera's voice was filled with frustration as she spoke the next words.

"The Creator took hundreds of years to gather strength into himself, shaping that power and then allowing it to spread throughout the void that was Creation at that time. From that power shapes emerged. Whirling balls of gas of different sizes, intensities, and brilliance. Floating clouds of dust and rock. Balls of dirt, water, air, and fire, that spun and circled. And while the Creator was once again disappointed because he knew the location and disposition of every celestial body that was formed from his power, he looked on as the dragons discovered these new creations. The dragons moved from body to body, determining the shape and scope of each of the newly made places, giving the things names. The Creator was disappointed that the names were part of his knowledge before the dragons even conceived of them or gave them voice. He knew the order in which the dragons would experience the bodies and knew the manner in which they would investigate and learn. The frustration with his knowledge and infallibility grew and he still did not have the answer to his questions. Was he truly the apex of Creation?"

Halicon's next words shook Ayden.

"As the dragons made their way through Creation naming things and debating amongst themselves over those names, the Creator again lost interest. He fell into his own thoughts, and felt himself disconnecting from that which he had made. One thought kept nagging at the back of his mind so much that it began to consume all of his thoughts. With all that he had made, he knew the names before the concept of naming began. He knew what the dragons would do before there were dragons. He knew the shape of each celestial body before the thoughts would even enter his mind.

However, one thought continued to nag at the corners of his mind. If the Creator was truly all-knowing, if he was truly all-powerful, if he was truly without limit, then how could he question whether or not he had limitation? If he had no limitation, he shouldn't even be able to question that truth. The very fact that the Creator could conceive of something beyond his knowledge or something beyond his power was the very proof that he needed that it actually existed."

When Pyrrus spoke again, the words were contemplative and pensive.

"The Creator and Tarot had spoken of this often. Tarot's supposition had been that the Creator's thirst for knowledge and understanding of himself made the possibility of something outside of his understanding a possibility. It was just a matter of the Creator's own questions manifesting themselves into reality. All the Creator had to do was to deny the possibility that any such quantity of control or understanding were outside of his reach, and the possibility would cease to exist. For Tarot, that logic was clear because in the mind of the dragon, there was nothing beyond the Creator's grasp. That was how the dragons were made. That is what they understood. However, if the dragon could conceive of a manner in which the doubts could be banished, then it must have been so. But no matter how the Creator tried to deny the existence of anything outside of his knowledge, the more the thought bore into his mind. Doubt became possibility, possibility became certainty, certainty became inevitability. There was something beyond the Creator's knowledge, and he became obsessed with finding it."

Raenera's voice came next, filled with irritation.

"And so the concept of the Living Cosmos came into focus. And yet the Creator still was unsure whether it existed before the concept came to his mind or whether it existed in spite of him. This thought consumed the Creator for a millennium more. The Creator had to know what this Living Cosmos was, how it came into being, what its boundaries were, and what its goals were. The very fact that the Creator did not simply know was vexing. But how could the Creator understand this thing that he did not understand? He had never had to learn before. He had never had to understand before. Knowledge simply existed. Understanding simply was.

Now the Creator had to determine a path by which he could create understanding. It was a new problem to be solved. His first problem."

Emries' voice was proud.

"The Creator did not simply know the Living Cosmos or understand the Living Cosmos. There had to be another way for the knowledge to come into being. This was when the Creator's thoughts turned back to the dragons. He had been detached from them for so long, he had neglected to see their progress. That neglect in itself was a surprise to the Creator. Had his obsession clouded his knowing? However, as soon as his focus returned to the dragons, so did his knowing. He knew all that they had done, knew all that they had named, but for the first time He knew something new. The dragons as they were taught by Tarot and taught by one another were lesser than their older compatriot Tarot, and of course were lesser than the Creator. But it seemed that this lack of quality created in the dragons a tribalism, a feudalism, and a uniqueness in the way that each dragon viewed Creation. This uniqueness created division. What was once ordered discussion and debate over names had become squabbles and eventually open conflict."

Talisia gave context and permanence to the situation.

"Through the conflict between the dragons, the Creator became aware of the conflict within himself, and that more than anything finally cemented the fact that the Living Cosmos was real. In that moment, the Creator knew that the only way to truly understand was through conflict. The dragons had taught the Creator that. However, at that time, the Creator believed that this internal conflict that stretched back to the beginning in the form of his own uncertainty about his own existence and its limits, had created the Living Cosmos. And so, if conflict had created the Living Cosmos, so too must conflict be used to understand the Living Cosmos. The conflict that the dragons represented however was too limited, too personal, and too irrelevant for the ideas that the Living Cosmos would represent. Those thoughts, those concepts, those ideas that the Living Cosmos represented could only be understood if the conflict could threaten the whole of Creation as well as the Living Cosmos itself."

Pyrrus spoke next, clear disappointment in his tone.

"As the Creator took in the sights of his domain, he began to question the supposition of creating a conflict that could threaten that which he had made. Could he himself construct something that would be able to unmake himself? The question tore at him. Should he not know the answer? And if the answer was no, should he not already know that? The fact that he did not know the answer ultimately meant that it was possible. That meant that the Living Cosmos could be moved to act against him. To the Creator, there was no way that he could destroy himself, which meant that the Living Cosmos had to be moved to destroy him. The thought of it was exhilarating. So for millennia the Creator planned, determining a path to discover the truth of the Living Cosmos, incite it to act, and then through the conflict between them learn the truth about the Creator's own nature and that of the Living Cosmos. It was a plan befitting the power of the Creator, and while it would take untold millennia for it to come to fruition, the Creator was a patient being, and this was the only thing that truly mattered."

Talisia once again spoke, the words dripping like venom from her lips.

"The Creator needed agents to sew conflict through the whole of Creation. The path was the one begun by the dragons, but limited by their design. They would squabble and fight, but they would never consciously harm one another. And the power that they had while considerable could not create the conflict on a grand scale as the Creator needed. And so he crafted two sets of beings. The first set of beings were the Children of the Creator. The five of us that you see before you are the beings that were made to spread strife and conflict amongst the stars. But we were initially a disappointment. We would pose ideological conflicts, debate and discuss, much as Tarot and the Creator had at the dawn of time. So the Creator began to push us, push us to prove our theories. So we, the Children of the Creator went forth, creating life, shaping worlds, and seeding Creation with our progeny. Our little model worlds that followed our doctrine implicitly were impressive, but ultimately disappointing. Yes, the worlds worked the way that we wanted them to, because we designed them. That proved nothing. We were all right, and we were all wrong. And so it was I that interjected the first act of sabotage. Pyrrus' world fell apart at my touch. It was the beginning, the first act of open conflict between the Children of the Creator, and our father was delighted. But as the conflicts began to spread amongst all of the worlds touched by the Children, the Creator began to see that the shape of his conflict was not bringing him any closer to the necessary point of entropy. So the second set of beings came into being."

As Emries spoke, Ayden noticed Halicon staring off into the Heavens beyond, disconnected from the retelling of the impossible story of Creation.

"The Servants' purpose was to nudge the conflict in the right direction, towards entropy. These beings could not have wills of their own that would influence the conflict, they simply had to do what they were ordered to do. However, after a time, the Children of the Creator began to see patterns arising from the appearance of the Servants. The Servants were steering conflicts, and the Children wanted to understand why. The Children were intelligent beings after all, and thus would wish to learn all they could about what the Creator wanted from them; if only in a selfish and vain attempt to win the conflict that raged between them. And so, the Creator pulled back the Servants and let the entropy fade from Creation. The Children were once again left to their own devices, striking at each other in subtle ways."

Raenera continued next, letting her hand reach out to indicate all that lay beyond.

"The Children and the dragons, they played amongst the stars until such time as the dragons themselves became foils of the plans of the Children. The dragons knew that they were the oldest and thus the most favored of the creatures, but the creation of the Children left them feeling outside of the Creator's love. They felt as though they had been replaced. And so, the Creator made for the first of his dragons great treasures that contained small pieces of His divine power. The Creator also gave the dragons the ability to go where they wanted, and do as they pleased. The dragons would avail themselves of this ability, placing them in direct conflict with the Children and furthering the pattern that the Creator was desperate to see finished. While this was originally nothing more than an annoyance for the Children, it eventually began to draw their focus away from the conflict that the Creator wanted. The first thought that came to the Creator's mind was that perhaps the dragons had served their purpose and they needed to be eradicated. However, the path to entropy returned to the Creator's vision, and the Creator saw the dragons for what they were. They were tools of the entropy that the Creator wanted. They could serve the purpose that the Creator had originally intended for the Servants, until such time as the Servants could be reasserted without drawing the suspicion of the Children. The Creator forbade the dragons from going to any world without permission of the inhabitants there, and forbade them to leave without that same permission. It did not take the dragons long to find ways out of the second part of the bargain, as the Creator knew they would. But the Creator needed the dragons to believe that they had a measure of self-determination in the face of what was coming. In the beginning the Creator allowed the dragons to kill the one that made the deal for their arrival, and to keep killing until they found a being willing to release them from their deal. Then the Creator imposed upon the dragons the rule that would be the first true step on the path to entropy. The dragons had to receive permission to leave from the same being that granted them permission to stay. This necessitated the dragons tying themselves to the one who made the deal through the use of the treasures gifted to them by the Creator. The divine power could grant long life, vitality, even imperviousness to injury and immortality if the right combinations of powers were applied. All of this was the Creator's plan, and once the dragons were in their proper place, all eyes turned to a small planet in an insignificant part of Creation called Loinn."

When Talisia spoke again, the pride was evident, as was the chilling glee.

"Loinn began the path that the whole of Creation is on now. It was the first long stride toward the entropy that the Creator desired. It created true strife between the Children, the dragons, and the beings of the Creation. It emboldened Emries to defy the will of the Creator, and it made the one called Dorovar, the one creature that could embody the entropy the Creator needed, and bring the Children to heel, freeing their power for use in the great upheaval that would come. And yet the Living Universe still had not revealed itself. No matter how many worlds Dorovar destroyed, how many beings he condemned to his so-called Chorus of Souls, the Living Cosmos did not reveal itself. Entropy was fast approaching, but the Creator could see no purpose to it. And so, the Creator imprisoned Dorovar until such time as his entropy influencing abilities were needed. He had already seeded the path with the information that Raenera and I would need to make use of Dorovar for the ultimate expression of that entropy, the death of the Creator, but we waited for the time to reveal itself. That revelation as it turned out was sooner than any of us could have imagined."

Emries' next words brought Ayden's thoughts and memories into focus.

"The second step on the path to entropy played out on another small rock floating in the nothingness; the world called Onea. There Halicon and I played out our piece of the game, the piece that has led us all here. The war between brothers, the war between light and shadow, and the birth of the man named Aerith Seth."

Halicon finally returned to the conversation, and as he spoke, a small green flame appeared in his hands.

"The Living Cosmos, it seems, had been watching the destruction wrought by the dragons and the Children and the one called Dorovar. So, in the darkest place in the whole of Creation, this little spark appeared. It escaped the notice of the Creator, which means that it could not have come from the Creator. It had to have come from the Living Cosmos. And I found it there as I explored the space between the worlds, the places outside of the Creator's light. I took this power into myself, made it one with that power that had come from the Creator, and the knowledge I had gained since gaining sentience, and I called that power the Blaze. Once I had touched the Blaze, I began to see its imprint everywhere in Creation. There was no telling how long the Blaze had been there; perhaps it had been there from the moment that the Creator willed it into existence. But it was part of every world, every star, every being. It seemed as though it was the stuff that held the whole of Creation together, filled in the cracks, made the movements of the celestial bodies possible. So when I came to Onea to fight against my brother and advance the conflict that the Creator craved, I brought with me with Blaze. From that foundational power I built my first phasia, and the destruction they wrought was terrifying. In time though, one of my phasia did not want to kill any longer. He took the powers that made him and walked away, to live life a different way. His child became Aerith Seth, and Aerith Seth had power unlike any that had ever been seen in Creation. It did not come from the Creator, it did not come from the dragons, it did not come from the Children. It was something different, something new, and it vexed the Creator all the more."

Emries continued the tale.

"The war raged on Onea for too long, but the Creator watched intently. For the first time while he knew everything that would unfold on that world, there were pockets that had unclear outcomes. Everything was around this Aerith Seth. There was this bubble of uncertainty. So, the Creator pushed at the edges of the bubble to see if he could still make happen when he wished. And while events would unfold as the Creator willed, the exact path of that unfolding was never certain. For a being who knew everything, even the slightest uncertainty was invigorating. The entropy that the Creator wished was fast approaching. It was time to reintroduce the Servants. The manner in which they were reintroduced however had to be done in such a way that the Children of the Creator no longer viewed them as monolithic. After the fall of Onea, the Creator elevated heroes from that world into the Heavens. He had used Gwydeon Sandar as a trial of his plan, a plan that would introduce these mortal beings as vessels for the Servants. And as he had seen and as he knew, the Creator was inwardly pleased that the Children assumed that some measure of the mortal being's essence remained despite being the host for one of the Servants."

Pyrrus continued.

"And so we were all of us deceived. None of the beings that were inhabited by the Servant survived. They were shells, nothing more. They spoke and acted as they had in life, but they were totally and completely under the sway of the Creator, furthering his plans, and ensuring that entropy continued in the manner in which it was destined. The final greatest expression of this control was through the woman who in life had been known as Sabrina Binosear. She was selected to be the Spirit by the Creator in an effort to push Aerith Seth down the path he needed to walk. But she was also selected for a very special purpose. She was to be in the right place at the right time to absorb the powers of Halicon."

Halicon's tone was grim, defeated.

"Though the powers of the Spirit had left her, Sabrina was still a servant of the Creator. She was still nothing more than a hollow shell that would entrap my powers. Each of the children would fall in turn, their powers absorbed by those who would further the Creator's pattern. The hosts would become disconnected from the limitations placed on the Children by the Creator, and they would spread like a plague through the world, passed from the disease carrier on to the next host. And on and on and on until it reached its ultimate expression of destructiveness. Some of the Children saw this passing of power as an opportunity. Talisia crafted her daggers, Pyrrus tinkered with technology from long dead worlds, and Raenera crafted continuations of her plans. Again we were placed in the positions that we were needed to be in by the Creator, and now all of us have passed our powers on."

The Golden Throne hummed again.

"Entropy Approaches. Soon the Living Cosmos Will Come. Soon the True Expression of the Creator Shall Be Known by the Whole of Creation."

Emries approached Ayden.

"Your time as a member of the Servants is at its end, Ayden Seth. You must now move on to the final part of your path. The Creator has allowed you to retain a fragment of your soul to prevent Aerith Seth and the rest of your connected family from feeling the deception that had been perpetrated upon them. However, once you take the next step, all will be revealed, though it will be too late for anyone to prevent what is coming. You will go now. The one called Wolf is waiting for you. He will explain the next part of your path. You will follow. You have no choice."

Emries touched Ayden on the shoulder, and Ayden could feel power being pulled from him. He suddenly felt smaller, diminished in all ways. Tears poured from his eyes as the divine light was replaced by remorse for the terrible actions done in the name of the Creator. The moment the process was complete and all of the power of the Will had been drawn from Ayden's body, Emries' eyes flared, and Ayden was pushed through a swirling white portal that appeared suddenly behind him. The portal closed, leaving the five apparitions with their Creator.

"The Inheritors Shall Know What They Must, and the Disciples Shall Be Denied the Knowledge That They Must Never Be Allowed to Know. All Comes to Pass as I Have Seen."

The Golden Throne flared once more, and each of the apparitions solidified, large wings sprouting from their backs, and cruel masks appearing to cover their faces.

"My Servants Now Must Ensure That All Comes To Pass As It Must. All Deformity Must Be Removed Now That The Final Piece Has Been Set Upon The Board. Emries, My Voice, You Will Go To Kill Your Old Nemesis. Logan Ranthall Must Not Be Allowed To Impede The Progress of the Entropy. Kill Him."

The Voice disappeared from the Heavens a moment later.

"My Spirit and My Wrath, Pyrrus and Talisia. In Life You Were The Deadliest of Enemies. You Were Dedicated to Ensuring That You Were The Only Ones Who Could Shape Creation, And That Conflict Has Given Rise To the Greatest of Possibilities. Go. Take With You the Whole of the Angelic Host. Descend Upon the Place Called the Heart of Stone. Wipe It and Its Interference from the Face of the World. There is to be Nothing Left of the Place When You Are Done. Do Not Launch Your Attack However Until the Bearer of Talisia's Power Has Inflicted It Upon Its Intended Victim."

The Spirit and the Wrath were gone a moment later.

"Raenera, My Will. Your Chosen Vessel Has Begun To Doubt the Path You Set Him Upon. He Has the Power to Stop the Spread of Your Plague. That Must Not Be Allowed to Come to Pass. Go. Eliminate Gideon Viruci, But No Harm Must Befall the One Called Jillian Corven. She Still Has Much Work Ahead of Her. Take Her to the Place Prepared for Her and Await My Command."

Once the Will was gone, the apparition of Halicon was left with the Golden Throne.

"And Now, You, My Greatest Champion, the One Who Has Laid Open the Path For My Greatest Ascendency, My Hope, You Will Go To Where

You Discovered the Blaze. You Will Wait There, Spreading the Knowledge of My Works. The Living Cosmos Must Come Now. Must Make Itself Known. There is No Other Way. There is No Other Path. Entropy is Upon Us All. Soon There Will Be Nothing. Not Even The Living Cosmos Should It Refuse To Reveal Itself. Go, My Hope. Go and Bring Back The Only Thing That Matters. The Validation Of All That I Have Done, and All That I Am."

Tears of the Flickering Flame

Year Five of the Just Emperor Kaitain "Dragonsbane" Lorien, Creator's Calendar Year 1872

The Imperial Army under the command of Kaitain Lorien marched quickly and without the benefit of rest from the capital of the Kingdom of Blood Zevarit, across the border into the Kingdom of Steel Celidar. Though the men were on a forced march, their limbs did not ache and their stomachs did not rumble. No matter the number of miles that the soldiers walked, it felt as though it were the first mile, and they knew that once they reached their destination they would be prepared to fight to the last for their emperor. The men marched through the night in the wake of the defeated and fleeing Army of Steel, and the only stops made were those to cut down the cowards that fled in the face of the might of Emperor Kaitain Lorien. Most of those caught and summarily executed by the Imperial Army were commoners who were armed with little more than shovels and pitchforks. The few members of the regular Army of Steel that were captured put up modest resistance before being overcome. They at least went down like warriors. The orders had come directly from the Emperor that none of the captured members of the army, be they soldier or commoner were to be granted any quarter. They were rebel combatants and were due the justice they had earned for themselves. That would be true of all of the enemies of the Emperor, no matter where they hid from his justice. The Imperial Army had been shown the way. Despite the losses suffered in Aldere, despite the losses in the war with the dragons, and despite the open conflict with the Dark Gods, the Emperor of Cadaria Kaitain Lorien continued to fight for his people. He had destroyed the scourge that had been the Church of the Creator, eliminating the lie that had held the people of Cadaria in bondage for far too long. Only someone as powerful and brave as Kaitain Lorien could have wrested control of the future of his people away from the apocryphal worship of the Creator. There were some within the ranks that were calling Kaitain the God Emperor of Espre. Perhaps that was the truest definition of what the man had become to his faithful. He had transcended simply being their leader. He was their savior, their deliverer, their living god. Only Kaitain could shape the future for his people.

By sunset of the following day, the Imperial Army had reached the borders of the city of Celidar. While there were no defenses left in the whole of the kingdom to muster against the Imperial Army, Kaitain called for a hold on the advance. The army would camp for the night in the small city of Celin on the outskirts of Celidar. It took only an hour for the Imperial Army to forcibly evict all of the citizens from the town. The emperor felt it important that after such a hard march that his soldiers would have real beds to sleep in for the night. Those members of the public that were not willing to sacrifice for the good of the very soldiers that were guaranteeing their freedom were considered traitors and summarily put to death for their villainy. Such affronts to the public good could not be tolerated. The emperor was building a new and better world for all that lived upon Espre, and those who did not believe in that vision of a free and prosperous empire could not be allowed to see its birth. The Imperial Army would become the just sword through which the righteous fury of the God Emperor would be visited upon the enemies of peace and harmony. Only through the destruction of dissent, through the elimination of disloyalty, and through the removal of all disharmonies could that new peaceful world be born. It didn't matter how many had to die to make that vision come into focus. What mattered was the purity of the realization of that vision, and the dedication and loyalty of those brave enough to walk the path that led to that realization. The Imperial Army were holy warriors on a quest to create a peaceful tomorrow where killing and death would no longer be necessary. Where everyone thought alike, valued the same things, and were singular in their devotion to their living god and deliverer from the darkness, the God Emperor Kaitain Lorien.

Kaitain of course took the largest house for himself, making sure that there was enough room for Alise to have a room of her own so that Kaitain could feel safe as he slept. Of course, Alise knew that Kaitain would not sleep through the night. Alise would stay awake through the night knowing that the man would pace up and down the halls all night long. For the two, the hours would pass very slowly, Kaitain's mind filled with all of the options for the future. In Alise's mind, there was very little that was ahead for any of them except death. But in Alise's mind, the death could only come from one place. It would come at the hands of the increasingly unstable and powerful Tess Annis. That girl would be the end of them all.

As for Tess, now that she had accepted who and what she truly was, there were pieces of her physical manifestation that no longer required her attention. The concepts of eating and rest were now foreign to her. This must have been how it felt to be a Child of the Creator, to be apart from the petty needs of the mortal world. To see everything else as beneath you. For so long Tess had felt out of place. She was an outsider in the Citadel of the Dark Gods, trying to find her place amongst those who had lived mortal lives. Tess was thought to be half-mortal, but that was a lie. Tess was never mortal, even in part. She had more in common with the woman she had thought she loved, Camille Sandar. Camille was born in the Heavens and was at least partly divine. Yes, she had been born to parents who were once mortal, like Tess, but they were both ascended beings when she was conceived. The only real differences between the two women was that Camille was born in the Heavens, and the Tess's mother had been a Child of the Creator. Perhaps that was why Tess had been so drawn to Camille. Perhaps that was why Tess thought that she had loved Camille. However, now Tess understood that love was a phantom, and it was not for those like Tess. The Children of the Creator did not love; could not love. They spoke about love and devotion, but the capacity for those kinds of emotions were alien to them. Tess found the paradox fascinating. How could beings like the Children of the Creator who did not have the capacity to feel love create beings like humans who seemed to be predicated on that emotion? Perhaps the very emotions that were central to humans were nothing more than a distraction that prevented humans from being able to truly see the nature of Creation. Emotions had clouded Tess's mind for so long, but now that they were being stripped away, she began to see clearly.

She saw the motivations circling around her. She saw Kaitain Lorien's pettiness and limited scope of vision. No matter how Tess tried to educate Kaitain about how his desires did not match his actions, he would not learn. He still thought like a mortal, driven by greed and driven by vengeance. Tess had hoped that once the so-called emperor's brother had been eliminated that Kaitain would be freed of the limitations on his vision, but it had been futile. All through the march from Zevarit to Celidar, all Kaitain could talk about was returning the Empire of Cadaria to its former glory, eliminating the traitors who had prevented him from leading the empire to a new prosperity. If anything, Feyd's death had done nothing but reinforce Kaitain's petty need for glory. True power did not need recognition. That was the Creator's ultimate failure. The Creator and the Children all wanted to be lauded. They all wanted recognition for their deeds. But so long as those with power sought adulation or validation for their deeds, they would be limited to avenues that created those responses. Tess had found her path beyond such concerns. She had Cedric Binosear to thank for that. He had shown her the truth about power. It was quiet. It did as it willed. It owed no one and desired nothing. True power simply was. Tess would become that true power that would mold and shape Creation. She needed nothing, wanted nothing, and could not be swayed from her path.

Tess looked out upon the world around her and let her eyes fall out of focus. She thought about the new Creation that she would build. Would she fall to the same temptation as the Creator? Would she seek validation for her deeds and betray that which she knew about the essence of power? Would the small parts of her that were still mortal crave company, or emotion, or something to aspire to? Perhaps Tess needed more time among the mortals to purge the last bits of her that were still mortal. It was not enough to simply numb herself to the emotions, as they would eventually resurface. They would need to be purged, removed, eternally banished from her if she was going to be true to the power. Tess could not just be a being that was inhabited by power. That was the road to failure. As Tess continued to consider, she thought that perhaps the new version of Creation should be without mortal beings. Was that the Creator's true failure? Was the fact that he created the dragons his downfall? Did seeing what he made through the eyes of imperfect creatures make Him imperfect? It was as though the light suddenly filled Tess's mind. That was the truth of it. In the beginning the Creator had been perfect, had been singular, and had been a true custodian of power. The Creator had been power in the truest sense of power. However, the Creator diminished himself. When he created the dragons, he used them to name things, and to explore that which he had made. And so, the Creator became corrupted by that imperfect vision. The more he troubled himself with the world of the mortals, the more mortal he became. That was what had led Creation to this failed point. The Creator was no longer worthy of being called the Creator. He had become too mortal, troubling himself with the affairs of the dragons, the Children, the Dark Gods, and the mortal beings of all of the worlds. That was why Tess had become necessary. It was all clear now. The Creator had fulfilled his purpose and it was time for him to be replaced. Tess was to be the new Creator, and she would not repeat his mistakes. There would be no mortals in the Creation that Tess would oversee. There would only be peace.

Tess suddenly became aware of a new presence. Someone had come for her, and she had been expecting it. She turned toward the city of Celidar and began walking slowly. Two of the members of the Imperial Army attempted to stop her to ascertain whether or not she had the emperor's permission. With a wave of her hand, the two men exploded into fountains of blood. They were simply mortal anyway, completely beneath her notice. All of the mortals would soon cease to exist anyway. As she walked, Tess barely acknowledged the sounds of yelling that went up from other guards posted around the town's perimeter. Someone had seen what she had done, but it mattered little. All that mattered was the person that had come for her. Her destiny.

* * * * * * * * * * * * *

Logan Ranthall stepped from the portal into the empty receiving hall of the Palace of Celidar and looked around idly. This had been the home of Jerrard and Erika Mystic, two of his great friends. But the palace felt heavy, angry. Logan could feel power all around the palace, including the room he was in. Looking over his shoulder to the throne, he could feel his stomach turn. Emries had been here, had been sitting on the throne.

Logan knelt down and put his hand on the floor, letting his perception spread through the structure of the place. The palace had so many good memories, but the pain was also clear. It sat upon the surfaces of the place like a stain. He could see the murder of Devlin Rannoch at the hands of Tess Annis. He could feel the death of Sabrina Binosear. And then his heart froze. Logan felt the death of Jerrard Mystic at the hands of his own child, followed by the death of Erika Mystic at the hands of Feyd Lorien. While Feyd had held the blade that killed Erika, it was really Emries that motivated the act. More unnecessary losses. Logan's mind kept coming back to Sabrina. She had done so much for those who were still fighting. He missed her terribly. However, now was not the time for such thoughts.

Logan slowly walked through the receiving hall, and pushed the door open that led to the grounds of the city. Tess would already know that he was in Celidar. He could have used a portal stone if he wanted to disguise his arrival, but there was no need for that. The city of Celidar was quiet, the streets empty and very few lights shining in any windows. The hour was late, but not so late that a major city should have been that quiet. Logan feared perhaps that he had come too late, that Tess had already done terrible things to the people of Celidar. After a moment of taking in the character of the city, Logan thrust his hands into his pockets and slowly walked in the direction of the city gates. Logan could clearly feel the bright shiny beacon of power that was Tess Annis. It was clear that the girl cared little about hiding her location. She was standing in a clearing between the capital city of Celidar and a small town to the west. Logan was not in a hurry to reach the confrontation, so he kept his pace even, his footfalls sounding impossibly loud in the empty streets and alleys. Once Logan had emerged through the city gates into the plain that lay beyond, he could feel the cold wind begin to whip around him. It actually felt good to just walk around again. He spent so much time using portals to move from place to place that he had lost something of his life before the war between Emries and Halicon entered his life. Logan had been fighting for so long, but he could also assuage his soul with the knowledge of all the good that he had done. He had given so many people the opportunity to find new lives, to make the choice that was denied to him. How many soldiers had come to the Order of the Flickering Flame disillusioned with the horrors that they had seen in the world? How many men who had spent the better part of their lives with blood on their hands were reborn by using those same hands to create rather than destroy? So many had died through the actions and inactions of Logan's life, and he carried each and every one of those losses in his heart. Some of his allies had tried to find their redemption through victory against their enemies. Others had tried to find redemption by ensuring that there would be a world once the conflict was over. Logan chose to find his redemption by making the quality of any world that would follow better. Less soldiers and more farmers and carpenters. Less killers and more healers. Why would it matter if the Creator and the Children were gone if their terrible legacy continued through the actions of the people who remained? The only way to make a better world was to make the people who inhabited it better.

As Logan continued to walk in the direction of the blinding power that Tess Annis represented, worry entered his mind for the first time since arriving in Celidar. No matter what he had accomplished up to this point, none of it would matter if he failed here. Tess Annis was a danger to everyone and everything that called Creation home. She needed to be stopped. Logan wasn't sure that he was up to it, but there was no one else. Aerith couldn't be risked yet; he was still needed for Dorovar. Rhain, Wolf, Cedric; how their powers would help to shape the rest of the war was still unclear, but they could not be risked on something like this. As powerful as the remaining members of the phasia were, they were no match for Conquest let alone Tess Annis. No, just as Pike had been Logan's responsibility, so too was Tess. Pike was family, and so was Tess. Logan had to ensure that she would not be able to hurt anyone else. And though she was unlikely to listen to reason, just as with Pike, Logan had to give her a chance. If Logan didn't try to bring her back to reason, he would be denying everything that he stood for, and everything that the Order of the Flickering Flame stood for.

It took only a few minutes to cross the plain to where the girl in the simple white dress stood waiting for him. Behind where she stood, Logan could see and hear a mass of activity. Soldiers were being roused from their beds and pressed into action. Regimental leaders were shouting at their soldiers to form ranks and prepare to march. Regardless of the flurry of activity behind her however, Tess stood like the eye of the storm, her dress not even being moved by the cold breeze that moved the long blades of grass at her feet. The girl's eyes never left Logan as he approached, but

Logan did not share her gaze. He kept his head down and his eyes on the patch of ground in front of his feet. He knew where she was, Logan didn't need to look. Several feet from where Tess Annis stood, Logan stopped. He kept his hands in his pockets, but finally looked up to meet the girl's gaze. Her eyes glowed with brilliant golden power, turbulent and full of violence, but the rest of her countenance was placid.

"You are Logan Ranthall."

The girl's tone was calm, dispassionate, and unnerving. She did not put any power into her voice, but Logan could hear her clearly as though she were standing right beside him.

"My father told me stories about you," Tess continued. "Many of them were unkind. But the other members of the Dark Gods spoke very highly of you. I think perhaps my father did not understand you, because he did not understand himself. I understand why you killed him, and I hold no malice toward you over it. He was an evil man."

Logan tried not to let his disappointment show on his face.

"Your father wasn't an evil man," Logan said finally. "But he was troubled. He had seen many things during this war that made him make decisions that were not in his best interests. I don't begrudge him the hate he had in his heart for me. I'm sure I earned it. But once he became a servant of Dorovar, I could not let him continue to sacrifice the innocent in Dorovar's name. I took no pleasure in killing him. He was my friend. He was my family. And I mourn his loss."

Tess cocked her head to one side.

"Why would you mourn him? Despite what you may think of my father, Conquest is what he always was, it is what he always would become. It was inevitable. Just as this is what I was always meant to become. You are under the false assumption that people have a best version of themselves. They do not. They have what they were made to be and nothing more. Whether it is by the will of the Creator, or the will of the Children, mortals are nothing more than collections of destinies that lead them to inevitable conclusions. They can fight against that destiny and cause themselves and others considerable pain, but in the end they will be what they must be because that is what the Creator decrees. Even me, even you. You are here because the Creator wants you to be here. You are here because the Creator wants you to try to kill me."

The girl blinked once, the light in her eyes intensifying.

"But you are not here to kill me."

Logan considered for a moment but did not let any emotion register on his face.

"Then why am I here, Tess?"

The girl smiled. It was an eerie smile that threatened to freeze Logan's blood.

"You are here to bear witness," she began, her voice deathly serious. "I have come to be in this place, as the visions have led me. I recognize this place, this field from the dreams that I have been having for so long. This is the place that I will achieve the fullness of my power. This is the place from which I will shake the Heavens and begin to remake reality into the shape that it should be. You, Logan Ranthall are the final witness, and it is fitting that you are. The man who killed my father. The man who stood against a Child of the Creator when that was thought impossible. The man who stood between so many worlds at the same time, trying to make them all fit together. You are the ultimate expression of everything that is wrong with the Creator's vision of reality. The ultimate expression of what it is to be mortal. You strive to be better yet are held back by your failings. You want the best for all people, and yet you kill to create that vision of the future. You are so firm in your beliefs that you attempt to shape reality around you. In one breath you decry the dogma of the Church of the Creator but with the next impart your own with the Order of the Flickering Flame. That is why you are the perfect expression of the mortal world, and the only one worthy of being witness to my ascension. You are the embodiment of hypocrisy, a mass of contradiction, and the fullest expression of the mortal need to constantly reach for those things beyond your grasp."

As her final words left her lips, above the plains storm clouds began to roll in. The sounds of thunder echoed in all directions and angry red lightning lanced between the black clouds. The tapestry of stars in the sky beyond the clouds disappeared, replaced with a field of crimson. From behind Tess, the Imperial Army had rallied quickly under the orders of their leaders and marched upon the plain. With weapons drawn, the soldiers formed a circle around Tess and Logan, some pointing their weapons at her, others pointing weapons at the stranger. As the Imperial Army was an army made of soldiers from each of the kingdoms, some shields and banners were emblazoned with the crests of those kingdoms while others were emblazoned with the imperial symbol. Beyond the ranks of troops, Logan could see a man running in their direction trailed by another form. The man broke through the ranks of soldiers, the young woman behind him armed with terrible looking metal claws strapped to the backs of her hands. Logan recognized the man immediately as Emperor Kaitain Lorien. He ran up behind Tess, wrapping his arms around her.

"You cannot stop me now! I have it, it is mine!"

The man's voice was wild, full of madness. Tess struggled against Kaitain's grasp for a moment but the look on her face did not change. She spoke, her words barely above a whisper, but Logan heard her clearly.

"You see, Logan," came the cold hard voice, "destiny. Kaitain has seen this moment, lived for this moment, but was unable to understand this moment. All he knew was that he would hold a girl in his arms, a girl he believed would forge his path."

Kaitain screamed again.

"You will never prevent my ascension to god-hood!"

Tess's voice came once more.

"You see? He is a puppet just as you are, just as my father was. Kaitain could only see this moment, surrounded by a mountain of dead troops representing the different kingdoms. What he never realized, and will never have a chance to, is that the army was not an assemblage of the Great Kingdoms attempting to destroy him. It was his own army that was only trying to protect him and facilitate his mad vision."

Tess's eyes flashed and suddenly every member of the Imperial army dropped to the ground, the life stolen from them. While Kaitain paid no notice to the fate of his soldiers, the woman with the claws spun around looking in all directions, her mind whirling. Fear was etched on her face, but fear had stolen any will she had to act.

"I will unseat the Creator and this world will become mine! I will save us all from the Dark Gods!"

Kaitain's voice trailed off after his last words, and then confusion filled his eyes. Everything had led him to this point. All of his scheming, all of his cruelty, and all of his single-minded devotion to his own desires crystallized in this singular moment. Logan recognized the look in his eyes. He had seen that look many times before. It was the look of a man that had just come to the realization that his path would end in a way opposite that which he had expected. It was the look of thwarted destiny. It was the look of denied desire. The next moment Tess's eyes flashed once more, and Kaitain Lorien was gone. A plume of blood was all that was left of the man who had been the cause of so much death. Tess stepped out of the puddle of blood that had once been the Emperor of Cadaria and closed the distance between herself and Logan. Finally, the two stood face to face.

"So you see, Logan," Tess began, "this is the price of prophecy. This is the price of destiny. And this is the price of providence."

Logan nodded. He withdrew his hand from his pocket and in it was a black dagger. He held the dagger up between he and Tess.

"Do you know the litany of the Order of the Flickering Flame, Tess? Do you know what it means?"

Tess blinked wordlessly.

"When I was born, I was but a flickering flame, unsure of its direction but yearning to be more," Logan recited. "From my infancy, I grew, I learned, and the flickering flame changed; it spread its wings and became the mighty Phoenix. But from the day those wings spread to catch the air, I knew that there was a great fate waiting beyond; beyond what I knew, beyond my perception. I would make the most of my time as the Phoenix;

learn all that I could learn, live a life that would make me worthy of what would come after."

Logan let the words sink in for a moment.

"When I wrote that, I was trying to sum up for the people who came to the Order how I had gotten to this point in my life. I always thought I was one thing on the verge of being something else. I was a farmer who was destined to be a hero. Not out of need for glory, or for fortune, but to earn the love of a woman. As you say though, there is a price for destiny and for providence."

Logan began to recite again, keeping his body still, making no moves toward or away from the girl.

"The Phoenix is not eternal. It returns to Flames when its life is ended, only to be reborn once more to continue its works."

Logan sighed.

"And I died. I died at the hands of the man I had served. Emries stood over me as I slept, wrapped his hands around my throat and squeezed until there was nothing left of me."

Logan smiled as he began to recite again.

"We do not live but one life. Like the Phoenix we live many. Some ending in fire, others in ashes, but all ending and beginning anew. My life before was the Phoenix. Now I am the flickering flame waiting to be reborn. Only through my deeds shall I become the majestic Phoenix once more."

Logan paused for a moment and then a serious look came to his eyes.

"Like me, you have lived many lives too, Tess. Like the phoenix. You have been a daughter, an emissary, a tool, a student, a savior, a murderer, a destroyer. And this moment, you are waiting to be reborn. We both are."

Logan looked down at his palm. The dagger changed the next moment, the hilt of the dagger disappearing, only to be replaced by another blade. As the change was taking place, Logan began to recite once again.

"I shall walk this world, the flickering flame. I shall lift up those who cannot rise by themselves. I shall use this flickering flame to bring comfort to those who have none, to shelter those who know only the ravages of the world. I am the flicking flame, and yet I am so much more."

The change in the dagger complete, it floated from Logan's hand and positioned itself between the two powerful beings, like a fulcrum of the two opposing views.

"That is where we diverge, Tess," Logan said finally. "However misguided, hypocritical, or contradictory I may be in my actions, I seek to comfort, shelter, and protect."

His next words were angry.

"Let this flickering flame be a beacon to all those lost in the darkness and let it lead them back into the light. Through these deeds and through grace this flickering flame shall spread its wings once more to become the mighty Phoenix, whose might shall protect all those who take shelter in its magnificence."

Logan took hold of the center of the dagger and stepped forward so that the tip of the blade was against his chest at his heart and the other tip was at Tess's heart.

"This is what we will decide here and now, Tess. Is the world one that is to be protected, or is it one that is to be destroyed. You have all of this power at your disposal. You could heal the sick, you could stop the wars and the suffering and unite us so that we might find a better way. You could be the Phoenix that spreads its wings to protect everyone. But you don't want to do that. Life is messy. People are messy. Emotions are messy. It's easier to just kill everyone. Just burn everything down. No people, no life, no mess. Just silence."

Logan pushed forward the dagger piercing the skin of both of them.

"And for what? What would it have all been for? My sacrifice. Your father's. The sacrifice of everyone who came before you that made you possible. The sacrifice you forced on Camille by taking Devlin from her in a fit of jealousy."

Tess's eyes went wide.

"No love," Logan continued, "no faith, no hope, no triumph. Yes, we feel pain, but we feel it so that we can know the power to overcome it. Yes, we struggle, only so that we can know what it means to be better than we think we can be. If you could only see the potential that you are squandering. Pike believed in you, so did Sadrina, and Darrien, and Midarin, and Gwydeon, and Wolf, and Lissa, and Mirana and Liara. And Camille. Camille believed. Cedric believed. I believe."

Tess's jaw went slack. Logan reached out and put his hand on Tess's shoulder, the dagger still pressed between them.

"Until again I shall return to the flames."

Logan pulled Tess forward that moment, the dagger thrusting deep into both of their hearts.

* * * * * * * * * * * * *

For a moment, Logan believed he was dead. There was nothing, only blackness. He floated in a sea of nothingness, detached from his body and his mind. But there, at the very edge of his perception was the little green flame of the Blaze. He didn't so much move towards the flame as it just simply was closer. He imagined sitting in front of it as he had often done with a small candle in the depths of the conclave of the Order long ago. He would sit for hours, staring at the flame, trying to understand it, trying to understand himself. There were many times he would hear Elwyne's voice in his head telling him that there wasn't enough depth within him to understand. Her teasing voice always made him feel better that he didn't know what he was supposed to do. After all, he was just a farm boy from a little town. He wasn't important really; he never had been. Perhaps though, that was the very reason he kept succeeding where others failed. He did not want power. He did not want glory. The Order of the Flickering Flame was a thing that he created that he wanted to surpass him.

"And now you hold the most incredible power in the palm of your hand."

Logan realized after a long moment that the voice had come from the green flame.

"But is what you will do with it any better than what the one you took it from intended? More conflict. More death. More destruction."

Logan's mind did not waver, and his thoughts remained clear.

"It isn't my power," he said finally. "It isn't meant for me. It isn't meant for Aerith, or for any of the Dark Gods or the Children, or even the Creator. It's a power that shouldn't be. Because no matter whose hands hold it, there is only one outcome. Destruction."

There was silence for a long time.

"And yet, you still hold it," the flame answered.

Logan considered.

"Because there is still a terrible purpose ahead for me. And I know, the longer I hold this power, the more tempted I'll be to use it. It's part of me now, how can I keep it from those who would misuse it though their aims would be good?"

The flame pulsed with light for barely a moment and then was still.

"You must choose, Logan Ranthall. Are you a Phoenix, or are you a flame? Are you a crusader or are you the crusade? Will you be true to your message, to uplift, the shelter, to protect, to be the beacon, or will you fall to your desire to force those things into being?"

Logan didn't hesitate. The words never came from him however. In his mind's eye where the green flame spoke to him appeared a black shroud that looked like a cloak, with it was a trio of pulsing lines of energy that wove together in intricate patterns. Lastly was a golden shimmering energy like that of curtain of falling rain. When the green flame spoke again, Logan could feel rather than hear the sorrow. But the sorrow was not coming from the flame, it came from his own heart.

"The path you choose to walk, you must walk alone. To protect those who love you. To shelter those who would use what you know from themselves. To be the true light in the darkness of this dying world. But you must also return to the flames. You must truly be the flickering flame, barely seen, barely warm, barely anything more than the potential for something more."

Logan knew that moment what was expected of him. Touching the shimmering golden rain, he could feel the power of the imperfect Dragon's Tear, the power that had once inhabited Tess Annis. With that power he could remake reality, but he would only do so to remake his own. The golden light flared, and the black cloak disappeared. It flared once more and the trio of mingled lines of power also disappeared. The next task was the hardest. It felt like a betrayal. It felt like an admission that everything he had done before was nothing more than a lie. But this was the only way. The flash of golden light came once more, and the flickering green flame was gone. In his mind's eye, a box appeared, a strong steel box with a heavy lid and a lock that could not be picked or forced open. Into that box he pushed the golden rain, sealing it tight. The box would only be opened once, and when it was, everything would change forever.

* * * * * * * * * * * * *

Logan stood on the bloody plain, the body of Tess Annis at his feet, and the broken pieces of the dagger lying beside her. Already the black storm clouds had begun to clear away. Logan felt different, diminished, human. His body ached, and his stomach rumbled. He couldn't see as far or as clearly as he did only moments before, and his mind was no longer filled with the thoughts of others. He was just himself once more. He began to slowly walk to the west, ignoring the unconscious form of the woman with the claws on the backs of her hands. He could tell that she was still breathing at the very least, and he knew that she would wake up eventually. She would have to find her own path. Logan would walk his alone from that point forward. As he bundled himself up against the suddenly very cold wind, he let the last words of the litany hit the air, more true now than they had been at the moment he wrote them all those years ago.

"I am the flickering flame, and yet I am so much more."

Appendicies

Dramatis Personae

<u>*The Imperial Court*</u>
Terrik 'Godslayer' Lorien
Emperor Lorien I

Liette Lorien
Wife of Terrik Lorien
Empress of Cadaria
Seer

Kaldawyn Lorien
Emperor Lorien X
Father of Ender Lorien

Ender 'Justhand' Lorien
Emperor Lorien XI
Father of Feyd and Kaitain Lorien

Meara Lorien
Wife of Ender Lorien
Mother of Kaitain and Feyd Lorien

Kaitain Lorien
Emperor Lorien XII
Father of Marlae Lorien
Adoptive Father of Quyhn Lorien
Twin Brother of Feyd Lorien

Irene Drage
The Ethereal Sorceress
Court Sorceress
Protégé of Alistair Ravenheart

Galen White
Member of the Imperial Guard
Personal Guard of Felicia Lorien

Geoffry Aramour
Imperial Historian and Bard
Master of the Shadow Guild

Alise Modrall
Personal Assassin of Kaitain Lorien

<u>*The Lordhill Rebellion*</u>
Feyd Lorien
Prince of Cadaria
Brother of Kaitain Lorien
Overseer of Lordhill Province
Father of Felicia Lorien

Felicia Lorien
Princess of Cadaria
Daughter of Feyd Lorien
Host of Nightwing

Quyhn Ravenheart Lorien
Sorceress
Ward of the Empire
Voice of the Emperor
Daughter of Alistair and Estelle Ravenheart

Dominique Arais Lorien
Wife of Kaitain Lorien
Former Mistress of Seraph Kore

Rhionna Winter
Personal Protector of Quyhn Ravenheart
Archer from the Army of Fire

Connor Peregrim
Lord of Lordhill
Former General in the Imperial Guard

Gabrielle Peregrim
Lady of Lordhill
Cousin of Kaitain Lorien

Arent Fox
General in the Rebel Army of Lordhill

Strum Anvilguard
General in the Rebel Army of Lordhill

The Knights of the Flashing Blade

Bernhardt Yeoman
The Moonstone Knight
Kingdom of Iron, Pellatori
Wielder of the Hammer Gravity

Chelsea Zarova
The Garnet Knight
Kingdom of Fire, Saldarine
"The Wolf of Saldarine"
Wife of Seraph Kore
Wielder of the Katars Tenacity
Personal Protector of Dominique Lorien

Devlin Rannoch
The Onyx Knight
Kingdom of Night, Galateria
Half-Dragon
Wielder of the Kopesh Discipline

Gregor Quicksilver
The Ruby Knight
Kingdom of Blood, Zevarit
Husband of Hannah Ironheart
Paladin of the Church of the Creator
Son of Ivan Quicksilver
Wielder of the Greatsword Valor

Hannah Ironheart
The Celestine Knight
Kingdom of Stone, Albitonin
High Priestess of the Church of the Creator
Wife of Gregor Quicksilver
Wielder of the Mace Spirit
First *Chosen One* of Espre

Leonora Wastri
The Jade Knight
Kingdom of Soul, Oradrim
Wielder of the Naginata Wisdom
Trained by Cedric Binosear

Jaccob Aldora
The Topaz Knight
The Flying Kingdom, Hedorah
Former Member of the Academy of Arcane Arts
Wielder of the Double Sword Temperance

Natalia Pressen
The Sunstone Knight
Kingdom of Gold, Bellnoc
Master of the Shadow Guild
Wielder of the Rapier Perseverance

Orren Eldrath
The Sapphire Knight
Kingdom of Ice, Rashaleb
Former Member of the Academy of Arcane Arts
Wielder of the Long Sword Courage

Seraph Kore
The Emerald Knight
Kingdom of Water, Thorigald
Husband of Chelsea Zarova
Wielder of Twin Sword Patience

Tolon Morr
The Amethyst Knight
Kingdom of Steel, Celidar
Former Gladiator
Wielder of Battle Axe Strength

Vallic Ultiv
The Serpentine Knight
Kingdom of Steam, Iltorp
Wielder of Scythe Harmony
Alias of Jeroch Yetre

Xaran Firesoul
The Tiger's Eye Knight
Kingdom of Knowledge, Menoris
Blind Since Birth
Wielder of Staff Faith

Gabriel Shadowfall
Member of the Imperial Guard
Personal Guard of Marlae Lorien
The Ruby Knight

Ivan Quicksilver
Former Ruby Knight
Father of Gregor Quicksilver
Advisor to the Dark Court

Tutio Illik
Former Onyx Knight

Heremon Tal
Former Amethyst Knight

The Academy of Arcane Arts

Alistair Ravenheart
Grandmaster of the Academy of Arcane Arts
Master of Water
Imperial Sorcerer
Husband of Estelle Ravenheart
Father of Quyhn Ravenheart

Estelle Ravenheart
Sorceress
Wife of Alistair Ravenheart
Mother of Quyhn Ravenheart

Fiona Ebonsight
Master of Fire
Mother of Aris Ebonsight

Aris Ebonsight
Master of Air
Daughter of Fiona Ebonsight

Jastra Mythryn
Master of Energy

Ashinica Maupin
Master of Stone
Member of the Imperial Family

<u>*The Seers*</u>

Jehna Feris
The Dark Seer

Jania Maldovrin
Oldest of the Maldovrin Triplets

Jerrica Maldovrin
Youngest of the Maldovrin Triplets

Jordyne Maldovrin
Middle of the Maldovrin Triplets

<u>*The Dragon Hunters*</u>

Jillian Corven
Self-Titled Lady of Cadaria
Wielder of Scaleripper
Leader of the Dragon Hunters

Kiara Aren
Dragon Hunter
Former Priestess of the Creator

Angelina Lynn Sydor
Dragon Hunter

Jacqueline Escandi
Dragon Hunter
Former Member of the Iron Legion

<u>*The Chorus*</u>

Dorovar
The Destroyer of Worlds

Pestilence
The Grey Man
Carrier of the Crawling Plague

Famine
Formerly Isabel Relin
Carrier of the Wasting Disease

Death
Formerly Ardis Franel
The Collector of Souls

Jerah
Alias of Caris

Conquest
Alias of Pike Rhuiden

Haricos
Member of the Adhradair

Redissa
Member of the Adhradair

Coriden
Member of the Adhradair

Faelara
Member of the Adhradair

Zaraven
Member of the Adhradair

Drust
Member of the Adhradair

<u>*The Hand of Chaos*</u>

Dimitri Sulano
The Voice of the Lost

Syren Belloch
The Priestess of Blood

Torda Safrick
The Master of Secrets

Xavier Cormea
The Corruptor of Souls

Erik Relcan
Pursuer of Lost Love
Former Personal Assistant of Hannah Ironheart

Seraphina Masile
Second in Command of the Hand of Chaos

Korin Melcab
Captain of the Imperial Guard

The Children of the Creator

Emries
The First *Coromor*
Creator of the *Erieal*

Halicon
Formerly known as Shau-ling
Father of the Phasia
Powers imbued to Rhain Seth

Talisia Masile
The Dark Goddess

Pyrrus
God of Light
Powers imbued to Wolf Ranthall

Raenera
Goddess of Order
Powers imbued to Gideon Viruci

The Phasia

Rhain Seth
Mistress of the Blaze
Former Personal Guard of Marlae Lorien
Daughter of Aerith Seth and Bryn Aplee

Jeroch Yetre
The Lord Shadow
First Born of the Phasia
Father of Hawk Yetre

Bryn Aplee
The Lady Fox
Member of the Brotherhood of Phasia
Former Lover of Aerith Seth
Wife of Grawn Aplee
Mother of Gideon Viruci

Ellis Chandara
The Lady Leopard
Member of the Brotherhood of Phasia
Mother of Korrd Ranthall

Grawn Aplee
The Lord Shark
Member of the Brotherhood of Phasia
Husband of Bryn Aplee

Warron Ysamaran
AKA Blade
The Lord Boar
Member of the Brotherhood of Phasia

Basille Mystic
The Lord Raven
Member of the Brotherhood of Phasia
Father of Jerrard Mystic

Farax Soar
Creator of the Snags
The Lord Vulture
Member of the Brotherhood of Phasia

The Flame
Kamen
Personal Guardian of Shau-ling
Keeper of the Hall of Terrors
Originally known as Kamen, Member of the Brotherhood of Phasia

Zarsi Aeron
The Lord Cobra
Member of the Brotherhood of Phasia

Aldridge Farran
The Lord Hawk
Member of the Brotherhood of Phasia

Saurn Macco
The Lord Viper
Member of the Brotherhood of Phasia

Caris Vale
The Lady Wolf
Member of the Brotherhood of Phasia

Erdric Yarrow
The Lord Scorpion
Member of the Brotherhood of Phasia

Taron Steen
The Lord Jackal
Member of the Brotherhood of Phasia

Draven Batoe
The Lord Crow
Member of the Brotherhood of Phasia

Rane Larion
The Lady Falcon
Member of the Brotherhood of Phasia

Stryfe Cadre
The Lord Python
Member of the Brotherhood of Phasia

Grimm Salde
The Lord Bear
Member of the Brotherhood of Phasia

Cash Griffon
The Lady Lynx
Member of the Brotherhood of Phasia

Nightwing
Member of the Dark Riders
Shau-ling's Assassin

Hawk Yetre
Son of Jeroch Yetre and Caris Vale

Natalie Yetre
Daughter of Jeroch Yetre and Ellis Chandara

Jessica Chandara
Daughter of Ellis Chandara and Grawn Aplee

The Court of the Dark Gods

Sadrina Annis
Queen of Mythryn
Wife of Pike Rhuiden

Darrien Annis
Half-Dark Goddess
Daughter of Pike Rhuiden

Tess Annis
Half-Dark Goddess
Daughter of Pike Rhuiden

Alderin Terian
Dark God
Son of Aryx and Diana Terian
Protector of Darrien Annis

Camille Sandar
Dark Goddess
Daughter of Gwydeon and Midarin Sandar
Protector of Tess Annis

Serrina Mistic
Dark Goddess
Voice of the Dark Council
Daughter of Jerrard and Erika Mystic

Mirana Ranthall
Daughter of Wolf Ranthall and Lissa Terian
Twin of Liara Ranthall

Liara Ranthall
Daughter of Wolf Ranthall and Lissa Terian
Twin of Mirana Ranthall

The Celestial Court

Marlae Tamerlane
The Divine Empress
Chosen Representative of the Creator
Daughter of Kaitain Lorien

Ayden Seth
Son of Aerith Seth and Bryn Aplee
The Will

Anabel Binosear
Sister of Cedric Binosear
Mother of Cairyn Binosear
Daughter of Aerith Seth
High Council to the Divine Empress

Azure
God of the Heavens
Advisor to the Divine Empress

Krysis
God of the Heavens
Advisor to the Divine Empress

Terrance Aldora
Brother of Jaccob Aldora
Advisor to the Divine Empress

Isabella Ranthall
Advisor to the Divine Empress

The Dark Gods

Aryx Terian
White Lightning
Fire *Erieal* of the First Generation of the Prophecies
Husband of Diana Geoffry Terian
Father of Lissa Terian
Father of Alderin Parran
Former Host of Nightwing

Diana Terian Geoffry
Wind *Erieal* of the First Generation of the Prophecies
Sister of Arathorn Geoffry
Wife of Aryx Terian
Mother of Lissa Terian
Mother of Alderin Parran

Pike Rhuiden
Water *Erieal* of the Second Generation of the Prophecies
Refugee from the Dark Mirror
First Cousin of Logan Ranthall
Eldar Merin's Former Husband
Husband of Sadrina Annis
Father of Darrien and Tess Annis

Gwydeon Sandar
Brother of Angels
Husband of Midarin Rice Sandar
Father of Nathaniel Sandar
Father of Camille Renar
Also Known as Wynne

Midarin Rice
Wife of Gwydeon Sandar
Mother of Nathaniel Sandar
Mother of Camille Renar

Lissa Terian
Fire *Erieal* of the Third Generation of the Prophecies
Daughter of Aryx and Diana Terian
Wife of Wolf Ranthall

Sabrina Binosear
Third *Chosen One* of the Prophecies
Refugee from the Dark Mirror
Daughter of Cairyn Binosear

Wolf Ranthall
Son of Logan Ranthall and Elwyne Tamerlane Ranthall

The Forgotten

Aerith Seth
The First *Chosen One*
Husband of Bryn Aplee
Father of Ayden Seth, Cedric Binosear, Anabel Binosear, Gideon Viruci

Taya Viruci
Daughter of Gideon Viruci and Erika Belnosian
Refugee from the Dark Mirror

Logan Ranthall
AKA Dane Rhuiden
Second *Chosen One* of the Prophecies
Brother of Korrd Ranthall
First Cousin of Pike Rhuiden
Father of Wolf Ranthall
Leader of the Order of the Flickering Flame
Refugee from the Dark Mirror

Jerrard Mystic
Son of Basille Mystic
Husband of Erika Belnosian
Father of Serrina Mistic

Erika Belnosian Mystic
Wife of Jerrard Mystic
Mother of Serrina Mystic

Other Cast

Cole Breon
Freelance Assassin
The Living Shadow

Liandra Nightshade
Freelance Assassin
Death Blossom

Dane Rhuiden
Monk
Leader of the Order of the Flickering Flame

Blade
Merchant
Purveyor of Oddities
Alias of Warron Ysamaran

Isa Shar
Companion of Vallic Ultiv
Alias of Ellis Chandara

Evan Sinn
Inheritor of Aerith Seth's power
The Voice of the Creator
Husband of Meredith Heron

Taya Mystic
Daughter of Jerrard and Erika Mystic

Meredith Heron
Emissary of the Creator
Wife of Evan Sinn
Murdered by Dorovar

Tera Dawnrunner
Guardian of the Council of the Winds
Guardian of the East
Last of the Tigrelle

Jander Eveningstar
Guardian of the Council of the Winds

Eldar Merin
The Spirit
Best Friend of Elwyne Tamerlane
Wife of Pike Rhuiden

Leane Torne
General in the Army of Rama
Former Member of the Army of Brea

Nathaniel Sandar
The Lord Ram
Third *Coromor* of the Prophecies
Son of Gwydeon Sandar and Midarin Rice
Brother of Liette Forer

Gwillim Sandar
Earth *Erieal* of the Third Generation of the Prophecies
Son of Korrd Ranthall and Gabrielle Crill
Adopted Son of Midarin Rice

Storm Mystic
Son of Jerrard and Erika Mystic
Water *Erieal* of the Third Generation of the Prophecies

Jared Vale
Son of Caris Vale and Cedric Binosear

Cairyn Binosear
Daughter of Anabel Binosear
Niece of Cedric Binosear
Queen of the Kingdoms of Kandor, Trelon, and Marcwell
Wife of Pike Rhuiden
Mother of Duncan Rhuiden and Sabrina Binosear

Sabrina Binosear
Former Host of the Spirit
Third *Chosen One* of the Prophecies
Sister of Duncan Rhuiden
Daughter of Pike Rhuiden and Cairyn Binosear

Duncan Rhuiden
Heir to the Kingdom of Marcwell
Brother of Sabrina Binosear
Son of Pike Rhuiden and Cairyn Binosear

Talon Aielin
Wind *Erieal* of the Second Generation of the Prophecies
Best Friend of Pike Rhuiden

Arin Domae
Fire *Erieal* of the Second Generation of the Prophecies
Former Soldier of the Army of Brea

Gideon Viruci
Earth *Erieal* of the Second Generation of the Prophecies
Killed in Battle with Shau-ling

Baeta Catrinel
High Priestess of the Church of the Creator

Aelind Torral
Assistant to the High Priestess

Reverend Mother Amalia
Priestess of Hedorah

Heralds of the Creator

The Voice
Formerly embodied by Evan Sinn
Currently embodies Gregor Quicksilver

The Will
Currently embodies Ayden Seth

The Wrath
Destroyed by Aerith Seth

The Spirit
Formerly embodied by Sabrina Binosear
Currently embodies Eldar Merin

The Council of Winds

The Elder Dragon Tarot
Leader of the Council

Mariti Brightblade
Second in Command of the Council
Companion of Tarot

Khalas Skydancer
Friend of Xaran Firesoul

The Demon Dragon Shadowweaver
Chief Opposition to Tarot

Krangoth Granitewill

The Arcane Dragon Serentis
Ally of Mariti Brightblade

Brux Mightytide

Charnada Ivorytooth
Ally of Shadowweaver

Stormbane the Traitor
Ally of Shadowweaver

Sheyruushk Bottomdweller
Ally of Khalas Skydancer

Aspertis the Just
Ally of Mariti Brightblade

Derelor the Manipulator
Ally of Shadowweaver

About the Author

Brian Kershner is a life-long dreamer, writer, and problem-solver. He grew up absorbing anything and everything he could get his hands on, and as a child of the Star Wars era he constantly wanted to see the worlds beyond the little Indiana town he grew up in. There was no adventure too far, and no problem too big.

Emboldened by parents who always supported his curiosity and his thoughtfulness, Brian found himself bounding from Space Camp to Laser Summer Camp to Athletic Training Camp to Piano Lessons to Football Practice to Basketball Practice to Choir Practice and back again. Despite all of the roaming and traveling, his family remained close-knit and supportive.

Though he flirted with the idea of becoming a doctor, Brian's attentions always fell back to the computer world. He got his first computer when he was six, and not long after found his way into a word processing program and began crafting his own fantastic worlds and even more fantastic characters.

As he has grown and changed and experienced life, so too have his characters. He continues to write, craft, and create; whether it is websites for his customers, or characters and worlds for his audience.

www.ingramcontent.com/pod-product-compliance
Lightning Source LLC
Chambersburg PA
CBHW072333020726
47506CB00004B/867

* 9 7 8 1 9 4 2 0 8 2 2 7 9 *